The
Horizon
Conspiracy

I wrote this!

M A CLARKE

First edition published in November 2016.

ISBN: 978-0-9929585-4-1

CONTENTS

"We've all been sorry, we've all been hurt.
But how we survive is what makes us who we are."

- Rise Against

PART ONE

1
ZOEY

"I've been a hostage for six years."

There. She'd said it. Now, how would he react?

He scoffed. The bastard was actually smirking.

She glared at him. "How is that *funny*?"

"A hostage? Isn't that a bit melodramatic, Zoeykins?"

"Don't call me that."

"Okay," he said, raising his hands in submission. "Zoey… Explain to me how working here makes you a hostage?"

"I didn't choose to be here. Who would?"

"Well, I did!"

She waved impatiently. "Yeah but you're weird. You love your nerd stuff."

He propped himself up in the bed beside her. "I actually prefer the term *geek*, Zoeybuns."

Another flash of anger. "And I prefer *Zoey*!" She muffled his chuckle by shoving a pillow into his face.

The anger was already draining, though. As annoying as Ben could be, she liked how her troubles seemed to shrink when in his company.

He escaped from the pillow and grabbed her around the waist, pulling her on top of him. His blue eyes closed as he leaned in to kiss her. Zoey didn't resist.

"So I'm a nerd, am I?" he smirked again.

"Yes." She squeezed his thigh between hers. "You're all *terabyte this* and *gigahertz that*."

"Ooh I love it when you speak dirty to me."

She smiled, and kissed him again, but it was feeble.

He noticed, and stopped to look her in the eye. "Come on, what's wrong?"

She rolled off him, staring at the ceiling. "It's this place, Ben. Don't you ever miss the sight of trees… the sound of birds?"

Propped on an elbow, watching her, he shrugged. "I can go to the rec room for that. We recently added a module for underwater sea creatures. It's just like *being* there, I swear."

She exhaled a disgruntled sigh. "It's not the same. Sitting in a chair in front of a glorified cinema screen. Gah, you don't understand…" She turned away from him. "I want fresh air whenever it suits me, not just at allocated time slots. Living underground is so unsatisfying."

He leaned over, tilted her chin and kissed her. "You seemed pretty satisfied last night."

She giggled, and pushed his chest away. "Stop it. I'm being serious."

"Did I ever tell you how beautiful your eyes are?"

He's such a charmer. IT nerds aren't supposed to be this confident! Zoey welcomed the distraction, but she had to get to her lab before someone came searching. "I have to go…"

He didn't seem fazed. "They are, you know. Green eyes to pierce the soul… I could get lost in your gaze, Zoeybuns…"

"*Zoey*," she scolded. "You have no idea how off-putting that is." She rolled away again, slid out of the bed and plucked her underwear off the floor.

Ben leaned against the headboard with his hands crossed behind his head. "How did you never get a boyfriend in school?" he said, eyes sweeping her body.

A warm flush swept through her. "I wasn't interested in boys back then."

He leaned forward. "Oooh, do tell."

Zoey hesitated, glancing at the floor. A wavy blonde haired, silver-eyed girl flickered in her mind. *Annie…*

"Maybe another time." Zoey picked up her trousers and lab shirt and carried the bundle into the bathroom.

She splashed her face with water and put both hands on her hips. The cold lighting did no favours to her pale complexion. She cocked her head at the mirror, probing around her boringly slim waist. *Why couldn't I have been born a little curvy, at least?*

Not that Ben seemed to mind. And he appreciated her one redeeming physical feature, those green eyes. She leaned over the sink for a closer look. *I swear they are getting duller down here… I hate this place.*

Six years she'd lived underground. What sort of life was that?

She jumped in the shower, brushed her teeth and got dressed. No need for makeup, that would only get you laughed at, but she tied back her brown hair in a ponytail. Practical and professional, the same way she started every day.

Ben was dozing in the bed when she emerged from the bathroom. He usually worked nights, but he always made it to the canteen in time for the lunchtime meal. That's where they had first met, a couple of years ago, but their relationship had progressed from friends-with-benefits to something more serious in the last few weeks.

She leaned down and pecked him on the cheek. He opened his eyes a fraction, smiling. "See you at lunch?" he murmured.

"Mm," she nodded.

He gave a dreamy sigh as he closed his eyes again.

Zoey left his apartment, peeking down both corridors to make sure it was clear, then scurried towards the labs, passing her own dorm along the way. There was no policy forbidding relationships with co-workers, but she didn't like the attention it brought. So far, no-one seemed to have noticed, and she hoped to keep it that way.

I tried to open up to him, and he didn't take it seriously. Well, how could he? A *hostage*, come on. It sounded so ridiculous out of context.

She passed through the sliding doors labelled *Data Analysis* and made her way to the lab where Nadia was already sitting at her computer screen.

"Morning," Nadia said, not looking up.

"Hi," Zoey replied, reaching for the computer's power button. She froze, noticing a small hand-written post-it note stuck to the monitor.

Come see me. - M

Zoey plucked the note off the screen and stared at it. She swallowed back bile. *What the hell does she want?*

A knot formed in the pit of her stomach. Better to get it out of the way. She marched straight back out of the lab.

"Where are you going?" Nadia said, but Zoey was already halfway out the door and didn't stop.

Two levels up, in the finely furnished administration floor, she came to the door labelled *Margery Blunt, Public Relations.* She rapped on the door with a clenched fist.

"Come in," Margery's muffled voice replied.

Zoey took a deep breath and strode inside.

"Hello, Zoey." Margery sat behind an oversized mahogany desk in front of a floor-to-ceiling virtual fish tank. "Please shut the door."

Zoey closed it and stood before the desk. *She's had more Botox since last I saw her.* "What do you want?"

Margery's thin red-lipped smile held firm. "I'm going away on a little business trip," she said, interlocking her fingers on the desk. "I'll probably be gone for three months. I just wanted to make sure everything was okay with you."

"Right," Zoey scoffed. She spread her hands, gesturing to herself. "Well, I'm fine. Can I go back to work now?"

Margery raised her finely plucked eyebrows. "Isn't there anything you want to tell me? This could be your last chance for some time."

Zoey hesitated. *Does she know about Ben and me?* "I… no. I'm just really busy at the moment."

Margery's penetrating gaze fixated on her. She gave an almost imperceptible shake of the head. The smile vanished, replaced by a snarl. "Come now, who do you take me for? You're fucking that IT monkey."

"So what if I am?" Zoey snapped. "It's none of your business, Mother!"

Margery glared at her. Zoey held her gaze, defiant, but the knot in her stomach pulled tight.

At last, Margery's scowl softened. "Of course it's not," she said, with a little shrug. "You may fuck whomever you wish. At least it's a man, this time."

Zoey reddened, fists clenched at her sides. "He's hardly the first…" *I gave my virginity away just to make you angry, but even that didn't work.*

Margery smirked. "Yes, I remember your little jaunt with the boys down in *R&D*. I was almost proud of you then. Finally learning how to use that tool between your legs for its true purpose: getting what you want."

"There's a word for that, Mother. *Slut.*"

Margery gave a quick wag of a finger. "Slut is a word men use to describe women who have more power than they can handle. It's little more than a form of jealousy." Margery leaned back in her chair. "So, tell me about him."

"Why?"

"I'm curious. What do you talk about?"

Zoey frowned. "Why do you care? Is this why you summoned me here, just to talk about my love life?"

"Does he know who you are?"

"No," she muttered. "Of course not."

"But these techy sorts are clever, you know. He might figure it out."

"He won't," Zoey insisted quietly.

"You know how dangerous it is for you to get close to people here. If someone were to realise who you are, it would cause a lot of… problems. For me."

"I know, Mother."

"So there'll be no more talk of *hostages,* will there?"

Zoey's heart jumped. She gaped at her mother.

Margery laughed, a throaty cluck that jangled the nerves. "Come now, dear. You're surprised? I thought you might have learned by now that nothing gets by me, unless I want it to."

"Have you bugged his room?"

"Of course I have," Margery said. "I don't trust him."

"But why don't you trust *me?*"

Margery looked astonished. "How can you ask me that? I don't think I can ever trust you again, not after…" Her lip curled in disgust.

"Her name was Annie, Mother. You can't even say her name, can you?"

Margery's jaw clenched as she ground her teeth.

"It's been *six years,* Mother. Have I not done everything you wanted, without question? Why won't you give me this small piece of freedom to enjoy a relationship? I don't have anything else to live for down here!"

Margery's eyes narrowed, her lips forming a thin line. "Freedom? Did I not remove your father's tracker?"

Zoey's hand went instinctively to her thigh, where the tracker chip used to live. "Yeah. But now you're *spying* on me!"

"Freedom is earned, girl. Don't stand there snivelling and whinging about a mere six years. You don't know how fortunate you are."

"*Fortunate?*" Tears were threatening in the corners of Zoey's eyes, and she wiped at them furiously. "In what way is living here *fortunate?*"

"Zoey, keep your voice dow—"

"I'm trapped with no friends, no contact with anyone outside, Ben's the *only* one who gives a shit about me, and the worst thing about it all is—"

"Zoey, be qui—"

"—I'm trapped here with my *bitch of a mother!*"

Margery stood and spoke in a guttural growl. "*Catherine!*" Dead silence.

Zoey crossed her arms tight against her chest and squeezed her eyes shut, desperate not to cry. The use of her real name sounded unfamiliar and wrong. She'd forgotten how long it had been since someone last used it. Her heart pounded against her trembling arms.

"Look at me," said Margery.

Zoey slowly unfurled her eyelids and despaired, feeling two trickles drip down her cheeks. She didn't look at her mother, though. She watched a big virtual shark glide past behind her.

Margery tutted. "So close to the hump, don't fall apart on me now, girl. Although I suppose it would be easier if you did. You really are more trouble than you're worth."

Zoey swallowed the scratchy lump in her throat. "If you don't want me here, then let me go."

Margery made a disgusted grunt. "Not this again. You have nowhere else to go, dear, and you know it."

"I could go *anywhere*, Mother." Now she looked at her. "You wouldn't ever need to see me again. Isn't that what you want?"

"What a lovely fantasy this is! Yes," Margery waved a mocking twirl of her fingers through the air. "And you could travel the world with a handsome man at your side, fucking in meadows and rolling through the flowers."

"You don't even know me…" Zoey whispered, dropping her chin, and wiping her eyes.

"No, I suppose I don't," Margery mused. "And I don't ever intend to. You know full well that if I let you go, your father will find you and I simply cannot allow that to happen." She was suddenly around the desk and standing inches away.

Zoey recoiled at the stench of perfume and touch of her mother's spiny fingers gripping her chin.

"Enough of this nonsense," Margery hissed. "I want you

to know that I understand how you feel better than you could imagine, and I will allow you to continue seeing this Ben, if that's what you wish. But be mindful of your pillow talk. I won't tolerate any more mention of *hostages*. *No more,* Catherine. Do you understand?"

Zoey nodded.

"Good," Margery said, releasing her grip. She straightened herself, eyeing Zoey with deep suspicion. "Don't think I won't still be checking up on you while I'm away. Behave yourself."

"Yes, Mother," Zoey mumbled. "Can I go now?"

Margery waved her away. "See you in three months."

Don't hurry back. Zoey turned and swept out the door, barely resisting the urge to slam it shut.

At her midday break, she found Ben in the canteen, munching a sandwich, dropping crumbs onto the keyboard of his laptop.

"You slob," she said, sitting on the bench opposite.

The babble of voices echoed through the cavernous room, dozens of scientists and technicians all eating their lunch.

"Hey," he smiled at her briefly, then squinted back at his screen.

She tore open a packet of Cheetos and slumped over the table. The day was dragging, and a foul mood had settled on her ever since the encounter with her mother that morning. She couldn't tell him about that, but perhaps Ben would brighten her day. "What ya doing?" she asked.

"Reading about the Second Cold War."

Zoey raised an eyebrow. "That sure sounds fun."

"I know!" he said, missing her sarcasm. "Isn't it fascinating to think that we came so close to nuclear war? I mean *this* close." He pinched his fingers almost together for emphasis.

"Fascinating's not the word I'd use. More like

terrifying?" Zoey said.

He went on, gesticulating with his hands. "It happened before, you know? Back in the seventies, between America and Russia. Even back then, people predicted a second conflict between the old rivals, but when China got involved, things became *way* more volatile."

"You're a real dork for this history stuff, aren't you?" Zoey said.

"The merger of continents *is* historic, Zoey! Euromerica's sole reason for existing is to send a big *fuck you* to Neo-Asia." He laughed. "'*Anything you can do, I can do better*', you know? Global dick-measuring."

This wasn't Zoey's idea of brightening her day. "Do we have to talk about this? I'm not in the mood." She tossed another Cheeto into her mouth.

Ben said, "Ooh, let's have one of those?" She held the bag out to him, and he took a few. "Thanks. Okay, what do you want to talk about?"

She shrugged. "I dunno."

They sat in awkward silence for a while. *Great. Now what?*

He snapped the lid on his laptop shut, leaned forward and spoke very quietly. "What did you mean earlier, about being a hostage?"

She coughed on a Cheeto. "Oh, nothing." Her eyes watered as the dry snack tried forcing its way down her windpipe. She coughed again. "I was joking."

"You okay? Want me to slap your back?"

She gave a dismissive wave. "No, I'm fine," she croaked.

"Here," he offered his bottle of water, which she gulped gratefully.

Well, that didn't seem suspicious at all. Eventually, she recomposed herself. "I just feel like this is a dead-end career for me. That's all I meant."

He nodded thoughtfully. "I guess it sucks that we have to stay underground for so long. But the work they do here is cutting edge stuff. Way better than those CERN boys next door. One day, we might change the world!"

"Heh, sure. You with your underwater simulations and me with my reams of paperwork."

He chuckled. "Well, maybe not us." He glanced around the room. "We're among some of the smartest people in the world though... see that guy?"

She turned to see a lab coat walk past carrying a steaming baked potato on a plate.

Ben said, "He's leading a team several levels down that are trying to create a miniature black hole... can you imagine it?"

Zoey shrugged. She knew all about the ambitious lower level eggheads. Her job was to analyse their research data and pick out anomalies. She was just a cog in the machine though, at the end of the day. One that could easily be replaced if her mother allowed her to leave, which was never going to happen.

"And then there's *that* guy," Ben went on. "I heard some rumours about him."

She followed his pointing finger. "Oh. I've seen him," she said. "He's experimenting with electro-particle emitters. They've been trying to develop a method of targeting living tissue; another futile attempt to cure cancer."

"Cancer, eh?" Ben rubbed his chin, following the guy as he walked past.

"Yeah, they're always trying to cure cancer," Zoey explained. "They've been developing this machine for the last four years. Trying to harness electricity instead of drugs. It's a bad technique, they should just move on, already."

"Sounds like you know a lot about it," Ben helped himself to another Cheeto.

"I have to analyse the data, I can tell when they're chasing their tails."

"You don't approve?" he frowned.

"It's not that I don't approve, I just find it all tedious and hubristic."

He raised his eyebrows and laughed. "I guess it is. Besides, some could see the dangers of such a machine. If that technology fell into the wrong hands…" He trailed off, leaving Zoey a little confused.

"What do you mean?"

He glanced up at the wall clock and said, "Never mind. I better go. Meet me at the elevator tonight at midnight."

"The elevator?" Zoey cocked her head.

"I have something I want to show you." He gave her a cheeky smile. "Say you'll be there?"

"Sure."

"Good. See you later Zoeykins."

"*Zoey*," she growled as he scampered off. But her curiosity had been roused. *What does he have planned, I wonder?* The anticipation was enough to perk her mood for the rest of the day.

***

At midnight, Zoey waited by the huge industrial elevator that linked the labs with the surface and the numerous levels beneath them.

He showed up ten minutes late, puffing and panting. "Sorry, I couldn't get away from Jon. He sure does talk."

They were alone by the elevator, so they shared a quick kiss.

"What did you want to show me?" she asked.

"It's a surprise," he grinned and gestured her into the elevator like a gentleman. He swiped his keycard, pressed the upmost button, and the doors slid shut.

Zoey's stomach fluttered. "We're going to the surface?"

She was only allowed up there on scheduled breaks, along with the rest of the technicians, but Ben had unrestricted access because the communication antennas needed regular maintenance.

His grin widened as the elevator jerked into motion.

Zoey tensed. *Oh god, what if Mother finds out?* "I'm not allowed…"

"You are if you're with me," he said, taking her by the hand. "No-one will care."

Mother certainly would… She kept silent. She'd told him too much already, Margery was at least right about that. *Gah! Screw it, she's not here now. Besides, she said I could be with him, I just have to mind my tongue, that's all.* She shivered with excitement and squeezed his hand. Grinning like a couple of school kids, they rode the elevator up to the surface.

The doors opened onto the lobby, empty at this hour except for the receptionist and a couple of guards. Ben gave a casual nod to the closest guard and strode up to the desk.

"Evening Mary," he said to the middle-aged woman typing on the computer. What she had to be typing after midnight Zoey could only guess, but she hoped she didn't recognise her.

"Hello Ben," she smiled at him. She glanced at Zoey's nametag and raised an eyebrow. "*Data Analysis?*" Back to Ben, "What are you up to?"

"Jon sent me to take some readings. It's easier with two pairs of eyes, and everyone else is busy or sleeping, so I've brought Zoey here to help me out." The lie rolled off his tongue like butter, and Zoey got the distinct feeling that he'd done this before.

Mary the receptionist gave a knowing smile and clicked a button. The door behind the desk buzzed open.

"Cheers, Mary! See you in the morning. Let's go."

Ben led her through the door to a garage home to a couple of 4x4s and three snowmobiles. He found two helmets and handed her one.

She hesitated. "Where are we going?"

"You'll see." He grabbed two fur-lined coats hanging on a hook and when they were wrapped and helmeted, they jumped onto a snowmobile. Ben reached back and positioned Zoey's arms around his waist. "Hold me tight!" He clicked a button on the snowmobile's screen and the garage door opened to the sight of moonlit mountains.

Zoey interlocked her gloved fingers and squeezed him, giddy with excitement. *The outside!*

Ben revved the engine and sped out into the freezing air.

Oh my god. It was beautiful beyond words up here on the top of the world. All around them the snowy alpine mountains loomed like jagged teeth, glinting silver under the light of a bright half-moon. Stars scattered the sky above, twinkling and shining.

The snowmobile went over a bump and Zoey's stomach dropped. She squeezed Ben tightly as they tilted down a slope and picked up speed. She leaned around him to see a cluster of wooden cabins approaching. Firelight danced in the windows of two, but the other three were dark.

Ben pulled up beside one of the occupied cabins and shut off the engine. They dismounted and pulled off their helmets. Zoey gulped down the fresh air, beaming.

"You enjoy that?" Ben asked.

"Oh hell yes."

"Heh. Wait there a sec." He bounced up the steps to the front door, knocked and opened it without waiting for a reply. "Only me, Carl. You got the spare key?" Ben disappeared inside. He re-emerged a moment later. "Thanks buddy, see ya tomorrow." He closed the door and bounded back to her, offering his hand. "Come on."

"Who's that in there?" Zoey took his hand and walked with him.

"Who, Carl? He's a spotter. Four of them live here, but they take shifts, so tonight we can use Patrik's cabin. He won't mind." He shot her a wink.

Zoey bit her lower lip, trying to conceal her excitement.

Ben led her across the hard packed snow to one of the empty cabins, unlocked it and they closed themselves inside. It was dark and the pleasant musk of burned wood hung in the air. Ben flicked on an orange coloured electric lantern and knelt beside a log stove.

Zoey glanced around the living room. A mounted deer's head looked down at her from one wall, and several animal skins decorated another. Opposite the front door, a window looked out onto the mountains, while the neighbouring cabins could be seen through the two windows either side of the front door. "So, what's a spotter?" Zoey asked.

"They just keep an eye on things out here. Snow levels, weather patterns, they carry out controlled demolitions to keep the mountain safe, y'know?"

"Huh. Never thought about that before," Zoey mused.

"Downsides to building a giant underground complex inside a mountain," said Ben as he struck a match. He lit a couple of firelighters and threw on some kindling. The log burner fizzled to life. Ben shut off the electric lamp and shadows danced around the cabin, cast by the flickering flames.

Before long, warmth emanated from the stove and the cabin filled with a cosy glow. Zoey took off her jacket and gloves and reached out towards the fire. "Oh that's good... I can't remember the last time I felt the heat of a real fire."

"Nothing like it, eh?" Ben grinned. "Now for a little something..." He wandered over to the open-plan kitchen area, which was just a sink and some cupboards. Out of one, he pulled a bottle of single-malt Scotch.

"That isn't yours," Zoey said, raising an eyebrow.

"Patrik won't mind," Ben said as the cork popped. "Besides, he owes me a favour." He poured two generously sized glasses and handed one to Zoey. "Cheers."

They clinked, and Zoey took a sip. It burned her throat. "Wow," she wheezed. "I haven't drank anything this strong, um, ever."

"Wait there." Ben opened the front door, reached up and snapped off an icicle. He broke it in half and put it spike-down in Zoey's glass.

"Thank you," she smiled.

They curled up together on a worn, soft couch in front of the fire.

Zoey took another sip of the whiskey and already felt its effects on her head; a pleasant hazy sensation behind the eyes.

This had the potential to turn into a wonderful night.

They both started speaking at the same time.

"I'm really looking forward to—"

"There's something I wanted to ask…" Ben trailed off.

She chuckled. He scratched the back of his head.

"You first," she said.

"No, go on. What are you looking forward to?"

She touched his hand. "Thanks for bringing me out here. I'm looking forward to spending a night outside for once. I never get to do this."

"I know," he said. "Living in the dormitory must take its toll. Air conditioned air really gives me a headache after a while."

"I know, right?" she exclaimed. "It's not natural. How can we live *here* and not use the air. Ever since they closed off the vents, the facility has become completely self-contained, cut off from the surface. I hate it. Six years and--" She stopped herself. *Mind your tongue!* "Anyway…what were you going to say?"

He considered for a moment, then spoke softly. "Zoey, I was thinking about what you said this morning. About you being a hostage."

Oh god, don't bring that up again now. "I really didn't mean anything by that. I was just cranky."

"Huh," he said. "Seemed pretty serious to me."

"No, I really dunno what I was saying," she insisted. *Mother might be listening!* "That time of the month, you know?"

"Relax, it's okay if you don't wanna talk about it."

"It's not like that," Zoey said, squeezing the glass and

downing the drink. "Can we just change the subject?"

"Woah, take it easy," Ben said. "At this altitude, it'll go right to your head. But on the plus side, mountain air first thing in the morning cures a hangover like that." He snapped his fingers and grinned.

She forced a smile.

"Okay," Ben said, rising to his feet. "I'm gonna get some more wood from the shack next door, and while I'm out there, I'll think of something else to talk about. You wait here and *relax*."

"Okay," she leaned back into the couch, and Ben laid a deerskin blanket over her legs.

"Good. Be right back."

When the door closed, Zoey inhaled a deep breath and poured herself another glass. Ben's questioning had sobered her up instantaneously. She took a sip, then another, until her head began to swim lightly once more. *Mother won't have bugged this place, surely? But I can't take any chances.*

"No, you're not spoiling this," she said aloud, rubbing the spot on her thigh where the tracker chip used to be, just beneath the skin. *She's gone for three months. I gotta make the most of that. I've earned* one *night of enjoyment, at least.*

She glanced out the window, admiring the gorgeous moonlit peaks against a black sea of twinkling stars. *You'd never see a night sky like this in Berlin.*

Something bumped the roof.

Zoey glanced up, frowning. Something outside scraped, followed by a soft *clank*.

"What the hell?"

She flipped the blanket off, put the glass down and went outside.

"Ben?" she called, looking towards the woodshed. She couldn't see any movement, so stepped down onto the hard packed snow to get a view of the roof. The chimney puffed orange-hued smoke into the sky, and next to it she saw the silhouette of something protruding from the wooden beams. *Is that a mini dish?*

"What's up?" Ben said.

Zoey jumped. He had appeared from the side of the cabin, carrying a bundle of logs under one arm. "You scared me!"

"Sorry," he said. "Aren't you freezing?"

"What's that?" she said, pointing at the dish on the roof.

"A data antenna." He offered his hand. "Shall we?"

"What does it do?" she probed, ignoring his hand.

Ben hesitated. "It transmits data."

"Duh. What data?"

He scratched the back of his head. "Wanna get back to the loveshack?" He tried a wink, but Zoey was having none of it.

"*Loveshack?*" She laughed. "If you think you're getting lucky tonight, you better tell me what you were doing first. I heard something on the roof. Were you messing with that up there?"

"Okay, okay… I was going to tell you anyway," he straightened his back. "I made it."

She suspected he was trying to impress her. But her immediate reaction was simple confusion. "You made it?"

"Yeah," he grinned. "It's awesome, isn't it? I use it to send data to the ShadowNet."

Zoey eyed him blankly. "Err, okay."

Ben groaned. "Do you know what the ShadowNet is?"

"I've heard of it." She narrowed her eyes. "I thought it was used by criminals…"

"Well, yeah it is," he said with a dismissive wave. "But it's also full of information. Stuff you can't find on the Net."

Zoey crossed her arms. "So why are you accessing the ShadowNet out here in the middle of the night?"

"Because if I use the work network, I'd be fired!" He laughed.

She looked from him, to the roof, back to him. "That's going to extreme measures, you know?"

"Yeah, I know."

She waited for him to elaborate, but he didn't. "Wait a second, so you brought me out here just to install your stupid little antenna dish?"

He clasped his chest in feigned agony. "Wow, right in the feels. I spent months on that. Hey, I didn't make you leave the nice, cosy cabin I prepared just for you."

"I just heard a noise, and… I was looking at the sky, and thought you might show me some star signs or something romantic."

He walked up and squeezed her hand in his glove. "Sorry. I don't really know any. You do like it up here though, right? I thought the *cabin* was romantic."

She softened at his touch. "Yeah, it really is."

"Beats being stuck down there, right?" he gestured to the ground at their feet.

"Oh yes."

"Come on, I'm freezing. Aren't you cold?"

"Mmm," she nodded.

"About time we warmed up, eh?" He winked.

"Definitely," she agreed.

They went back into the cabin and locked the door.

Afterwards, they lay together naked and tipsy under the deerskin blanket, the windows steamed up and the fire crackling.

For the first time in six years, Zoey felt genuine happiness. Being outside, in the company of a lover, enjoying a naughty night of passion. Little things, really. A bunch of intricate details that added up to something huge in her mind: freedom.

Ben took a swig from the bottle, and offered it to Zoey.

"No, thanks," her head was spinning very pleasantly, either from alcohol or recovering from what Ben had just finished doing. As she lay staring at the ceiling, it occurred to her that he hadn't really answered her question earlier.

"So why use the ShadowNet?"

"Well, I probably shouldn't tell you this…" He looked sideways at her.

"But you're going to," she encouraged him.

He glanced left and right, then spoke in a conspiratorial whisper, "I'm a member of Binary Eye."

Zoey scrunched her upper lip. "And that means?"

"Seriously? Don't you watch our YouTube videos?"

"No, some of us have actual work to do around here," she said, yawning. "What's Binary Eye? Some hacker group?"

He raised a finger. "I prefer the term *Truth-Seeker*. And we're not a group, we're a *collective*. But yes. The less poetic version is a group of hackers."

"Oh, you're a poet, too?" she said dreamily, resting her head on his chest. "Tell me a poem."

"I don't know any," he replied.

"Make it up," she said, closing her eyes against the steady rise and fall of his breathing.

"All right, then…" He started stroking her hair and chanted softly:

"I met this girl called Zoey, in the work canteen,
I like her eyes, they are very green…"

She would have laughed, had she the energy. The gentle vibrations of his voice sent her into a doze.

"I like her messy hair, it's long and nice and brown,
She wears a pony-tail, but I prefer it when it's… down."

Zoey exhaled a breathy sigh and drifted to the edge of unconsciousness.

"I'm curious about her, so I took her to the mountain,
I wonder… Is she really Zoey? Or could she be…"

She was asleep before he finished.

***

CRASH!

Frigid air engulfed the cabin through the burst-open door.

Zoey jolted awake on the couch.

"Here they are," a muffled voice said. "Grab him!"

Torchlights flashed. Men in black helmets stormed in.

"Miss Blunt! Are you okay?"

"What?" She spluttered, pulling the blanket up to her chest.

Ben yelled, "What the hell!" He was in the other chair, his face illuminated by the laptop screen, wearing nothing but his boxer shorts.

Two men seized him by the arms and dragged him out of the chair. At least four more helmets armed with pistols began searching the room.

"Get off him!" cried Zoey.

"Miss Blunt, please get dressed," the apparent leader said. He turned to his men. "Get the computer," he ordered. Another man marched over and picked it up off the table.

Zoey's heart pounded. *Who are they?*

"Put that down!" Ben said, struggling in the grip of the two helmeted brutes.

"Shut up," the leader said. He turned to the one holding the laptop. "What's the damage?"

"Just forums, sir. ShadowNet connection."

"Where's the transmitter?" a helmet demanded of Ben.

Ben stood defiant. "Fuck you, who even are you?"

Ben's interrogator punched him in the stomach. "Don't make me ask you again, son."

Zoey let out a cry. "Leave him alone!"

"Miss Blunt, please get dressed," the leader repeated, offering her a gloved hand.

She slapped it away. Pain seared through her finger bones. "Ow," she winced. He wasn't wearing a glove, his hand was made of black metal.

"You like this?" the leader asked, flexing his prosthetic

fingers. His tone was all smugness. "This is your father's latest work."

Wait a second…oh my god. Zoey covered her mouth with her hands.

Ben coughed. "Fuck… the transmitter's on the roof, asshole."

"Go," the leader gestured to another man, who disappeared outside.

"Mother…" Zoey mumbled.

"Miss Blunt, I won't ask you again." He picked up some of her clothes and shoved them into her lap.

They're Mother's men. Which means… "Don't hurt him! *Please don't hurt him!*" Zoey shrieked.

"Sorry, Miss. But he knows who you are."

"*And whose fault is that you prick!*" Zoey yelled. "You didn't have to call me Miss Blunt!"

"He already knew," the man with the laptop said. He spun it around so Zoey could see the screen.

A photo of her sleeping right here on the couch was shown under a heading which read *"Is Catherine Blunt still alive?"*

She choked back tears, looking at Ben in horror. *He has no idea what he's done.* "I…Ben…"

"I'm sorry, Catherine… I didn't mean…" he said, but Zoey interrupted.

"*Please!*" she begged the helmeted leader, standing up and grabbing his cold metal arm. "Please don't kill him! *Please!*"

The helmet tilted up and down, studying her naked body. "You brought this on yourself. Take him outside."

"*No!*" Zoey shrieked.

"What? No, please." Ben stammered as they dragged him through the door.

Zoey burst past the others and followed them into the freezing night.

"Let him go you bastards!" Hands seized her and held her back.

They threw Ben onto the snow next to another man. *Must be Carl, the spotter from the other cabin.* His head sat crooked above his snapped neck.

Ben's eyes were confusion and terror. He scrambled onto his knees as the leader with the metal arm sidled up behind him and gripped him around the chin.

"Ben!" Zoey cried.

His eyes met hers a split second before the leader twisted his grip.

Crack.

Ben slumped over dead on the ground.

The men released their grip on her. Zoey buried her face in her hands and cried. "Not again. *Not again!*"

"Grab a blanket, cover her up for fuck's sake." Rough hands wrapped her in the deerskin. The world was blurry through her tears.

The leader said, "Margery wants her locked in her dorm before sunrise. And make *this* look like an accident. Set off some explosives up the slope there. Send the whole lot tumbling down the mountain.

SIX WEEKS LATER

2
THE MOUNTAIN FACILITY

"ETA ten minutes, Agent."

"Roger that," Frank replied through his headset.

"Oh God, oh God," went the kid, jackhammering both feet against the metallic cargo bay floor. "Can't believe I volunteered for this."

"Relax," Frank said. "Tuck your thumbs inside the straps of your chute and breathe, like this."

The kid mimicked Frank from the bench on the opposite side of the fuselage. He inhaled two short breaths then shook his head. "It's no good, man. I gotta occupy my mind or something." He pulled out his tablet for the sixth time and manically thumbed the screen.

Bloody kids. "Put it away," Frank ordered. "I need you to start focusing."

"I'm focused, just checking the brief again," the kid tried to insist. "Also, I can't stop thinking about that picture. You know, of the Blunts' daughter."

"It was grainy as shit and she didn't even have her eyes open," Frank reminded him. "That could have been anyone, anywhere."

"I know, dude, but it might have been here. The guy who posted it said he worked in a science facility. And Margery Blunt works here!"

"The Blunts are not our concern. We're here to keep

tabs on their medical research, nothing more."

"Do you think we'll see Margery Blunt down there?"

Frank crossed his arms. "Intel says she's away. And if I do my job properly, nobody should see us down there. What's with this obsession with the Blunts, kid?"

"Are you kidding me? All my tech back home is branded Blunt. They're the best. Or, they were. The company went a bit downhill after Sid and Margery split." He gave a nervous laugh. "Imagine bumping into her, man. 'Oops, don't mind me! I'm only here to steal your private files!'"

Frank didn't see the funny side of that. Meeting the business tycoon during an unwarranted infiltration would cause irreparable damage to Europa's public profile. She had enough media connections to drag Europa's image through the dirt. It was no coincidence that Frank had been sent here while they knew she was abroad. "Put the tablet away. You're here to do a job, not surf the bloody Net."

The kid sighed, put the tablet back in his pack and hung his head. His feet resumed their erratic dance.

"It's Jimmy, right?" said Frank.

"Yeah. And you're, um, Agent Hawkins?"

"Frank'll do."

"Right."

"You say you volunteered for this?"

Jimmy squeaked a nervous laugh. "Yeah. They said if I do three field missions, they'll cut my sentence in half."

"Good move, I'd say."

"Glad you think so. My brother would kill me if he knew where I was right now…"

"Why's that?" Frank probed, feigning interest to keep the kid's mind off punching a hole through the aircraft floor with his twitchy boot heels.

"Because Europa caught me. He's never been caught."

"Your brother's a hacker, too?"

"Heh, yeah. Thinks he's better than me, and well, I suppose he is considering I'm the one sat here and he's…

God knows where."

"You dunno where he is?"

"Somewhere in Korea. He ran away there, supposedly for the fast Net access. He was always a bit of a loner." Jimmy smiled at the floor. "Still love 'im though, we stay in touch online. He has a pretty dark view about Europa."

"Is that so?" Frank said, resisting the urge to yawn.

"Yeah, you may call me your techie sidekick or whatever, but he'd call it unjustified kidnapping."

Frank snorted. "Europa caught you breaking into their network, and they arrested you for it. You only have yourself to blame, kid."

Jimmy quietened. "I know." He rubbed his hands together. "I just want this whole ordeal to be over with now."

"ETA five minutes, Agent," the pilot buzzed in Frank's ear.

"Roger that."

"Shit, shit, shit," yammered Jimmy, drumming his hands on his thighs.

Frank unhooked himself and strode across the cargo hold to sit next to the fidgety teenager. He flexed a bicep in front of Jimmy's nose. "You see this?"

The kid froze. "Um, yes."

"How'd you think I got that?"

"By working out?"

"Yeah. Training. Hard work. Six hours a day, six days a week, whenever I ain't in the field."

"Good for you, man," the kid squirmed, scratching the back of his neck.

"How long do you spend looking at that screen all day?" Frank asked.

"Jeez, man, are you my mom?"

"How long?"

"I dunno," Jimmy gave Frank a petulant wide-eyed shrug. "Same as you? Probably more? I live on my computer, man."

"Exactly," Frank jabbed a finger towards Jimmy's forehead.

The kid flinched.

"I dunno what you did to get caught up with Europa, kid. But, if the chief decided to assign you to be my tech, you must be bloody good at it. And that's why you're here. When we get down there, you have a job to do, and I expect you to do it. It's my job to keep you safe." He pointed his thumb at his own chest. "And I'm bloody good at that."

Jimmy's feet stopped tapping.

"This is a recon mission, very routine," Frank said.

"You mean breaking and entering."

"That's one way to put it. We call it tactical infiltration. You do what I tell you, when I tell you, and we'll be just fine."

Jimmy exhaled, and nodded quickly. "Okay, dude. Just get me to the server farm."

"Atta' boy." Frank slapped him on the shoulder.

"ETA one minute, Agent."

"Roger that," he replied.

A red light above the bay door illuminated the cargo hold.

"Up," Frank said, rising. He clicked his retractable black visor into place. "Press here, by your neck."

The kid fumbled with the button until the visor snapped into place. Frank did a quick final check of the kid's chute pack and skysuit, then positioned Jimmy's hands so they were holding his shoulder straps.

The aircraft slowed to a hover, indicated by Frank's stomach churning at the sudden decrease of speed.

"Help me push." Frank braced against the back of the snowspeeder, which was secured to a rail with a nylon cargo net. Together, they heaved it towards the rear of the hold.

The ramp door opened in front of them and the throbbing *wub-wub-wub* of the propellers pounded through

Frank's skull.

Evening sunlight glinted off the snowy peaks of the mountains, casting a fiery glow into the hold. The cargo net danced wildly in the chill wind that gusted in.

"Oh God!" cried Jimmy, recoiling and stumbling onto his arse and crawling backwards.

Sorry, kid. You ain't getting out of it. "Got a runner back here, mate," Frank said into his mic. "Give us a nudge?"

"Heh, roger that, Agent," said the pilot. "Initiating tilt."

Frank strode over to the kid, who had his back flush against the secure pilot's cabin door. "Better to get it over with. Let's go." He gestured to the open ramp.

The mountains seemed to slide upwards. The sky disappeared as the ground tipped further into view.

"Oh shit man!" Jimmy whimpered.

"Let's jump, kid."

"I've never done this! Aren't you supposed to do it tandem for your first jump?"

"That's what the skysuit's for. It'll sort you out."

The kid slipped on the rapidly tilting floor. His panicked eyes followed the snowspeeder as it rolled along the rail, down the ramp and disappeared from sight.

He ain't gonna jump. "It's a VTOL, kid. Vertical Take-off and Landing."

"I can't do this man!"

Frank laughed. "You ain't listening. There is no can't here. She can tilt right over and spit us out whilst still hovering in the same spot and there's nothing you can do to prevent it." He considered throwing Jimmy out himself, but managed to restrain the urge. "So long, kid."

With that, Frank sprinted down the sloping floor and dived into the frigid alpine sky. He tucked his arms in and nosedived.

The sun set a dozen peaks on fire, glowing across the mountainous horizon. As Frank plummeted into a high valley between two great ridges, the fiery ball disappeared and the world turned a shade dimmer.

Above the roaring wind, Jimmy's wail came through Frank's headset, signaling his defeat to the tilting aircraft.

Frank grinned to himself.

The skysuit's flaps opened automatically, guiding him towards a flat perch of snow right beneath his belly. A manmade slab of circular concrete marked his landing zone.

The snowspeeder's chute deployed far below and he saw it land in a puff of white powder next to the concrete. As Frank's own chute opened, his stomach turned upside down and wedged itself in his throat. He descended to a gentle float just above the ground and dropped onto his feet in the soft, unspoiled snow. Buttons on the side of his pack and on the snowspeeder collapsed both parachutes back into their respective packs. He unclipped the cargo net from the snowspeeder and rolled it into a compartment.

Jimmy's scream pierced his ears in the headset, but even when Frank switched it off, he heard the kid's voice echoing off the mountainside.

"Aaaaiieeee!" Jimmy wailed before the chute cut him off. It snapped open like a gigantic bird's wing over Frank's head, bringing the kid to a gentle cruise beside him. The chute slowed him down with such calculated precision, that he landed as lightly as you would step off a curb.

Jimmy stood trembling, before stumbling to his knees in the snow. He fumbled his visor out of the way and puked on the snow. "Ugh, man."

Frank hit the contract button on Jimmy's pack and the chute folded itself away. *These skysuits really are the tits*, Frank mused. He was far from a technophobe and certainly appreciated it when it made his job easier.

Jimmy groaned, wiping his mouth.

"Better out than in," Frank slapped him on the shoulder.

"I'm pulling out, Agent. See you at the rendezvous." The VTOL, a small black speck high in the sky, drifted away.

"Roger that. Out." Frank stashed their chutes on the

snowspeeder, grabbed his equipment backpack from its storage box and chucked it up onto the raised concrete slab jutting out of the ground. "This is our point of entry and escape. Come on." He climbed up.

He hunkered to examine the square grate in the centre of the slab. *Same as when I left it the last time.* The hinge screamed as he lifted it open. A cavernous ventilation shaft plunged into pitch darkness straight down into the mountain.

Jimmy scrambled up to join him, and peered inside. He gulped. "Is it deep?"

"Let's see." Frank leaned over and flicked on his shoulder flashlight. He aimed it down the hole and shone it across the smooth metal walls of the circular shaft.

Thank fuck for good Intel. The fans are gone. Last time Frank was here, he'd had to navigate through three sets of industrial fans in order to reach the bottom, but they had since been removed. *Glad I don't have to do that again, especially with the kid.*

Jimmy was staring agape down the shaft. "So, how deep is that?"

"About fifty metres."

"Fifty…" Jimmy swallowed his words, or bile, Frank couldn't tell which.

"This'll get you down safely." Frank reached into his pack and handed Jimmy a black metallic cylinder. "It's called a zip-winch. Strap it to your wrist, like this." He clipped his own onto a slot in the skysuit's sleeve.

Jimmy shook his head vigorously. "What the hell, man? You said this was a routine recon mission. Jumping out of a plane may be routine to you, but I prefer doing shit like that in a videogame. And now you want me to throw myself down a death pit that leads God-knows where?"

"It connects to a series of vents, right above the air filtration room. That section of the facility has been abandoned, but we still have to be quiet while we're in the vents. We have to crawl to the server farm. You were briefed on all of this."

Jimmy scratched the back of his neck and sighed through clenched teeth.

Frank sympathised with the kid. A little. But he had a job to do. "Come on, we'll be in and out of here in under an hour. Assuming you're up to the task?"

"I'm a hacker, man... not some secret agent."

"And a bloody good job, too. Listen, I can't get the info I need without you, so when you're done whinging like a lost puppy... like I told you in the plane, it's better to get it over with." He gestured to the square hole at their feet.

"All this for some cancer research..." Jimmy muttered. He clipped his zip-winch on so that the cylindrical canister could be gripped in his hand, the same as Frank. Jimmy's white knuckles threatened to pop through the skin. "They better have something else worth stealing down there, man."

Jimmy shuffled towards the grate and sat down, dangling his legs through the hole. His eyes flicked to it but then he looked up into the distance, jaw clenched.

"Unleash the tethers," Frank said. He guided Jimmy's hand down towards his ankles, through the grate and clicked the button on the winch.

Three pronged cables spat out of the cap, tipped with metallic gyroscopic ball-bearings which stuck to the walls and pulled taut.

"See?" Frank tugged Jimmy's arm. "Strong as hell. Now jump in and let it take you down. Press this button to slow down before you hit the bottom. And remember, try to stay quiet."

"Shit, man," Jimmy wiped his mouth, and inhaled a deep breath. He glanced at the hole and hesitated.

I'm gonna have to push him...

"Oh fuck it," Jimmy said, and slipped over the edge. He plunged into the shaft and disappeared with a yelp.

ZZZZZZZZZZZzzzzzzziiiiiiiiiiinngg.

The zip-winch cables unravelled, allowing a smooth but

rapid descent. At the same time, the ball bearings slid down the walls, whining just like a zip. Jimmy reached the bottom in less than three seconds.

"Woah!" he wheezed, his voice echoing up to Frank. "Holy crap!"

"I said be quiet," Frank hissed. "Move aside, I'm coming down."

Frank glanced around the darkening mountainside. *Might catch the last of the light if we're quick enough.*

When Jimmy had moved out of the way, Frank jumped in with the zip-winch raised above his head. He clicked the cables out in mid-air and they snapped against the walls, jolting his shoulder as they took the brunt of his weight. Dangling from the winch, he shot down the ventilation shaft and joined Jimmy at the bottom.

With a click of a button, the cables detached from the walls and retracted into the winch's cylindrical casing.

"Now what?" Jimmy whispered in the dark.

Frank flicked his shoulder light to night mode, casting a red glow on the walls and the kid's baby-smooth jawline. At their feet, two square-shaped ventilation tunnels led away in opposite directions. Frank pointed at the one on their left. "This way."

Frank tossed his backpack into the vent, got down on hands and knees and crawled inside.

*   *   *

It took twenty minutes of cramped, awkward navigation to reach the server farm. If it weren't for the frigid conditioned air constantly billowing through the ventilation with them, Frank would have worked up a nasty sweat.

"Routine, my ass," Jimmy complained from somewhere behind. "In and out in an hour, my fat ass."

"Shut it," Frank snapped. He was trying to listen for voices on the other side of the sealed grate blocking their path to the server room. Through the tiny slits in the grate, he could see down a single row of server banks. Nobody in sight.

He took a micro-welder from the backpack and used it to melt the bolts in each corner of the grate. It hissed and sent a sharp tendril of pungent smoke into his nostrils.

"All these seals we've been burning through," Jimmy said. "They must be to do with the EMS."

Frank was losing patience with the kid. Despite his constant reminders to be quiet, Jimmy not only complained at every opportunity, but he had this irritating habit of talking with vague acronyms that went over Frank's head. This time, Frank replied by jerking his boot back until it struck something soft.

"Ow!" Jimmy grunted. "Sorry, man…"

"For the love of fuck, be quiet."

Frank tugged the grate loose and turned it flush against the vent wall. Now he had a clear view of the server farm. They were in a corner, almost ceiling-height, overlooking the last two rows of machines. The air conditioned room hummed with the gentle whirr of electronics, and the soft ambient glow of red LEDs.

He couldn't see any CCTV cameras covering this particular row, so he eased himself out and dropped to the ground. He slung his pack onto his back, then turned to help Jimmy down.

Frank made a sharp zip gesture across his lips and glared at the kid. Jimmy nodded.

Frank gestured to the row of machines and turned his palms to the ceiling. *Which one?*

Jimmy shrugged. He took out his tablet and cable, hunkered down beside the nearest terminal and plugged into it. Data streamed across a window of the unrecognisable operating system. The kid flexed his fingers then started tapping the screen in a whirlwind of motion.

Within seconds, he was copying files, indicated by a loading bar and animation of alien letters running over the screen like something out of a cheesy sci-fi movie.

Frank questioned the kid with a thumbs up, thumbs down gesture. Jimmy didn't seem to notice. He was frowning intensely at the screen, apparently lost in his work.

He knows what he's doing. Frank checked the corridor beyond the thick glass window that ran the length of the farm, scanning for wandering scientists. Empty. *It's early evening, most of 'em should be having dinner. Just like I planned.*

A jab on Frank's leg made him turn around. Jimmy was staring up at him, tilting the screen so Frank could see. A text window overlapped the copying animation, with a typed message in it.

`'Horizon'` mean anything to you?

Frank racked his brain, but the word didn't connect with anything. He shook his head.

Jimmy bit his lip, and went back to work while Frank kept a lookout.

The room flickered red. Frank assumed it was the LEDs of the server banks and thought nothing of it until it happened again. And again.

He glanced out of the window, and saw that the corridor walls outside the room were also flashing red. A cold chill swept through his spine. *That's a fucking alarm.*

Frank's ears popped as every one of the thousand or so computers in the room abruptly switched off and the room went dark. The red light from the silent siren outside lit the room in intermittent flashes of crimson.

"Fuck!" Jimmy cried. "What happened?"

"Someone knows we're here."

3
ESCAPE

The ache in the back of her neck spiked whenever she turned her head, so she tried not to move it unless absolutely necessary. She hunched over her desk, typing one sentence after another with trembling fingers. Now and then, they tensed up and she had to clench them into fists.

How much longer could she go on like this? Suicide had never crossed her mind despite everything that had happened. Yet Zoey felt claustrophobic, so stifled and suffocated beyond words that she assumed it was only a matter of time.

Getting out of bed every day proved to be the toughest challenge, and it got a little harder every morning.

One day I'll just wake and be unable to get up. I'll just lie there until I die. And nobody will care.

Yet so far, she'd managed to keep going. Did that make her a fighter? If so, what was she fighting for?

This is no life. This is no fucking life...

"Earth to Zoey!"

Zoey jumped in her seat. Her colleague Nadia was standing beside her, holding a manila folder which she had just slapped onto the desk. "Sorry. What?"

"You were really zoned out there. Wow, you look pale,

are you okay?"

"I'm fine. Did you need something?"

"Just seeing if you want a coffee?" Nadia stretched her arms. "I gotta fuel up for my all-nighter, you know?"

"Uh, sure. Thanks."

Nadia squinted at Zoey's screen, then gaped. "You're still on section two of that Bio report?"

"Um, yeah," Zoey clicked the cursor onto a new section and stared at the list of numbers, but they all jumbled into a mass of gibberish before her eyes. Her temples throbbed.

"Are you sure you're okay?" Nadia asked.

The phone rang.

Zoey leaned back in her chair, shaking her head. She fumbled with the handset and answered, "Hello?"

"Catherine, are you alone?"

Mother…

Zoey spoke sideways to Nadia, "Sorry, I have to take this."

"No problem. I'll go get that coffee." She picked up the folder and sauntered away.

Zoey took a deep breath. "I'm alone, Mother."

"Good. I don't have time to explain, but you need to get to your dorm room."

"What? Why?"

"What did I *just* say about my time? Listen, get up, go to your dorm and lock the door. I'll send a man to pick you up. Hold on." The phone went dead, as if Margery had muted her.

Zoey massaged the back of her neck as she waited.

The phone clicked and Margery spoke again, this time in a more urgent tone. "Catherine, you must do as I say. Security has reported activity in the, what did you call it?" She seemed to be speaking to someone else in the room. "Right, the EMS system."

"What's that?" Zoey frowned.

"The Environment Management System, apparently." Margery sounded impatient. "It's the ventilation ducts…

temperature control for the server room. Will you stop talking over me, I can't explain all of that!" She snapped at the other person. Then back to Zoey, "We think it's an infiltrator, Catherine."

"Like a spy? Am I in danger?"

"Don't be ridiculous, nobody knows you are alive, except…" Margery trailed off.

"Except Dad," Zoey finished. A small light ignited deep inside her. *Did he finally come for me?*

"Hold on."

The phone went quiet again, but not silent this time. "Mother?"

She heard Margery speak, her voice distant and tinny. "Why can't I see them?"

"Must be in a blind spot," a man said.

Zoey listened, straining to hear the conversation.

"Confirmed breach. They're transferring files."

"Which sector?"

"It's the *R&D Archives.*"

"Twelve terabytes already."

"Are the Horizon files backed up anywhere else?" said another man with an air of authority.

"Yes sir, we have multiple backups spread ac—"

"Then shut it down. *Now!*"

A pause followed, then, "It's shutting down, sir."

"Purge the facility," said the authoritive man, his voice cold and hard. "Sound the five-minute warning for management. The intruders cannot be allowed to leave."

"But Henry," Margery shrilled. "Catherine is there!"

"She's played her part. It'll all be for nothing if Horizon gets leaked. Is that on mute? *Christ,* hang up the ph—"

Click.

A beat later, a siren exploded through the room. It blurted sharp honks loud enough to rattle the windows. A red pulsating light cast deep shadows across the floors and up the walls.

Deafened by the wail, Zoey dropped the handset and

covered her ears. The noise drove out all but a single thought:

This is how I die, then.

She remained rooted to her chair as technicians appeared in the corridor outside, shuffling towards the emergency exit. Some were still slurping their coffees as they bundled along, white coats flickering blood red like sheep led to the slaughter.

Two figures caught Zoey's eye. Dressed in black, a tall muscular man brushed past her colleagues, heading in the opposite direction. Following in his wake, a shorter, younger-looking man weaved between the jostling flow of bodies. *They're the spies!*

The fire in Zoey's heart flickered again.

She sprang to her feet. Zoey barged through the door into the throng of people and pushed her way through, eyes locked on the two strangers.

"Zoey!" Nadia said as Zoey bumped into her, nearly spilling the coffee cups in each hand. "Where are you going?"

Zoey ignored her and pressed through the remaining cluster of people and emerged at the back of the press to an empty corridor. The siren wailed in her ears as she jogged around the corner just in time to see the shorter man in black entering a door.

They're going to the old ventilation room.

She bolted for the door and jammed her arm in it just before it swung shut. She squeezed through and entered a dark, musky corridor. As the door closed behind her, the alarm faded to a distant and muffled wail.

She heard the men speaking somewhere in the dark ahead.

The first voice was deep and gruff, and he talked with a thick British accent. "This panel leads to the shaft. Pack your shit away, we're getting out of here."

"Just a second," the younger one answered. He sounded like an American teenager.

Something heavy and metallic clattered to the floor, echoing through the darkness. Zoey couldn't see much so she walked with her hands out in front, feeling for the edge of the next doorway.

"I'll go up first, so I can pull you through the gap," the older man said. "Wait for me to get clear."

"Okay," the other replied.

Zoey heard a metallic *clang,* followed by a drawn-out *züing* which sounded a bit like a zipper.

She fumbled through the doorway and saw a figure kneeling on the floor, his face illuminated by a computer screen.

"Hey!" she called.

"*Fuck!*" the young man spun to face her and Zoey was half-blinded by a soft red light. She squinted against it, and stumbled through the darkness towards him.

"You have to help me get out of here. Please take me with you."

"How did you get in here?" he said, glancing up to the ceiling and back at her.

She made it across the room to him, and saw that the red light was a night-mode flashlight mounted on his shoulder. A metal grate was lying on the floor beside him, under a square hole in the ceiling.

This must be how they broke in.

"Please, I have to get out," Zoey pleaded. "I don't think we have much time."

"It's not up to me," the young man said, fidgeting with his tablet.

"Where did your partner go?" she said, studying his face in the dim light. *He can't be much older than sixteen.*

"Just a second." He frantically typed something on the tablet's screen.

"Jimmy?" The gruff British voice echoed down the shaft. "What the *fuck* are you doing? Get up here!"

"I'm coming!" Jimmy said. He jabbed a button on the tablet which said *send,* before standing up. "Sorry, Miss. I can't take…" He squinted at her. "Oh my god. You're Catherine, aren't you?"

Zoey recoiled. *How can he possibly know that?* "Um, no. My name's Zoey. Please, if we don't get out of here, I think we're going to die."

"*JIMMY!*"

"Shit," Jimmy slapped a hand over his mouth and flapped the other one at his side. He stuffed the tablet inside his backpack and pulled out a metal cylinder. Zipping it up, he handed the bag out to her. "You better carry this."

She took it, confused. "Why?"

"Just put it on and follow me."

He jumped at the hole in the ceiling and pulled himself up.

Zoey slung the backpack on and reached up. Jimmy grabbed her by the arms and helped her climb into the chilly ventilation shaft. High above their heads, she saw a red light shining down.

"Jimmy if you don't get your arse up here in five seconds, I'm leaving you behind!"

"We're coming!"

"What the fuck do you mean '*we*?'"

Jimmy aimed the cylinder above his head and – *twang!* Something shot out of the end, attached to cables.

"Climb on my back," Jimmy said. "And hold on tight as you can."

Zoey did so. Her heart beat against his back as she wrapped her arms over one shoulder and under his other, squeezing his skinny chest.

Zoey's body jerked upwards in the dark. She cried out in surprise as her feet lifted off the ground. Clinging the guy's neck for dear life, she tried to swing her legs around his body but the force was too strong. She hugged him with all her strength as they shot up into the air.

Zzzüüüüüüinngg!

They came to a stop, dangling just below the ceiling of

the cavernous shaft.

"Who's *she*?" the British guy demanded.

"It's Catherine Blunt," Jimmy wheezed. "Take her, man. I'm slipping!"

Rough hands seized Zoey under the arms.

One of the cables snapped. Zoey shrieked.

Jimmy dropped a few feet and Zoey slipped out of the other man's clutches. He managed to grab her by the hand, and she dangled from his iron-like grip, accidentally kicking Jimmy who hung on just below her waist.

"What's happening Frank?" Jimmy cried.

"The tethers are coming loose," the bigger guy said, straining as he took Zoey's weight.

"Don't let me go!" she begged. She swung against the shaft wall, her wrist burning from the pressure.

Twack! Another cable broke.

Frank strained to pull her up. "Jimmy, you idiot, they're only designed for *one person*!"

The backpack snagged on the hole. Frank tugged, but she was stuck.

"Help me Frank!" wailed Jimmy.

The last cable went *twang!*

"*Ahhh*!" Jimmy screamed.

Zoey felt him drop away from her. She instinctively looked down.

"Jimmy!" Frank shouted.

Jimmy tumbled down the shaft in freefall. His scream echoed off the walls until it abruptly cut off with a sickening *thud.*

Oh my god.

Frank gave a mighty heave. The backpack gave way and her head popped out into freezing air. She fumbled for a grip on the floor, touched icy cold concrete. He wrenched her out of the hole and she sprawled on her side looking up at the starry sky and jagged snowy peaks.

"I…I'm sorry," she stammered.

The mountain rumbled.

The concrete slab she was lying on cracked violently, splitting out from the edges of the hole.

"The fuck?" Frank said, stumbling backwards. "Move!" He lunged at Zoey, shoving her hard.

They both slipped off the slab just as a huge chunk of it fell away, plunging into the shaft. A deep throated roar ruptured from the hole, but it seemed to come from all across the valley, echoing around the mountains.

Mother… what did you do?

"Fuck me. We have to move, now!" Frank barked, staggering to his feet against the vibrating ground, hauling Zoey with him.

He dragged her to a sleek, black snowspeeder parked on the snow.

She climbed on behind him, while he tried starting it. The engine sputtered out. "It's dead!" He whipped out a kick-starter pedal and gave it a hard yank with his boot heel.

Still nothing.

A noise like an approaching hurricane whirred up behind them. Zoey craned her neck around and squinted at the nearest peak above them. A puffy cloud of white powder drifted into the sky from off the mountains surface. It was growing rapidly.

Avalanche…

"Fuck!" Frank jumped off the snowspeeder. He released the brake and it started sliding down the slope very slowly. Grabbing the handlebars he leaned into it and pushed.

"I'll help you!" Zoey said, scrambling off and adding her own modest effort.

The speeder crept along, picking up speed. The ground rumbled through Zoey's feet, heavy vibrations coming from deep beneath the mountain.

"Oh god!" she panicked.

"Get on!" Frank yelled over the din of approaching thunder.

She jumped on the back seat and grabbed him around

the waist as soon as he was in front. He kicked the pedal again. Nothing.

A thunderous roar split the air behind them. *It's almost on top of us!*

Frank kicked again.

The engine screamed to life.

Frank revved the throttle. Zoey nearly fell off the back. She grabbed hold of Frank's shoulder as the snowspeeder sprang forward.

A cold blast hit the back of Zoey's neck. She caught a terrifying glimpse of the icy wall of death bearing down on them. Chunks of ice and snow spat over their heads and thudded into the ground all around them.

The speeder accelerated. Zoey lost all sense of direction and tried to focus on just holding on.

They careened down the mountain at breakneck speed ahead of the avalanche.

The speeder jerked sideways as Frank manoeuvred to avoid crevices and juts of rock.

At last Zoey sensed the danger retreating behind them.

They reached a wide plateau dotted with boulders and shot into the open space. Zoey glanced behind and saw a sprawling cloud of moonlit mist rising high above them, blocking out the view of the mountain.

As the avalanche struck the flat ground, it lost its momentum. A plume of snowy mist billowed into the sky and dissipated far behind them. An echoing rumble ricocheted off the surrounding peaks before finally diminishing to nothing, and all Zoey could hear was the whine of the snowspeeder's engine.

***

Frank weaved the snowspeeder through a tightly packed evergreen forest, until they emerged in an icy clearing on the top of a sheer cliff. The view overlooked a forested valley, a vast carpet of trees ran up against a jagged peak which stabbed the starry sky several miles away.

He pulled up in the middle of the clearing and shut off the engine.

Zoey sat frozen on the seat, clutching him round the waist. Neither of them moved for a while, only breathed. The echoes of the avalanche died away, until the night air finally stilled.

A deafening silence settled on the clearing. As the adrenaline wore off, Zoey began to shiver.

The speeder creaked as Frank stood up and dismounted. He took a step away and held his arm up as if checking his watch. He tapped his arm agitatedly and cursed under his breath. He turned to Zoey, scowling. "So what's your story?"

Zoey hugged herself. "My name's Zoey. I'm just an analyst—"

"Don't gimme that bullshit. The kid," Frank paused, closing his eyes for a moment. "…Jimmy died trying to get you out. Are you Catherine Blunt or not?"

Zoey swallowed. *He doesn't know me. So Dad can't have sent him. And Mother, she was so angry. I need to know if I can trust him…* "Who do you work for?"

The agent shook his head as he stormed towards her. He grabbed her round the throat and dragged her off the bike. Choking, she scratched at his arm and dug her heels in but his strength far outweighed hers.

He leaned her out over the edge of the chasm.

"If the next words out your mouth ain't a yes or a no, I'm gonna drop you, understand?"

"Yes," she wheezed, heart racing.

"Are you Catherine Blunt?"

She sensed the deathly drop beneath her and believed he would do it. *So what choice do I have?*

"Yes," she said. "I'm Catherine."

Frank didn't kill her.

He setup a tent in the clearing, illuminated it with a small hanging battery lantern from the inside. The white canvas glowed like a Chinese lantern in the snow. "We'll sleep here tonight," the agent said.

"Shouldn't we get out of here?" she asked, shivering.

"I should have been at the rendezvous with the kid about…" He checked his wrist watch, then shrugged. "Now, I guess. My comms is fried, so I can't even contact anyone. I'm onto Plan B here." He rubbed his forehead. "There's a spare skysuit in there. It'll keep you warm. I'll wait out here while you change."

Zoey took another look around the clearing. *So peaceful.* She inhaled the cold scent of fresh snow and pine needles, recognising the significance of the moment. *I never meant for anyone to die because of me… thank you for getting me out, Jimmy.*

She crawled inside and changed into the black skysuit. It felt strong and insulated, but it hung off her frame a few sizes too big. "I'm done."

The agent crawled inside and zipped the tent up. He collapsed on his butt, then lay down on his sleeping bag with one hand behind his head. He looked to be about forty, with a stubbly square chin and off-kilter nose. *Probably had a few fights in his time,* she mused.

She still didn't know who he was. She hugged her knees. "So, um, your name is Frank, right?"

"Yup."

"And um, Plan B… What are you going to do with me?"

He watched her a moment. "I don't know. Tomorrow, we'll catch a train to the border. We have a safehouse there."

"Who is 'we'?"

"Europa," he said.

The government agency… She frowned. "Why were you investigating us?"

"That's classified."

"Oh. Right."

He grunted. "Still, wasn't worth losing the kid over." He rubbed a hand down across his face. *He feels guilty.* "Who the fuck rigs a science lab to self-destruct?" he mumbled, looking at Zoey.

She swallowed and looked away.

"And you," he said. "What were you doing there?"

Zoey — *No, my name is Catherine* — felt a shiver crawl up her back. Six years of torment had crushed her spirit to a point she thought she could never recover from. But she was out now.

She gritted her teeth. Tears formed in the corners of her eyes. "My father. It was all his fault."

4
A FATHER'S FAILURE

EIGHT YEARS AGO

"As you know, Mr. Zhin," Sid Blunt steepled his fingers, eyeing the Korean businessman projected on the wall of his study. "While *Blunt Electronics* operates out of Berlin here in Germany, we are bound by Euro-American trade laws. As far as I see it, what you bring to the table is the opportunity to establish a presence in Neo Asia."

"And that is an exciting prospect," added his wife Margery, sitting beside Sid at the table.

"Of course," Zhin's projection said. "You require someone with experience in the art of uniting opposing forces, and I think you'll be hard pressed to find a more suitable partner than myself."

"We quite agree," said Margery, bowing her head.

Zhin smiled. "I'm glad to hear it."

"May I ask what your thoughts are on the development of artificial limbs and prostheses?" Sid inquired.

"I can't say that I've ever given it much thought. I wasn't aware that *Blunt* invested much in medical technology. With all due respect, I thought you just sold phones to teenagers."

"It's something I'm hoping to expand into," Sid explained.

"Is there a market for it?"

"I believe so, yes."

"Sidney, is this relevant?" Margery said.

"I want to hear his opinion, dear."

Zhin chuckled. "Please, I am always interested in new enterprises, particularly if they are of benefit to people. But I'm afraid my knowledge on medical technology is limited, at best."

"Never mind then," Sid said. "There will be plenty of time to enlighten you, if we partner up."

"Of course," Zhin replied.

"Thank you for your time," Sid said, reaching for the call button. "We will be in touch."

"I look forward to working with you."

Sid ended the call and the study turned a shade darker. "Lights on," Sid commanded, and the small chandelier lit up, illuminating the book cases and vintage globe.

Margery cocked her head with one raised eyebrow. "What was that?"

"What?"

"You veered off-topic."

"So what?"

"Do you really think a man like that is interested in hearing about your fanciful side projects?"

"He said he was interested!"

"He humoured you, Sidney. He was being gracious." She rubbed her forehead. "I hope you haven't squandered this incredible opportunity. He'd be perfect."

"He's rather arrogant. I haven't agreed to anything yet, and he's *looking forward to working with me*."

"You must be joking?" Margery said. "The man is responsible for uniting the Koreans. I'd say he's earned the right to display a little arrogance."

Sid scoffed. "No one man could be praised for the Korean Unification. That was the result of years of negotiations from dozens of countries. Who told you Zhin was involved?"

"I made a contact at the BBC. Louise Stone." Margery gave a smug smile. "She's an up and coming global reporter, gaining quite a reputation. If she says something is true, then it probably is. I just know we are going to get along *exquisitely*."

"Well done. She sounds—"

"But we're not discussing Louise, Sid. We're discussing Horatio Zhin. He tipped the scales in the Korean debate, if nothing else." She walked around the desk to stand in front of him and placed both hands flat on the table. Leaning forward, she said, "That man is changing the world, Sidney. You would do well to partner with him."

Sid knew she was right. With Zhin's Asian influence, Blunt would become the largest electronics brand in the world, and be free to sell to any continent without restrictions. The notion was both exciting and daunting.

Margery leaned back and crossed her arms. "I see you have your doubts."

"Of course I do. This is not something I can decide lightly."

"What is there to decide?" Margery spread her palms. "Do you want us to live *here* for the rest of our lives?"

We live in a mansion…

"I don't want Catherine to lose her head," Sid answered at last. "She needs to keep her feet on the ground, understand the value of hard work."

"Don't use our daughter as an excuse to quell your ambition. Where's your *drive?*"

"You haven't seen what I've got my tech team working on. These new prostheses are going to make a big difference to amputees' lives. Doctor Gunther claims to have fully-functional finger simulation working in conjunction with the body's original nerve system. It's incredible, Margery. We're going to help a lot of people."

She looked bemused. "Philanthropy. Is that your idea of a business model?"

"Blunt is the third most profitable corporation in the

world, Margery. You do realise that, don't you?"

"I do. But it's not like you can claim responsibility for your father's genius now, is it?"

Sid gaped. "How dare you?"

"I'm sorry, dear. It's just you lack everything that Horatio Zhin possesses." She turned and swept out of the room. "What are the plans for dinner tonight, Bernard?" she called as her footsteps clacked across the marble hallway.

Sid leaned back in his chair and sighed through gritted teeth.

She's right and you know it. The Blunt brand needed to penetrate the Neo-Asian market, and Zhin might just be the man to help him do it. Sid didn't have to like him in order to work with him. But setting up the deal would involve a lot of travelling to and fro, wrapped up in negotiations for the next few months. *I hardly see Catherine as it is. I want to be around to guide her.*

A hulking dark-skinned man appeared in the open door and knocked.

"Come in, Arnie."

Sid's personal bodyguard, Arnie Dillon had to duck under the doorframe to enter. "Hello, sir." His deep throaty voice and Maori accent emanated a gentle strength.

"You can call me Sid at home, Arnie. Please close the door."

Arnie shut the door and clasped his hands in front of his waist. "I know I can, sir."

Sid smiled. "Do you miss your family back home?"

Arnie blinked. "I… Sir, you know they disowned me."

Sid flushed with embarrassment. "Oh, yes, of course. I'm sorry, Arnie."

"You know I'm so grateful to you for hiring me," Arnie said. "I appreciate it every day."

Sid shook his head. "Arnie, please forgive me. I'm just in a bit of a predicament. I didn't mean to bring up old history."

"Without our history, we are nothing," Arnie said.

Sid looked at him thoughtfully. "How profound."

Arnie bowed his head. "In Maori culture, our ancestors are very important. The elder in my tribe used to teach us all about it. Then again, he also used to say that God's child was a tree that held up the sky. If you believe that horseshit, you'll probably believe anything, eh?"

"I suppose so!" Sid chortled. "Catherine seems to enjoy your stories, though."

Arnie's mouth flapped open like a fish. "Sir, I'm sorry. Was I out of line to tell her—?"

Sid waved him quiet. "It's fine, Arnie. I want her to learn about other cultures. Stories drive the imagination and I believe you are a good influence on her. By all means, tell her as many tales as you like."

Arnie clasped his hands together again. "That means a lot to me, sir. I am growing fond of Catherine. She particularly likes the story about Ruapehu and the mountain lovers."

"You'll have to tell me it sometime." Sid sighed.

"What's troubling you, sir?"

"It's my wife… She believes that we should partner with Horatio Zhin, and I know she is right."

"And that's a bad thing, I take it?"

"If I make the deal, I'll be dragged into a whirlwind of meetings and negotiations all across the world. My work on the prosthesis project will grind to a halt. On top of that, I'll hardly have any time to spend with Catherine."

"You're a good man, sir." Arnie frowned, appeared to want to say something else, but didn't.

"What is it?" Sid probed.

"Well, sir. It seems to me that Margery is well suited to that sort of thing."

"That's for sure. Inheriting a global enterprise was never on my list of life-goals. I'm doing my best, but she's the one with the mind for it."

"Then why don't you send her instead?"

Sid blinked. "That could work." *Why didn't I think of that before?* Margery had always wanted to be more involved with the business. Sid resisted while his father was alive, trying to prove that he could be a capable heir to his corporation. *But it was Father who arranged our marriage. He saw her potential as an asset.* "She's been very beneficial to my marketing team."

"Use the right tool for the job, eh?"

"Is that a Maori phrase?"

"No, sir. I believe it's American."

They laughed. "Well, thank you Arnie. I will certainly consider that." He checked his watch. "Damn, it's nearly 3'oclock and I haven't finished going over these reports. Would you mind taking the car to pick up Catherine from school? She is bringing a friend with her for dinner tonight I believe."

"It would be my pleasure, sir." Arnie smiled and ducked out of the room.

Sid was still in the study when he heard the front door open.

Arnie Dillon's deep voice resonated through the hallway. "Home sweet home, Catherine."

"Thanks Arnie!" came his sixteen year old daughter's reply.

Sid rose and went into the hall to greet her.

"Welcome home, dear." Sid's gaze went immediately to the angel standing beside her.

"Hey Dad, this is Annie," Catherine introduced him. "She's the friend I told you about."

Annie's sparkling blue eyes gazed out beneath blonde curls, tied at the back in a long ponytail. Her soft pink lips curled in a gleaming smile as she held a hand out to greet him. "Pleased to meet you, Mr. Blunt. Your home is amazing!" She spoke with a hint of an Eastern European accent.

Sid blinked. "Thank you." He reached out and squeezed her hand. Her skin felt like silk. She wore a tight fitting zip-up hoodie which was half undone, revealing a glimpse of cleavage. Sid averted his eyes. "Catherine tells me you've recently moved to Berlin, is that true?"

She pushed a lock of hair behind her ear. "Um, yes. I got held back a year in Czechoslovakia. My parents sent me here to improve myself and the school just transferred me to Cathy's class a few weeks ago."

"We're totally like, the odd-ones out in the class, Dad. I'm the youngest and she's the oldest."

"Eldest," Sid corrected her.

"Yeah, I meant that." Catherine raised an eyebrow. "Uhh, you two can stop shaking hands now."

Annie giggled. A sweet sound that set Sid's ears to singing.

He released her hand and composed himself. Then he spotted the pair of Blunt earphones dangling around Annie's neck. "Aha, good choice."

She gave a little confused frown at first, glancing down at her chest. "Oh, these?" She held up the earphones, and drew the Blunt smartphone out from an inner pocket inside the hoodie. "Ohhh, of *course*. Your company makes these, right?" She turned to Catherine excitedly. "I forgot your dad was famous!"

Catherine smirked. "It's no big deal."

"This is so *amazing*!" Her eyes darted around the room as if she didn't know where to look. "I can't believe how lucky I am." She covered her mouth with a hand.

Sid realised she was on the brink of tears. "Hey now, relax."

"Are you okay?" Catherine asked.

"I'm sorry, yes," Annie said. "It's just, I moved here, and I don't know anybody, and then I meet you, and we got on so well so fast, and now I'm in your huge house and I just…oh my god." She threw her arms around Catherine. "I'm just so happy!"

Sid chuckled at Catherine's bemused face peering at him over her new friend's shoulder. "I'm glad to see Catherine with a friend as well. She doesn't have many."

"*Dad!*" Catherine hissed, her cheeks reddening. "Come on, Annie. My room's up here." She made for the staircase, pulling her friend by the hand.

"It was nice to meet you, Mr. Blunt!" Annie said over a shoulder, as the pair scrambled up the stairs.

"Likewise," Sid called after her.

"Do you need me for anything else, sir?" Arnie said.

Sid turned to his bodyguard. "No, thank you. Go and relax."

"Thank you, sir." The big man smiled and ambled away.

Sid started for the kitchen, when he spotted Margery standing in the doorway to the living room.

"So, what do you think?" she asked, holding a glass of wine against her shoulder.

"Are you drinking already?" Sid frowned.

She let out an exasperated sigh. "Oh, Sidney, it's just a glass before dinner. You didn't answer my question."

"What do I think of what?" He followed her into the living room.

"Annie."

They sat down on the sofa.

"She seems like just the sort of friend that Catherine needs."

"Really." Margery took a sip, eyeing Sid. "What makes you say that?"

Sid hesitated. "Catherine has always been a bit... socially inept."

"*That's* putting it lightly." Margery's tone was scathing.

"Annie seems energetic. Bubbly. She should be a good influence on Catherine."

Margery only shrugged.

Sid cleared his throat. "I have an idea I wanted to share with you."

"Have you now?" Margery swirled her glass.

"Yes. Regarding the partnership with Horatio Zhin. I want you to meet with him."

"Me?"

"Yes. I mean, I think with your experience in communications and vested interest in the company..." He gathered his thoughts. *I have to convince her this was my idea. I need her respect.* "Father believed in you. Blunt is your future just as it is mine now. We cannot continue to grow without the Neo-Asian market, and Zhin is our way in. Will you meet with him, Margery?"

She watched Sid with narrowed eyes. "I'll need a bodyguard. I'm not travelling abroad without some security."

"Of course, would you like to take Arnie with you?"

She shook her head. "He's your lapdog. I want my own."

"Okay, of course. So, you'll meet Zhin then?"

She handed Sid a glass and filled it with wine before topping up her own.

"Yes, dear. I will do this. It's a great idea."

Sid smiled, relieved. "I'm glad to hear it. A toast, then. To our future."

"To the future," Margery raised her glass.

Clink.

SEVEN YEARS AGO

"So how was the flight?" asked Sid.

"Adequate. At least they had a bar." Margery took off her jacket and hung it in the wardrobe. She pulled out her hairclip and her long brown hair fell about her shoulders. Sid liked it that way.

"You look nice."

Margery gave him a sour look. "Please, Sidney. Nobody looks nice after an eight hour flight." She sat on the edge of the bed and pulled off her shoes.

"Are you jetlagged?"

"No," she sighed. "I managed to nap on the plane. But I'm not happy about missing the Indian market meeting just because it's Catherine's birthday. That made me look weak, Sidney."

Sid shrugged it off. "Zhin will manage without you for a few days." He sidled up to his wife and put his hands around her hips. "Catherine isn't home for at least an hour, you know."

Margery turned away. "I couldn't be less in the mood for this right now, Sidney."

This response was unexpected and caused a flash of paranoia to flare in Sid's head. He stepped back. "Really? Why not?"

Margery rose and opened her closet to pull out a new blouse. With her back to Sid, she said, "I told you, I'm not in the mood."

"We haven't seen each other in over a week."

"Well, whose choice was that, dear?"

Sid opened his mouth to retort, but had nothing.

She turned back to him, holding a cream coloured blouse, one of her more casual outfits. "Would you mind…?" She trailed off. "Oh, forget it." She began to undress in front of him.

Margery had a fantastic figure for a woman in her late forties. Sid ogled at her from across the room, the muscles in his groin gently throbbing. If only she was happy to see him.

"I have some good news from Japan," Sid tried.

"Oh yeah?" she said flatly, unclipping her bra strap.

"Professor Tenji from Kitsanagi Technologies wants to look at my prototypes."

"The prosthetics?"

"Yes, he wants to meet and discuss a potential manufacturing deal. I'm sorry I sent you to India alone, but I will be with you in Japan next week. That'll be an important one."

Margery tossed the bra onto the bed and with one hand on her hip glowered at him, topless. "You are so out of touch. Japan is barely holding its place in the market these days. India was *the* important one. I had to explain to the head of India's biggest superstore that my daughter's birthday takes precedent over our multi-billion dollar deal." She touched her forehead. "It was beyond embarrassing."

Sid took a step towards his wife, driven by an urge to comfort and convince her that he had everything under control. He had to impress her.

She looked up, alarmed. "What are you doing? How many times must I tell you no?"

"Don't worry," Sid reassured her. "Zhin called to say that talks went smoothly, but the Neo-Asian committee needs time to make a final decision. They'll be on board soon enough."

"You are probably right. Horatio is a master of words." Margery's eyes glazed over somewhat. She turned back to the wardrobe and selected a new bra, slipping it on while Sid stared at her back.

"So it was a good decision to partner with him?" Sid said.

"Definitely."

"Okay, then." *A master of words. Is that the sort of man she really wants?*

An awkward silence followed as Margery finished dressing with her back to Sid.

"Right then," she said at last, brushing down her front. "I have a meeting with Louise now, to make sure our daughter's birthday is covered in the press tastefully and minimally. Don't you have some presents to wrap?" She swept passed him.

"Um, yeah." Sid followed her out of the room.

The truth was, Sid had prepared Catherine's presents earlier that morning with the help of Arnie and two of the serving staff. A huge pile of wrapped boxes awaited her in the living room, neatly stacked from largest to smallest in a pyramid.

While Margery and the reporter chatted privately in one of the studies, Sid busied himself with prosthesis reports. He knew there was a future for this technology and couldn't understand why his wife showed no interest in it. It was as if anything that involved helping other people bored her. *If that's true, how can I love someone like that?*

And yet…

Catherine arrived home from school with Annie, their laughter in the hallway announcing their entrance.

Sid inhaled deep, wanting to enjoy the next few hours with his daughter. He strolled out to greet her. "Happy Birthday, my wonderful daughter." He spread his arms wide and she came in for a hug.

"Thanks Dad!"

"Seventeen! I can hardly believe it," he said, kissing her

forehead. He looked up and waved. "Hello Annie."

She tucked her hands behind her. "Hi, Mr. Blunt." Today Annie wore jeans and a zebra striped top, both of which hugged her curves.

Sid pulled his attention back to Catherine. "Your mother flew back especially to see you."

"Oh. Yeah?" Catherine forced a smile. "Didn't she have an important meeting?"

"Yes, but you are more important. Now, before you two rush off, you may want to go into the living room…"

Catherine chuckled and brushed a loose strand of hair behind her ear. "You're still doing that for me, Dad?" Sid and Annie followed her in, where a pyramid of gifts awaited. A big chocolate cake had been laid out on the coffee table.

"Thank you Dad! I don't even know where to begin."

She started from the top, and worked her way down. Sid watched from the sofa, smiling whenever Catherine made eye contact, but otherwise fending off an ever gnawing sense of discomfort. *Margery should be here for this. At least Annie is here.*

Catherine's friend was sitting cross-legged on the carpet next to the shrinking pile of birthday presents. Sid caught himself taking longer glances at her.

He stood up. "Excuse me for a moment, girls."

He went to his study and retrieved a sealed box for a brand new Blunt smartphone. On his way back to the living room, he met Margery and Louise Stone coming down the stairs.

"Ah, you must be Mr. Blunt," said Miss Stone. "It's wonderful to finally meet you."

"Likewise," Sid smiled, shaking her hand. "I hope you'll make Catherine look good in the news?"

She laughed. "I'm sure you'd prefer that days such as these are kept as private as possible. That's the approach I will be taking."

"Oh yes, of course. Thank you for helping us out."

"It's my absolute pleasure," she beamed. Her elegant British accent reminded Sid of the King of England.

"If you don't mind, Sidney," Margery said. "Louise has a flight to catch."

"Yes, I have a live report tonight in London."

"Wow, good luck."

"Thank you. We must talk again sometime when your prostheses are ready for the world."

Sid flustered, shocked that Margery had told her about that.

"Yes, soon enough," Margery led her to the door where a driver awaited to take Miss Stone to the airport and then she was gone.

"You told a reporter about my prostheses project?" Sid gaped. "It's still top secret."

"Not just any reporter, Sidney. She's *my* reporter."

"I hope you made her sign a non-disclosure agreement."

"Relax, of course I did. She can be trusted. You'll appreciate her when the time comes." She looked down at the smartphone box in his hand. "What are you doing with that?"

"Oh, this? I wanted to give Annie something. She's in there with Catherine."

"Our latest phone model? The one that's still under development." She crossed her arms. "I suppose you intended to make her sign an NDA as well?"

Sid blushed. "They'll be released to the public next week. This isn't the same."

"Hm." Margery let it slide, thankfully. They went into the living room and re-joined the girls.

"Here, Annie. This is for you." Sid held the box out to her.

"What? Really?" Her eyes lit up as she read the label. "The B96! These haven't even been released yet!"

"I know. It's our way of saying thank you. You almost feel like part of the family now."

Annie leapt up and wrapped her arms around his neck.

Sid tried to ignore her firm breasts prodding him in the ribs.

"Thank you," she exclaimed.

"I thought you'd like it," he said, gesturing to the phone. "It has the best camera money can buy. Your parents back home will be able to see you more clearly now whenever you call them."

"Oh my god, it even has night vision. Cathy, check it out!"

"That's awesome," Catherine beamed, scrunching up more wrapping paper and adding it to the pile. "Take one of us!"

Annie held out the phone and took a selfie of them both.

Sid couldn't remember the last time his family were in the same room like this and he desperately wanted to enjoy the rare moment of togetherness. But Margery's behaviour had filled him with a sense of doubt and the next few hours passed him by in a dark haze.

After a sumptuous meal and gratuitous amount of cake, the girls went upstairs to try on Catherine's new clothes and take more pictures with Annie's phone. Sid and Margery retired to the living room and settled in separate arm chairs watching television.

Sid turned the volume down, and looked across at his wife.

"What is it, dear?" she said.

He wanted to retain eye contact as he asked the burning question on his mind, but he just couldn't. Instead, he glanced down at his glass and muttered, "You and Horatio Zhin…"

"Excuse me? Was that a question?"

He gritted his teeth and said more clearly, "You and Horatio Zhin. Are you…?" *Just say it.*

She watched him intently from across the room. Sid

swore he caught a glimpse of a smirk playing on her lips. That made it even harder to ask.

It was Margery that broke the silence. "You don't even have the balls to ask, do you?"

Sid clenched a fist against the armrest.

"Turn it up," she pointed at the television. "Louise is on."

"What? No, we need to talk about this."

"About what? If you have something to say, either say it, or turn up the fucking TV so I can listen."

Sid hesitated. He did neither.

"Fine," Margery said. "Volume up."

The television amplified and the interview on the screen grew louder.

"...I'm standing across the river from Thames House, the British Secret Service building in London," Louise Stone said. "Or should I say the new Europa headquarters. Ever since the Second Cold War, there have been numerous Euromerican diplomats demanding the formation of an institution to keep our borders safe. With the combined forces of the CIA, MI6 and even certain members of Russia's KGB, *Europa* is the answer to those demands."

"It sounds very James Bond, doesn't it?" the news anchor said. "Is it wise to broadcast the location of their HQ like this, Louise?"

"Well, Johnathon, this building is more of a symbol than anything these days. Today's announcement is a political move. It's a show of strength. Nothing like this has ever been tried before. The combined forces of three major superpowers is Euromerica flexing its muscles to say, *"Look, you may have united Korea, but we're still bigger than you."* That's one way of looking at it, in any case."

"Ha!" Margery clapped. "She's brilliant."

"Thank you, Louise," the anchorman took over the screen. "That was Louise Stone, reporting live from London. In other news..."

Margery stood up. "Well, isn't she just something?"

"Where are you going?"

"To the bathroom, dear. And after that, I might go to bed. I don't think I want to be in your company this evening."

Sid grimaced. "What sort of marriage is this turning into? We barely see each other and when we do, you don't even want me in the same room."

"Oh, you noticed that?"

Sid sputtered, trying to think of a way to prove his strength. "Look. Don't think I'm stupid, okay? I see what's going on."

"I don't think you do," she said as she strolled out of the room. He heard her footsteps climbing the stairs.

I'm not paranoid. She is sleeping with Zhin, and wants me to confront her about it. How could she do this to me?

Sid took a sip of his wine with a trembling hand and spilt a drop down his chin. He flung the glass sideways and it smashed against the wall. It left a red spatter that dribbled down in thin rivulets onto the cream carpet.

Arnie Dillon rushed in from the hallway. "Sir, are you okay? What happened?"

"Nothing, Arnie. Just lost my temper."

"Understandable, sir."

"You heard that, I assume?"

"Yes, sir. Is there anything I can do? I can't help feeling somewhat responsible…"

Just then, a loud *thump* came from the ceiling, followed by a shriek. Sid looked up. Arnie's eyes went wide and he dashed back through the door. Sid bolted to his feet and followed him. As he came to the foot of the stairs, he heard Margery stomping across the landing.

"*Sidney!* Get up here right now! Arnie, *fuck off*, this is a family matter."

Sid ran up the stairs two at a time, passing Dillon on the way back down. "What on earth is going on?"

"It's your *daughter*." She grabbed his upper arm and led

him to Catherine's room. The door was ajar, and Margery barged it open.

Catherine and Annie were in the middle of getting dressed, and they both froze when Sid entered. Catherine stood on one side of the bed wearing only her underwear. Opposite her, a topless Annie stood gaping, her bra dangling loose around one arm in the mid-process of strapping it on. Her panties were back to front suggesting they had been put on in some haste.

"Wha...?" He couldn't make sense of the scene.

"I found them on the bed," Margery pointed for emphasis. "*Fornicating.*"

Sid's eyes went to Annie. She cupped an arm over her breasts, her face bright red.

Margery grabbed Sid's chin and turned his head to face her. "Our daughter is a *dyke.*"

"*Shut up!*" Catherine yelled. "And get out of my room!"

Margery spun on her heel, marched across to Catherine and slapped her hard across the face. As Cathy raised a hand to her cheek, tears spilled from her eyes, while Margery stood glaring.

Sid watched, lost for words and feeling quite out of his depth. His eyes were drawn back to Annie, who was gathering up her clothes and putting them on as fast as she could.

"You don't have to go," Sid said. "We can talk about this."

"There is *nothing* to talk about," snarled Margery.

Annie pulled her jeans on and slipped her top over her head. She said, "I'm sorry, Cathy. I should go."

"Yes." Margery aimed her fierce gaze at Catherine's friend. Sid felt like stepping between them, but thought better of it.

Margery approached Annie and spoke with a quiet, cold authority. "You are never to step foot in my house again. Is that understood?"

Annie nodded.

Margery glared point-blank for an uncomfortable amount of time. "Now get out."

Annie cautiously stepped around Margery and picked up her bag. She gave one last nervous glance at Catherine, then made for the door. Her eyes met Sid's for a moment, glistening wet with frightened tears. Sid started to go after her, but stopped at the top of the stairs. He shouted down, "See that she gets home, Arnie."

"Will do, sir."

The front door slammed shut.

Sid felt embarrassed that the servants would all be hearing everything, so he eased his daughter's bedroom door closed to be alone with his family.

Margery's hissing voice cut through the silence.

"This is not how I raised you, young lady."

"I told you not to come in when my door is closed." Cathy sniffed.

"I will do what I please in *my* house, Catherine. And while you live under this roof, you will do exactly what I tell you."

"What *we* tell you," Sid corrected.

Catherine frowned at him, wiping a tear from her cheek.

Margery went on, "We've given you so much. Too much, I see that now. Your father has spoiled you rotten today and *this* is how you repay us?" She paused to rub her forehead. "I'm putting an end to this clown's education. You're going to boarding school to learn some discipline."

Sid sputtered, "Margery, now wait just a—"

"What?" Catherine gaped. "You can't do that to me!"

"Nobody's doing anything," Sid assured her.

His wife turned on him, stone faced. "You've always been too *soft* on her. It's for her own good, you stupid man."

Sid spread his hands in confusion. "Where is this coming from? Since when do you decide what happens to our daughter without speaking to me first?"

"Since you proved you were incapable of having a spine.

Someone needs to be the man in this family." Margery stormed from the room.

"*I hate you!*" Catherine screamed after her.

Sid stepped further into the room. "I won't let her send you—"

"Thanks for the moral support, Dad! You just stood there while she *humiliated* us."

"I... Look, if you and Annie are, you know. I don't even mind—"

"Just get out!" Catherine shoved him in the chest. "Get out, get out, *get out!*" He stumbled backwards into the landing and she slammed the door in his face.

I'm losing control of my family. He clenched a fist at his side. "You belong here, this is your home," he said to the door. "I won't let her send you away. You hear me, Catherine?"

No response.

He went to the master bedroom and found Margery standing with her arms crossed.

"We are not sending her to boarding school," he said.

"Give me one good reason why."

"She's too old for one thing. And she's doing well at college, why make her start over from scratch because of this... this incident?"

"This incident," Margery repeated.

"It's just a phase," Sid said dismissively. "Didn't you ever, you know... when you were younger?"

"No."

"Really?"

"*No.* It's disgusting." She shook her head. "That girl requires discipline, and you'd let her get away with murder. If you won't send her away, I want her chipped."

Sid raised his eyebrows. "Chipped? Like a dog? You want to spy on our daughter?"

"Yes. Use one of your new models, the one's with the lifetime battery."

"Don't you think that's an extreme reaction?"

"I believe tonight's *incident* more than justifies it. It's not extreme, it's called parenting."

Sid decided this was better than the alternative. "Only if you let her continue seeing Annie."

Margery narrowed her eyes at him. "*Seeing* her?"

"I didn't mean it like that. They are friends, Margery. Catherine doesn't have many friends. We should support her."

"I will not condone *that* behaviour in my house, Sidney."

"And what about *your* behaviour," Sid growled, a flash of anger searing through him.

"What about *my* behaviour?" she retorted in a whisper.

They stared at each other for a moment. Sid ground his teeth. "Are you sleeping with Horatio Zhin?"

"No. But I want to. What are you going to do about it?"

Sid was speechless. A jagged stone had lodged itself in his throat.

"I thought so." She turned away from him.

"I won't send Catherine away," Sid said. "I will chip her. But only if she stays here. This is her home."

"Fine, but the slut is forbidden from ever spending the night."

"Annie is her friend."

"I won't allow it, Sidney."

"She can't stay over, then. But we're not breaking their friendship."

Margery gave a resigned sigh, and began removing her earrings. "Fine. Now leave me."

Sid walked out and closed the door with deliberate and difficult gentleness.

Walking slowly down the landing, he inhaled five deep breaths to steady his heartrate. When he felt ready to break the news about the chip, he rapped on Catherine's door.

Catherine answered softly. "What?"

"It's me. Can I come in?"

After a long silence, the door clicked open.

***

"What does it do?" Catherine asked.

"It's a health-monitoring device. It's mostly used for elderly people in care homes and sick people. It lets the carers keep a remote eye on their condition."

She frowned. "Why do I need one? I'm not sick."

Sid hesitated. "It also contains a GPS."

"*What?*"

"Listen, it's not as bad as you might think. I would never, *ever* use it to track your movements, unless I had a very serious reason to."

"Such as if I want to go to Annie's house. This was Mother's idea, wasn't it? I can't believe you'd let her do this to me, Dad!"

"You broke her trust, Catherine. She needs you to earn it back, that's all. And hey, I've fitted this to some pretty famous people, don't you know. Celebrities are *asking* to be chipped. It protects them from kidnappings. Who's that singer you like, Tracy Wingdings?"

Catherine chuckled. "Tracy Winghams. Has she got one?"

"Yup. Same model I'll give to you."

She considered that. "Will it hurt?"

"Nope. It's just a tiny microchip. No worse than getting a jab."

Catherine chewed her lip.

"I will not send you away," Sid went on. "I mean it. I will *never* let anything like that happen to you. But this is the compromise. And this way, you'll still get to see Annie."

"You swear, Dad?"

"I swear it."

"It's not what you think. Annie and me. She was just... teaching me."

Annie popped into his mind again, naked, lying on the

bed. "It's okay," he sputtered. He caressed her cheek where Margery's slap had left a sore hand print. "I don't want this to be the memory you have of this day."

"Thanks, Dad." She closed her eyes. "Okay, I'll do it. I'll get the chip. Maybe I'll tell Annie to get one, too. She's convinced she'll be famous one day."

"You shouldn't tell anyone about it, Catherine. It's supposed to be secret. If people know, then it becomes meaningless."

"Oh. Okay. I won't tell, then."

"That's my girl." He patted her hand.

SIX YEARS AGO

Sid couldn't file for divorce until he made sure that his assets were safe from Margery. He'd made the mistake of embedding her deep into the Neo-Asian establishment along with Horatio Zhin, but he still maintained a strong hold over his prosthesis department, which had gone from strength to strength in a very short space of time.

He now had military contracts across Euromerica, and was fitting veterans with his cutting-edge artificial limbs. Blunt's public image had skyrocketed, and even Margery had shown some level of interest in where he had taken that branch of the business.

He hardly saw her these days.

She and Zhin travelled the globe together, and had established distribution in India, Japan, Malaysia, Taiwan and Singapore. Now that the Blunt brand was continental, they were generating more money than ever before.

They hadn't cracked China yet, though. The heart of Neo-Asia. His marriage was like a tire around his neck threatening to drown him, but he couldn't cut the rope until she secured China. It was just too big.

On the day before Catherine's graduation, Margery and Zhin flew to China.

"Just you and me then," he said to Catherine over breakfast that morning. "We have the whole house to ourselves."

Catherine gave a feeble smile. "Yeah."

"Is something wrong?"

"No. Just nervous about tomorrow."

He reached across the table and patted her hand. "You're gonna do fine. I know it."

"I want to make you proud, Dad. I even thought I could show Mother, but she obviously doesn't care."

"She cares," he lied. "She just has important work to do. It's unfortunate timing…"

"She's horrible, Dad. I don't even know how you can love her."

"Catherine!" he scolded. But he regretted the outburst immediately. "Look, your mother and I are going through a rough patch. But we love you. You need to know that."

She watched him. "You've never been a very good liar, Dad." She got up and left the room.

***

A dozen camera's flashed as they threw their hats into the air.

Catherine and Annie hugged, smiling and whirling around the crowd of students. They bounded over to Sid, standing with Arnie Dillon and the other parents.

"I did it, Dad!"

Catherine flung herself into his arms and he squeezed her. "I'm so proud of you. I told you you'd be fine, didn't I?"

She beamed at him, and turned to the big Maori. "Look at my scroll, Arnie."

"Congratulations, my Ruapehu," he rumbled.

"Well done, Annie," Sid said.

"Thank you Mr. Blunt!" she curtsied in her dark gown. A boy from her class asked if he could take a photo with her and she scurried away with him.

"Dad, since Mother's away, is it all right if Annie comes over later?" Catherine asked him quietly as the rest of her class tossed their hats again and posed.

Sid glanced at Annie, who met his eyes with a cheeky smile.

"Of course," he swallowed, smiling at his daughter.

"Thanks Dad," Catherine threw her arms around him again. "You're the best."

"You're very welcome. Now, stand over there. I want a memento of this."

"Me too!" Annie cried, jumping in beside Catherine.

Sid snapped a photo of the two girls standing side by side in their graduation gowns and hats, overflowing with pride.

"We're going to go out for some drinks with everyone after this. I'll try not to wake you when we come home tonight!"

"Go have fun. You earned it."

Catherine and Annie interlocked arms and floated back amongst their peers.

Arnie drove Sid home, and they enjoyed a quiet meal with the servants.

"That was delicious," Arnie said. "Thank you, sir."

"You've been a loyal friend, Arnie. I should be thanking you for everything you've done this year."

"Come on, sir. I'm just doing my job."

"I hope we mean more than just a job to you?"

Dillon nodded. "Oh yes, sir. I almost think of Catherine as a little sister. I only wish you and Margery could... Well. I'm not sure what to suggest about her, to be honest."

Sid shook his head. "Let's not get into that. I want to enjoy this week while I can."

"Fair enough."

"I tell you what, take the day off tomorrow. I'd like to spend the day with Catherine, just the two of us."

"Thank you sir. I appreciate that."

At around midnight, Sid fell asleep in his empty bed.

He awoke at two in the morning. He made out a silhouette of someone standing by his desk, fiddling with something. He sat bolt upright in bed. "Who's there?"

"Shhh, it's me," said a soft voice. Annie turned around and strode over to the bed. She flicked on his bedside light, illuminating the bedroom in a warm orange glow.

Sid squinted at the brightness. His mind felt foggy from sleep. "What are you doing here?"

She pouted. "You said I could come, remember? Because your wife isn't here." Sid smelled fruity alcohol on her breath. She tussled her head and blonde hair fell about her face in long curled ringlets. She gazed at him with sparkling blue eyes, wearing a short black skirt and white top that accentuated the shape of her modest round breasts.

"Where's Catherine?"

"Sleeping in her room." Annie stepped closer and pulled her top off over her head and dropped it on the floor. Underneath, she was braless. Sid licked his lips.

"You shouldn't be here," he said.

"Why not?"

"Because you're Catherine's friend. It seems… wrong."

She gave a coy smile and sat on the bed. "Isn't that what makes it exciting?"

It took all the strength Sid could muster to ask, "Why are you here? Tell me the truth."

Annie slid forward and put her hands on his chest. "I've never been with a millionaire, before."

"Billionaire," Sid corrected.

She gasped.

"How old are you again?"

"I'm nineteen, Mister Blunt."

Sid's resistance was slipping away. He longed for her. And she was right; the wrongness was a major part of the attraction.

Annie leaned in close to his ear and whispered, "I want this."

"Come here," Sid said.

Annie obliged. She pulled back the duvet, climbed onto her hands and knees and crawled across the bed to him. Sid's erection stabbed against his briefs. He wrapped an arm around her waist and pulled her nipple into his mouth, sucking gently. Annie moaned.

"Oh, Mister Blunt. That feels so good."

She helped him to pull down her skirt, until she was wearing nothing but a white thong.

"No more talk," he said. *If you stay quiet, I can pretend this was just a wild dream.* He reached over and flicked the light off.

She bent to kiss him. With one hand around his neck, she slid her fingertips down the length of his chest and belly until she touched the tip of his erection. Sid shuddered. He flipped Annie onto her back and tore down her thong.

She wrapped her legs around his waist and he lost himself to her.

***

Vvvrrrt. Vrrrrt.

He awoke to an empty bed and the sound of his phone vibrating across the bedside table.

Vvvvrrrt.

Sid flopped out a hand and fumbled to pick up the cell phone.

"Hello?"

"Sir! Are you okay?"

"Arnie?" Sid propped himself up. "What's wrong?"

"I'm on my way over now, sir! Don't worry, we can fix this. I have Doctor Gunther with me, and most of the prosthesis team locked themselves in the labs."

"What are you talking about?"

Then he remembered something. A nagging thought. *What was Annie doing to my desk last night?* Frowning, he got up and inspected it. Nothing seemed to be amiss.

"You said I could come, remember?" said Annie. Her voice came through the ajar bedroom door unnaturally loud. *"Because your wife isn't here."*

Sid's blood turned to ice.

"It's your wife, sir," Arnie went on. "She's instigated a hostile—"

Sid tuned out. He dropped the phone and opened his bedroom door, listening.

"You shouldn't be here," he heard himself say. It seemed to be coming from downstairs, possibly being blasted through his sound system.

What the…?

Sid inhaled a deep breath, his mind racing.

"Isn't that what makes it exciting?" her voice boomed.

He flung his night gown on and bolted down the stairs.

By the time he reached the living room, it was filled with the sound of Sid and Annie's intense groaning and squeaking bed springs. The recording blared throughout the house, and the home video of his adultery played projected on the blank living room wall.

Night vision? She recorded it on the phone I gave her!

Sid shouted, "Stop." The video ignored him. "*Stop!* Pause, switch off, goddammit!" He scanned the room searching desperately for the remote control. It was nowhere to be seen. Annie yelped in pleasure, her voice blasting out from the sound system so loud Sid thought the windows might shatter. *Where's the goddamn remote?*

"Argh!" He reached up to the hanging projector, grabbed it with both hands and tore it down from the ceiling. The image of Sid's thrusting buttocks disappeared from the wall, but the terrible moans continued to deafen him.

"Dad?"

He spun around. Catherine stood in the doorway in her

pyjamas. *How much did you see?*

"Catherine!" Sid blurted. "Someone's broken into our house. This is some sick, disgusting joke." He stumbled towards her. She was right about him; he couldn't lie to save his life.

"I saw you," she said, backing away.

Sid groaned across the speaker system.

Catherine screwed up her face. "I saw you and *Annie*." She covered her ears, gagging.

"Catherine, please."

She turned and ran from the room.

He followed her. "Please, Catherine! Let me explain!"

She ran into the downstairs bathroom and slammed the door before he reached it. It locked shut with a *click*.

Sid banged on the door. "Catherine! Please! It's not what it looks like."

"I saw exactly what it looked like, Dad!"

The recording of Annie let out a shuddering moan, which echoed through the house.

Sid couldn't hear any more. He went to the staircase, opened the cupboard beneath it where the trip switches and circuit breakers were. He frantically drummed his fingers down the switches, flipping them all to the *off* position, until finally the horrendous recording cut off.

In the silence, Sid collapsed onto his butt and breathed a sigh of relief. *It's too late. The damage is done.*

He knocked on the bathroom door again, but Catherine gave no reply other than a quavering, "Stay away from me!"

Sid went to the kitchen to pour a glass of water. As he downed the glass, he peered out of the window that overlooked the back garden. Annie, Louise Stone and Margery were all sitting in garden chairs, relaxing in the morning sun. A trio of suited men stood in bodyguard formation behind each of the women.

Margery looked in at him and waved.

She came home early? Sid's stomach turned upside down.

Sid rubbed the sweat from his forehead, and walked outside.

"Good morning, dear," Margery greeted him in a tone of bored disappointment.

"M-Margery," Sid stammered. "What the fuck is this? Why aren't you in China?"

Annie replied first. "Sorry, Mr. Blunt. But I really want to be famous…" She turned to Stone, who was tapping at a tablet computer. "Is it ready?"

"It's ready," Stone said, looking to Margery.

Sid gaped. "You want to blackmail me with a sex tape? Oh my god."

"You pathetic worm of a man," said Margery. "Seduced by this brainless, pretty thing."

"Why are you doing this? What do you want?"

Margery leaned back in the chair. "I think it's rather obvious, don't you?" She gestured to an empty chair.

Sid swallowed bile, and took a seat.

"Now, then," Margery began. "To quell your fears about China, let me just say that it no longer concerns you. After last night's events, it's become remarkably clear that you no longer care for this marriage."

"Oh, *please*." Sid said. "You've been screwing Zhin for months. Why else would I have done it?"

"Do you have any evidence?" Margery cocked her head. "No. So in the public eye, you would be the bad guy here."

"This is insane."

"Shut up," she said. "I'm divorcing you Sidney. And I want everything."

Sid sputtered. "You can't have *everything*."

"I know," she admitted. "Your little team of scientists have sealed themselves away, and refuse to correspond with me or Horatio. So congratulations. You've secured yourself a nice little pension. I will not fight that, as a token of respect."

"Mother? Dad?"

Sid spun around to see Catherine walking across the

grass towards them.

"What's going on?" Catherine paused a moment. "Annie?" She sped towards her friend with furious intent.

"Catherine," Annie said. "I'm sorry, but I—"

Catherine slapped Annie across the face. "How could you! You were supposed to be my friend!"

The two tangled up in a messy scrap that lasted several seconds before Margery signalled to one of her men, who pried the girls apart.

Catherine was in tears, and Annie looked mildly ashamed. Only mildly.

"I just," Annie said slowly. "Really want to be famous…"

"By being a slut?" Cathy cried. "Where's your dignity?"

Margery stood up. "Enough. You," pointing to Annie, "Shut the fuck up. Catherine, sit down and pay attention. You need to understand what is happening."

Catherine sat, guided by one of Margery's men. A knot had begun to tighten in the pit of Sid's stomach. Their presence unnerved him.

When Margery seemed satisfied, she continued. "Your father arranged our marriage for a reason Sidney. He understood your capabilities as much as he did mine. But I'm afraid I've outgrown you."

"Look, Margery. If you want to take the Neo-Asian market share, I would be willing to accommodate that. You and Horatio worked so hard, I feel as though you've earned that. But this threat of the sex tape…"

"You'll be publically humiliated Sidney."

Annie piped up, "I thought you were uploading it anyway? That was our deal!"

"Please be quiet," Margery lifted a finger at her. Back at Sid, "I'm afraid Neo-Asia is not enough, Sidney. Horatio and I will of course be partnering up once this sorry mess is dealt with. But we have our sights set on something much larger. Breaking Blunt into fragments will hinder us beyond repair and I'm just not willing to let that happen."

Sid grimaced. He crossed his arms and leaned back in the chair. "I still own the business. It's my name, not yours. Even if you let this out, it's just a scandal that'll blow over in a couple of months, perhaps a year."

Margery sighed. "That was actually the best offer I am willing to give you. The alternative…" She waved a hand.

The three goons un-holstered their pistols.

Sid froze, eyeing the gun barrels. "You're not serious."

"Mother!" Catherine cried.

"You don't seem to understand the lengths I'm willing to go to get my way in this matter, dear."

"So, what? You're going to murder me?" Sid gripped the armrests. "You're aware that if I die, Catherine inherits everything. You won't get a thing, Margery."

Margery grinned. "I'm so glad you said that." A goon stepped up behind Catherine, grabbed her around the neck and planted a gun against her temple.

Annie shrieked and her chair toppled over as she got out of the way. Louise Stone casually moved aside as well.

"You bastard!" Sid leapt out of his chair to lunge at the gunman, but a second one darted between them and aimed a gun at his forehead.

"We're running out of time, Sidney. I know your lapdog Dillon is on his way here. And if he arrives, this will turn into a shooting gallery. Someone dies here today. I'm letting you choose."

"What has gotten into you? We are a *family*!"

"Mother…" Catherine said. "Take me with you."

"Why?" Margery said.

"Because…" Catherine made eye contact with Sid, and his heart melted. "Father will do anything you ask, so long as I'm okay. Isn't that right, Dad?"

Sid felt tears welling up. *My poor, sweet girl.* "Yes. I'd do anything for you, my daughter."

"Interesting," Margery mused. "Perhaps you do take after your mother more than I realised. You see Sidney, even your daughter has more backbone than you." She got up and walked over to Catherine. The gunman released his grip and stepped back. "I do have a place for you. A job, actually. It's about time you learned something of the real world."

"Please, Margery. I won't let you take her away from me."

"It seems that decision isn't up to you, Sidney."

"Wait," Annie said. "This means you don't need the video of us."

"How observant," Margery said. She nodded to the gunman, who strode up behind Annie and grabbed her by the ponytail. "Just in case you have any doubts of my resolve, Sidney."

"What?" Annie said. The gunman forced her forwards. Annie stumbled onto her knees. "But I did everything you asked! Please!"

"You fucked both my daughter and my husband," Margery said. "Which means you fucked me. I'm afraid no-one fucks with me anymore."

Sid met Annie's terrified wide eyes as tears streamed from her face. She wailed as the man pressed the gun against the back of her head.

"No!" Sid and Catherine cried together.

The gun went off and the grass turned red.

As the report faded away, Catherine's wail filled Sid's right ear.

Margery stepped in front of Sid, filling his vision. "I'm not taking anything that isn't already rightfully mine. Catherine will come and work for me, and you will be left to carry on with your little philanthropy project in peace, so long as you stay out of my business. Assuming you want your daughter to remain alive, you'll provide Horatio and me regular access to your technology. I have some practical applications for those prosthetics. Have we finally come to an agreement?"

Sid was thunderstruck. He nodded, trembling in front of his wife.

"Good." Margery spun on her heel. "Louise, don't look so shocked. You knew what you were signing on for when you joined me."

"Y-yes, Ma'am," Stone said.

"How would you suggest we explain the sudden disappearance of my daughter in tomorrow's headlines?"

"Umm… I don't know."

"How about: 'Armed gunmen break into Blunt mansion. Daughter killed. Father stricken with grief. Hands business over to entrepreneurial wife.' Something along those lines, I think. Come along, we'll iron out the details on the plane."

Two more armed men appeared from nowhere carrying a body bag. They went straight to Annie's corpse and started zipping her inside.

Sid averted his eyes.

Margery offered her hand to Catherine, who had slumped onto the ground. "Come now, dear. Be thankful it wasn't you."

Catherine took her mother by the hand, and stared back at Sid with an intense terror. He could hear their conversation echoing in his mind:

"I will not send you away." Sid said.

"You swear, Dad?"

"I swear it."

Margery led Catherine towards the house. Over her shoulder, Margery said, "Arnie will be with you soon, Sidney. I'm sure he'll help you pack your things."

PRESENT DAY

Dawn broke in Berlin. The sun hadn't quite crested the horizon, but its soft glow reflected across the glass skyscrapers and off the silver TV-tower ball. Alexanderplatz looked so peaceful from the hundredth floor, but it did nothing to stop Sid's hands from shaking. He stood by the office window sweating, his receding hair a tangle, shirt untucked and tie dangling loose about his neck.

He hadn't slept. Not since he'd seen the news on television late last night about *CERN*. There had been a massive earthquake or explosion—nobody knew which yet—deep in the mountain nearby and thousands of people had been killed.

It's where Margery had taken Catherine. Now he had no idea whether she was alive or dead.

He used to be able to tell because of the tracker chip in her thigh. But Margery had surgically removed it at Catherine's request and since then he'd gotten a photograph every morning just as she was waking up to prove she was still alive.

Those photographs were the only thing keeping him under their influence. If Catherine died, he had no reason to keep up the charade.

Catherine… my poor, sweet daughter.

Staring out of the window, a tip of sunlight pierced the horizon and Sid believed he was the first person in the city to see it. *Not a bad view, if it's to be your last…*

"No!" he said aloud, turning back to his computer and

slumping down in the chair. *He'll call, he always does.*

He must've dozed off because the next thing he felt was a rush of panic as his computer's incoming call alert jolted him awake.

He fumbled to answer it. "Yes? Arnie, tell me you found something. Where—" He cut short when Margery appeared on the screen.

"Hello, Sidney."

The name stabbed him like ice through the chest.

"Oh, come now. Don't I even get a hello?" The woman looked like a mannequin. Smart crimson jacket, blood-red lipstick, hair pulled back revealing an imposing forehead. "It's been so long since we last spoke. I'd be lying if I said you looked well."

"This has been the most stressful night of my life." Sid's strained voice squeezed out of his throat. "What the hell happened?"

"Oh, we had a little incident at the facility. Everyone is dead."

Sid stared, thunderstruck. His jaw moved wordlessly. "C-Catherine… is she…?"

"I'm afraid so. Nobody made it out of there alive. It's sort of why I'm calling, you know. We've had a long talk, Horatio and I, and we've decided we no longer need you. So, it doesn't really matter if Catherine is alive or not, now does it?"

An intense numbness overtook him. He buried his face in his hands.

"I suggest you call your lapdog back. He's only going to find snow and rubble out there. The good news is that the media is blaming CERN, at least. So you don't need to worry about any of this tracing back to you." She smiled out of his screen.

"I-I'll talk to the press. You won't get away with—"

"And tell them what?" she interrupted. "Will you tell them that I had your foreign schoolgirl mistress murdered?"

"I… no, but Catherine—"

"Catherine died six years ago, remember? You want to reveal the fact that you helped cover it up? What else could you tell them? Let's see…"

"I… you can't…"

"I'll take this opportunity to remind you that I have the most respected journalist of our time in my pocket, and she has already written our version of this story. It's been online for an hour and will soon become fact. If you talk, you will kill your reputation and probably go to prison. There's no version of this where you come out on top. So no, you won't talk, Sidney."

"Don't call me *that.*" He didn't want to cry in front of her, so he jerked to his feet. His chair slammed into the glass window behind him and it juddered. Sid shoved it out of the way and turned his back to the monitor to gape out at the city.

"There's always another option," Margery's cruel voice spoke softly through the speakers behind him. "They do say that what goes up must fall back down. You made a good go of it in the end Sidney, despite losing me. That's quite a view."

He saw her sinister smile in the reflection. She ended the call and disappeared.

"Fuck!" he cried, bursting into tears. He trembled with grief, turned to the desk and was about to sweep everything onto the floor when he caught sight of the framed photo beside his monitor. Catherine smiling in her graduation gown. He'd had Annie edited out of it.

He clutched the photo and caressed the glass.

He slapped himself across the face. *Keep it together man. Until you know for sure. Arnie is there, he'll find her if he can.*

His computer eventually beeped. *Finally!* Arnie Dillon's message was simple:

```
Can't    talk.    But    can    confirm,
Catherine's    alive.    I'm    watching    her
tent.      Gear      suggests      Europa
```

involvement. Should I engage?

"Ohh!" Blunt collapsed back in his chair. His shoulders slumped and every muscle in his body relaxed at once. Europa could be a problem. But right then he only had a single priority. He typed up a reply – Please bring her back to me. Do whatever it takes. – and hit send.

The overwhelming sense of relief replaced all thoughts of throwing himself through the window.

PART TWO

5
THE MOUNTAIN FOREST

She slept in fits and starts in the frigid sleeping bag on the mountain, catching snippets of a dream involving Ben and a helicopter. He was trying to show her the beauty of the mountain, but she could never quite see what he was looking at. Whenever she tried to stand beside him, the helicopter blocked her way with its thundering propellers, and when she tried to run towards him her feet were too heavy to move. Intense frustration.

Agent Hawkins stirred. His movement woke her.

She sensed it was still dark, not yet dawn, but kept her eyes closed trying to bring back the dream of Ben.

The tent zip opened and Frank stepped outside, presumably to relieve himself.

It must be time to leave soon. He said we have to catch a train.

She didn't know where they'd find a train station halfway up a mountain, but after telling him a bit of her story of how she ended up working in the facility, he'd been adamant about bringing her to his superiors for protection.

Bang!

Cathy jolted upright. The gunshot echoed outside the tent.

Another *bang!* And a *clang!*

"Fuck!" Frank cursed, somewhere nearby outside.

"Frank? What's happening?"

"Stay down!" he roared.

"Catherine?" called a voice, deeper and farther away,

somewhere behind her. "Catherine! Are you okay?"

"Arnie?" she said. "Is that you?"

"Yes, it's me Catherine!" He sounded relieved. "Has he hurt you? I'll kill him if – ah!" *Bang! Clang!*

Frank bundled in through the tent and almost tackled her to the ground.

"You fuckin' coward!" Arnie bellowed. "If you hurt her I swear to God I'll rip your head off!"

"Arnie, it's okay! I'm fine!" She looked at Frank. "Right?"

He whispered, "He's here for you. Why?"

"It's Arnie, my father's bodyguard."

"Catherine!" Arnie's voice grew louder as he approached the tent.

Frank pulled a pistol from his sleeping bag and pointed it at the tent wall, towards Arnie's footsteps crunching through the snow.

"No!" Cathy said. "Arnie, stay back! Please don't hurt him," she begged Frank.

"He just shot at me."

"Let me talk to him, please. Arnie! Stay where you are, don't come any closer! I'm coming out."

She grabbed the combat boots he had given her as part of the skysuit and made to stand, when Frank grabbed her arm. He raised a finger, a gesture of *wait a second*. He gathered his pack, slung it onto his back and manoeuvred behind her. Then he tapped her on the shoulder which she took to mean, *go*.

She exited the tent, Frank close behind.

The biting air snapped her cheeks like frozen irons. She caught a strong whiff of gasoline. The ledge they had slept on plummeted straight down into a steep forested valley a few paces away, guarded by a tall peak that loomed directly ahead, silhouetted against the pale sky.

Frank spun her one-eighty degrees to face the forest as he wrapped a bulky arm firmly around her neck, using her as a shield. With his other hand he pointed the pistol at

Arnie.

"What the hell?" she squeaked.

"You bastard," Arnie growled. He stood between their tent and the forest in ankle-deep snow, aiming a huge rifle at them. "Let her go or I will shoot you in the face."

"No you won't," retorted Frank. "You couldn't even hit me when I was having a piss."

Arnie took an angry step closer. "Let her go!"

"I dunno about you," Frank went on. "But I generally don't trust blokes who shoot at me first thing in the morning. So until you put that gun down, I ain't letting go of shit."

"Both of you put the guns *down!*" Cathy cried.

Arnie's eyes darted from Frank to her and back again, flickering between rage and concern.

"Arnie. Please, it's okay," Cathy said. "It's so good to see you again."

That seemed to calm him somewhat. "My Ruapehu…"

A tingle rippled down Cathy's spine. She hadn't been called that for so long. There was something nostalgic about it, reassuring. "Please put down the gun."

Arnie lowered the rifle, but kept his suspicious eye on Frank. "You're Europa, right?"

Frank didn't answer, but Arnie took that as a yes. "Thought so. I recognised that beaut'." He gestured to the snowspeeder with the barrel of his rifle, before slinging it on a strap over his shoulder.

Frank cautiously lowered his gun and released Cathy. "How the fuck did you find us out here?"

"Chopper's heat sensor picked you up."

So that explains my helicopter dream…

"How'd a piss-poor shot like you wind up a merc?" Frank scathed. "You ruptured my fuel tank. We needed that to get off this mountain."

"I haven't slept all night, give me a break." Arnie squinted with one eye. "Sorry about that."

A moment passed, and Cathy thought the two of them

might actually laugh. At least the tension lifted.

"So, what now?" she asked.

"Catherine, your father sent me to find you," Arnie said. "I'm here to take you home."

"Home?" Cathy frowned, trying to digest the notion of going back to the man responsible for putting her in this diabolical situation to begin with.

"I tried to come sooner, I really did. Your father planned a rescue for a long time."

"Arnie, it's been *six years*!"

"I know," he admitted. "But your father—"

"I don't *care* about Dad. He did this to me! This is all his fault, him and Mother. I'm not going back to him. Not ever." She stepped backwards and bumped into Frank. "If it weren't for Frank and Jimmy... His partner died getting me out, Arnie. He was younger than me."

"Don't you realise they were probably the reason Margery had the place destroyed?" Arnie said. "They're Europa spies!"

"Margery Blunt had authority to destroy that facility?" Frank said.

"Yes," Arnie said. "She's been running the place for years."

"And you work for her husband?"

Arnie's face dropped. "*Ex*-husband, yes. But Sid had nothing to do with this."

"But he knew Catherine was alive in there," Frank went on. "Which means he knew her death was a cover up. Why would the head of a mega corporation fake his own daughter's death, I wonder?"

"He had no choice," Arnie growled through gritted teeth.

"What about you?" Frank asked Cathy. "I'll bet you know more about that place than anyone."

"I... I was just an analyst. They were conducting research."

"Research they wanted to protect so badly, they were

willing to murder everyone inside? What the hell were you doing down there?"

"Jeez, am I under arrest or something?"

"Not yet," Frank said.

"Wait just a second," Arnie said. "Catherine's been a prisoner against her will for years."

"It wasn't entirely against my will…" She sighed. "I chose that."

"Why?" Frank said.

"Because she was going to kill my dad!"

"Who, Margery?"

"Yes." Cathy felt sickened at having to bring up such painful memories. "She murdered my best friend right in front of me. She was going to kill him too. I saved him… and he never bothered to save me back."

"Catherine, that's why I'm here…"

"Well, it's too late, Arnie. I'm out now. A man died to help me. He was a total stranger, but he did more to help than my own *father*."

"So, that's it?" Arnie spread his arms. "You're just going to go with him? A Europa agent."

She hesitated.

"Look me in the eye," said Arnie. "And tell me this is what you want, my Ruapehu…"

She didn't want any of this. All she wanted was to be left alone. She wanted to get away from everyone and be somewhere where there weren't people trying to tell her what to do. But six years in the facility had at least taught her how to make the best of a shit situation.

Right now, her slightly less shit option was to go with Frank. She could tell Europa everything she knows, and maybe they'd arrest her mother for what she'd done. *That* would feel good.

"I'm sorry, Arnie." She stepped in front of Frank again.

"I can't let you take her!" Arnie insisted, drawing a pistol.

"The girl's made her decision, mate," said Frank.

Cathy felt a little tug at the small of her back as Frank retreated towards the precipice of the cliff. "What are you—?"

"Let her go!" Arnie aimed the pistol at them.

"Nope," said Frank.

Cathy felt a prick in her upper leg a split second before Frank spun her around and threw her off the cliff.

She caught a blinding glimpse of the sunrise peeking behind the mountain and clamped her eyes shut.

Then she was falling.

She screamed.

The snowy forest hundreds of feet below rushed towards her. The wind in her ears drowned out all other senses. Then all the air in her lungs was forced out and she gagged, almost swallowing her tongue.

A tree rushed up to catch her. She tumbled through a cap of freezing snow. Spindly branches scratched her face and tore holes in her skysuit around her arms and legs. She struck a more solid branch and came to a jarring halt, dangling several feet off the ground.

"What the fuck!" she shrieked.

"You okay?" Frank said.

Somehow, he was still directly behind her. She squirmed to look back, and realised that they were attached at the waist.

"No I'm not okay!" Her arms and legs were bleeding from a dozen light scratches.

"Sorry. But he was going to shoot at me again. I took pre-emptive action."

"By jumping off a cliff?"

"Relax. The parachute worked, didn't it? Get ready, I'm going to cut you loose."

"What? Wait a—"

Click.

Cathy fell another six feet and landed on her ass on a bed of snowy pine needles.

Frank cut himself free of the tangled parachute and

dropped down beside her. He offered a hand and pulled her up.

"All good?" he asked.

"No…" She exhaled a breath, the adrenaline shaking her hands. They were under a canopy of snowy trees, so she couldn't even see the ridge that they had jumped off. Arnie was somewhere up there.

Cathy winced as her left cheek began to throb.

"Let me see that," Frank tilted her chin and leaned in to look at her cheek. "It's not deep. Here." He made a snowball, squeezed it into ice and pressed it gently to her wound. The pain numbed.

"Thanks," she said. Blood rushed to her cheeks, she sensed them reddening.

"Come on, we have a long walk ahead of us now." Frank led the way deeper into the forest.

***

They trekked through the icy underbrush for several miles. Occasionally, Frank had to carve a path through deep snow drifts so Cathy could follow.

It was hard work, but at least the forest sloped gently downhill. When the sun started to wink through the treetops, Cathy asked, "Are we going to miss the train?"

"We'll miss the one I intended to catch, yeah," said Frank. "But there'll be another."

"Where exactly do we catch it? There can't be many train stations up here."

"You'll see. Mind if I ask you a question?"

She hopped over a fallen log. "What about?"

"Well, you obviously don't think much of your parents. Why is that?"

A flash of anger overcame her. "Have you ever been a hostage?"

"Yes, actually."

"Well, I bet you never had to fake your own death."

"Twice."

She was flabbergasted. "Okay Mister Jason Bourne, what about—"

"Who's that?"

"He's a spy. From an old series of books. They even made some movies, you must have heard of them?"

"Nope."

"Hmm. I don't suppose you get much time for fun in your job?"

"Not really. Too busy babysitting privileged brats these days it seems."

"Excuse me?" She stopped and planted her hands on her hips.

He glanced over his shoulder with a grin on his face. "What?"

"You don't know anything about me!"

He stopped to brush snow off a tree stump, then sat down facing her. He counted off several facts on his fingers. "You're Catherine Blunt. Daughter of one of the wealthiest men alive. Probably had a butler?"

We had three...

"I can tell by your face that I'm right." He shrugged. "It's not your fault. Kids these days, dunno how good they got it. Even Jimmy," Frank's face dropped. "Poor fuckin' kid, he was soft as they come. Brought up on video games and the Net, everything he could ever need at his fingertips."

"What's wrong with that? The Net is a pretty incredible achievement."

"Yeah, yeah. I know. But it's just digital information, floating nowhere. Unless I can physically touch something with my bare hands, I can't fully trust it." He flexed his fingers and balled them into fists for emphasis. Then he gave a dismissive wave. "I always thought I was raised the wrong side of the millennium."

That was quite profound for someone she assumed was just a brainless hunk of muscle. He reminded her of Arnie, who would sometimes come out with these peculiar phrases or sayings from his former life in New Zealand. "What are you?"

"What?" He frowned.

"I mean, what's your job title?"

"Heh. I'm an infiltrator. First man in, first man out."

"I can't believe guys like you still exist. Don't get me wrong, I'm glad that you do, otherwise I'd still be stuck in there… But can't a hacker just do your job for you?"

"Don't let technology fool you. You can have all the surveillance, computers, drones and cameras that you like, but without men on the ground, how will you ever know what you're seeing hasn't been manipulated or faked? Look at you, for example. You're supposedly dead. Yet here you are."

She considered that. "So, you don't trust computers at all?"

"They have their place. They're another tool, useful in the right hands." He shook his head. "Just not mine. I bet that Arnie fellas the same, he seemed to know how to handle himself."

"He's the toughest guy I know," Cathy said.

"Can't aim a gun to save his life though."

Cathy pouted. "He'd probably beat you in a fight."

"Heh. Not sure I'd wanna find out, to be honest. I can see why your father hired him."

"I don't want to talk about my father…"

"Yeah, yeah. Daddy issues."

She glared at him. "You're very condescending, you know that?"

"Sorry, I'm in a bad mood. This mission's been fucked right from the start. Let's get you on that bloody train."

6
TRAIN

Frank escorted the girl to the edge of the forest where he paused to survey the area.

Ahead of them stretched a plain of patchy brown grass dotted with splats of snow. The horizon was jagged peaks in all directions, but nestled at the base of the hills were a cluster of small buildings surrounded by a wire fence.

Frank pointed to a dark opening in the base of rock. "We have to get to that tunnel," he said.

"Okay," she said, rubbing her thigh.

"It's not much farther, then we can relax on the train."

She sighed with relief. "That sounds good to me."

Frank glanced up at the sky. *No sign of that guy's chopper. Can't hear it, neither.*

"We should try to be quick. Let's go."

"Lead the way."

He jogged out into the open, making straight for the yard of buildings. Intel had learned of this place via satellite surveillance and knew it was unoccupied. The train went through twice a day heading across the border into Germany farther down the line. This abandoned loading yard was the best place to board without being seen.

They reached the fence without incident.

Cathy puffed and hunched over clutching her knees. "How much farther do we have to go?"

"We'll get on here." He purposely avoided using the word *jump*.

She frowned, put her hands on her hips and looked

around, breathing heavily. "What? This doesn't look like a station."

Frank hunkered down to the wire fence and heaved it up, making a gap. "Under you go."

She hesitantly crawled through the dirt, making cute wincing noises as she went and Frank squeezed himself through after.

The empty yard was cut in half by the train tracks which led between a bunch of containers and storage shacks before diving into the mountain itself through the maw of the tunnel. A set of overhead cables and signals bridged the tracks at the tunnel's mouth, and a maintenance scaffold granted access to them.

Frank led her to the scaffold. "Up we go."

"Wait a minute," she said, freezing. "This isn't a station. And this is a freight line, isn't it?"

"Yep."

She swallowed. "The train isn't gonna stop here, is it?"

"No."

Her pretty green eyes turned into dinner plates. "Frank, I'm not jumping onto a train!"

Not quite as dumb as I thought, then. "Sure you are. I'll help you, don't worry."

"Frank!"

"It'll be fine," he said, ushering her onto the ladder. "I've done this before."

There was a deep rumbling in the tunnel.

"Listen, it's coming. Unless you want to walk twenty more miles, I suggest you get your arse up there."

She reluctantly scaled the scaffold ladder, grumbling and stuttering.

At the top, Cathy crawled on her hands and knees and leaned back against the rock wall directly over the tunnel. Frank hunkered beside her.

"You already base jumped off a cliff today, this'll be way easier!"

She glared at him. Apparently that wasn't a convincing

argument.

The rumbling escalated, vibrating the scaffold under Frank's feet.

"I'm starting to think I should have gone with Arnie," she said.

The freight train rumbled out of the tunnel making any more talk difficult over the noise.

Frank hopped over the barrier and rested his toes on the plank. Cathy looked terrified as he helped her over and they stood with their backs against the railing, poised to jump. She squeezed the blood from his hand.

It took several seconds for each car to pass below them. The train couldn't be doing more than fifteen miles per hour.

Frank watched each carriage, waiting for an empty one. Something above them caught his eye, a flickering in the sky. Frank frowned, shook his head and focused on the train again.

An empty container trundled beneath them and Frank shouted "Go!"

But Cathy didn't budge.

"*Go!*" he repeated.

She was frozen solid.

They missed their chance. The next container was full of iron beams, and the next, and the next.

"We can't miss the next one! Don't make me push you!" he warned.

"I'm scared!" she wailed.

He cupped her chin and turned it to his face. "Relax! I've got you, okay? You can do this."

She trembled, staring at him with those big striking green eyes. He rather liked looking at them.

Focus you idiot.

An open container emerged. Empty. "This is it!"

He nodded at her. She nodded back.

They jumped.

Cathy's wail stabbed his eardrum.

They landed hard and rolled. Frank cupped an arm around her and took the brunt of the impact when they struck the metal wall of the container, knocking all the wind from him.

No harm done. They were on the train.

"See?" he said, catching his breath. "That wasn't too bad."

She coughed. "Oh god. You really know how to treat a lady."

He stood and offered her a hand up. "I'm trying my best."

Lying on the floor of the container, she looked past him and frowned. "What's that?"

Frank turned and saw the flickering again. A shimmering haze floated in the sky seeming to follow the train. It grew bigger as it approached, and Frank heard a whine of engines.

A hatch opened inside the haze and that hulking Maori bloke peered down at Frank from inside a flying vehicle. The haze shimmered again and for a brief moment Frank made the outline of the craft, a VTOL with twin turbine engines instead of propellers, and the most sophisticated stealth chassis he'd ever seen. You could see the clouds right through it.

"Is that Arnie?" Cathy said.

Arnie shouted something, gesturing wildly at someone else inside the VTOL. He stepped out and descended on a cable towards them.

"Oh you gotta be kidding me," Frank said. "Your father must really want you back."

"I'm not going back!"

I ain't returning empty handed. Chief's gonna be pissed that I lost the kid, I gotta get this girl back and find out what the fuck is going on.

Arnie swung down onto the container behind theirs and landed on its roof.

"Stay here!" Frank barked. He darted at the wall and

vaulted up, scrambling to his feet on the roof of the container.

Arnie, still attached to the cable, steadied himself and eyed Frank with furious determination.

The wind whipped past the two men as the train picked up speed. Between the *cu-chunk, cu-chunk* of the train wheels and the whining thrusters of the VTOL above them, they shouted at each other.

"I don't want to fight you," Arnie started. "Just give me Catherine."

"I don't wanna fight you neither. But you can't have her."

A beat passed. Arnie reached for his pistol at his belt.

Frank charged him down.

He ploughed into Arnie's stomach in a rugby tackle and they sprawled out on the roof of the container. Frank slammed Arnie's arm into the floor and the gun spiralled out of his grip and tumbled off the train.

Arnie swung his weight and toppled Frank sideways. He came face-to-face with the mountain wall rushing past. He rolled away as Arnie lunged. Frank kicked Arnie's feet out from under him and the big man slammed onto his back. The cable went taut and Arnie slid backwards along the floor away from Frank.

Frank followed and swung his boot at Arnie's jaw but the Maori blocked with a bulging forearm and roared in pain. The cable tightened and yanked Arnie to his feet and into the air. The pilot must have pulled up because Arnie shot over Frank's head and dangled away from the train over the grassy plain.

"Look out!" Cathy cried.

Frank glanced ahead and ducked. A concrete tunnel engulfed them. Darkness swallowed Frank for a few seconds before he emerged in daylight again.

Arnie was swinging back towards the train like a wrecking ball. Frank skipped sideways to avoid him.

Arnie regained his feet and unclipped the cable. The

VTOL slurped it up like spaghetti and it disappeared.

Arnie raised his fists and the two men squared off again.

Frank swung. Missed. Arnie jabbed him in the chest, then kneed him in the stomach. Frank recoiled and shifted his weight. Arnie stepped forward and made to swing but Frank ducked and kicked Arnie in the knee. He yelped in pain and swung a wild arm that caught Frank in the side of the neck.

Frank staggered and spun, precariously close to the edge of the container. A sledgehammer of a fist caught Frank in the side of the head and he lost consciousness for a second.

"Arnie! Don't hurt him!" Cathy's voice came out of the darkness and was swallowed by the wind.

Frank was on his back staring up at the passing clouds. Arnie loomed over him.

Arnie lifted his boot above Frank's face, leaving his 'nads open.

Frank booted Arnie in the balls as hard as he could. He was wearing some kind of protective armour, but the force was enough to send him off balance. Frank hunkered and sprang. He threw his entire weight at the hulking Maori and shoved him towards the edge.

Arnie stumbled backwards. He stepped into thin air and fell off the train. A sickening *thud* clanged out as his body struck a passing metal post. And he was gone.

Frank heard the engines above him roar as they changed direction. The stealth VTOL fell behind, slowing to a hover. The train sped on and left it behind.

Staggering to his feet, Frank climbed back down into Cathy's container and fell over. *Haven't taken a beating like that for a while.*

"Oh my god, Arnie!" Cathy cried, covering her mouth.

Frank looked up at her, his vision swimming. *How the fuck did he find us?* He inhaled a breath, trying to stay conscious. But it was too much effort.

***

The train pulled up at a depot in a small German village on the edge of the Alps just before sundown.

Frank and Cathy snuck away and made their way to the Europa safe house. Little more than a wooden cabin on the edge of the village, it blended in with the rest of the quaint buildings perfectly. Except for the helipad on the roof, which Frank thought gave the whole place away.

"*Velcome* Agent Hawkins," greeted Helga, a woman built like a medieval blacksmith. "You are late."

"The mission went tits up," Frank said, brushing past her and into the hall. "I lost the kid."

"Oh no," Helga clutched her chest. "And who is *zis?*"

"This is Catherine Blunt," Frank said. "Priority one protection."

Helga raised her bushy eyebrows. "*The* Catherine Blunt? Pretty for a dead girl, no?"

Cathy blushed.

"You got a panic room here?" Frank asked Helga.

"*Ja.*"

"Show her to it."

"Frank," Cathy said sheepishly. "Don't lock me up…"

"I'm not locking you up. I'm protecting you."

"Yeah, but a panic room? My dad won't be able to find me now, surely?"

Frank eyed her. "Hopefully not." *His bodyguard hadn't been easy to shake off.* "It'll only be for a short while, until I can get you a chopper out of here. I have to make a call. Helga, where's the phone?"

"That way," she said, pointing to one doorway. "Catherine, *zis* way please." She walked out of a different door and Cathy followed.

Frank went to find the phone and dialled in his code number.

To the desk monkey that picked up, he said, "It's Agent Hawkins, connect me to the chief."

He was transferred to his boss, a woman whose real name he didn't even know. When she answered, she did not sound pleased.

"What the hell happened, Agent?" she said as way of greeting. "The CERN facility disaster is all over the news. I thought I could count on your discretion."

"You wanna hear my side of it or not?" Frank wasn't in the mood for a bollocking.

"Watch your tone." She paused a moment, then when she spoke again, her voice had softened. "Yes. What can you tell me?"

"The *fuck* did you get me into, Chief? The whole facility was rigged. I did my part, got the kid in and as far as I know he did his job too. We transferred a shitload of data before the whole goddamn place exploded. I lost the kid."

"You lost him?"

"He's dead."

"Shit." She drew out a breath. "That's not good. I'll have to put you through the psych evaluation when you get back to London."

"Fuck that, I'm fine."

"You know its protocol."

"Sod the protocol, just tell me you got the data? At least tell me you got *something* out of this clusterfuck of a mission?"

"We received a substantial datapacket," the chief said. "Our analysts began decrypting it yesterday. But they claim it's incomplete."

"Incomplete?" Frank frowned.

"There are corrupt sectors of data where information should be, but the actual files are only ghosts."

"That means less than nothing to me, Chief."

"Never mind. Do you have the asset's laptop?"

The asset, Frank thought in disgust. Where was her humanity? He was a fucking kid. "Yeah. I got Jimmy's computer in my bag. He was a bloody genius. We'd only been in the server room for two minutes, and he picked out something almost straight away."

"What did he find?" asked the chief.

"A key word, or a name of something. Jimmy said there were a lot of files relating to it. H- something." Frank clicked his fingers. "Horizon. That was it. Your techs find that anywhere yet?"

"Not that I'm aware of. I'll pass it along."

"Think it means anything, Chief?"

"Running a search now. There's hundreds of companies and references to 'horizon' online. It's too generic."

Typical. Generic means it'll be easy to overlook whatever it is they're trying to keep secret. Hide in plain sight and all that.

"The truth is," the chief went on. "Without the rest of the data, I'm not sure how useful the information is gonna be."

"You want me to upload it from the kid's computer or some shit?"

"No need for that. I'm sending a chopper to bring you back tonight. I want you de-briefed and in psych by tomorrow morning."

"There is one other thing," Frank said, leaning back against the wall. "I picked up a hitchhiker. And you'll never believe who she is."

***

Frank and Cathy parted ways in London.

Cathy was taken in to protective custody to be interviewed. Meanwhile, Frank had an appointment with the chief, followed by three gruelling hours in the *Anti-Dream Machine* courtesy of Europa's own Doctor Frankenstein.

Whenever a field agent was 'exposed to mortality', they

had to be evaluated for signs of post-traumatic stress and other such conditions. The ridiculous contraption nicknamed the Anti-Dream Machine was designed to flood your conscious and subconscious mind with peaceful images and soothing music to the point of there being no room left for any negative thoughts.

Frank had been in the machine twice before and every time the procedure became more nauseating than the last.

Finally, somewhere around three in the morning, he was relieved from duty and prescribed five days leave.

"Are you fucking kidding me?" he argued. "I'm in the middle of a mission. We have a witness to a potential mass-murder and you're sending me home on fucking *leave*?"

"You are not my only agent, Frank," the chief reminded him. He'd hoped to observe Catherine's interview, to see what more she had to say about her captivity, but the chief wouldn't have it. "Go home. Sleep. And I'll see you in five days."

So he went straight home to his luxury apartment opposite Europa HQ on the Thames.

"Welcome home Agent," greeted his household AI.

"Shut the blinds," he commanded, and the blinds slid shut.

Frank went straight to his bed and collapsed onto it.

"Would you like a wake-up call?" inquired the AI politely.

"Fuck no," answered Frank. He rolled over and closed his eyes.

He dreamed. Abstract sensations of paranoia and fear kept him in a restless daze until dawn when he finally passed out properly for a few hours.

Sunlight squeezed in through the slatted blinds and woke him before midday. Groggy and pissed off, Frank wandered into the kitchen in his boxer shorts to make a coffee and something to eat.

He sat down on his gargantuan sofa in front of his

football field size television and turned it on.

He caught about three seconds of a news report before the room went abruptly dark.

The blinds slammed shut. The TV went black.

Frank sat upright. *What the –*

The TV flicked back on. Static set the room alive with flickering light and white noise *hissed* across the room, deafeningly loud. He leapt to his feet blocking out the cacophony with both hands over his ears, then the room went silent.

A message played on his TV.

It was made of short clips of different shows and movies, single words cut into a mishmash of accents from movie stars. Frank squinted at the screen.

"Frank – I know – who – **YOU** –are. I know – who – you- work FOR. – Meet – me – at the - Zoo – in – one – hour. **COME. ALONE.** - Do –not – keep – me – waiting!"

7
FIRST STEPS

Arnie Dillon dreamed of snow and pain.

Light flashed behind his eyes, and faces drifted in and out of sight. He heard voices, distant and hectic. "*A pulse... alive...call Blunt, ask him...*" He caught snapshot glimpses of mountains, and the sky, and he was flying.

Fire erupted in his legs. A nurse loomed over him. "*...50 mils of...for the love of, his eyes are op... hurry u...*" A kaleidoscopic blur of colours and acidic patterns swallowed the nurse's face before Arnie's world faded to black.

The Europa agent's scowling face floated out of the dark. Catherine's kidnapper. He meant Arnie unfathomable malice. Arnie *had* to defeat him to rescue Catherine.

The kidnapper was strong, but Arnie knew he could overcome him. He *had* to, because Mr. Blunt had put his faith in Arnie to bring back Catherine, no matter the cost. Failure was unthinkable.

In the hazy darkness of the morphine dream, he relived the brutal brawl atop the alpine train. The mountainous setting strengthened Arnie's determination; he was Taranaki personified, fighting Tongariro to save his Ruapehu.

But like Taranaki in the Maori legend, Arnie was defeated. The kidnapper beat him down and shoved him into oblivion. Arnie tried to scream but no sound came out of his throat. He fell backwards off the train, glimpsed the sky overhead and the signal post that flew at him before the meaty *crunch* –

He sat up violently, gasping for breath.

He was in a hospital bed under a pristine white sheet. *I'm alive?*

"Thank Christ," he said, clutching his wheezing chest. He took several deep breaths as he waited for his heart to calm.

He had the spacious recovery room to himself. Very modern, very clean. The wide mattress offered a perfect balance between soft comfort and firm support. A wide television hung from the ceiling at the foot of the bed and to his right a window overlooked a grassy field. From his viewpoint, he could see a tree-lined pond with several ducks bobbing on its surface beneath a blue sky dotted with puffy white clouds.

Am I still in Switzerland?

A tube and needle ran into his arm, connected to a suspended bag that drip-fed clear liquid into his veins. He wasn't in any pain, but the hospital gown suggested he'd undergone an operation of some kind. Examining his arms, he saw only bruises. *I got off lucky,* he thought, shaking his head.

He threw back the sheet to check the rest of his body.

He looked at his legs, unable to comprehend the sight of them for a moment. They weren't his. In their place were a set of grey plastic prosthetics strapped to two tiny stumps.

Arnie froze in absolute shock. "What… *the fuck!*" he stammered.

A surge of hot panic engulfed him. With a hammering heart and trembling hands he reached forward to touch the lifeless, grey plastic. The thigh felt silky smooth and all wrong compared to his leathery brown skin. The ball-joints at the knees and ankles looked flimsy and weak.

He winced and pulled his hand back. A throbbing sensation began in his upper thigh. But how could that be?

He didn't have thighs any more. It intensified and crawled down his legs, twisting into a calf cramp. The pain extended down further until it reached his ankles, his feet, his toes. *What is happening?*

All at once, every invisible muscle in his legs seized up.

"Aaaagh!" he screamed, clenching his fists and thrashing on the bed in uncontrollable agony.

He was vaguely aware of the door opening and sensed people entering the room, but he couldn't pull his head up off the pillow because his spine and neck had turned to stone.

"He's spasming," said a female nurse.

Arnie's arms flailed wildly and he felt his fist connect with something soft.

"Ow!" yelped a male voice.

"Stay back!" said the woman. "Increase the drip, let's get him stable again. Mr. Dillon? Try to relax. It's just ghost-pain. A trick of the mind. How's that sedative?"

"He should be feeling it now," said the man, whose voice had turned nasally.

"Good," said the woman. She leaned into Arnie's line of sight. "There, Mr. Dillon. I've increased the painkiller. Take a deep breath."

The pain eased off very slowly. The fire in Arnie's legs dwindled to a tolerable smoulder.

"That's it. Relax," she said again in soothing tones.

Arnie heaved himself into a sitting position and exhaled a long, heavy breath. "What happened to me, doctor? Where are my legs? *Why did you take my legs?*"

"Please," she patted her palms in the air, gesturing him to calm down. "You suffered a grave injury."

He swallowed. Glancing at the plastic legs triggered his stomach to churn. He dry retched over the edge of the bed, coughing up tiny globules of bile. "Ugh," he groaned.

"I'll call Mr. Blunt," said the nasally man. He had opted to stand by the door, far away from Arnie's bed, and held a bloody tissue against his nose.

"Did I do that?" Arnie asked. "Sorry."

"It's okay," the man waved it off, and stepped out of the room with a phone to his ear.

"Where am I?" Arnie said.

"Not far from Bern," said the woman. "A private facility."

"How long have I been here?"

"Overnight. This must be very difficult for you, I expect."

You got that right. "Why did you have to take my legs? The rest of me feels fine."

"You were lucky. Relatively speaking, of course," she added. "You arrived with a shattered pelvis, and your knees were... irreparable. Both of them. Your pilot said you fell off a moving train."

"Yeah, that's the last thing I remember," said Arnie.

"You were delirious and in severe shock. It can happen when the body suffers a tremendous trauma," she explained. "It's fortunate you were travelling by air, so we were able to operate within an hour of your injury."

"Am I going to get that ghost-pain regularly? Fuck that was painful."

"Actually, you should talk to your boss about that..." She trailed off as the male nurse returned, talking on the phone.

"Hold on, I'll plug you in," he said. He inserted the telephone into a slot on the side of the television, and Sid's face appeared on the screen.

"Arnie? Oh thank goodness, you're awake."

"I'll give you some privacy," the woman smiled, and followed the man out of the door.

"How are you doing, Arnie?" Sid asked.

"Sir, I... Not good, actually."

"What a ridiculous question, I'm so sorry. Are you comfortable, at least? If you need anything, make sure you ask. It's all going on my bill."

"Thank you, sir." Arnie didn't know what to say. He'd

expected Sid to be angry about his failure to rescue his daughter. "Sir, I am sorry about Catherine. I couldn't save her…"

"I know," Sid said. "But at least we know where she is, thanks to you. The tracker is still active, for now."

Thank God. He'd almost been too slow to see the agent's intention to throw himself off the cliff with her, but Arnie had just managed to shoot a bug into Cathy's leg before they fell. "Where is she?"

"London, at Europa HQ," replied Sid. "I'm keeping my eye on her location. But I can't imagine what she's going through. I need to get her back more than ever."

"I wish I could help, but it could take months for me to learn to walk on these." He gestured to the awful prosthetics. "I'm getting ghost-pains already. The nurse said I should talk to you about that. Why?"

Sid nodded thoughtfully. "I have a confession to make, Arnie. When I learned of your injuries last night, I made a difficult decision on your behalf."

"What decision?" Arnie cocked his head a fraction.

"About your legs. They told me that they could save one, but not both."

"She told me that both of my knees were 'irreparable,' sir."

"I told her to say that, but seeing you now, I realise I cannot lie to you. I ordered them to amputate both of your legs."

Arnie's throat went dry. "Why? Why would you do that?"

"Because I *need* you, Arnie. I realise the terrible irony, but the truth is you'll adapt much quicker to double prosthesis than you would with only one."

Arnie opened his mouth but nothing came out. A whirl of emotions struggled for dominance inside his head, a complicated mix of shock, bewilderment and anger… "That makes no sense whatsoever. How could you do this to me?" he murmured.

"My new prototype is ready, Arnie. The team finished it last month and we've been waiting for the right volunteer. Look, I know you didn't *volunteer* but… I hope you can forgive me."

Arnie shook his head. "You took my *legs*. This is a lot for me to take in, sir." Arnie rubbed his forehead. *Mr. Blunt has always looked out for me. I cannot blame him for my mistakes.* "I failed Catherine. Had I been stronger, I could have saved her. This injury was my fault."

"Do you still want to help me get Catherine back?" Sid said quietly.

"You know I do," Arnie said. "But I'm in no state to save anyone right now, sir. I mean, *look* at me."

"I see you Arnie. And I see what you can become. With my new prototype, you *will* be stronger."

"What kind of prototype is it?"

Sid paused. "I think it's better if you see it. Doctor Gunther is on his way. I can see I have upset you, and I fully understand why," Sid said, leaning closer to the screen. "But please know that I care deeply about your well-being Arnie, and when you see what my team has come up with, I pray you'll forgive me. Let's speak again tonight, after your initiation."

"Okay, sir."

Sid smiled sympathetically, then the screen went blank.

Arnie at in silence on the bed, staring down at his missing legs. When he tried to move them, the grey prosthetics twitched. A mild throbbing accompanied every effort. *My nerves are attached somehow, but they're not very responsive.* What could Sid's prototype be?

He leaned forward to shimmy the legs into a more comfortable position, but as soon as he touched them, another burst of fire seared up his non-existent muscles.

He clenched his teeth and slammed backwards into the pillow, wracked with debilitating pain.

***

"Ah, there is ze man himself," Doctor Gunther spread his arms in greeting as Arnie rolled to a stop in front of him.

Various apparatus designed to help patients walk and exercise were stationed around the physiology gymnasium. Gunther was waiting in a large open space, standing next to an enigmatic lump taller than himself, hidden beneath a canvas sheet.

"Hello Doctor," Arnie said. They had met a few times before in Sid's laboratory in Berlin. "I never thought I'd ever become one of your patients."

"Quite!" the doctor beamed. "Zis is a very exciting time."

"Maybe for you, bro," Arnie brooded.

Gunther's demeanour didn't change. "Well, let me take a look at you," he said brightly, hunkering in front of Arnie's wheelchair. He popped some horn-rimmed spectacles onto his bulbous nose and leaned in close to examine Arnie's stumps. "Very gut, very gut indeed. These are exceptionally clean cuts."

"Thank you," replied the woman standing behind Arnie. "My name is Doctor Judy Abel. I've heard a lot about your work, so it's an honour to meet you Doctor Wiesmann."

Gunther stood and offered his hand. "Please, call me Gunther, Doctor Abel."

"And you may call me Judy. We are all friends here."

Arnie felt a tinge of ghost-pain in his toes as he imagined tapping them with impatience. He glanced down, reminding his brain that his legs were not there and the sensation vanished immediately. It seemed to him that the pain occurred more frequently and intensely when he had the prostheses attached.

That made him rather anxious to see what Gunther had underneath that sheet. *Can we get this over with for the love of mercy?* He cleared his throat.

"My apologies, Mr. Dillon," Gunther sang, shimmying over to the sheet. "Let us get you acquainted with my masterpiece, shall ve? Behold," he said, grabbing the sheet. "Your new legs!" He whipped the sheet away with a flourish.

A pair of sleek black prosthetic legs, streaked with silver stood upright on the floor. Where the thigh met the waist, a rounded bowl curled up into a skeletal frame of torso armour with adjustable straps.

Arnie gaped in awe. He'd never seen anything like it, but he knew straight away that he liked what he saw.

"Yes!" exclaimed Gunther. "He is impressed! Combat prosthesis V1.0." He pointed to the bowl in the centre. "Full-integration with the spinal column and nervous system eliminates phantom limb syndrome. The brain is tricked into believing the limbs are still present and functional, which has the added benefit of drastically reducing the recovery time."

"By how long?" Arnie asked.

"You could walk out of here tomorrow, Mr. Dillon."

"Jesus. Wait, did you say *combat prosthesis?*"

"Yes. Zis project was sanctioned with the intention of aiding prematurely retired soldiers. The prototype has been designed from the ground up for bilateral transfemoral amputees."

"Sorry doc, I'm not so hot on the lingo…"

"Double amputation, above the knees," Judy said, gesturing to his stumps.

Gunther glided his hand down vertically an inch away from the metal legs. "As you can see, they fully replace human appendages. But more than that, they *improve* on the original concept."

"What material is that?" Judy asked, stepping in for a closer look.

"A carbon fibre composite crossed with titanium alloy. Very strong and not overly heavy."

"It's incredible," she said. "And this framework supports

the spine?"

"Yes. It is of course an unfortunate necessity to provide additional support to the upper body when replacing leg bone and muscle with metal."

"And that's a lot of metal," Arnie said.

They turned to him as if remembering he was there.

"Fortunately, Mr. Dillon is a very strong patient." Doctor Gunther smiled. "Shall we get you calibrated?"

Arnie didn't know what that meant but he said, "Yes."

Judy wheeled him closer to the legs, and two strapping physiotherapists helped to lift Arnie out of the chair. They lowered him gently into the bowl seat.

Arnie saw the array of tiny needles lining the bottom of the bowl, carefully spaced to line up with his stumps.

Doctor Gunther leaned over to adjust them, making sure everything lined up correctly.

"This vill sting a bit," he warned.

They lowered Arnie onto the nerve connectors.

He grimaced through the initial shock. A sharp, jarring jolt of cold shuddered through his nervous system. For a moment it paralysed him and his vision went black.

But the moment passed and he exhaled a short series of gulping breaths.

"Ow," he wheezed.

"Vell done," said Gunther, smiling. "The worst part is over." He tightened the straps until they fit snugly around Arnie's lower back and over his shoulders.

When the physiotherapists stepped away, Arnie was standing upright, a head taller than he had been prior to the operation.

"How does it feel?" Gunther asked, holding his elbow with one hand and touching his chin with the other.

"It feels… good." Arnie relaxed into the seat. The framework around his torso supported his back comfortably, and he had a surprising amount of movement. He could swivel left and right and lean forward and backwards with ease.

"Would you like to try walking?" Gunther inquired.

Arnie tried taking a step, but the legs were lifeless metal. They didn't budge. "I can't," he said, frowning.

"That's because they're not switched on, yet." Gunther pushed the glasses back onto his nose and stepped forward. He reached for Arnie's crotch, about where his belt buckle might be, and released a small compartment in the bowl. Inside was a panel and digital display, flipped upside down so that it appeared the right way up to Arnie. "Push here when you are ready," Gunther said.

Arnie pushed the button.

A sensation rippled through his legs in what could only be described as anti-ghost pain. Arnie felt his legs come *alive*. "Woah," he said, and stamped his foot. It cracked a dent in the floor which spider-webbed out from his heel.

Doctor Judy jumped back in alarm. Gunther only grinned.

"Holy shit," Arnie said, stepping to the side. He wobbled a bit but remained upright, spreading his arms wide as if balancing on a beam. Whenever he felt like he might topple over, the legs automatically adjusted and kept him from falling. "This is incredible!"

"Calibration successful," beamed Doctor Gunther. "Why don't we go outside before we break some of this expensive-looking equipment, hmm?"

Gunther led the way to a side door that opened out onto the grassy field. Arnie followed, taking slow, deliberate steps and ducked under the door.

A fresh breeze caressed his skin. "Holy crap, I can feel the wind on these things!"

"Gut!" said Gunther. "Zat is the neural sensors. You can disable them if you like, but they are in place to help alleviate phantom discomfort. Go now, walk!"

Arnie strutted across the grass. It felt like walking barefooted, only his feet were black metal oblongs leaving footprints in the soft soil.

"Now try a little faster."

"Okay." Arnie moved towards the duck pond and made a semi-circuit of it at a steady jog. The legs made hydraulic *fw-shoosh* sounds as they extended and contracted with every bounce.

"Very gut! Now, try a jump."

"A jump?" Arnie said, dubious. *I was just in surgery this morning, and now I'm jogging around outside.* "All right." He turned to face Gunther and Judy, who were standing on the other side of the duck pond. Arnie did a little hop.

"You can do better than that!" Gunther called. "*Higher!*"

Arnie jumped again, this time gaining about four feet of air from a standing position. "Woah!" Arnie said with a laugh.

"*Higher!*" Gunther shrieked.

"All right you crazy old git," Arnie muttered. He looked at the duck pond. Must've been twenty feet wide. Impossible for an ordinary person to jump that far. Yet Arnie somehow knew…

He ran for the pond, churning up grass and soil as his feet dug in with every step. He charged forwards, thinking *clear it*. The legs obeyed. They sprang at the last possible moment and Arnie sailed high into the air. He cleared the pond and then some, flying right towards Doctor Judy and Gunther.

"Oh shit!" Arnie cried as he plummeted straight towards them.

Judy yelped and darted away, but Gunther grinned up at him, unmoving.

Arnie slammed into the grass in front of Gunther, and the feet sunk half a foot into the ground. The legs and body framework absorbed the impact and Arnie stood upright looming over Gunther as he burst into an excited cackle.

"Vell done! Very gut! You are a natural."

"That felt good. Really good." Arnie reached forwards and shook Gunther's hand vigorously. "Thank you Doctor."

"You are most velcome."

Arnie couldn't wait to call Sid and tell him that he was ready to go after Catherine once more.

Wait 'til we meet again, Mr. Kidnapper...

8
BROTHERS

"Oh wow," Dan exclaimed to his computer screen, watching a pair of incomprehensibly attractive Japanese women—dressed as seductive ninjas—making out. He loosened his belt and shoved his hand down his pants.

It was three o'clock in the morning and the city of Seoul bustled with noise and night life on the streets outside. Traces of light burst across the ceiling every time a car drove past his apartment, casting shadows of the empty soda cans across his desk. The A/C unit rattled in the ceiling and raised voices somewhere outside suggested a group of drunk idiots were walking home from a nightclub.

Dan blocked everything out with his pair of Blunt circumaural headphones and turned up the volume of *Yuki vs Kaname : Tongues of Fury.*

An invasive message popped up in the corner of the screen:

Jimmy says, "u there?"

"Goddamn, little bro', not now." He ignored the popup until it faded away, but a few seconds later, another one appeared.

Jimmy says, "Code 48 dude."

Dan's hand froze. He read the message twice to make sure he was seeing it correctly. You didn't joke about Code 48. He had to acknowledge it.

He dug his hand out, stopped the video and brought up

his messenger app.

Dan says, "Gimme deets."

Jimmy says, "Europa caught me snooping. im on some mission in the alps."

Dan says, "Europa caught u?? WTF were u doing?"

Jimmy says, "no time 2 expln. plz bro. accept wot im abt 2 send u."

Dan says, "What is it?"

Jimmy wants to send you 1'722'684 files. Do you accept the transfer? Y/N?

Dan hit Y without hesitation.

Dan says, "200TB?? That'l take all night to send."

Jimmy says, "just get the ghosts. Europa want this stuff, but if u have it, u can blackmail 'um yeh?"

Fucking hell this was some deep shit his little bro had gotten himself into. They'd always agreed to help each other out if either of them got caught by the *fedz*. But blackmailing *Europa*? Could he even do that? Binary Eye's code of honour dictated that he try. Hell, Jimmy was his little brother, he couldn't just leave him in their clutches.

Dan says, "I'll try, little bro. where exactly are you now?"

Jimmy says, "some facility in the mountains. Switzerland. right now, a server farm. dis agent hawkins guy dusnt even relize wot im doin. Thinks im uploadin to Europa, haha."

Dan says, "Be careful you idiot. Upload SOMETHING or they'll notice."

Jimmy says, "hes standing right behind me, LOL."

Dan stopped typing. He didn't know what Jimmy was

using on his end, but if the app had popups like the one he used, then even an idiot would be able to see that Jimmy was talking to someone instead of doing whatever job he was supposed to be doing.

The files ticked over, so far he'd received about 10 gigabytes of data. *What's he sending me, I wonder?*

Dan watched the files filtering through his firewall and virus scanner, each one slotting into place on his encrypted backup drive where he could sift through them later. He caught a glimpse of a filename and it jogged his memory. *Horizon? Where have I seen that before?*

Dan navigated to the file dump and ran a search for Horizon. 22 results popped up. The files were encrypted though, so he couldn't see their contents yet.

Jimmy says, "u still there, bro?"

Dan says, "Yeah. Found mention of Horizon. Sounds familiar…"

Jimmy says, "omg. wasnt Bennit0 lookin into dat?"

Dan snapped his fingers. That was it, Bennit0, one of his online hacker buddies had released a few snippets of information regarding a secret project called Horizon a month or so ago. It was typical conspiratorial bullshit, the kinda thing that crops up online all the time, and most people didn't care for it. But Bennit0 stopped coming online shortly after, and no-one had seen or heard from him since.

Jimmy says, "just asked hawkins. He dusnt no anything about horizon."

Dan says, "how are you talking to me and he doesn't even realise? Hes gotta be a total idiot."

Jimmy says, "he is! Oh shit, brb"

Dan checked the files were still transferring. Whatever Jimmy was doing, the connection remained active for the next five minutes, until Dan received one final message.

Jimmy says, "shits hit the fan,

```
we're escaping.  Help  me  bro,  FIND
FRANK HAWKINS."
 Jimmy has gone offline.
```

The connection terminated.

In total, Jimmy had sent Dan 263 gigs of encrypted data, and a batch of micro ghost files worth 86 terabytes. It wasn't much, but with any luck, there'd be something vital in there which Europa would be desperate enough to exchange for Jimmy.

Europa. *The fedz.* Dan swallowed. He glanced behind him, checking the door was bolted. He'd never been caught hacking in his life, and didn't intend to start now.

It was time to flee again.

He bundled clothes into a rucksack, packed up his laptop and external drives. With a final glance around the pit he'd called home for the past nine months, he went outside and caught a taxi to the airport.

***

Dan hunched in the plastic departure lounge seat staring at his laptop screen in horror.

Word of the accident at the alpine research facility had spread across the Shadow Net and the conspiracy nuts were riling themselves up. CERN had imploded. Was Jimmy there? *Please let this be a horrible coincidence.* His brother had never mentioned CERN in their chat, but his last message to him—"*shits hit the fan*"—replayed over in his mind, and Dan feared the worst.

Skimming through the Eye's forums, Dan saw that CERN seemed to be the most common topic, and each argument boiled down to whether it really was an accident or not:

Reno: CERN have killed us all!! They

made a black hole in there lab and now were all DEAD!!1!1 BYEBYE EARTH

Roofey: Um, what are you talking about?

Herbert472: their* and we're* dumbass

Reno: THEY MADE A BLACK HOLE, BUT THEY'LL COVER IT UP JUS WAIT N SEE

Frellig: Actually something has happened. An explosion triggered an avalanche. But Reno you moron if they made a black hole, we'd all be dead already. Derunox is looking into it right now.

Reno: NO SAY YER PRAYRS COZ THIS IS THE END

Roofey: What kind of accident? Don't they do crazy experiments up there?

KRUG: something like this was bound to happen eventually. those stupid scientists knew what they were doing and didn't care even if they do make a black hole. now we all get to suffer the consequences of their actions.

Frellig: Theres no fucking black hole you idiots.

Derunox: CERN is fucked.

Dan sent a private message to Derunox, hoping the legendary hacker would be online.

He replied instantly.

Derunox says, "Bergazoid, sup?"

Bergazoid was Dan's online alias. A relic nickname from his childhood which played on the fact his surname was Bergman. He'd never bothered to come up with anything better.

Bergazoid says, "You know any more

about this CERN thing?"

Derunox says, "I've been digging around a bit. I'm putting an article together, it'll be online within the hour."

Bergazoid says, "Please, dude. I'm boarding a flight to London in twenty minutes, can you tell me what you know?"

Derunox says, "Why are you going to London?"

Bergazoid says, "It's my brother, Jimmy. He sent me a Code 48… Europa captured him and put him to work."

Derunox says, "No way, J-Lord got himself caught? That's the third this month. We're dropping like flies."

Bergazoid says, "I know, but dude, it gets worse. He contacted me while on some mission… in a facility in the alps."

Derunox says, "Oh."

Dan rubbed the back of his neck and glanced up at the departure board. His gate was being called.

Bergazoid says, "Please man, I need to know if my brother is okay. Do you know anything about what happened?"

Derunox says, "I'll tell you what I know, but you gotta keep this to yourself until I publish it, okay?"

Bergazoid says, "I'll be on a plane for the next seven hours and there's no way I'm risking an airliner network. I'm offline until tomorrow after this."

Derunox says, "All right. Well, it wasn't CERN. Never mind what all the news reports are saying, the facility that imploded was not CERN. It was a private subsidiary."

Bergazoid says, "Really? So why is it being reported as CERN?"

Derunox says, "That's the question. And I think it has to do with who was running the subsidiary… Margery Blunt."

Bergazoid says, "No way!"

Derunox says, "She has a background in social media and journalism, then ups and disappears six years ago to focus on some 'personal projects'. Now this accident has brought her into the spotlight a bit."

Bergazoid says, "You think she's framing CERN?"

Derunox says, "I don't think framing is correct. This feels more like an accident that she's covering up. CERN is the scapegoat. Hard to be sure, but the pieces fit."

Dan shook his head. He had seven hours to worry about conspiracies, but right now he needed Derunox's help.

Bergazoid says, "I need a favour, dude."

Derunox says, "You want help finding your brother."

Bergazoid says, "Yes… I have the name of a Europa agent, Frank Hawkins. Can you get me his address?"

Derunox says, "You call that a favour? O_O"

Bergazoid says, "I know its asking a lot. But I need to find Jimmy. He sent me a load of data that he pulled from

```
the facility. It could be related to
your cover up theory. I'll give you
access to it if you help me find this
Hawkins guy. Deal?"
```

There was a long pause. Dan fidgeted in his seat, watching the last of the other passengers file through the gate. He needed to get going or he'd miss his flight.

```
Derunox says, "I'll see what I can
find out."
Bergazoid says, "Thank you. I owe
you big time for this dude."
Derunox says, "Yeah you do. Fly
safe, dude."
```

Dan slapped his laptop shut and ran for the gate.

***

He squirmed in his coach-class seat, trying to get comfortable. He'd been on the plane for three hours and desperately needed sleep. His lanky height meant he had to sit up straight so as not to squash his knees against the chair in front; a posture that felt completely at odds with his natural slouch position.

He stretched one leg out along the aisle and closed his eyes.

"Excuse me, sir?" Someone rudely shook him awake.

"Huh? What?" he said groggily.

"You can't put your leg there, sir," said the stewardess, offering him a sardonic smile.

"Sorry," he squirmed around some more and finally found a position where his legs could half stretch under the seat in front and his head could tilt against the side of his chair.

At last, he dozed off. His subconscious wandered into the past and he dreamed.

He was just nine years old, watching television in the living room with his younger brother Jimmy, while their mother prepared dinner in the kitchen. A news report showed a local fugitive being transported to the county jail after being caught robbing a gas station.

Dan gawped at the girl with long flowing black hair flipping the bird to the cameras and wrestling with the officers as they bundled her into the back of the cop van. "She's pretty," he mumbled.

Jimmy grinned through his gap-tooth. "You love her!" he cried, giggling. "Mom, Dan wants to kiss a *girl!*"

"No, I don't!" Daniel clocked Jimmy round the back of the head. "You're such a little nub."

"I'm no nub. I'm gonna free her," Jimmy boasted and Dan burst out laughing.

"Free her? You mean bust her out of jail? There's no way you could do that. You can't even bust the Circle K without my help."

The dream rewound even further to another night where the two boys snuck out of the house to practice their hacking on the local convenience store.

"Keep your eyes peeled!" Dan whispered as he hunkered beside the network box on the side of the building, and started fiddling with the wires.

"Roger, roger," Jimmy said, imitating the stupid robots from an old Star Wars movie, looking left and right up the alleyway.

Dan connected the box to his netbook and initiated a program he'd written himself. It gained access to the store's local network, adjusted the prices of their favourite chocolate bar and then covered its tracks. Very sophisticated stuff, for a nine year old.

Dan liked the way Jimmy looked up to him during those mini adventures.

But that all changed one night.

As the two brothers sat up late, bathing in the glow of their netbook screens on each layer of the bunk bed, the little shit had burst into a fit of uncontrollable laughter. The bed shook and rattled as Jimmy bounced up and down.

Dan leaned over the side and glared upside down at him. "What are you doing?" he hissed. "You'll wake up mom!"

"I did it! I did it I did it *I did it! Ha haaa!*" Jimmy grabbed his netbook, turned it over so Dan could see. "Look!"

Dan squinted at the screen. A fuzzy image of the county jail cell block displayed in a window next to a terminal full of text—Jimmy's code. Every jail cell door was open, and the inmates were waking up and peering out. Dan recognised the black haired girl as one of them.

"No way!" He fell out of the bed and landed on the floor with a loud *thump*. He scrambled up and climbed into Jimmy's bed. "Is that footage *live?* How did you break through the firewall? What's their encryption?"

Jimmy put the netbook on his lap and clicked the terminal shut, hiding his code. "I ain't telling you!"

Dan gaped at him. "Tell me you little twerp. There's no way you could have done this." He tried to grab the netbook from Jimmy, but he tugged it back.

"Get off!" Jimmy yelped.

"Show it to me!" They scuffled, fighting over the little computer as the bed frame rattled some more.

The landing light clicked on, and the bedroom door opened. Jimmy snapped the netbook lid shut, but too late.

"What are you two still doing up?" their mom asked sleepily. "And what have I told you about computers after bedtime? Daniel, get back to your bed and go to sleep!"

The dream flicked forward to the following morning, when Jimmy's antics were all over the local news. Some of the inmates had vandalised the police station during their escape and they issued a public warning about the fugitives now loose on the town.

The cops traced the hack to their house. Jimmy was too young to be prosecuted, but they confiscated his computer and Jimmy earned a black mark on his citizen's record that would never be wiped clean.

"We can't let that happen again, Jimmy," Dan said to his little brother that night. They were both sitting on his top bunk, surfing the Net on Dan's computer. "We mustn't ever be caught. Next time, they won't go easy on you."

"I know," Jimmy grumbled. Then he smirked. "I totally did it though."

"It's no good if you get caught," Dan insisted. *But yeah, you did.* He didn't want to sound bitter. He wanted to be proud of his brother's natural talent, but found it distressingly easy to slip into jealousy instead.

"I learned about something today," Dan said. "It's called the Shadow Net."

"What's that?" Jimmy asked, his eyes eager.

"It's like a secret side of the Net," Dan explained, punching in an IP address. "Think of it like this: the Net is a busy freeway, and the Shadow Net is a tunnel buried right beneath it."

"Cooool," Jimmy cooed.

Dan brought up a website titled *Binary Eye*. The banner at the top of the page showed a logo of an eye peering through a flaming brick wall. *A firewall*, Dan mused. "Check it out. These guys know how it's done. They *never* get caught."

"Who are they?" Jimmy asked.

"They're the real deal. They could have released that girl in their sleep, they're *that* good."

"Wow," Jimmy marvelled, leaning closer.

"But," Dan went on. "She was a criminal. She didn't deserve to be free, not really. These guys only hack bad people."

"What kind of bad people?" Jimmy asked, frowning.

"I don't know. But look. They have a list for nubs." He clicked to another page. The banner at the top changed to say *Initiation Missions*. Each 'mission' was numbered for difficulty. "If we do all of these beginner hacks, they'll let us in. We should use it for practice."

"Yeah!" Jimmy whispered excitedly.

"I bet I can finish them all before you can."

Jimmy grabbed the bedsheets. "No way! I will beat you!"

"Well, you don't even have a computer you little nublet." Dan snapped the lid shut and the room darkened. "Go on back to your bed."

Jimmy clambered off the bunk and climbed under his blanket. Dan waited until he was sure his little brother had fallen asleep, then he opened his netbook again, scrolled back to the top of the mission's page and clicked on #1. *I need a head start, anyway.*

The bedroom light flicked on and for a split second Dan saw Jimmy leering at him. His brother spoke, a dozen different voices spilling from his mouth in nonsensical chattering gibberish.

Dan jolted awake and head butted the airliner seat in front of him.

"Easy there, Mister," said the passenger next to him. "We've arrived."

Dan glanced about the plane, which had touched down, parked up and come to a stop outside Heathrow Terminal 5.

Sweating, he gathered up his bags and joined the herd.

***

Dan got himself a cheap dorm bed in London's city centre. As soon as he'd dumped his bag, he bought a coffee and sat down in the hostel's café to check his email.

Derunox came through for him, and then some.

```
Do what you will with this. But if
you get caught with it, you're on your
own. And I expect to see what your
brother dug up soon. Sharing is
caring! -Derunox.
```

He'd sent Dan a list of personal information on this Agent Hawkins guy. Dan now knew where the guy lived, what his latest assignments were and even when he was due for leave. It turned out that the agent had been taken off his mission and ordered to stay home for a few days.

That would make him much easier to isolate.

He typed up a reply to Derunox.

```
Thanks dude, I've attached access
deets to my remote server where the
datapacket is stored. Just do me a
solid, and don't publish ANYTHING to
the Net until I've got Jimmy back.
Should only take a day or two. Peace.
- Bergazoid.
```

Dan spent the next hour downloading various video clips from famous movies, then used a video editor to line them up into a harrowing message, intended to scare Agent Hawkins into meeting him alone.

Hawkins' apartment had all the luxuries you'd expect from a state of the art new build, including a simple AI to control things like the heating, the shutters and the entertainment system. *These fancy ass places, with everything networked, I can even add a little flair...* Dan planted his video message as a virus inside the AI and set the shutters to close when the agent was in the room.

Now all he had to do was wait for Hawkins to trigger the message and show up to make the exchange: the data for Jimmy. In the meantime, he needed a disguise...

9
THE ZOO

Frank arrived at London Zoo wearing civvies and a hidden earpiece. He queued up behind a line of excited kids, bought a ticket and marched through the turn style.

"Visual confirmed, I see Hawkins," reported an agent in his ear.

"Roger that," replied Jones, sitting in the comms van somewhere nearby. "Frank, touch your face if you can hear myself and Agent Willis."

Frank scratched his nose.

"Comms are good," confirmed Willis. "Follow the path, Frank. I'll be watching out for any tails."

Frank stalked along the path with his hands in his pockets, heading past a row of tall bird cages. *I should be at home chilling out, or better yet, working the mission. What fucking luck to be dragged into this on my downtime.*

He weaved between a family watching some meerkats and rounded a corner past the hippo pond. He eyed everyone he passed. Mothers pushed prams, kids ran to and fro, the odd elderly couple ambled along. Very busy. *A good place to talk if you don't want to risk getting hurt,* Frank reflected. That meant his stalker was intelligent, but not very brave.

Frank, already in a bad mood after his psyche evaluation would have appreciated the chance to knock someone out.

"No sign of activity yet," Willis reported.

"Copy that," said Jones. "Where is Agent Hawkins

now?"

"Just approaching the penguin colony."

Come on, whoever you are. Let's get this over with.

Frank glanced towards the penguin enclosure as he passed. A semi-circular fence overlooked the animals below, sunbathing on the artificial rocks or splashing about in the icy blue water. A solitary man stood against the railing looking over the edge at the birds. He caught Frank's eye because the long brown trench coat and wide brimmed hat he was wearing didn't match the white sneakers on his feet.

"Frank Hawkins, come here," said the man without turning around.

Frank stopped.

"Do we have contact?" said Willis. "Potential suspect at the penguin enclosure."

Frank approached the man and leaned against the railing next to him. "So, who the fuck are you?" he asked, peering down at the penguins.

"It doesn't matter," said the man. He spoke with an American accent. "I have something you need, and you have something I want. Let's trade."

The man's voice was odd. He sounded strained, as if trying to put on a menacing tone but hadn't quite got the hang of it. Frank took a sidelong glance at his face and saw, to his amusement, the bloke was wearing a huge pair of dark sunglasses. The caricature spy look was complete. The stubble-free chin also suggested he was pretty young, early twenties at the most.

"A trade?" said Frank. "What sort of trade?"

"Contact confirmed," Agent Willis said. "Hawkins is talking to a man, medium build, trench coat. Standing by to engage."

"Wait for Frank's signal," reminded Jones. "Don't blow your cover unless absolutely necessary."

"Let me make this as simple as I can," said the suspicious man. "Europa captured one of my people, and I want them back. In exchange, I'll give you the missing data that you failed to retrieve from your last mission."

How the hell can he know about that? "So, you're with those hacktivist muppets? I shoulda' guessed." *Jimmy was one of them too...*

"Muppets?" the man said, but it came out closer to a squeak. He composed himself and regained his phony deep voice, "Could a muppet hack into a Europa agent's safehouse?"

"That was a neat trick with my TV," admitted Frank. "Did you do that all by yourself?"

A smile played on the man's lips. "Europa should know better than to house their agents in civilian buildings. Hacking your apartment was a breeze."

"So it *was* you," Frank mused, turning his back to lean the opposite way on the railing. He patted his right leg, a signal to Willis, who was hidden somewhere among the other visitors.

"Frank believes he's our man," said Willis.

"Keep your eyes peeled for any accomplices," ordered Jones.

Frank went on, "What makes you think I have authority to just release one of your buddies?"

"You might not," the man admitted. "But your superiors will. And if you value your career, you'll convince them."

"I don't see why you had to drag me into this," Frank argued.

"Because Jimmy Bergman is your partner."

Fuck. "You know Jimmy?"

"Yes. I know Europa have other members of Binary Eye too, but I'm only asking for him. I'm offering you a fair deal: the missing data for Jimmy."

I can't tell him that Jimmy's dead. Gotta' stall him... "Let's say, for argument's sake, I agree to help you. How do I know you're not bullshitting me about the missing data? Can you prove that you have it?"

"I can prove it to you right here and now with a single

word," the man boasted.

That took Frank by surprise. "How?"

"Horizon."

Frank blinked. *Who is this guy?*

The man grinned. "You don't know what it means, do you?"

"Do you?" Frank growled, leaning closer with clenched fists.

"No!" the man said, raising his hands. "I swear. But I want to know. Give me Jimmy, and I'll give you the data so you can carry on doing your job."

"You're pretty brave to threaten a Europa agent," Frank said. "Or just stupid."

"I hope you're not underestimating what we could do to you, Mister Hawkins. Your personnel records are in the hands of the Eye, and will be distributed across the Net within the hour if we can't come to some sort of agreement. You'll never function as a spy again."

Frank seethed. The man's getup and attitude were a complete mockery of everything Frank stood for. These technophiles had no idea what sort of shit he had done to protect them during the Second Cold War. He couldn't give him Jimmy, and Frank was supposed to just let this arrogant dork destroy his life for that? "Who the fuck are you to threaten *me*?" he asked, grinding his teeth.

Frank grabbed the man by his throat and in one swift movement, dangled him over the railing.

"Agh!" the man choked, clutching at Frank's arm.

"Contact! Situation has dissolved!" Agent Willis babbled in Frank's ear.

Frank tore the earpiece out and threw it to the ground. "Tell me where the data is or I'll break your scrawny neck."

"Wait!" begged the dangling man. He didn't weigh much, must be skin and bone beneath that big coat. "I really do have the data. I'll give you it. Just give me back my little brother!"

Frank frowned. "What?" He plucked the sunglasses from the man's face and for a split second Jimmy stared back at him.

Frank let go.

"Ahh!"

Splash.

Penguins squawked and flapped their wings in panic.

Agent Willis sprinted up to Frank out of a crowd of onlookers. "Agent Hawkins, why did you do that?"

Frank didn't know how to start. He was reeling from the shock and a massive pang of guilt. He ignored Willis and jumped over the railing instead. He landed on a rocky island next to a startled penguin. Jimmy's brother was flailing around in the water, being drowned by his trench coat.

Frank plucked him out, leaving his hat bobbing on the surface, and hauled him onto the rock, where he coughed up half of the pond. His streaky black hair clung about his face.

"Sorry about that," Frank said. "You look just like Jimmy. A bit older, I guess. What's your name?"

"I'm two years older," he said between coughs. He hacked up a final bit of phloem. "My name's Dan."

"Nice to meet ya, Dan." *Fucking hell. I've got some real bad news for you, mate…*

"Hawkins!" Willis called from above. He stood among a few amazed children and some very confused parents staring down at them from the railing.

"We're fine," Frank said, giving him a dismissive wave.

"You brought backup!" Dan said with alarm.

"Of course I did, I ain't a bloody fool." Frank rubbed his chin, trying to find the best way to tell this kid that his brother was dead. "Listen, about Jimmy—"

Zzzzzstt.

Frank's tongue stiffened and the penguin enclosure turned fuzzy. The next thing he knew he was staring up at the sky, with Agent Willis shouting, "He's getting away!"

Frank blinked several times and staggered to his feet. "Did that little shit *taser me?*"

"He went that way!" Willis yelled, pointing to a door marked *Feeding Time.*

Frank shook the cobwebs off and bolted through the door.

He charged down a maintenance corridor and burst out into a tunnel aquarium. Lying on the floor in a sodden heap was the kid's trench coat, and he spied the lanky kid barging through the exit on the far side end of the room. Frank ran after him.

He kicked open the door and caught sight of Dan weaving through the crowds lined up outside the elephant paddock. Frank pushed his way through causing a ruckus, which sent the elephants trumpeting and several angry shouts from upset parents. Frank squeezed out of the bustle into a wide open path some twenty paces behind Dan.

The lad ran around a curving path and briefly disappeared from sight behind some trees but Frank soon caught up and re-spotted him making for the zoo's exit. Security guards at the gate scrambled to their feet as Dan bolted past them and by the time Frank arrived, two of them were blocking the way, armed with batons.

"Move it!" roared Frank, shouldering through both and sprawling them on the concrete.

Frank charged out into the street and followed two more security guards who were chasing the hacker. At a busy road junction, the two guards stopped, looking left and right. Frank slowed up before he reached them. *They've lost him.*

Frank scanned the area, searching for lanky men among the bustling shoppers and tourists. No sign of him.

"Fuck," he cursed, halting and turning around. He happened to glance at the pavement and spied some very faint watery footprints leading into a clothes store. Frank followed them and strode into the store.

"Welcome to Winghams Wonderstore!" said a cheery clerk. "Let me know if you need any help today, sir."

Frank ignored her, and looked at the floor. The footprints were swallowed by the carpeted threshold between the door and the shop floor. He scanned the room, noticing an overwhelming abundance of pink clothing.

A high pitched shriek came from the fitting rooms at the back of the store.

Frank weaved between rows of skirts, t-shirts and underwear and approached the fitting room area where two shop assistants were having an animated conversation involving a lot of hand gestures.

"I couldn't stop him, he just ran in!" one said.

"Well I'm calling security," said the other, and reached for a phone.

Frank planted a firm hand on the desk, startling a yelp from the young girl. "Excuse me," he said, apologetically. "Did a young man just come through here? Bean pole, wet black hair?"

"Um, yes," she said, clutching the phone. "Do you know him?"

"May I?" Frank said, gesturing towards the changing rooms. Without waiting for an answer, he slipped past and walked into the area beyond. Rows of pink curtains lined both sides of the corridor, some splayed open, but three were drawn. "Dan?" he said. "Come on out. We need to talk about your brother."

Frank approached the nearest curtain and just as he got there, a woman opened it and scurried out clutching a pair of trousers. "Sorry, Miss," he said and moved aside to let her pass. When she was gone, he dropped to the ground and peered beneath the next curtain. A pair of slender legs and bare feet looked back at him. He spun to look under the only other drawn curtain and saw nothing.

Gotcha.

He stood up, went to the curtain and flung it open.

Dan was crouched on the bench, armed with a black pistol. Frank dodged sideways by instinct and Dan darted from the room. He got three paces before Frank tackled him to the floor from behind. He disarmed the lad with a swift jab to his wrist and sent the gun bouncing over the carpet.

"Let me go!" Dan cried, writhing to break free but Frank pinned his head to the floor.

"Calm down!" Frank barked. "We need to talk about your brother."

"You caught him, but I'll never go with you!"

"Shut up and *listen to me*. Jimmy's dead."

Some of the shop assistants had gathered at the entrance to the fitting rooms like a flock of curious geese. At this, some gasped and covered their mouths.

Dan's body went limp as if all the strength had been sucked out of him.

Frank let go and climbed to his feet. Dan remained flat on the floor.

Frank bent to pick up the gun—it was actually some kind of blocky-shaped stun-gun with a squared off barrel and a battery attached to its side—and stuffed it inside his jacket.

"Come on," Frank hooked a hand under Dan's armpit and hoisted him upright.

Dan stared at him with resigned eyes and an upturned mouth. *He looks numb, but not surprised. He must have suspected this.*

"Let's get out of here and find somewhere to talk," Frank said, leading him past the shop assistants, who offered sympathetic expressions. At least they weren't going to call the cops now.

***

They went to a nearby park and found a bench off the path. Frank slumped down onto it. Dan stayed standing, his head hung.

"How did he die?" Dan asked the ground.

"Do you really want to know?"

Dan didn't move.

"Sit down, kid," said Frank with a heavy sigh.

Dan ran both hands through his hair and dropped onto the bench next to Frank.

"Jimmy was a bloody good kid, right to the end," Frank said. "You should know, he died saving someone else."

"Really?"

"Yeah. And I'm sure she is hugely grateful for it." Frank spared a thought for Cathy and realised he didn't know where she was. She might be locked up in some Europa cell for all he knew.

"Who did he save?" Dan asked.

"I can't tell you that."

"It's not right." Dan shook his head. "What you're doing to us."

"Right and wrong ain't for us to decide, kid."

"How can you say that?" Dan frowned. "You kidnap people, and then make them work for you."

"Not me. My higher ups." Frank didn't feel comfortable justifying himself, probably because he knew his argument was weak as shit. "Look, I didn't exactly sign up to Europa to force kids into working for us."

"So you're just a soldier? A mindless drone who carries out his orders, even if he doesn't actually agree with them?"

"Your brother was a criminal," Frank reminded him. "You're all criminals. At least Europa puts your skills to good use instead of locking you up. We keep you out of prison and doing something beneficial to society."

"You're no good to society when you're dead," Dan said flatly.

Frank rubbed his hands together and leaned forward.

"Look. I'm really sorry about your brother. He was the first tech I ever lost…" The pit of his stomach churned. Frank couldn't remember the last time he felt this close to chucking up.

"Your apology won't bring my brother back," Dan's voice was soft and breaking. "The worst part is he died for *nothing*."

"That ain't true," Frank stood up. "Cathy would be dead if it wasn't for him. And so long as you give me the data, I can get to the bottom of this Horizon bullshit. I *have* to."

"Cathy?" Dan said.

Oops. "Yeah. Never mind that. Look, kid, you know I have to bring you in, right?"

"Fuck you," Dan said, rising to his feet. "You think I'm gonna just let you take me?" He fumbled inside his pocket, then gasped when he realised it was empty.

Frank pulled out the stun-gun and held it up. "Looking for this?" He pulled it back when Dan lunged to grab it.

"Give that back, I need it!"

Frank turned it over in his hand, checking out the details. It didn't look anything like a traditional Taser what with it being pistol-shaped, and the battery had naked wires protruding from it. "This looks custom made."

"That's because I made it."

"Well that can't be legal," Frank said. "I'm gonna hold onto this." He put it back inside his jacket pocket.

Dan made a frustrated grunting sound. "You're an asshole, man. I should kill you for what happened." His face contorted in a pained grimace, clearly fighting back tears with considerable effort.

Frank felt another stab of guilt. "Look, kid. I won't pretend to know what you're going through. And I am genuinely sorry for what happened to Jimmy. But I can't let that shit eat me up. I have a job to do, and right now it involves finding out what the fuck Margery Blunt was hiding in that facility. I need that data, okay?"

Dan had been fidgeting and inhaling deep breaths, but

now he looked at Frank with a puzzled expression. "You said her name was Cathy… Surely not Catherine Blunt?"

"Goddamnit," Frank cursed. "Look, you need to forget I said that. How did you even figure that out?"

"It all makes sense now!" Dan said. "Bennit0, he posted pictures of a girl he claimed to be Catherine, like, two months ago." He added, under his breath, "Bastard even claimed to be screwing her… But he also leaked information about Horizon. Bennit0 must have been working at that facility!"

"I don't know what you're on about."

"Bennit0 found out something that he shouldn't, I bet you anything," Dan said. "And I don't know what happened to him, but he hasn't been online ever since he posted that. If you're 100 percent certain that you rescued Catherine Blunt, then she might know what happened to him. *And* she must know something about Horizon."

"She's being held at Thames House for questioning. If she knows anything, Europa will find out."

"Questioning?" Dan looked alarmed. "Is that spy-talk for 'tortured'?"

"What? No, kid, who do you think we are?"

"I've read things, dude."

"On the Net, I assume?" Frank said sardonically.

"Where else?" Dan said.

"Good for you."

"My brother helped rescue Catherine *Blunt*…" Dan gave a stifled laugh. "Oh my god."

Frank knew he'd be in deep shit if this kid were to go back to his hacker buddies and tell the world that Catherine was actually alive. *Then again, maybe that would be the right thing to do.*

"Look, I think we're done here. I gotta take you in."

"Wait, wait, wait." Dan stepped back holding up two index fingers. "I've had an idea just now."

"What is it?" Frank folded his arms across his chest.

"What if I were to go with you? Willingly."

"Um, that would be better than me having to knock you out and carry you."

"Don't do that! I want to help you figure this out." Dan paused a moment, and his tone changed from excitable to serious. "I have to."

"I'm not sure I want another tech…" Frank said.

"This isn't about you. I'm not doing it for you."

Frank smiled sadly. "You're doing it for Jimmy."

"Yeah."

Who was Frank to argue? If this kid wanted to help, so be it. "All right, kid. Let's go see the chief."

10
PRESSING MATTERS

Margery Blunt sat cross-legged on the sofa beside the reporter Louise Stone, sipping a glass of wine in front of her suspended television. She wore a crimson blouse, her dyed black hair draped loose about her shoulders.

She eased into the chair and got to work. "Let's see what you have."

Stone sat with her BluntBook on her lap, mirroring the screen onto the television so that Margery could see. "Okay, this is my voiceover, regarding CERN." She pressed play.

A video of Stone talking to the camera played on the screen. She was sitting at a table in some hotel room, but that didn't matter—they were only going to use the audio of this and overlay it with helicopter footage of the avalanche.

"*As you can see, the devastation to the surrounding mountainside is catastrophic. There were no survivors at the research facility, in what is believed to be Euromerica's biggest international disaster since the super continent merger. Now the question on many people's minds is also one of the most controversial: How did this happen?*"

Margery rolled her eyes. "Melodramatic, much?"

"Really?" Stone chewed her lip.

"Yes, but it's your style, I suppose." Margery considered losing the part about 'how it happened,' but realised that focusing on the *how* would conveniently distract the mobs from the *where*. She took a sip of wine. "It's fine. What's next?"

Stone brought up a selection of videos taken outside the UN building in Vienna. "I managed to interview a few of the protestors. I was thinking, since everyone has a different view on the event, we can show a few examples of what people are saying."

Margery sat a little more upright. These had to be chosen *very* carefully. "Show me."

The first video started rather shakily, as if the cameraman wasn't quite finished setting up, during which Stone's voice could be heard asking, "*Why are you here today then, sir?*"

The camera finally settled amid the crowd of dozens of jostling picketers. A bearded man waving his crude sign that showed a stylised graphic of a sun, took his place in front of the camera.

"Sell it to me, big man," Margery smirked.

"*Close down CERN!*" he shouted. "*We've said it for years – what good is scientific discovery when it costs lives! For too long they have meddled with God's plan, it's time we heeded his signs.*"

A din of agreement chimed up from the people around him, before the camera jerked to the side and then cut to black.

"The religious approach?" Margery hissed through gritted teeth. "I don't like it."

"It was quite a common viewpoint, I'm afraid," Stone said.

"What is that symbol he's carrying?"

Stone paused the video so they could look at the man's picket. "Oh, it's a new-age religion or something. There were a lot of them there today. I believe it's called *New Dawn.*"

"New Dawn…" Margery repeated. She stared at the symbol of the sun rising over a field. A stylised depiction of a horizon. That struck a chord with Margery. *I'll have to remember this for later.* "What else did you get?"

Stone played another clip, this time of a young couple

sporting peace symbols drawn onto their cheeks in felt pen.

"*Love thyself, man! We don't need technology, only love!*" The girl then shoved her tongue down the man's throat.

Margery was disgusted, and glared at Stone.

"Sorry, I guess I won't use that one."

"No."

Stone played a few more clips, each one showing another zealot spouting similar gibberish about God.

"Hmm, this is all feeling a bit samey." Margery swirled her glass.

Stone scrolled over the thumbnails and stopped on another clip. "Ah, this was a little different."

The video played, showing a man in his fifties, this time in a less crowded area, off to the side of the main throng. He had red raw eyes and a brown beanie hat on.

He took the hat off and clutched it in his hands. "*I lost my wife and daughter,*" he mumbled. "*They were on a hiking trip, on the mountain. And um, they were in that area. They should've been home yesterday, but I haven't heard from them since the avalanche. I just know they were killed up there.*" He broke down into wracking sobs.

Margery stuck her tongue into her cheek. "I can't imagine there's many like him. But that is a refreshing change from all of the Bible bashers. Did he have any more to say?"

"Yeah, a little bit." Stone clicked up another video.

The same man appeared on screen, having composed himself. This time he looked angry. "*The people at CERN have paid for their arrogance with their lives. But my family was innocent.*"

On the video, Stone asked, "*What would you say to the Euromerican government, if you could?*"

"*Our government need to put tighter restrictions on these so-called researchers. We don't need them running dangerous experiments on our doorstep!*"

"That's good," Margery said. "Use him at the end to

drum home the point."

"Okay," Stone said. She added, "Um, may I ask, just to confirm… what is the overall point?"

Margery lowered her glass mid-sip and turned towards the young reporter with deliberate slowness. "You should know that."

"Ah, well, yes. I think I do, but—"

"So, what do you think we are doing here? Take a stab."

Stone hesitated. "We're implicating CERN."

"Correct."

"But CERN itself is still mostly functioning."

"So?"

"So, won't people suspect something is wrong?"

"They already suspect something is very wrong with CERN. You said it yourself, the religious sheep are all over this incident like a rash, and we must play with the cards we are dealt."

"I just thought, seeing as it wasn't CERN's facility that got destroyed, a little ambiguity would lend some credence to my report…" She trailed off.

Margery's knuckles were white as she squeezed the stem of her glass. "I pay you to make *facts*, not add fuel to *rumours*. There are very few people still alive that know about our facility." She glared hard at Stone. "*Very* few."

"I know," Louise flustered, gesticulating in agreement. "We have contained this."

"It's just that if someone at CERN were to speak to the press, it wouldn't take long for the truth to come out."

"Let us deal with that," Margery spoke as if comforting a child that had awoken from a bad dream. Louise wasn't stupid, it's why she chose her in the first place, but sometimes she could get concerned with ideas that were above her station. "Just do your job." Margery pointed at the television screen, and finished the last gulp of her wine.

"Yes, ma'am." Stone unplugged the laptop and picked it up as she scurried from the room. "Oh, hello Mr. Zhin."

Margery turned to see Henry leaning against the

doorframe in his charcoal suit. "Miss. Stone." He nodded as she slipped past him into the hall. He cocked his head to watch her go, then smiled back at Margery. "Impressively done."

Margery draped her slender arm over the back of the couch. "Snooping again, are we dear?"

"You know I love watching you work." Henry closed the door and strode across the room, making for the liquor cabinet.

Margery raised her empty glass to him. "Be a dear, and top me up."

He poured himself a whiskey and leaned his rear against the mahogany. "I have a mind for something a little harder." He downed the glass in one and studied her with a long, enigmatic look.

His stony features were difficult to read at the best of times, but his body language and lack of response to her request for more wine told her he was preoccupied.

Margery plonked her empty glass down against her thigh. "What's wrong?"

"She has a point, doesn't she?" Henry gave a curt point with one finger extending from his whiskey glass. He poured himself another. "If the right person at CERN spoke out, we'd be in trouble."

"I suppose so, yes. It's nothing we can't handle, though, right?" It loathed her not to be certain.

"I just got off the phone with your ex-husband."

It was a drastic change of subject that caught Margery completely off guard. "Oh?"

Henry took a seat in his armchair and crossed his legs. He didn't say anything more.

Margery inhaled a deep breath, acutely aware of an intense anger within Henry, and she wanted nothing more than to help alleviate him of the burden. But how could she unless he told her what the matter was?

"Come now," she jabbed her glass onto the coffee table and sat upright in the couch. "Tell me what that bumbling idiot has done now."

"He's gone after your daughter."

Margery scowled. "My daughter was at the facility. The place is nothing but a craterous ruin now. What do you mean he's *gone after her?*"

Henry pulled out a handheld recorder and raised it to the ceiling. He clicked a button and Sidney's unmistakably grating voice played through the living room's speaker system.

"I'm done with you people," Sid spat. "You can't tell me what to do any more, and you won't be receiving any more of my research."

"What makes you think you can just walk away from this?" Henry's cold voice replied.

"Because you don't have Catherine anymore."

"She's with God now. You have my condolences, Sid."

"Is that what you think?" Sid shrilled. "You underestimated her, just like you underestimated *me.*"

"What are you talking about?" Henry replied in a bored tone.

"Catherine is with Europa. She'll be telling them the truth about Margery. They'll have all the evidence they need to bury her for deception and murder."

"Won't Catherine's very existence implicate you as well?" Henry pointed out. "You helped cover up her death."

"I'm beyond caring any more. All I want is Catherine back. You need to let me try."

"I didn't realise I was stopping you."

"Ahe," Sidney said. "Don't play coy with me. I'm not an idiot. You thought Catherine was dead, and so you have no more use for me. Margery called me the other day, trying to get under my skin. She wants me to kill myself. Well, I won't! Not while Catherine still breathes."

"If you want to talk to Margery, why did you call me Sid?"

"I never want to speak to her again. You can tell her I'm

still here, and if she wants to send a goon to finish me off, she had better think about whether she likes the idea of living in a German prison for the rest of her life. Because if I don't get Catherine out of Europa's custody, that's exactly where she'll end up!"

"I suppose I'll pass the message along. Might I inquire as to the method in which you intend to assault Europa?"

A moment of silence passed at the other end of the line. "No."

"All right then. I will give your regards to Margery. I'm hanging up now. Do take care, Sidney."

The recorded call ended.

"Catherine is *alive*?" Margery blurted.

"It would seem so. Unless he is lying?"

"He wasn't," Margery shook her head. "He was never any good at lying. I was the one who told him that Catherine was dead, and I saw how he reacted. She's the only thing keeping him going. But now she's with *Europa*?"

"How do you suppose he'll try to get her back? Can that Maori of his do anything?"

"Arnie?" Margery scoffed. "That dim-witted fool is loyal to a fault, but he's no match for Europa."

"So you're confident Sid will fail to retrieve her?"

Margery bit the end of her thumb. *It would be better if he did get Catherine back. How much had she told them already?*

"Why do you look so afraid, my dear?" Henry smiled at her.

"Because my daughter is in the hands of the one group of people that could stop us, Henry."

"Do you think I would let that happen?" He raised his eyebrows.

I was wrong. He's not angry at all. He was toying with me. "You're not the least bit concerned."

"No."

"Why?"

"Sidney has dug his own grave, if he thinks he can attack Europa without consequences. After I spoke to him, I made a call to Europa's Chief. She and I had a little talk about the future."

A smile tugged at Margery's lips. "Really?"

"She's on board. In exchange for a place on the Guest List, she's agreed to help rid us of our problem with Sid."

"Excellent." Margery's anxieties were slipping away. "What about CERN?"

"They were handled a long while ago. The EAU has been aware of the energy production element of Horizon since the beginning. They're practically chomping at the bit to get their hands on our supply."

"What's the latest from Tunisia?"

"The solar plant is 75% operational. We are almost ready to initiate Phase One."

"I had an idea about that," Margery said, remembering the zealots from the video. "Have you heard of the New Dawn movement?"

"No?" Henry cocked his head in curiosity.

"I think they could be very useful to us."

"Interesting. Tell me about it later." Henry curled his index finger in the air. "Come here."

A pleasant shudder swept down Margery's spine. She got up off the couch and sashayed over to Henry. Standing before him, she placed her hands on both armrests and leaned forward, allowing her hair to form a curtained tunnel pointing at her cleavage.

Still got it, she thought as Henry took a long glance down her blouse.

"I'm going to miss you," he said.

"What?" she said, standing upright.

He reached forward planting his hands around her waist and pulled her closer. "You need to retreat to Cloud Lodge for a while."

"By myself?"

"Yes, just in case Europa come sniffing. We have to play this next part very carefully." He caressed her thighs, massaging them with experienced fingers, and slid them behind to squeeze her buttocks. "I'm going to record my speech there. I'll join you as soon as I can."

Margery climbed into the armchair, pushing her knees down either side of him and pressed herself against him. "When do you want me to leave?" she murmured in his ear.

"First thing tomorrow," he said, clawing at her back.

"Then we had better make the most of tonight," she said, and kissed him.

PART THREE

11
EUROPA HQ

As Dan approached Thames House, the looming brown-brick building that overlooked the river, his feet started to feel like cinderblocks. Every instinct told him not to go inside, because this was the home of *the fedz*.

And yet on he walked, one heavy step at a time, following Agent Hawkins right up to the front door.

Well, a side door actually. Frank led him around to a barred window and flashed his ID to the guard inside, who buzzed them in.

Jimmy piped up in Dan's mind, *What're you doing, bro?*

Infiltrating the enemy.

You're crazy!

"I know," he muttered.

"What?" Frank said, pausing in the threshold of the door and turning around.

"Nothing," Dan said, hoisting his backpack higher on his shoulder and gripping the strap.

Frank glanced at his bag. "That's your computer, right?"

"Yeah."

"Let's get it scanned." He went inside.

Dan hesitated long enough for the door to almost close. A second before it dead-bolted, he slapped out his palm to stop it and pushed his way into the lion's den.

His heart accelerated as he scanned his bag through security. It was just like an airport, except he and Frank were the only passengers. The guards outnumbered them four-to-one.

"Afternoon Agent Hawkins," one greeted Frank with a smile, as Frank emptied his pockets into a tray beside the metal detector. "Aren't you on leave?"

"Gotta see the chief," Frank said and stepped through.

"Ah," the guard nodded. "What's this, Agent?" He picked up Dan's EMP-gun out of the tray. The sight sent Dan's heart into overdrive and a cold sweat formed on his back. *If they find out what that really is, I'll be deported.*

"Oh, it's the kid's Taser," Frank said.

"It's not standard issue," the guard said. "So I'll have to keep it here until you leave."

"Fair enough," Frank said, stepping through the metal detector arch.

What? No! Dan clenched his teeth, watching the guard lock the custom gun in a safety box. He'd hoped to somehow get it back into his possession while inside this building, but there'd be no chance of that now.

The guard turned to Dan and waved him forward.

Dan's throat turned to sandpaper as he stepped through, but the machine didn't beep.

"Who're you, then?" the cheerful guard asked.

"I'm—" Dan croaked. He cleared his throat.

"He's a product of the modern age," Frank said.

"Another asset?" The guard's eyebrows raised. "Jeez. How many are out there?"

"Less every day, thanks to you people," Dan said.

The guard blinked.

"Come on, this way," Frank said, roughly spinning him by the shoulder and leading him deeper into the hive.

They passed by offices and Dan spied the sort of equipment they were using—old hardware running obsolete operating systems. Nothing made by *Blunt*. He couldn't believe it. This was the cutting edge governmental intelligence agency? *This?*

The sight of middle aged men and women typing on such defunct hardware calmed his nerves somewhat.

Maybe taking these jokers down would be easier than he originally anticipated, even without his EMP-gun. At least he still had his laptop, loaded with ready-to-use viruses.

They rode an elevator up to the fifth floor and exited into an identical-looking corridor. Finally, they came to a door marked *Processing* and Frank held open the door for him. Inside a forty-something woman with greying hair curled in a bun looked up from a reception desk. "Hello Agent, what brings you to me today?"

"Got another one for ya." He gestured to Dan.

"Ah, one moment." She picked up a handset and pressed a speed-dial button. She exchanged a few words with the person at the other end, then hung up. "Okay, someone's on the way to conduct the interview. You can wait through there." She gestured to a side door and they both went inside.

It looked like an interrogation room, complete with a wide mirror on one wall, a desk and some uncomfortable-looking metal chairs. A cordless telephone rested on the desk next to a tablet computer dock.

Dan dumped his bag on the desk and paced the room.

Frank leaned against the wall and crossed his arms. "Nervous?"

"No," Dan lied.

"Heh," Frank said.

Outside the door, Dan heard an agitated voice. A man asking, "Where is he?"

Dan looked to Frank, whose grin faded and he stood up straight.

A moment later, the door burst open and a pale bespectacled man stormed in. "Frank! What the hell happened out there today?"

Frank held out his hands. "Relax, Jones. Cripes man, you'll give yourself an aneurism."

Jones flapped his arms wide. "And it'll be your fault!" He wore a creased white shirt and clutched a folded laptop in one hand. Dan recognised him as a technician, someone that might actually speak his language.

"I brought him in, didn't I?" Frank said.

Jones saw Dan for the first time. "This is the hacker that broke into your apartment?"

"Hi," Dan said. Then, recalling some distant memory of social interaction, he offered his hand.

Jones frowned, but gave it a brisk shake. "Why isn't he in handcuffs?"

"Because after I chased him across half of London, he volunteered."

"What?" Jones narrowed his eyes at Dan. "Why?"

Because I want to burn your organisation from the inside. "Because I want to help. I, uh, know about Horizon."

Jones' eyes went wide. He scurried to the door and eased it shut before taking a seat at the desk. "Are you serious? How do you even know that word?"

Dan took a seat opposite, and pulled his computer out of his bag. "Jimmy Bergman was my brother. He transferred me a datapacket." He patted his laptop—at least three years newer than Jones'—and leaned forward in the chair. "It's the data you are missing."

Jones looked to Frank. Frank's eyebrows said *told ya so*.

"So, you're just offering to give the data to us?" said Jones.

"Uh huh."

"That doesn't seem likely. I've met many of your sort before, you don't do anything unless there's something in it for you."

"It's like I said, I want to help. I'll give you the data…" *And a virus or two.* "…in exchange for becoming Frank's partner."

Jones scoffed. "That seems even more unlikely. You've gotta be pretty high up in Binary Eye's chain of command with your skills."

"We don't have a chain of command," Dan laughed.

"Aha, so you admit you're one of them."

Damn, he caught me there. "Look, does it matter? I'm here

to make a trade. I have important information you need, why do you care what my reasons are?"

"Because it's not how this usually works." Jones leaned back in his chair, and Dan saw bemusement in his face. "We've never had a volunteer before."

"So? I can be the first."

"It's not that simple. I can't trust you. You hacked into one of our agent's private homes. Frank, surely you don't want this kid with you in the field, not after the last one?"

A flash of anger ripped across Frank's face. "The last one was Dan's *brother*. I watched him die, for fuck's sake."

"Is that what this is about? You don't owe this criminal a thing."

Frank clenched a fist and growled. "Yes I do."

Dan swallowed. This Frank guy seemed pretty honourable. *He feels legitimately responsible for Jimmy. And he feels guilty…*

Jones and Frank stared each other down but eventually Jones cracked and turned away. He returned his attention to Dan. "Look, I'm sorry about your brother. But put yourself in my shoes. I'm responsible for any of the techs we bring in from outside. I have to make sure we have, well, something to ensure their loyalty. Did you ever wonder why your brother cooperated with us?"

Dan blinked with realisation. "Um, no actually."

Jones sighed. "We had to tell your mother that we had her son in custody, of course. Jimmy went crazy when he found that out and begged us not to. He said it would break her heart."

Dan inhaled a sharp breath. She was the reason he fled to South Korea in the first place. He had to stay away in order to keep her protected from himself.

"So," Jones went on. "We came up with an alternative solution. Instead of informing her of Jimmy's arrest, we told her he'd volunteered to help us. She never knew that Jimmy had been dragged from his apartment at four o'clock in the morning by a team of armed infiltrators."

"Fuck," Dan wiped his mouth. *Jimmy must have been terrified.*

"That's what happens when you mess with us," Jones said matter-of-factly. He gave an almost apologetic shrug.

Dan swallowed the lump in his throat. He had to stay focused if he was to convince them to let him join. "Look, what does that have to do with me right now? I still want to help. I have to get to the bottom of this Horizon conspiracy."

"Who said anything about a conspiracy?" Jones asked.

"It's fucking *obvious*! You don't know anything about it, do you? You *need* me. I'm motivated."

"By what?"

"By revenge! Justice! Call it whatever you want, but my brother died in that place, because of Margery Blunt or her superiors or whoever. They're hiding something, and I *have* to expose it. I stand a much better chance of doing that if I work with you, but if not, I'll just go back out there and do what I can by myself."

"What makes you think you'll be allowed to leave this place?" said Jones.

A harrowing silence settled over the room.

Jones turned to the mirror behind him. He nodded once.

A moment later, the door opened and a smartly dressed blonde woman marched inside. She had a militaristic air about her, a strong posture and fierce blue eyes. Dan guessed her age at about fifty.

"Chief," Frank greeted her.

Jones rose to offer her his chair.

She took it and sat opposite Dan, clasping her hands on the desk between them. Dan held her gaze for an uncomfortably long few seconds.

So this is Frank's boss, the head of Europa.

"My condolences," the chief said softly. She had a subtle rasp to her voice, and spoke with a strong London accent. "I chatted to your mum this morning. I had to tell her about Jimmy, and arrange her compensation package. She

160

was upset as you can imagine." She cocked her head a fraction at him and gave a wan smile. "Never expected to be meet her other son today. You must despise me."

"A bit, yeah," he stiffened. "You're the one who's kidnapping us."

"You don't kidnap criminals, you *catch* them. I have captured dozens of you over the last three years, and I can't honestly say that I've trusted a single one."

"You can tr—"

She held out a hand. "You're not joining us. Protocol dictates that any criminal who volunteers obviously has an ulterior motive. Top that with the moral implications of hiring a grieving mother's only remaining son, I just won't do it."

"You've seen what I can do," Dan insisted.

"Yes, I have." She gave a fleeting angry glance at Frank. "Your little stunt at my agent's home will not go unpunished."

Dan gulped. "What are you going to do to me?"

She leaned forward across the desk.

Dan instinctively leaned away.

She smiled. "We'll just take this." She snapped Dan's laptop off the desk and held it over her shoulder for Jones to take.

"What? You can't have my computer!"

"Yes we can. Be grateful we're only taking that, Mr. Bergman. She leaned around and said to Jones, "Take it to your team, have them analyse the data and match it to the rest."

"Will do," he said and walked out the door.

She spun back to Dan. "As soon as I have confirmation that the data is what you claim, you'll be deported back to America."

"*What?* No!" Dan cried. He couldn't go back there, not now. "Frank!" he begged. "You gotta let me join you. You *know* I can help!"

Frank waved him quiet. "Do I get a say here, Chief?"

"Hawkins," the chief glared at him. "You're on leave."

"I know."

Dan sensed she was mad at him, but there was respect there too. She clearly didn't want to hear him out, but resigned herself to it anyway. That gave Dan a glimmer of hope.

"Go on," she said.

"I ain't happy about being taken off the mission. I feel bad about Jimmy, and—"

"Good god Frank, have you gone soft?"

"No, sir. Well, maybe a bit. But Jimmy was a fucking good kid, and from what I've seen of Dan, he knows his stuff too. He'd be invaluable to my mission, and his brother died because of us. We owe him more than just a bloody compensation package."

The chief gave an exasperated sigh. "It's against protocol, Frank."

"Fuck protocol." He added, "With respect, sir."

Dan cracked a smile.

The chief and Frank looked at each other with comrade-in-arms wordless understanding. Dan chewed his lip, waiting in anticipation.

"I'm sorry, Frank. Times have changed." She stood up, and made for the door. "Stay here and keep an eye on Mr. Bergman until we have confirmation of the legitimacy of his data." She strode out.

Dan let out a hopeless breath. Frank clenched a fist and marched after her. With the door ajar, Dan could hear them talking in the reception beyond.

"What about Cathy?" Frank said.

"*Cathy*?" the chief replied. "You mean Miss Catherine Blunt."

"Where is she?"

"You're *on leave*. Miss Blunt no longer concerns you. I hope you enjoyed your little jaunt through the Alps. You did a good job getting her out of there unharmed, but your role in her safety is over."

"She could be integral to figuring out what's going on. If it wasn't for Jimmy, she would have died along with everyone else. Jimmy sacrificed himself for her. And now his brother wants to carry on. How can you just send him home?"

The chief's voice softened. "Look, losing the junior was rough, and I think you need time to get your head together."

"I'm fine. Put me back on the mission before our trail goes cold."

"The trail hasn't gone cold. You are not my only agent, Frank."

"Can I at least speak to her?" Frank asked.

"*No.* She's not even here. You were right about the tracker, we found one in her leg. I couldn't risk keeping her here, so I've transferred her to Plumpton this morning, as a precaution."

"I see."

"As soon as we've surgically removed the tracker, I'll have her quarantined in a secure location until we've extracted what she knows about this Horizon. Your part in this is over, Frank. Do I make myself clear?"

A moment of silence passed. Eventually, Frank resigned. "Yes, sir."

"Good. Now do your job, Agent, and let me do mine."

Dan heard a door closing as she left. Frank didn't return straight away.

Where did he go? Dan stood up and crept towards the door to peer out. The receptionist was still typing on her computer, but Frank was nowhere to be seen. Dan considered making a run for it, but this place was a maze. He wouldn't know where to go.

Frank appeared suddenly from an adjacent door, presumably leading to the room behind the mirror. "Get back in there," he ushered Dan away from the door as he returned.

"So is that it?" Dan asked. "I gotta just sit here and wait

to be deported?"

"Shh." Frank whispered. "We don't have much time. I just disabled the security camera. If you really wanna help, then follow me."

"What?" Frank re-opened the door and pulled Dan by the arm with him. "Kid needs a piss, we'll be right back."

"Okay, Agent," said the receptionist, barely looking up. "Huh? I don—*ow.*"

Frank squeezed his arm to shut him up.

Frank left *Processing* behind and instead of turning left the way they had arrived, he followed the corridor to the right. They passed a few doors, one of which was the men's bathroom and kept going.

Holy shit, he's breaking me out.

He pushed open an emergency exit door, and in the privacy of a switchback stairwell, he explained. "We're heading to the garage in the bottom level. I got a car we can use to get out of here."

"Where are we going?" Dan asked, scuttling down the staircase behind Frank.

"Plumpton. Catherine Blunt is my biggest lead, and for some reason, the chief won't even let me see her. That don't seem right." Frank flung himself around the next bannister, taking the steps two at a time. "Hurry up!"

"Do you think she's hiding something?"

"I might be wrong, but if I had to guess, I'd say she knows more about Horizon than she's letting on."

Dan fell behind. He passed a floor labelled 'G' with a subheading that said *Security*. Dan halted in the middle of the stairs. "Wait up!"

"What now?" Frank called, a whole stairwell below him.

"My stun-gun! They still have it."

"Forget about it, we don't have time."

"No, I need it! Do you have any idea how long it took me to build that?"

"We don't have *time!*" Frank growled, rushing back up the stairs towards him. "Soon as they find out you're gone, they'll put this place on lockdown."

Dan retreated to the door labelled 'G' and held his palms out in panic. "It's not just a stun-gun!"

Frank stopped at the top of the stairs and narrowed his eyes at him. "What is it, then?"

"It holds an EMP charge. It can disable electronic locks, things like that. It'll be useful to us!"

Frank considered that, glancing at the door. He let out a guttural growl. "Fine." Dan made to open the door but Frank pushed him back. "*I'll* get it. You meet me at the bottom of the stairs. Don't enter the garage without me."

"Okay," Dan agreed. He watched Frank go, then proceeded to the bottom of the stairwell.

He waited for a nerve-wracking five minutes before Frank finally reappeared.

"Did you get it?" Dan asked eagerly.

"Yeah," Frank said, handing him the EMP gun. "Come on."

They entered a sprawling underground parking lot. They passed several rows of cars before Frank stopped next to a black Mitsubishi Evolution with tinted windows. A really old one.

"What the hell is this?" Dan remarked. "This car must be ten years old."

Frank clicked the alarm off, sending the indicator lights into a blinking frenzy. "Eight," he corrected, popping the trunk. "In ya get."

Dan looked at the confined space. "Oh man, you gotta be kidding me."

"Nope."

Dan reluctantly climbed in and laid down.

"I'll stop when we're clear of the building, then you can ride shotgun," Frank promised. "Until then, stay quiet."

"Okay," Dan said.

Frank slammed the trunk shut and Dan's world went pitch black.

12
CONFINED

After Frank left her, she was taken to the Thames House medical facility where a kindly doctor conducted a routine physical examination, which included an x-ray and a blood test.

"It's not every day I get to treat a dead person," the doctor smiled as she typed some notes into her computer.

"Ahe," Cathy smiled back, hoping it didn't come across disconcerting because frankly that was a weird thing to say to someone, even in Cathy's position. *I didn't actually die, you know?* She hadn't met many doctors before, but they all had the same dark sense of humour, apparently.

After the x-ray, the doctor furrowed her brow, studying the screen.

"Is something wrong?" Cathy asked.

"Perhaps." The doctor eyed her quizzically. "You said your father implanted a tracker chip in the past, yes?"

"Yeah. But I had it removed over a year ago."

"Hmm," mused the doctor. "So how do you explain this?"

She swivelled the screen around so Cathy could see. A black and white fuzzy image of one thick vertical bone filled the image, Cathy's femur. But there was something else, too. A small black oblong nested under the skin, almost touching the bone.

"What is that?" Cathy asked, gulping.

"It's an x-ray of your left thigh," the woman replied.

"I know that," Cathy said irritably. "But what is that black thing?"

The doctor's smile faded, and her tone became accusatory. "You tell me," she said.

Cathy probed her leg instinctively with her fingertips. She was wearing a pair of jogger pants, which Europa had given her in replacement of their expensive skysuit. Both of her legs ached after the hike through the mountain with Frank. Worse still were the scratches and bruises inflicted on her by the tree branches after Frank threw her off that damn cliff.

As she ran her fingers across her thigh, each abrasion throbbed lightly, but a sudden flare of pain seared up at one particular spot at the front of her upper thigh. She sucked in a breath through gritted teeth. "I think I can feel that thing in there."

"You told me you weren't bugged anymore." The doctor's eyes never left Cathy's.

"I didn't know about this, I swear!" *How can this be happening? Mother had the chip removed. This is something else.* "Can't you take it out?"

"I could," said the doctor. "But it's not up to me. I need to report this immediately." The doctor swivelled the screen around to face her and picked up a telephone.

Cathy swallowed. She felt her stomach tightening up. "Please, Doctor. I don't know anything about this. It doesn't make sense!" The doctor held up a finger to shush her.

Cathy clutched a handful of hair on her head, wracking her brain, trying to remember how she could have been chipped again without her knowledge.

The woman spoke to someone on the other end of the phone. The short exchange ended with her saying, "I'll keep her here until they arrive." She hung up and gave Cathy an apprehensive look.

Cathy chewed her lip, butterflies fluttering around the knot in her belly. She hesitantly asked, "Who are 'they'?"

167

"Security guards."

The fluttering intensified, inching towards her sternum. "Why are security guards coming for me?"

"Just wait here," the doctor said. "There's nothing more I can do for you."

A few moments later, the door opened and three burly men entered, followed by a smartly dressed blonde woman.

The doctor leapt up, apparently surprised. "Chief!" she said, by way of startled greeting.

The blonde woman gave a swift downward gesture with one hand, and the doctor returned to her seat. "Miss Blunt?" the chief said, marching towards Cathy.

"Yeah," she replied, now looking up at the chief as she loomed over her in the chair.

"Please come with us. We are transferring you to a safe location for protection."

"Protection? Am I in danger?"

The chief cocked her head. "No, the protection is for us. Until I know whose monitoring that tracker of yours, I will not risk holding you here at Thames House."

"I didn't know about the tracker!" Cathy insisted. "I just found out myself, I—"

"It's irrelevant," the chief interrupted. "Please just come with us."

Cathy felt as small as a mouse, and timidly walked between the security guards towards the open door. "Where are you taking me?"

"You don't need to know that," the chief said, closing the door behind them.

***

The door to Cathy's cell banged open and she jolted awake. Her head felt fuzzy with the lack of sleep and her eyelids sagged.

Something flashed bright, temporarily blinding her.

She blinked, shielding her eyes. "Not again," she groaned.

Mr. Gruff came into focus, standing in the open doorway. One of her guards; she'd given him that name herself.

"What's with all the photo's you creep?" She heard the hysteria in her voice.

"Just orders," Mr. Gruff said gruffly. He slid the camera phone back into his pocket and walked out. The deadbolt gave a meaty *choonk* as he locked the door behind him.

Cathy lay back on the mattress staring up at the ceiling.

She had no idea what time it was. She'd been locked in this cell since yesterday, a small room without a window, somewhere underground. There was a strip bulb embedded in the ceiling, and it got brighter whenever Mr. Gruff opened the cell door. It returned to a dull state after he left again, leaving her in constant flat light that kept the tiny room neither dark nor bright.

Europa transferred her to this place under the claim that it was for their protection. The walls were embedded with lead, apparently, meaning it would be impossible for the tracker in her leg to be traced.

But who was tracking her? And had they been monitoring it during the time it took for Europa to transfer her?

It had taken over an hour to get there, travelling by armoured hummer in the middle of the night. Cathy had seen the transition from urban city to rural English countryside through the tinted windows.

The sight of so many trees had excited her—six years in an underground research facility will have that effect on you, she reflected—before they brought her to this miserable concrete bunker, a sprawling underground complex, and locked her in a cell.

So much for my short-lived freedom.

It was all Frank Hawkins' fault.

He had convinced her that coming to Europa would be for her own good. She suspected that he didn't mean for her to be locked up underground yet again, but it was still his fault all the same.

Maybe he put the tracker inside me? They had spent the night alone in the tent, could he have done it then?

"Oh, get a grip!" she said aloud to herself. Why would Frank bug her? He worked for Europa, and Europa didn't know about the chip, so it couldn't have been him.

So who did that leave? *Mother? Or Father, somehow?*

She found herself rubbing her thigh at the spot where the chip was located under the skin. She winced as the pain flared up again. It felt raw, like a fresh wound.

Wait a second.

She sat up on the bed and rolled down her pant leg to get a closer look. The dim light made it difficult to tell, but there was certainly a bloody scab around the spot where it hurt. It blended in with the rest of the scratches she'd received when Frank and she parachuted off the cliff.

That's when it happened! Arnie shot it into me!

He'd been aiming a gun at them both just before they jumped. It must have been some kind of tracker gun. She recalled the moment, and definitely remembered Arnie firing it a split second before she fell. She'd been so terrified of falling to her death that the pain in her leg had been shoved to the back of her mind. Then they fell through the trees, and all the other scratches had camouflaged the tracker chip wound, so she hadn't noticed it at all.

So Father is tracking me…

She wasn't sure how she felt about that. The last thing she wanted was to see him again, the cowardly fool. But that didn't really matter, because there was no way he'd ever get to her while she was locked in this cell.

At least her psychotic bitch of a mother finally had no idea where she was. She most likely thought Cathy was dead, and that was just fine.

Now all Cathy wanted was to get out of here and be left alone. Was that too much to ask?

When they let me go, I'm never going to be anyone's prisoner ever again.

She yawned. All this time to think was tiresome. Or maybe it was just the surreal interruptions to her sleep courtesy of Mr. Gruff and his camera. He'd taken at least six photographs of her now, and she had no idea why.

Nobody had hurt her, not physically at least, but being caged up again was definitely taking a toll on her mind.

Why didn't I go with Arnie when I had the chance? At least then, I'd be outside.

She lay back on the mattress and wearily closed her eyes.

***

The cell door unbolted and Cathy stared up at the ceiling. *How long has it been this time?* An hour? Three, perhaps? Rubbing sleep from her eyes, she sat up on the bed, expecting to see Mr. Gruff walk in with his camera again.

"Good morning," said a woman.

"Is it?" Cathy recognised the chief after blearily wiping her eyes. "What d'you want?" she said.

"Oh my, we are sleepy aren't we?" said the chief in a jovial tone. "Let me help you up."

Before Cathy could protest, the chief hooked a hand under her armpit and hoisted Cathy to her feet with surprising strength.

"I am sorry about confining you like this, but you understand why it had to be done, don't you?"

Cathy shook her head.

"It's because of the tracker inside you, of course," the chief said. "Until I knew for sure who was tracing your location, I had to keep you confined and out of reach of the GPS. Hence, the solitary confinement here in our lead-walled cell. I am sorry you had to go through that."

Cathy was still groggy from lack of restful sleep, but something nagged at the forefront of her mind that overshadowed any discontent regarding her confinement. She was more pissed off about her lack of privacy. "Why did he keep taking photos of me all night?" she blurted, pointing at Mr. Gruff.

The man was standing guard outside the cell door, and at the photos, he glanced over his shoulder to look at her. His stubbly chin protruded from his face almost as far as his nose.

"I ordered him to keep an eye on you," explained the chief. "We don't have surveillance cameras down here, you see. I just wanted to make sure you weren't doing anything… untoward."

Cathy frowned. "Really?"

"Anyway, I'm glad you accept my apology, and I'd like to invite you to return to the upper levels where a hot shower and a breakfast meal awaits you, Miss Blunt."

Cathy nearly pointed out the fact she hadn't accepted the apology, but the thought of food set her stomach to immediate growling, so she just nodded instead, and walked out of the cell.

The shower was glorious.

The breakfast even more so. Bacon and eggs and baked beans accompanied with freshly squeezed orange juice and two slices of toast. Cathy scoffed the whole lot down and sat back in the school-dinner style canteen where several other Europa employees were scattered, eating their own breakfasts.

When she was done, the chief invited her to a private office to explain the details of how they intended to proceed.

"So, when can I leave?" Cathy asked.

"Soon," promised the chief. "I just need to ask you a few questions."

"Okay."

"It's about your time at the alpine facility."

"Okay…"

"I would like to know about your involvement in the Horizon project."

Cathy frowned. "Horizon project? What's that?"

A moment passed where the chief said nothing, but looked at Cathy as if she'd grown an extra head.

"So you don't know anything about the Horizon project?

"No. What is it?"

"Never mind," the chief said, and promptly stood up and turned around to face her bookcase.

What was that about? Cathy thought that maybe she *should* know about this Horizon project, the way the chief had seemingly expected her to tell her about it. It sounded vaguely familiar, but only in the way that hearing an overused catch phrase was familiar. Maybe one of the research notes she'd read had been codenamed Horizon, but if it was, Cathy couldn't recall what it was about. She'd analysed literally hundreds of the things during her time at the facility.

"I was just an analyst," Cathy explained, trying to be helpful. "I mostly looked at energy readings and how different methods were applied to various types of matter. I don't suppose that makes much sense to you, though…"

The chief turned back around with curiosity in her eyes. "Tell me about that. What were they doing with energy?"

"Um. Well, I don't know exactly. But for over a year now, the team responsible for electromagnetic research had been trying to figure out a way to harness electricity into its most efficient form. I believe it had something to do with treating cancer patients."

"Cancer?" The chief furrowed her brow. "Are you sure that's what they were doing? What about solar energy?"

"Solar energy?" Cathy gave a stifled laugh. "Our facility was underground…"

"Right, but you had equipment on the surface. Did you have anything to do with the research related to solar energy?"

"No."

"Are you sure?"

"Yeah. Why are you asking me this?"

"You worked there for over six years, Miss Blunt. I assumed you might know something about the Horizon project."

"It's like I said, I analysed data. I looked for anomalies and made suggestions for how to improve the results. I was never assigned to any one particular project."

"Tell me about the cancer research, then."

"It's difficult to explain," Cathy said. "Most of the recent studies were related to the effects of electromagnetism on living tissue. Nobody really talked to me about it much, but I had a friend..." The words suddenly snagged in Cathy's throat, as she thought of Ben. She swallowed hard and forced herself to continue. "I had a friend who worked in the facility, and..." She choked again.

"It's okay," the chief said warmly. "Take your time."

"Look," Cathy said, struggling to hold back a tear. "I agreed to let Frank bring me to you because I thought you would want to know about my mother. I was her hostage. And she killed two of my friends..."

"You must have lost many friends in the accident," the chief said.

"Accident?" Cathy said.

"The incident," the chief corrected.

"No, you said accident." Cathy felt a hot flush of something close to anger. "What happened wasn't an accident."

"No, I suppose not."

"What happened there was... an atrocity."

"Yeah."

Cathy gave the chief a hard look. "You have to arrest my mother."

"I can't do that."

"What? You're the head of Europa, of course you can. She's a murderer!"

"Do you have any proof?"

"I'm here, aren't I? She made the whole world think I was dead, she covered it up."

"That's not the same as murder. Do you have any proof that she killed two of your friends?"

"I *saw* it happen, both times!" Cathy's voice cracked and a tear leaked out of one eye. "For God's sake, are you telling me that after what happened at the facility, after thousands of people have died, you're not going to do anything about it?"

"I said no such thing," the chief said. "I have my best agents looking into the incident at CERN. Is there anything you can tell me about the incident itself? I'd very much like to know who authorised the destruction of the place, but no doubt you'll blame your mother for that as well."

Cathy nearly said yes, but that wasn't strictly true. Cathy was speaking to her mother when it happened. Someone else gave the order to destroy the facility. In a rare moment, Margery had shown an inch of motherly compassion when she was told the facility would be purged. For once, Cathy had a reason to believe that somebody other than her parents was responsible for the shitty situation she found herself in.

What did she call him over the phone... she said his name right before the siren went off... *Harold? Or Henry? Yes!* "I think a man called Henry authorised it."

"Henry?" the chief said, raising an eyebrow. "Henry what?"

"I don't know. I just heard my mother say the name Henry, right before the whole place got destroyed. I wish I could tell you more."

"I'll add it to our intel," said the chief. "But I'm afraid a forename by itself may not be that useful."

"Whatever," Cathy said. She didn't want to talk about any of this. She wanted to get to the part where the Chief let her go and she could finally move on with her life and leave this whole sorry chapter in the dust.

The chief's telephone rang. She answered at once. "Yes?" Cathy heard a tinny but indecipherable voice shouting on the other end. "What? Already?" More panicked shouting. "Yes, for fuck's sake, sound the alarm. Get the others to their stations."

The chief hung up.

"I'm sorry Miss Blunt, but I'm going to have to ask you to return to your cell."

"What? Why?"

"We're under attack."

"*What?*"

The chief stood and went to the door, opened it and ordered Mr. Gruff to escort Cathy back to the lower level.

"Come with me, Miss," he said. "Quick like."

Cathy followed him through the bunker and down the stairwell all the way to the same cell she had spent the previous night.

"You aren't going to lock me inside, are you?" she asked, hesitating at the open door.

"You'll be safe here, Miss." He shoved her inside.

"Hey!"

The door slammed shut behind her and the ceiling light immediately dimmed again.

"Fuck!" Cathy cursed.

The floor trembled. Cathy staggered. "Woah..." Dust fell from the ceiling in a little puff. *Was that an explosion?* Before she had time to consider it, another tremor shook the walls. She backed away from the door, staring at it.

Someone outside the door screamed. It sounded like Mr. Gruff. Then something banged against the door. Cathy yelped.

The thick metal door buckled against the weight of something heavy on the other side. *DWANG! DWANG!*

The door burst open, swung violently around on its hinges and embedded itself in the concrete wall. *TWACK!*

Cathy screamed.

13
ASSAULT

Arnie stood in the cargo hold of the Blunt VTOL wearing his titanium legs. *Or is this sitting?* He figured he'd have time to work it out later.

The legs were switched on and he felt the AI's presence like an obedient dog in his mind, waiting for instructions. He thought about turning towards the peep hole and the legs obeyed. He couldn't see out of the window because he was too high, so he thought about bending down, but this time his legs did something else. Instead of bending at the knee, they contracted. The thigh sank lower, swallowing the shin until he was low enough to see out of the small, rounded window.

Rolling ocean waves spread out below their craft as it flew across the English Channel. Arnie could just about see white cliffs ahead of them, some ten miles away.

The pilot's voice crackled in Arnie's headphones. "Call from Mr. Blunt for you, Dillon."

"Put him through," Arnie said.

The headphones *clicked* as the channel switched, then he heard Sid. "Arnie, can you hear me?"

"Loud and clear, sir."

"You're approaching the coast now," Sid explained. "The last sighting of Catherine's signal is just a few miles inland. They sent me another photo just now… Catherine is being held in a cell. A fucking *cell*, Arnie."

"How does she look? Have they hurt her?"

"I... I don't think so. She just looks exhausted."

"And you've had no signal from the tracker since last night, sir?"

"No, it's still being blocked by something."

"She's probably underground," Arnie said.

"Must be."

Movement through the peep hole caught Arnie's eye. The chalky cliffs roared beneath them and the rushing sea was replaced by fields of grass whipping by below.

"Have you considered the possibility of a trap, sir?"

"Of course it's a trap," Sid said. "These photos they keep sending me. They're bait."

"And we're falling for it...?"

"They've underestimated us, Arnie. They've underestimated *you*. You have to go in with full force. The exoskeleton will protect you from most small-arms fire."

Arnie flexed the fingers of his right hand, encased in a metal frame that ran all the way up his arm and around his torso. "I will bring her back for you, sir."

"I know you will." Sid gasped. "The signal! It's back!"

"How close are we?" Arnie said, adrenaline kicking in.

"Not far. She hasn't moved far from where we lost the signal. It's near a small village called Plumpton."

"Sync the location to the pilot's GPS, so he can follow it. I want to drop right on top of them, sir."

As the VTOL cruised northwards following the source of Cathy's signal, Arnie made some last minute adjustments to his equipment. He clipped three concussion grenades and a pistol to his belt, and strapped an assault rifle across his front. He put a parachute pack on his back and clipped a handheld GPS scanner to his wrist, which showed a satellite view of the local area, as well as a blip indicating Catherine's tracker location. Together with the exoskeleton armour, he felt like the hero of a science fiction movie.

I hope Mr. Kidnapper is down there so I can kick his bloody arse.

The AI inside the legs buzzed with excitement, reacting

to Arnie's eager anticipation.

"Arnie?" Sid spoke up again through the headphones.

"Yes, sir?"

"You're approaching Catherine's signal now. I just wanted to say, good luck."

"Thank you sir."

"Bring her back for me…"

"You betcha."

"ETA sixty seconds!" the pilot buzzed through his headphones. *"Unclip yourself and wait for the green light!"*

Arnie took off the headphones and hung them on the wall, then put on his visorless helmet with retractable shades.

"Here we go." Arnie thought about facing the hatch and his legs turned for him. He stood motionless under the glow of the red light illuminating the cargo hold, waiting for the VTOL's bay doors to open.

A thin slit of light appeared in the floor, which quickly extended as the hatch slid open at his feet. Gushing wind pummelled the cabin and made Arnie's ears pop.

He stood on the precipice staring down at green fields rushing by, a thousand feet below. The ground slowed as the VTOL tilted its engines, slowing to a hover in mid-air.

The light turned green.

Arnie jumped.

He plummeted through the sky. The chute opened, but they hadn't done a live test jump with this much weight, and he immediately felt the difference between this and a regular jump. *I'm not slowing down…*

The grass rushed up to meet him.

He landed hard on his feet.

The impact crashed through his spine, protected and reinforced by the exoskeleton. His vision turned blurry from the intense pain, but the legs injected him a dose of something and his sight cleared in an instant.

He looked down. His feet were buried two feet into the ground. He plucked one leg out of the earth and heaved the other one up. The blip on his wrist scanner blinked, indicating Catherine's position nearby.

Arnie retracted his shades and glanced about. He stood in a field, a few trees in the far corner, no buildings in sight. English countryside.

He shrugged off the chute pack and left it in the grass, then started towards Catherine's location.

He came across a dirt track and followed it. It crossed the grass field and as Arnie clomped along it, he realised it suddenly dipped downwards into the earth ahead.

Shit, that's well camouflaged.

A concrete arch protruded very faintly from the ground, overgrown with grass like an oversized Hobbit-hole. He could have walked right by the entrance to the bunker if he didn't have Catherine's tracker for guidance.

He followed the track into the hollow, where it opened out into a tunnel leading downwards. At the end of the tunnel was a faint light, illuminating a metal door.

Arnie charged at the door.

His synapses buzzed with every step, and his titanium feet churned up clods of dirt. He ran at the thick metal door, and kicked it. *CLANG!* It dented, so he kicked it again. *CLANG!* The door crashed open and he barged inside.

"Hey! Stop –"

Arnie punched the first security guard in the face before he had time to aim his gun. A second one on the other side of the room fired, bullets bouncing off his armour. He clunked across the room and backhanded the guard across the head with a metal fist.

Yes, yessss! Arnie's blood roared through his veins.

A sign on the wall pointed in different directions. One arrow said *Confinement.* Arnie went that way.

CU-CHUNK, CU-CHUNK, CU-CHUNK. His metal feet stomped along the corridor tearing up chunks of concrete. He had a lot of adjusting to do before he'd be able to walk without breaking stuff, but this mission needed little finesse.

He came to an unguarded locked door. *I'll need to kick this down*, he thought to himself, and the legs did the rest.

CLANG!

The door flew off its hinges as Arnie booted it. It flew down the corridor and bounced into a Europa guard. The door smashed him against the floor and his gun spiralled away. Arnie stomped over him and carried on.

A guard surprised him by shooting him in the back. The bullet ricocheted away and bounced down the corridor.

"He's bulletproof!" the Europa guard said in alarm, and fled the other way.

Arnie considered going after him, but his priority was Catherine. He checked his wrist scanner, but Catherine's signal had disappeared.

She's gone deeper.

He found a stairwell and crashed his way down it, sometimes breaking the steps as he stomped down.

At the bottom, a cluster of guards had gathered, and they fired up at him with pistols.

Arnie ducked back taking cover behind a flight of stairs. He popped the pin off a concussion grenade and dropped it over the edge of the bannister.

"Grenade!" someone shouted, a split second before it exploded.

The shockwave ripped up the confined space of the stairwell and Arnie thought his head might pop. "Oww," he grunted, heaved out a deep breath and stomped down to the bottom.

Two of the men lay unconscious on top of each other in a heap, blood dripping from their ears. A third man stared up at Arnie in shock as he leaned against the wall on his arse, desperately trying to pull himself away. He didn't seem to know where to look at Arnie and kept flicking between the legs, and his upper body.

Arnie ignored him and entered the corridor in time to see the fourth guard locking himself behind a set of steel barred gates.

Arnie roared an old Maori battle cry as he ran at the gate and plunged his titanium boot right through the middle. The bars snapped like matchsticks. He flattened the gate and ducked through.

"Where's Catherine!" Arnie boomed.

The guard was now stuck between Arnie and another locked gate. He trembled with his back to the metal bars. "S-she's back there." He pointed a wobbly hand over his shoulder.

Arnie stomped towards him, and the guard skipped out of his way. Arnie kicked the second gate off its hinges and stomped through.

Cell doors lined the corridor, but only one was guarded by a man with a fat stubbly chin and carrying an assault rifle.

He took aim at Arnie and fired.

Bullets clanged off the exoskeleton, and Arnie put his head down and charged like a rhinoceros.

The man let out a scream as Arnie ploughed into him fists and head first. He punched the guard in the face and knocked him out.

He turned to the door that the man had been posted to and gave it a gentle kick. *DWANG!* He tried again, a little harder this time. *DWANG!* On the third kick, the door smashed open and buried itself in the concrete wall. *TWACK!*

An ear-piercing scream wailed out of the cell.

Arnie ducked under, squinting in the gloom. Catherine stood before him, gaping open mouthed. "Well, hello." He grinned.

"Arnie?" she said.

"I'm Arnie 2.0," he shot her a metal thumbs up.

"You're alive!"

"Bloody right I am. You gonna come with me this time, ya?"

She looked him up and down. "Are those your... legs?"

"They are now."

Catherine hesitated. "Those prosthetics, what happened to you, Arnie?"

"No time to explain. Come on, let's get you out of here." He held a hand out to her, but still she stood back.

"This is *Europa,* Arnie. Did my father know that before he sent you?"

"Of course. He wants you back. Now, can we go, or do I have to carry you?"

She blinked, fiddling with her hands. "Right. Yes. Lead the way."

Arnie turned and glanced left and right down both corridors. "Follow me."

He led her back the way he had come, following the trail of cracked footprints and unconscious bodies on the floor.

As he rounded a corner that led back to the stairwell, he had to stop. A blonde woman had appeared. She stood in the centre of a group of five Europa guards, armed with automatic rifles, all aimed at him. *No sign of Mr. Kidnapper. No reason for him to be here, I suppose.*

"Easy," Arnie said. "I'm taking Miss Blunt. Don't get in my way now." Then quieter to Catherine, "Stay behind me."

"Who are you?" the smartly dressed woman demanded. She had her arms folded, eyeing Arnie with wide, piercing blue eyes.

"Just a bodyguard."

"Is this Blunt's new technology?" She didn't need to gesture to his legs.

"Why would you think that?" Arnie asked. *Shit! They know I work for Blunt?*

"We found the tracker in her leg. Same one used in all of Blunt's GPS devices. We knew you were coming. But I never expected... this." This time she did gesture to his legs.

"Something else, aren't they?" Arnie grinned. "Now if you'll excuse us. We'll be leaving now."

He made to walk towards the stairwell between the chief and her armed men, when she stepped to one side, revealing another guard behind her. He wielded a very large rifle. *Shit!*

"Fire at will," the woman ordered. "Don't worry if you hit the girl."

Arnie whirled around, shielding Catherine.

DOOF! The massive gun went off and Arnie flinched violently against the weight of a fridge smashing him in the back. His armour dented inwards, but the round didn't penetrate.

He picked up Catherine and ran.

He bolted down the corridor away from the guards, and away from the *fucking anti-tank cannon.*

Catherine was petite and light, but even if she wasn't Arnie felt enough adrenaline coursing through him that he'd happily carry a hippo out of this mess with ease. He clomped past the cells and the unconscious bodies, heading deeper into the bunker.

"Do you know where to go?" Catherine wailed, as she bounced up and down in his arms, clutching his neck.

"Yeah, of course I do!" At the next junction he chose a corridor at random and went that way. The floor was sloped ever so slightly downwards.

"This really feels like the wrong way!" Catherine shrieked as more bullets clanged off the walls around them.

Arnie clomped on. He spotted a set of pipes running along the ceiling. *There must be an air vent chamber somewhere. That's my best chance now.*

He kicked in another door and found himself in a cavernous underground hangar. Helicopters with folded up rotor blades sat around idle in the spacious room. On the far side of the hangar Arnie spotted a wide elevator.

A way out!

Holding Catherine with one arm, he hastily unclipped another grenade and tossed it into the corridor behind them, then adjusted his grip on Catherine with both hands.

"Hold on!"

He sprinted, his legs ground up the concrete floor as they ran across the hangar, heading for the elevator. Someone behind them yelled "Cease fire! You'll hit the fuel tanks!"

BOOM!

The grenade exploded behind them.

Arnie reached the shaft and looked upwards. It was as wide as a bus, and some hundred feet up, it opened into light. Arnie thought *can I jump that high?* His legs attempted it anyway.

They retracted to the ground.

"Um, Arnie?" Catherine had time to ask.

The legs sprang. Arnie soared up the shaft and his question was answered: He *couldn't* jump that high.

Two spikes jutted out of his kneecaps just as he approached the wall of the shaft and dug themselves into the wall. He lurched against the impact, some two-thirds of the way up the shaft, stuck in the wall. Then the legs sprang again and he leapt out of the opening and into sunlight.

"Woah!" he exclaimed.

Catherine eyed him in terror, speechless.

"I didn't know they could do that." Arnie grinned. He readjusted his grip on Catherine, and bolted into the fields.

14
COLLISIONS

"S-slow d-d-down Aaaaar-kneeee." Cathy's brain had turned to scrambled eggs as she bounced up and down with every one of the bulky half-man-half-robot's enormous strides. She clung to his neck with her eyes closed tight.

"Sorry," he said. "But we have to get out of here. They'll probably send one of those helicopters after us."

Cathy opened her eyes and the world spun. Grassy green fields and hedgerows formed around her. They were approaching a gentle hillside of lush grass. Arnie's pace slowed to a brisk march and he started up the hill.

"Let me walk for a bit," Cathy said.

Arnie sucked air through his teeth. "I'm not sure that's a good idea. It's quicker if I carry you."

"My head is spinning, I'm going to throw up if you keep bumping me around like this!"

"Sorry," he grimaced. "How about if I..." He trailed off, his face contorted in thought. She frowned, wondering what he was doing, but something in his stride changed and Cathy felt herself drifting up the hill in his arms as if she were floating. Arnie's face relaxed and he raised his eyebrows at her in question. "Is that better?"

Cathy blinked. "Yes." She glanced down at his legs, which were making a hydraulic *hiss* with every step. "How are you doing that?"

"It's these legs. They're amazing, Catherine." He

sounded like an excited child. "I just think of something, and they do it. Right now I'm thinking of walking smoothly!"

Even his walking pace dwarfed that of a regular person's jog. The higher they climbed, the more of the rolling countryside Cathy could see, stretching for several miles in every direction.

Out here, staring across the peaceful greenery of the English countryside, she felt something that she didn't immediately recognise. As Arnie carried her up the hill, she wracked her brain, trying to put the sensation into words. When it hit her, a weight lifted that felt like a rush of clear wind breezing through her body.

Freedom. Right now, I'm free.
But for how long?

"Where are we going?" Cathy asked.

"Rendezvous. Mr. Blunt's VTOL is waiting on the other side of that village." He nodded at the cluster of old fashioned buildings to their right.

At the mention of her father, Cathy became nauseous. She tried to ignore it. "What's a VTOL?"

"Vertical Take Off and Landing craft."

"Like a helicopter?"

"It's more like a cross between a helicopter and an airplane. You'll see." Arnie came to a halt on the summit and gazed about. He must have been looking for the VTOL, Cathy mused.

"Please put me down."

Arnie lowered Cathy to her feet. She swayed once, but he steadied her with a gentle hand. After a few deep breaths, her head felt clearer. Arnie went back to peering around.

The fresh air filled her lungs and the nausea passed. *My god it feels good to be outside again.* "Thank you, Arnie."

He turned to her and smiled. "It's all good."

"I'm sorry I didn't come with you back on the mountain."

"It's all right, I'm uhh…" He glanced at her leg for a brief moment.

"You shot me, didn't you?" Cathy crossed her arms.

"Yes… I am sorry about that. I had to track you."

"I don't want to be tracked any more Arnie. Do you know how invasive it is? *Literally?*"

"You gave me no other choice." He gave an apologetic shrug. "Can you forgive me?"

"Not yet…" She looked him up and down, barely recognising him. Arnie stood about a foot taller than he did before and was covered from head to toe in some kind of metal armour plating. Metal legs, metal chest, metal arms, and his leathery brown face peered out from under a metal helmet. "You look…"

"Like Robocop?" he grinned.

She laughed. "I was just going to say 'different'."

"Good different or bad different?"

"I…" *How can I answer that honestly?*

His face dropped. "It's still me, *taina.*"

"I know it is," she said, unable to resist smiling at his use of the Maori word for little sister. She didn't have any siblings, but she liked it when he called her *taina*, anyway.

She wrapped her arms around his torso. It was like hugging a titanium bear. He squeezed her back, but his hands were cold, hard, and his elbows pinched her skin.

"Ow!" she gave a yelp and pulled away.

"Sorry," Arnie said, flustered.

"It's okay," she said, taking a step back and rubbing her side where it stung. "What happened to you, Arnie?"

"That Europa agent got the better of me, eh?" he said flatly. "I'll pay him back if I see him again, don't you doubt it."

"Frank's not a bad guy… At least, I don't think so, anyway. He was just protecting me."

"Well he fucked me up. At least I got some fancy new legs out of it, thanks to your dad. He's gonna be so happy to get you back."

No… I'm not going back there. She turned away and stared across the countryside.

"What's wrong?" Arnie said. "Don't worry about them. You're safe with me. They can't hurt you anymore."

"It's not that." She rubbed her eye with a finger, and placed a hand on her hip. "Ugh, god. Arnie, tell me something. Why did he send you? And don't tell me it was to rescue me."

He gave her a confused look. "Your father cares about you."

Cathy scoffed. "I spent six *years* working for those bastards because of him. If he cared so much, why did he wait so long? Why did he let Mother take me away in the first place!"

"He didn't have a choice. Please, Catherine, you don't know what he's been through."

"What *he's* been through?" she seethed.

"He loves you," Arnie said. "He wanted to get you out sooner, but he never dared sending me in for fear of your life. He built these soldier legs specifically for you."

Cathy pitied Arnie for believing that. "He was working on those prostheses projects long before I was sent away. It's part of the reason he and Mother couldn't see eye to eye. You must know that, Arnie?"

"Maybe so," Arnie said, nodding. "But I also know that he's desperate to get you back. You're his daughter."

"I wish I wasn't." She slumped onto her butt in the grass and buried her head between her knees. She sobbed, digging her palms into her eyes, disgusted at herself for being such a wreck. Arnie wanted to help, and he cared deeply, but that didn't change the fact that he was only here to bring her home.

Something beside her went *tsssst.* Arnie's legs hissing as they retracted, lowering his body towards the ground. He laid a hand on her shoulder.

"Catherine. We can't stay here. I'm going to carry you again, okay?"

"Mmm." She resigned herself to him.

He scooped her up, supporting her butt and lower back. As he bent down, she couldn't help noticing the compartment at his crotch area. Where his manhood should be. *Is that a trapdoor? A dick-door...* A gasp of laughter escaped as he lifted her off the ground.

"What?" Arnie smiled, oblivious.

"Nothing," she said, resting her head against his metal chest.

He set off at a steady, smooth jog. "Let's get out of here, my Ruapehu."

The word sent a hot shiver down Cathy's spine. *Ruapehu.* It was a name from a character in one of Arnie's Maori stories. "Tell me about Ruapehu, Arnie."

"Really? Aren't you a little old for story time?"

"Probably," she admitted. "But tell it anyway. Please?"

"All right," he said.

He recounted the tale of the mountains, Tongariro and Taranaki fighting for the love of Ruapehu. Arnie had always called her that, but she felt a closer affinity to the loser of the encounter, Taranaki, who ran away to be by himself, carving an entire valley in the process.

"I'm going to run away, like Taranaki," Cathy mumbled.

Arnie stopped mid-sentence and looked down at her. "What? Why would you say that?"

"If you take me home, I'm going to run away, Arnie. I'm twenty-three, I should have my own life by now."

To his credit, he didn't argue. But Cathy could tell that Arnie wasn't happy about this abrupt change of conversation. "Where would you go?" he asked tentatively.

"I don't know. New Zealand is nice, right?"

"It's beautiful," Arnie said wistfully. He nodded at the surrounding countryside. "You see this? Aotearoa is like England, only the sky is more blue. The bluest sky you could ever imagine, and trees greener than emeralds. Everything in New Zealand is more vibrant and full of life. It's the way the earth is supposed to be."

"That sounds amazing… Do you miss it?" she asked.

"Every day. But it's not my home any more. I cannot go back."

"I think we have that in common, then."

The hill flattened out and Arnie hopped over a fence and carried her into a field of grazing cows. The animals raised their heads from the grass and stared at Cathy with big round eyes. Some did a little skip and trotted away as the strange pair passed. *They've probably never met a cyborg before.*

Arnie's legs made a soft *cu-chunk* with every hydraulic step, but gradually a car's engine drowned the noise out. Arnie paused in the field. The engine's whine filled the air as it approached from somewhere to their right. Cathy caught a glimpse of a black car as it passed a gate in the hedgerow that outlined the field.

Vroooooooooommmmmmm – SCREEEEEEEEECCCHHH!

She heard the driver clunk the gearbox into reverse and the engine whined as the car careened back down the road and into view again. The windows were blacked out, so she couldn't see inside.

"Hold on, Catherine!" Arnie adjusted his grip, hoisted Cathy over his shoulder and burst into a violent sprint.

Cathy might as well have been caught in an earthquake. She bounced up and down across Arnie's shoulder as he fled across the field. She was facing backwards and so had a good view of the car as it smashed through the gate amid a spray of wooden splinters before turning in their direction and accelerating.

Arnie must have been running at 40mph. The car sped after them, cows stampeding in every direction out of its way. Arnie's clomping feet shot thick clods of mud into the sky. They landed like tiny bombs all around the pursuing car.

Arnie's legs sprang and without warning, the car shrank away from them as he and Cathy leapt high into the air.

Cathy shrieked. At the apex of the jump, her stomach turned over and the shriek cut off into a silent, breathless gasp.

They landed hard on the other side of a tall hedge.

THUD.

All the wind left Cathy's lungs as Arnie's shoulder pounded her in the stomach, and her neck jerked downwards forcing her nose into his armour plated back.

"*Owww*," she groaned, fighting for breath. The car was out of sight now, hidden behind the hedge, and Arnie broke into another run. "Stop!" she wheezed. Her nose screamed with pain, dripping blood. "Arnie, stop, *stop!*"

The hedge exploded open and the black car burst out of its leafy innards. Its tyres gripped the ground and the car lurched towards them.

"He's still after us! It's Europa!" Arnie boomed.

The car caught up to them and pulled alongside Arnie. It swerved sideways and nudged his legs.

"Agh!" Arnie staggered but kept going. The car swerved again, the driver trying to clip Arnie's legs with the bumper. Arnie hopped and soared over the car. He landed on the other side of it and kept running.

The car veered the other way trying to ram him again, but this time Arnie jumped forwards. The car swept sideways, narrowly missing Arnie's ankles.

The driver leaned out of the window and Cathy thought she recognised the man, but the way she was being shaken around made it impossible to be sure. He aimed something at them, which fired cables towards Arnie's legs.

He's trying to trip us!

The cables went taut and untethered immediately, Arnie's legs were moving too quickly to be stopped by such a contraption.

Then the passenger leaned out of the window. Cathy was trying not to throw up as her body was tossed around on top of Arnie's plated shoulder. She glimpsed a gun.

A spark *sizzled* through the air. Cathy's hairs stood on end. Arnie seized up. Cathy tumbled out of his grip and landed on damp, squishy grass. She bounced twice and skidded to a halt.

Dazed, she looked up to see the car sliding ahead of her. Arnie lay on his front in the grass, groaning. He staggered to his feet, shaking his head. He clomped over, bent down and studied her face. "Are you okay? Are you hurt?"

Cathy blinked. She touched her nostrils, and pulled blood away on her fingertips. "My nose. Is it broken?"

The car spun around in the slick grass ahead and aimed back towards them. It stopped about twenty metres away.

"No," Arnie said. "It's just bleeding. You'll be okay. Now go. Run. I'll deal with this and come get you. Find somewhere to hide in those trees!"

She spied a hill with a crown of woodland covering its summit, and started running.

"Cathy!" a voice called out. Not Arnie's. She didn't care. Ahead of her, the tree line beckoned. A small wood that could lead anywhere. *Freedom.*

"*YOU!*" Arnie roared behind her. "You did this to me."

Cathy reached the tree line and kept going. She slipped into the shadows, weaving between skinny tree trunks and crunching through a carpet of dead leaves.

Dimly behind her, the car's engine revved and screamed as it accelerated. She ploughed on, scrambled over a mossy log and ducked beneath a low hanging branch.

Behind her came the unmistakable crash of two heavy metal objects colliding with each other.

CRUNCHHH.

15
FLEE

Riding shotgun in Frank's Mitsubishi proved a lot more comfortable than being crammed in the trunk. "Thanks man," Dan said, clipping on his seatbelt.

Frank clunked the car into gear and they sped down a freeway out of the city.

Dan noticed the central gearstick. "*Stick shift?* Who drives a stick shift, man?"

Frank gave him a sideways glare. "This is a *real* car, not like those automatic toys you got in America." Frank caressed the steering wheel.

"Can't believe Europa's full of dinosaurs. Even your cars are old."

"This isn't a standard issue vehicle. I bought it for myself, something to play with on my downtime. And oi, it ain't *that* old," Frank argued. "It's the 2020 model, the last version they ever made. It's vintage, mate."

"2020?" Dan said, unimpressed. "That's when I was ten."

Frank shot him another quick glare, then revved the engine hard, accelerating past a few cars in the outside lane.

Dan suspected he was trying to show off, but it didn't work. "Whatever, man. It's just a car to me. Show me a laptop with a decuple core processor and a zettabyte of ram and then we'll be on some level of appreciation. Cars just aren't my thing."

"You kids these days," Frank muttered. "This wasn't built for speed, anyway. It was originally designed for manoeuvrability. A rally car, great off-road."

Dan looked at the freeway—miles of tarmac stretching on ahead. "That must be a useful feature," he scathed.

An hour later, they were ploughing through a farmer's gate into a muddy field.

"What the hell is that?" Dan cried.

"Fuck knows, but it has Catherine!" Frank said, wrestling the steering wheel.

"It looks like a goddamn cyborg," Dan pointed at the hulking metal monstrosity lumbering away from them at surprising speed. "Holy shit, it's fast!"

"Hold on." Frank worked the stick shift and revved.

Dan steadied himself by holding the dashboard and the handle above his head. The car bounced across jutted ground, picking up speed. The clomping cyborg was running straight towards a towering hedge, cornering himself.

"We've got him now," Frank said.

"What about Catherine?" Dan said. "How are we supposed to get her—"

The cyborg leapt over the hedge and disappeared on the other side. "Holy *shit,* did you see that?" Dan cried. "He cleared the entire hedge!"

"We can't do that," Frank said, narrowing his eyes. He put his foot to the floor.

"Um, Frank?" Dan pressed his head back against the rest, flinching away from the oncoming hedge.

They crashed straight through it. Dan's head was thrown forward and he almost head-butted the dash, but his seatbelt held him back, forcing the wind from him. They emerged on the other side as broken twigs and leaves scattered across the windshield.

Cows. Everywhere. The startled animals fled in all

directions as Frank switched gears again and found momentum on the grass. They shot across the field and caught the galloping cyborg up. Frank positioned the car alongside him.

Dan saw blood dripping from the girl's face as she clung to the cyborg's back. "Is he kidnapping her? That's not Europa, is it?"

"Course not!" Frank roared, and jerked the steering wheel. The car's front collided with the cyborg's legs. He stumbled but maintained his footing. Frank tried again but the cyborg jumped right over the car and landed on the other side.

"Shit," Frank cursed and tried again. Missed. The cyborg leapt forwards out of range.

"He's too agile," Dan observed.

"Not for long," Frank growled. He reached into the glove compartment and pulled out a cylindrical metal object with buttons on. He lowered his window and aimed the cylinder at the clomping cyborg.

Three pronged wires shot out of the device and attached to the cyborg's legs.

"Holy crap, what is that thing?"

"Called a zip-winch," Frank said through gritted teeth, wrestling with one hand on the steering wheel.

The wires tore loose, unable to stick to the galloping metal legs, and they pinged back against the windscreen with such force that it cracked. Frank flinched away from the wild wires as they contracted back inside the cylinder.

"Shit!" cursed Frank, dropping the zip-winch into his lap.

An idea came to Dan. He whipped out his EMP gun and set it to maximum charge. "Let me try with this."

Frank grunted agreement.

Dan wound down the window and leaned out, pointing the EMP gun at the cyborg's legs. *I hope this works.* He squeezed the trigger and an arc of lightning spewed out of the gun and struck the cyborg on the back of the knee.

He seized up and tripped. Catherine tumbled forwards into the grass as the cyborg landed flat on his face and slid along the ground.

"Woah!" Dan cried as Frank swerved violently to avoid crashing into them. Dan almost fell out of the car, but again saved by his seatbelt, he managed to swing back inside as Frank skidded to a halt.

"Good work, kid," Frank said. His eyes never left the cyborg, who was stumbling to his feet. The girl lay in the grass nearby. "Wait here," Frank ordered, and got out of the car.

Dan gulped, watching Frank take a few steps closer, then he froze. The girl and the cyborg exchanged a few words, before she got up and started running up the hill towards a cluster of trees. *Shit, she's running.*

"Cathy!" Frank yelled.

The girl didn't respond, but the cyborg did. "*YOU!*" he bellowed. "You did this to me!"

Dan frowned, confused. *Does Frank know this guy?*

Frank returned to the car and slipped inside. "Dan, get out. Go after her."

"What are you gonna do?"

"I don't know," he said, clipping the zip-winch to his wrist, and buckling his safety belt. "But you have to get out of the car right now. *Go!*"

Dan scrambled out and closed the door. He kept a wary eye on the cyborg as he scurried around the back of the car and started up the hill towards the girl. She was almost to the trees now. Dan holstered his EMP gun in his belt and ran as fast as he could.

A thunderous warcry bellowed out behind him. Dan stopped and turned back to see the cyborg slam a fist into his palm and pull a hideous face with mad, wide eyes and his tongue sticking out. Frank responded by revving the engine and accelerated towards him.

Frank's gonna ram him!

The car lurched towards the cyborg, who charged

forward to meet it.

The cyborg swung his leg out as if kicking a football. His foot struck the underside of the hood and the car backflipped into the air.

The car half rotated and landed in a crumpled heap on its roof.

CRUNCHHH.

Dan stared in dumbfounded horror. He stood rooted to the ground, his mouth gaping open, as the cyborg brute stomped towards the wreckage.

"Stop!" Dan squeaked. The metal-man glared at Dan, his eyes furrowed in a fierce scowl. Dan's bowels rumbled at the sight. He tried to take a step back and found his feet were concrete slabs.

The cyborg held his stare for a few agonising moments. Dan's skinny figure and terrified expression obviously did nothing to intimidate him. He snorted and continued marching towards the upturned car. Dan couldn't see Frank, nor any sign of movement inside. *What can I do against that?*

Dan turned and ran for the trees.

The girl had disappeared. Dan bolted into the woodland, hoping to find her. The air turned cooler as he entered the shadows. He scanned the trees, but saw nothing but clumps of tree trunks and fallen leaves.

"*Catherine!*" he called. The woods swallowed his voice, making no reply. Dan staggered into the brush, clambering through the shrubby undergrowth, deeper into the woods. "I'm a friend! We came to save you!"

He stumbled on, calling out now and then. The brambles kept snagging on his jeans, and his sneakers squelched in the soggy mud turning them from black to brown. He came to a fallen tree. With the intention of climbing over it, he planted both hands down on the top but reeled back, repulsed by the slimy wet moss. *Hacker's don't belong in the wild.*

He stood still, let his arms slump to the side and glumly

peered around the wood. *Push on, or go back?*

Faint gunfire sounded behind him. Dan counted twelve shots in total. After that, there was no more.

Frank might be nothing but a bloody pancake by now, at the hands of that crazy cyborg. Dan felt more than a little guilty about leaving him behind. But what good would it do to be torn apart along with Frank? *He's a tough guy. He might be okay…*

A tree branch snapped somewhere close by.

Dan jolted around, eyes wide. *What was that?*

He dived over the fallen tree and fell into a thorny bramble on the other side. Prickly needles stabbed him in the arms. "Ow, ow, ow," he whispered. He lie on his hands and belly in soggy leaves, trying not to move, listening intently; nothing but the gentle *hiss* of leaves swaying in the breeze.

He gulped. He raised his head until he could see over the log. The wood seemed empty. But there was a groaning sound. Faint and low, he thought it came from behind a thick tree to his left.

"Hnnn."

What is that?

"Hnnnnnn."

The sound was strained and whining. It wasn't the sort of noise he would have expected from the cyborg.

Dan crept out from behind the log, and made his way through the undergrowth, making a wide circle around the chunky tree. He came up against another tree, hidden from the source of the noise. He peered around for a look.

Dan saw a pair of bright yellow panties. Catherine Blunt's slender, pale legs protruded out of them. Her skin was flecked with light scratches and her pants were wrapped around her ankles as she sat with her back against the big tree.

Dan's mouth hung low. The only time he usually got to see a girl with her pants down was when he paid them for a lap dance.

Catherine held a long pointed branch, and wielded it like a dagger with the tip pressed against the bare skin of her upper thigh. She applied pressure and groaned again. "Hnnnnn." She pulled the stick away, tilted her head to the sky and exhaled a sharp breath. "Just do it. Get it over with," she muttered. She bounced her knees up and down rapidly. Dan stared, entranced.

Catherine placed the point on her thigh again, gripping with both hands. She raised the stick into the air, about to ram it into the side of her leg.

"*Wait!* What are you doing?" Dan cried, leaping from his hiding spot.

Catherine shrieked. She dropped the stick and gaped at Dan. She scrambled to her feet, trying to pull her pants up and tripped over into the dirt. She landed on her front with her butt cheeks pointing in the air. "What the fuck are you doing, you pervert!"

"I'm sorry! I wasn't – It's not like – No, you don't understand!"

She wriggled backwards away from him, struggling to get dressed. For some reason he continued approaching the young woman.

"*Get away from me!*"

He froze, taking in the image of Catherine Blunt, daughter of Sid Blunt, the boss of the biggest tech firm on the planet, scrambling through the dirt with her pants down. He uttered a nervous laugh.

She got up, pulled her pants up and slapped him across the cheek.

His vision flared, and his eyes watered from the pain. "*Ow!*" he wheezed, breathless.

"What's so funny, you freak?"

He rubbed his cheek. "I dunno, it's just…" He shrugged, gesturing to the general scene.

She faced him with flushed red cheeks and crossed arms. "Well," she said. "Are you here to capture me?"

"No."

"Okay. Well, then." She picked up the pointed stick. "Leave me alone." She marched past Dan.

"Where are you going?"

"What's it to you?" She didn't look back.

"Wait!" Dan followed her. "What were you doing with that stick?"

She didn't turn around, stomping through the undergrowth. "Trying to remove a tracker that's buried in my leg."

"Really? Why are you bugged? Who's tracking you?"

"It's none of your business." She stopped in her tracks and spun around. "*Why are you following me?*"

Dan stopped. She stared at him with bright green eyes, a glare that threatened to set him on fire. Dan was taken aback. He didn't expect her to be this cute. "Uhh." His mind had gone blank.

"Leave. Me. *Alone.*" She pointed the stick at his face to emphasise each word.

I could disable the tracker.

Before he could say it, her butt was swaying away from him again.

"Wait!" he blurted. "I can help you."

"Uuugh!" she cried, exasperated. "I don't *want* your help, I don't need *anybody's* help. Go away!"

"I can fry it! The tracker, I mean. I can deactivate it for you."

That caught her attention. Catherine's scowl softened and she searched his face. "How?"

"I have this." He held up the EMP gun.

"What is that?"

"It's, uhh…" *It's something I designed for breaking into ATM machines…* "It's a gadget that I made." *It produces a concentrated electrical current that feigns a digital skeleton key...* "It acts a bit like a Taser." *It lets me steal cash…* She didn't need to know that. "It's a miniature EMP. It looks a bit like a gun, but it's actually more like a tiny microwave on the end of a trigger."

Catherine gave the gun a wary look. "How stupid do I look? You think I'm going to just let you shoot me with that thing? It's probably some kind of tranquiliser, then you'll take me back to Europa."

"What? No, it's an EMP gun. We used it on that big metal guy earlier, when he was carrying you." She was shaking her head, her lip curled in disbelief. Dan went on, "Look, I really can help you. I'm not even with them!" He pointed wildly behind him.

"So you don't deny that *they* are Europa. Yet you're not *with* them."

"No!" Dan gritted his teeth. He inhaled a deep breath, eyeing the stubborn woman. "They killed my brother."

Catherine's eyebrows rose. She answered warily. "What has that got to do with anything?"

"Listen, I think we're on the same side here. You met my brother the other day. Jimmy?"

She gasped. "You're Jimmy's brother?"

"Yeah. He was sent on a mission with them to CERN. He ended up finding out about the existence of Horizon. It's some kind of secret underground project, or organisation. Like the Illuminati or some shit."

"How do you know that?"

"Because Jimmy sent the data to me. Whatever he dug up down there, they didn't want it getting out. He died because of Horizon. I joined Europa because I have to find out what it is."

"Why get involved?" Catherine asked softly. "Why put yourself in danger like that?"

"I'm a part of Binary Eye. We uncover the truth, no matter how deep it's buried." He stuck his chest out, but Catherine didn't show any sign of being impressed. "Uhh," he deflated. "Anyway, I'm involved now and I can't back out until I find what my brother died for." He scratched the back of his neck. "I was hoping you might know something."

She studied him closely, and he flushed red with

embarrassment. "I don't know anything about Horizon," she said. "But I know the facility wasn't CERN."

"For real?" *Derunox suspected that much.* "What was it, then?"

"It was a privately funded facility. I don't know why it's being reported as CERN, but I do know the person responsible for lying to the media about it."

"Who?" Dan said, growing giddy with excitement.

"My mother. Margery Blunt."

"No fucking way! Derunox was right!"

"Who?" Cathy frowned again.

"Oh, never mind. He's this guy on our forum. He had this crazy theory that the CERN disaster was a cover up. It tied up to another theory that you were still alive and being kept hostage by your own mother, and I mean, look at you! That one was true too." He shook his head slowly, looking Catherine up and down. "Oh, man!"

"Are you done?" She scowled.

"Sorry. I just. Wow. The conspiracy nuts will go apeshit over this."

"You're weird." Catherine looked up. The woodland was eerily gloomy under the shadow of the trees. In the dim quiet, helicopter rotor blades pounded in the distance. "Shit," she said. "They might be Europa, or worse…"

"What could be worse?" Dan said.

"My father wants to find me. That big metal guy is his bodyguard, Arnie Dillon. I've known him since I was young. He told me there was a VTOL coming to meet us at a rendezvous."

"Where's the rendezvous?" Dan asked.

"I have no idea. But…" She looked down at her leg, and rubbed her thigh with two fingers.

"Oh, shit. Unless we get that tracker out of you, the rendezvous will be wherever you are!"

"Yeah, I guess so." She glanced at her pointed stick, then back at Dan. "I want to borrow your EMP thingy."

He held it out to her. "Here."

She chewed her lip. "Actually, why don't you just do it?"

"Okay," he said. "Where is the tracker?"

"Here. I think." Cathy touched her thigh about midway between her knee and her hip.

"It might work best on bare skin," Dan suggested cautiously.

"Will it work if I keep my pants on?"

"Probably."

She scowled. "Then they're staying on."

"Okay." Dan hesitated. "You don't have a pacemaker or anything?"

"What? Do I look old enough to need a *pacemaker*?"

"Um, no." He tweaked the EMP charge to emit a medium strength charge, and pressed the muzzle against her jogger pants. "All right. Hold still."

Zzzzzuuuup.

A crackling bolt shot out of the device and burned a hole in her pants.

"Ow!" she yelped. She rubbed her palm on the smoking scorch mark.

"Are you okay?" Dan asked.

"Yeah. It's not so bad." Her pants had protected her skin from the worst of the heat. She eyed him eagerly. "Did it work?"

"Hopefully." He shrugged.

"Well, what good is that? Arnie might still find me!"

Dan's stomach dropped. "The cyborg guy? He's scary."

She smiled mockingly. "You're definitely not a Europa agent, are you?"

Dan scratched the back of his head. "I'm not cut out for this. This is the longest I've been away from my computer since... I don't know when."

"Zap me again to make sure. I don't want to be re-captured."

Dan placed the gun against her leg and squeezed the trigger. It sputtered. Not even a tiny spark came out. "Oh, shit, it's dead."

"Are you kidding me?"

"The battery's completely drained. I used up most of it zapping Mr. Metal."

The noise of the helicopter rotor blades grew louder as they approached.

"I won't be captured again!" Cathy cried, and darted into the trees.

"Wait up!" Dan ran after her.

They scrambled through the woodland as two helicopters roared overhead. The trees danced wildly in the wind, raining leaves all around.

A strange harmonic sound rumbled through the air, resonating in Dan's stomach. The helicopters' engines cut out together and the woods exploded in a cacophony of rending metal. The ground trembled from the impacts and a hail of debris ripped through the trees towards them.

"Get down!" Dan dived at Catherine and shoved her into the ground, instinctively shielding her from a spray of splinters.

Fwoosh!

His back seared with a sudden burst of heat which faded quickly. When he looked up, the woods were on fire around both crash sites thirty paces behind them.

"Holy shit," he gasped.

Catherine pushed him off, staring at the fire. "Oh my god."

"We have to get out of here," Dan said, rising. He offered her a hand up, "Come on."

She took his hand and climbed to her feet. "Where should we go?"

"Away from *that*," Dan pointed at the burning helicopter wreckages.

"I want to help you," Catherine blurted. She had a burning determination in her eyes, aided by the actual fire that was reflected in them.

"Oh, yeah?" he said.

"Jimmy died for me. I owe him my life. If I can help you

figure out what Horizon is, maybe I can pay off that debt."

Dan swallowed hard. "Okay, deal." He tried to recall his geography of England. "We should head south, there's a ferry crossing not far from here. We can get to mainland Europe, maybe head for the Czech Republic or something."

"Why there?" she asked.

"I know a guy that will help us." *Derunox. He has a copy of the Horizon data.*

"Okay." Cathy's eyes sparkled, and she bit her lower lip in a nervous smile.

Wow, she's even cuter when she's happy.

They set off through the woods, away from the burning helicopters.

"What's your name, by the way?" Catherine asked.

"Oh. I'm Dan. It's nice to meet you, Catherine Blunt."

She gave a nervous laugh. "You can call me Cathy."

16
CONFRONTATION

"*YOU!* You did this to me!"

Until the big man spoke, Frank had no idea who Catherine's captor might be. Even with the dark skin and bulging muscles, Arnie Dillon resembled nothing of the bumbling sniper that had tracked him down in the high ranges of the Swiss Alps. When Frank fought him on the train, he had managed to overcome him and trip him overboard. Now, somehow, that same man stood before him like a towering Terminator.

Frank ducked inside the car. "Dan, get out. Go after her."

"What are you gonna do?"

"I don't know, but you have to get out of the car right now. *Go!*"

The kid scrambled out and shut the door.

Frank clipped his zip-winch onto his wrist, then reached under the steering wheel and punched a flat rounded button with his palm. *Emergency signal. Chief better get here fast...* He turned back to face the Maori.

Dillon bellowed, bulged his eyes and hung out his tongue. He snarled teeth and crashed his fist into his palm. Frank vaguely recognised the gesture as a tribal war cry designed to terrify enemies, although you didn't have to be a history teacher to get the gist of a Maori threat.

He wants to fight. Maybe I can break his legs. Frank put it into first and slammed on the accelerator pedal.

The car lurched forwards.

The Terminator charged.

Frank gripped the steering wheel, aiming it right for the stomping metal legs. The Maori towered over the car, filling his windscreen and pulled back his leg moments before impact. Frank had time to think: *This was a mistake.*

Dillon's foot thrust into the underside of the bonnet. Frank's head smashed into the wheel. When his eyes reopened, he saw a blurry, cloudy sky spinning past, which turned green and then–*CRUUNNCH.*

Frank landed on his shoulder on the ceiling of the car, now upside down on the grass. His windshield had transformed into a web of frosted glass, but didn't shatter. He blinked, trying to focus. *The glove box. My gun.* Frank reached for it, but his shoulder made a nasty *click* when he tried to stretch, and it hurt like hell.

He shifted his weight onto his other side and went to reach with his left arm instead. He popped it open and the gun tumbled out, but before he could grab it, his car door burst open.

Dillon's scowling face loomed in. "Come here." He grabbed Frank by the dead arm and yanked him out.

Searing fire streamed from his shoulder and shot down the length of his arm all the way to Frank's fingertips. "*Aggh!*"

"Aw, what's this now?" Dillon feigned concern. "I think you have a broken arm." He dragged him backwards and dumped him on the grass. "That don't make us even yet." He loomed over Frank, blotting out the sky with his big head. "Oh, no. To be even, I'd have to do *this.*" Dillon took hold of Frank's good arm around the bicep in a vice-like grip. *He's gonna rip my fucking arm off.*

"No, don't!" Frank panicked. "I came to help Catherine!" His eyes threatened to pop out of their sockets. He winced under the Maori's iron grip.

Dillon frowned. "Catherine?" His face softened. The big man loosened his fingers around Frank's arm.

Dillon glanced towards the woods, and then checked his wrist where he must have had some kind of GPS monitor. "She's not far." He hauled Frank up by the shirt beneath his neck and glared two inches from Frank's face. "If anything happens to her, I swear I'll come back and finish this. Now, you wait right there." He dropped Frank to the ground, and fire flared through his busted arm like a backdraft.

The metal Maori clomped up the hill, leaving a trail of footprints.

Frank lay on the grass staring up at the clouds, his arm screaming.

So they were tracking her after all, Frank realised. *Dan. He'll kill Dan.* Frank didn't want another dead hacker on his conscience.

He rolled onto his good arm and hauled himself inside the car. He grabbed his pistol and from inside the car, fired it at Dillon's back. He emptied the magazine of all twelve bullets.

Most seemed to miss, while a few clanged off the Maori's armour.

Dillon turned around, crouched down and leapt into the air. He landed with a mighty thud that shook the car. "Get *out!*" Dillon reached in and pulled Frank out by the ankle.

Frank tried to kick him, but his head rang with tinnitus and he could hardly see straight. *I think I'm concussed.* He glanced around the sky. *Come on, Chief.*

"Do you want me to kill you?" Dillon bellowed in rage. He tore off his helmet and glared down at Frank with snarling teeth.

"I beat you before," Frank gloated. *Gotta keep him here.* "I could beat you again." Frank aimed the zip-winch at Dillon's neck and fired. The three pronged cables wrapped around him like a trio of tiny pythons, causing him to gag. Frank yanked the winch downwards, but without his strong arm, Dillon barely moved.

In a savage swipe, he tore free of the cables, which

retracted sharply back into the cylinder on Frank's wrist.

Dillon loomed over him with clenched his fists and Frank resigned himself to a terrible pummelling, when they both froze. A helicopter approached, its engines throbbing in the sky.

"You're fucked now, mate," Frank said. "Sounds like my backup's here."

"No," Arnie shook his head. "It's mine."

He clomped away, looking up at the sky. Frank craned his neck, trying to get a glimpse of the chopper, when he realised it wasn't a chopper at all.

Wind buffeted Frank in the face and the trees swayed violently against the gusts of twin rotor engines. *It's that stealth VTOL.* Frank recognised the shape as it landed on the grass in front of them. It wasn't entirely transparent, but rather seemed to reflect the immediate surroundings, and Frank could see the hazy colour of sky and clouds through its surface.

The rear hatch lowered, and the interior of the cargo bay revealed itself, entirely un-stealthed and visible. Three armed men wearing helmets and carrying assault rifles sat along the benches inside. Frank recognised mercenaries as soon as he saw them.

"Mr. Dillon!" One merc rose and strode down the cargo ramp. "We were waiting at the rendezvous, but then Catherine's signal started moving away. We traced it to here, but it just went offline. This was the last known location."

"What?" Dillon said, and checked his wrist. He tapped it angrily. "Her signal. It's gone." He turned to Frank. "This is your fault!"

He picked Frank up by his dislocated shoulder. Frank's world turned blurry through searing pain, but he distantly heard the hiss and crackle of his wrist communicator.

"Hawkins. Come in, Agent."

The Maori stared at Frank's wrist communicator, then tore if off. "What is this?"

"I'm here, hurry up!" Frank said.

Arnie squeezed the device in his palm and crushed it. He tossed it away.

The churning sound of a smaller craft approached. Frank forced a grimacing grin as two Europa transport chopper's appeared over the woods. "My backup."

"We'll be spotted!" cried the mercenary.

"Get him on board!" Dillon ordered, shoving Frank towards the ramp. "I'll deal with this." He took three strides towards the woods and crouched, ready to pounce.

"Wait, Dillon! No need!" The merc signalled into the back of the VTOL, shouted a command that sounded to Frank like, "Burn it!"

DRROOOOOM. A low-pitched hum vibrated through Frank's core, trembling his very bones.

The pulse spread outwards away from the VTOL, resonating in the air. The resonations lasted no longer than a few seconds, and when they ceased Frank's ears popped.

The Europa choppers' engines failed. The blades cut out and both helicopters plummeted under the canopy and disappeared in the soup of leaves. A plume of smoke billowed up out of the woods.

Frank gaped at the empty sky. *An EMP?*

"My legs!" Dillon cried. He was still crouched, but only the top half of his body was moving. He flapped his arms around and wailed, "You killed my legs!"

The VTOL seemed unaffected by the EMP. Its engines whirred on.

"Shit," cursed the merc. "You two, get Dillon! We have to move, now!"

The other two mercs sprang out and scurried over to the Terminator. The first one led Frank by gunpoint into the back of the craft. He didn't have the energy to fight back, and with his only chance of escape lying in pieces in the woods, he saw little choice.

Frank sat down and the mercenary tied his left arm to the cargo netting on the wall. Frank watched the two mercs outside fondle the clippings around Dillon's pelvis and haul his upper torso out of the metal bucket connecting him to the legs. They carried him with little dignity to the craft and set him down on a bench opposite Frank.

A merc used a control panel and the ramp hatch started to close.

"No!" Dillon bellowed, clutching the seatbelt with one arm to hold himself on the bench. "Catherine's still out there. Get your fucking arses into those woods and find her!"

The ramp froze, then reopened. The three mercs bustled out and ran away up the hill towards the smoking woodland.

Then it was just the two of them. Dillon glared Frank down from across the hold, a legless cripple in body armour.

"Didn't think I'd see you again," Frank said.

"Takes more than a train to kill a Maori," Dillon rumbled.

"Takes more than a car crash to kill me," Frank retorted. He looked out at his crumpled car. "Although you didn't have to smash it up. That car was vintage. I only came here to help Catherine."

"What do you want with her?" Dillon demanded. "You have no right to hold her prisoner."

"You know, I actually agree. You busted her out, right? I was on my way to do the same bloody thing."

Dillon's scowl suggested he didn't believe that.

The merc had tied Frank's good arm to the netting, and with his right arm busted, he had no way of untying himself. "Listen," Frank said, shifting in his seat. "I'm supposed to be on leave, officially. I only came here to help Cathy—"

"*Why?*"

Yeah, why? I'll lose my career for this. They'll think I've gone rogue. Chief's gonna suspend me, or worse, question my allegiance.

"What was she doing in that place?"

"She was a hostage," Dillon said. "Her own mother held her against her will for six years."

"She mentioned that. But her father is really to blame, right?"

The Maori slammed his fist against the wall. "Everything Mr. Blunt does, he does for Catherine. You know nothing about the situation."

Frank tried to ignore his throbbing arm. "I am trying to piece it together. That facility, where Cathy worked. I wasn't sent there to find her, I didn't even know she was there. We stumbled on information about something called Horizon." *Well, Jimmy did.* "Does Horizon mean anything to you?"

"No. Should it?"

"Probably not."

"Then what does that have to do with Catherine?"

"I don't know yet. But she seems to be caught in the middle of some fucked up shit. For all I know, her parents are the masterminds of some global conspiracy!"

"Mr. Blunt would not be involved in anything like that," Dillon insisted.

"Oh yeah, like you'd know, bright spark."

"He just wants his daughter back. Catherine should be with her family."

"You think so? She's run away from you twice, so from where I'm sittin' it don't look like she wants to be anywhere near Daddy. You gotta be an idiot if you can't see that, mate."

"Say that again, ya mongrel bastard," Dillon growled.

"Mongrel?" Frank scoffed. "That supposed to be an insult?"

Dillon's face contorted into a hideous grimace, and he let out a guttural shout. He pierced Frank with a terrible glare and chanted, "*Ka mate, ka mate! Ka ora, ka ora!*"

"What the fu—?"

Dillon clanged his metal arms together violently and

continued, never averting his mad eyes.

"*Tēnei te tangata pūhuruhuru! Nāna nei i tiki mai whakawhiti te rā!*"

Frank tensed and squirmed in the seat as the chant went on.

"*Ā, upane! ka upane! Ā, upane, ka upane, whiti te ra!*"

To end his haka, Dillon raised his arms in the air and snarled viciously.

Frank thought he might climb down from the bench and try fighting Frank. Even without legs, Dillon made an imposing figure, and with Frank's broken arm, he wasn't even sure whether he could take him on.

"You done?" Frank said, trying to keep his cool. Adrenaline pumped through his veins, making his body tremble slightly.

The Maori sat in brooding silence, watching Frank.

He held eye contact as long as possible, but caved from the intimidation and scanned the cabin. It was state of the art, more spacious and modern than Europa's version. "Blunt sure knows how to build tech, don't he? Wonder how much this baby cost."

"You can ask him when we get there," Dillon said.

"Heh." Frank figured that's where they'd take him. "Kidnapping a Europa agent, eh? That sounds like a smart idea."

Movement outside caught Frank's eye. He counted three men running back down the hill. "Doesn't look like Daddy's gonna get his daughter back yet, though."

"What?" Dillon pulled himself up and turned towards the cargo door.

The mercs each grabbed a part of Arnie's legs and struggled to drag them along the grass and up the ramp.

"We gotta get out of here," one wheezed, dumping the legs unceremoniously on the floor. "There's more choppers on the way!"

"But Catherine's still out there!" Dillon said.

"We looked for her, but she's gone."

"You morons!" Dillon seethed. "If you hadn't disabled my legs, I could have stayed behind and searched for her!"

The mercs didn't say anything. The one in charge twirled his fingers and said, "Get us out of here."

As the ramp closed, Frank took a last mournful look at his ruined car scattered across the grassy paddock. The hold door sealed shut, blocking it from sight.

And the VTOL lifted off.

PART FOUR

17
HITCHHIKERS

Dan and Cathy left the woodland and trekked for three hours across English farmland. Dan kept looking over his shoulder, afraid he might see the cyborg or a Europa helicopter chasing after them.

As his paranoia grew, Cathy's smile broadened. She seemed convinced that the tracker in her leg had been destroyed and thanked him over and over again.

"For the first time in forever, I'm not being watched!" She inhaled another deep gulp of fresh air.

"We don't know that yet," Dan warned.

"I do!" she insisted. "If Arnie was still tracking me, he'd have shown up by now. This is just exhilarating. Thank you, Dan!"

"Heh, you're welcome." He glanced back at a suspicious-looking barn they had passed a while ago, expecting the doors to burst open and the cyborg—*get it together!* Despite the circumstances, he was beginning to enjoy Cathy's upbeat company.

They arrived at a vibrant seaside town called Brighton just before sunset and checked into a cheap hostel for the night. They risked an exploratory walk around the town and discovered a quaint network of alleyways bustling with quirky shops that spilled out into the streets like a market.

"Wow, it's so crowded here," Cathy remarked.

"Yeah," Dan said, squeezing between some tourists. "I have to buy a new computer. Europa confiscated mine."

"Okay. I could do with some other clothes," Cathy shrugged at herself. "These aren't even mine."

A bedraggled, bearded man interrupted them from his jewellery stall. "A pretty bracelet for the pretty lady?" He held up a shiny bangle and pressed it towards Cathy's nose.

"Ah," she cooed. "It's lovely, but I don't have any money... sorry."

Dan found that hilarious, considering who she was. He let slip a snicker.

"What's so funny?" she said.

"I just assumed you would have, I dunno, stacks of cash."

"Well, I don't." She crossed her arms.

The hippy eyeballed Catherine.

"Come with me," Dan urged, feeling another case of paranoia.

He bought some batteries for his EMP gun and found an ATM machine in the sidewall of a closed bank. He pressed the gun muzzle against the card slot.

"What are you doing?" Cathy said, peering over his shoulder.

"Making a withdrawal," he smirked.

Zzzzzzsstt.

The machine beeped and started spitting out twenties.

"Oh my god, you thief!" Cathy said. "That's somebody's money!"

"This isn't anyone's money," Dan corrected her. "It was printed by a corrupt system built on lies and deception, and is insured by the Euromerican government. Whatever we take now will just get reprinted tomorrow. That's how the system works."

Cathy shook her head in bewilderment. "How do you know stuff like that?"

"I spend a lot of time online."

The machine beeped again and the money hatch sealed shut. Dan counted almost two thousand Euros worth of notes and gave Cathy half.

"Happy spending," he grinned.

Dan had always fantasised about travelling the world with a nice girl. He liked the romantic idea of exploring a foreign land together, treating her to exotic foods and sharing some unique memories. This fantasy existed on some kind of long-term vacation, not while trying to flee a country from a rampaging cyborg hell bent on capturing and/or killing them both.

And in his fantasy, they didn't sleep in bunk beds, in a grotty dorm shared by twelve other people.

"This is horrible," Cathy whispered from the bottom bunk. "Why can't we stay in a fancy hotel? It's not like we can't afford it."

The bed squeaked every time Dan leaned over the side of the top bunk to talk to her. "We have to keep a low profile," he explained. "ATM hacks get reported to the *fedz*. If we start flashing our cash around, it'll look suspicious. It's safer to blend in as lowly backpackers."

"I know, but c'mon," she whispered. She glanced at the other roommates, all chatting in French and German and Spanish. "They smell really bad." She curled her lip in a pout.

Dan chuckled. "They're backpackers. What do you expect?"

"I guess." She sighed and half-smiled. "It does feel quite adventurous. I've never travelled before. I wonder what France is like?" She put her hands behind her head and closed her eyes.

Dan fought the urge to watch her snooze and pulled himself away, making the bed give another tremendous squeak.

"Dan, stop wriggling about," she said. "This bed will make me go crazy."

"Sorry," he said, and switched on his new laptop. He secured the connection and went onto the Eye's forum to find a way of forging a digital passport for Cathy. As he worked, the others in the room dropped off to sleep one by one until it was just the two of them.

He fumbled inside his backpack and pulled out a small gift box. Carefully, so as not to make the bed squeak, he leaned over the side.

"I b—" *bought you something,* he finished in his head. Cathy was asleep. He put the box back in his bag and laid down. He stared at the ceiling for a while before eventually drifting off to sleep.

***

The following morning, they had a go at hitch-hiking. Ten cars drove by without stopping for Dan, but when Cathy swapped with him, it wasn't long before a truck pulled over to offer them a ride.

"Beginner's luck?" she said, coyly chewing on her lip.

The trucker took them to Folkstone where they bought two tickets to Paris, using the fake passport that Dan had acquired for Cathy. They rode the train through the Channel Tunnel into France, disembarking in the capital shortly after midday. They still had a long way to go, needing to cross the border into Germany far to the east, but Cathy yelped with excitement when they saw the Eiffel Tower, and insisted they go take a closer look.

"Woooow," she cooed as they strolled underneath the magnificent structure. "It's so much *bigger* in real life!"

Dan understood how to program algorithms to secure a public WiFi spot with military grade encryption, and he could explain all the flaws of the International Digital Freedom Rights Act of 2024... But standing beneath the Eiffel Tower, an intricate web of metal beams rising hundreds of feet into the sky, he became overwhelmed with the pure physical complexity of it.

He tried to stay cool. "Yeah, man. It's not bad." He had his hands in his pockets and casually glanced around at the four enormous metal feet holding up the tower. *Man, how did they build this back then?*

"Woah," his head spun and he stumbled.

"Careful!" Cathy blurted as he bumped into her.

"Sorry." He flushed. "It's big isn't it?"

"Yeah. I love it. Hey, I'll be right back, okay?" She ran off in the direction of a public bathroom. Dan watched her all the way, entranced by her brown ponytail as it swung from side to side.

The square beneath the tower was bustling with tourists, and Dan spied several merchants selling tiny miniature figurines of the Tower on keyrings. *Ooh, I can add that to it.*

He approached the nearest merchant and bought one of the smallest key rings. He glanced back at the bathroom, seeing no sign of Cathy. *Do it quick, before she gets back.* He whipped out the gift box and opened the lid. Inside was the bracelet that the hippy had tried to sell to Cathy back in Brighton. It had lots of empty little ringlets all around its circumference. On one of the rings hung a tiny red London bus that he had bought from a gift shop on the train. He added the miniature Eifel Tower to the ring next to it.

"What are you doing?"

Dan scrambled the bracelet back into the box. "Um. Nothing." He turned to see Cathy frowning at him.

"What was that?"

"It's nothing!" His cheeks burned red. He gulped, holding the box behind him. "Come on, we gotta get out of here. Time for you to get us a ride again!"

She beamed. "Haha, yeah?" She pushed a loose hair strand behind an ear. "Do you think it'll work again? The French might have a different taste to Englanders."

"I doubt that," Dan said.

An awkward silence lingered a moment.

"Okay... let's go, then," Cathy said at last.

They walked to the eastern edge of the city and picked a spot to try hitch-hiking. Cars passed by frequently, so Dan felt confident they wouldn't have to wait long.

Cathy plonked her bag down at her feet, and held a palm out to him. "Stand aside, Pastey." She pulled her hair band out, unleashing her shoulder-length hair. It was unkempt, and more than a little matted, but Dan liked it anyway.

She put on an innocent smile and stuck out her thumb.

The very next car to come along pulled over, a red Audi saloon.

Two guys were inside, and the passenger leaned out of the open window. "Bonjour! Où allez-vous?"

"Um, hi." Cathy said, biting her lip. "Do you speak English?"

The young man smiled warmly. "Oui! I mean yes! Where are you going?"

"We are trying to reach the German border," she replied, pointing vaguely down the road. "Do you have room for two?"

The guy seemed to notice Dan for the first time. His smile wavered, and he turned to the driver, who gave a casual shrug. The passenger turned back and answered gracefully. "Oui. Of course! We are going as far as Metz. It is not far to the border from there. Get in!"

Cathy turned to Dan, grinning. She shot two thumbs up at him.

Heh. It's good travelling with a girl.

As they cruised out of the city, they engaged in casual conversation with the French men. Cathy did, anyway. Dan tried to chime in with a comment now and then, but felt his responses were met with one word answers, and often the things they talked about didn't interest him. The French guys enjoyed wine, not Red Bull. They talked about their home town, which was apparently full of dance clubs and soccer matches.

When Cathy mentioned that she used to be a research analyst, the Frenchmen seemed impressed. Cathy told them that she hated it and fibbed about how she had finally quit, opting to seek out a new life.

"I can't be tied down any longer, you know!" she gesticulated.

"Oui, oui!" The passenger, whose name was René, agreed. "I know exactly what you mean. So, you are Swiss? We could speak in German if you like?"

Cathy laughed. "Oh no! I'm not Swiss. I am a mixed breed. My mother —" She gave a nervous laugh, and coughed. "My mother is English..." She seemed to be struggling with her words. "And my father is from Germany, originally. I, uhh…"

"Her parents are dead," Dan lied.

Cathy glanced at him, first with surprise. Then she nodded a sad smile which made Dan tingle.

"Yeah." Cathy leaned back in the car seat and gazed out the window at the passing scenery.

René turned to Dan, leaning against the backrest of the front seat. "That is sad."

"Yup," Dan raised his eyebrows. He decided to change the subject. "I'm a hacker." *Oh, good one. Discreet.*

"Really?" René's smile didn't seem genuine. He added in a rather mocking tone, "Are you like, one of those cyber criminals who are always on the news?" He slapped the driver on the arm. "Ce sont ces pirates appelés, Claude?"

Claude the driver chuckled. "Err, les yeux binaires?"

"Oui!" René clapped. "The Eye of Binary!" He grinned at Dan. "Don't tell me you are one of those geeky pussies?"

Cathy snickered, still facing the window.

Dan felt a flush creeping up his neck. "Um. You mean Binary Eye, I think." *Don't say yes, don't say yes.* "What if I am?"

René's smile vanished and he gaped at Dan. "Are you for real?" He turned to Claude, who was gazing in the rearview at Dan with wide eyes and his mouth curled in disbelief.

They both burst out laughing.

They think I'm a joke. Worse still, Cathy's sympathetic smile suggested that she agreed with them.

Anger flashed through his head. "So, what have you morons ever stood for? The Eye fights for the good of everyone. We uncover secrets that our government would hide from you—"

René interrupted. "They took down Apple's iService last month. Why did they do that? My phone did not work for an entire day because of those filthy *connards*."

"That was to protest their incongruous attitude to consumers," Dan explained. "They have been ripping people off for decades, and *you* sheep do nothing but feed their profits blindly!"

"My grandmother died that day," Claude said.

Dan's words caught in his throat.

"She was sick," Claude went on. "She needed to call an ambulance, but her phone couldn't make the call because hackers had taken over the service."

Dan blinked. *Oh god.* "That's... I mean—"

"That's awful," Cathy said. She reached around and touched Claude on the shoulder.

"I... I didn't..." Dan couldn't find any words of consolation. The atmosphere in the car weighed heavily on his conscience.

René and Claude burst into laughter again.

Cathy pulled her hand away. "Were you kidding? That's so mean!" She slapped Claude on the arm. "I can't believe you would joke about that."

"I'm sorry, that was too funny. You should see your face!" René pointed back at Dan, who could do nothing but digest his dignity.

"It was still really annoying, man," Claude said after they had finally stopped laughing. "Those hacker guys are the worst. Ruining everyone's lives for no good reason." He frowned in the mirror at Dan. "I may not have picked you up if I had known!" René shot him another slimy smile.

Dan flustered in the backseat, scratching his neck.

"I'm not like those guys. Apple was small time, man. I'm better than that."

"Oh yeah?" René said. "What can you hack? Show us some *mad skillz*," he mocked an American accent.

Dan glared at him. He looked to Cathy, who was staring out the window again, perhaps trying not to laugh.

"All right." He grabbed his backpack and pulled out a thick wad of bills. "This is three thousand Euros."

Cathy turned sharply to him.

René gaped at the money. "Where did you get that?"

"*Mad skillz.*" Dan mimicked, shooting him a smug smile.

Claude slammed on the brakes. Dan lurched forward and smashed his head on the back of René's chair. He dropped the notes on the floor and they scattered around his feet. The car stopped dead.

"What the hell man?" Dan said, bending to retrieve the notes from the floor. Something cold and sharp pressed against his throat.

He gulped. His adam's apple snagged against the blade of the flick knife.

Cathy shrieked. "What are you doing?"

"*Silence!*" Claude ordered. He was leaning back between the front seats, holding the knife with one hand against Dan's neck. "No more ride, American. Leave the money and go."

"Wha...?"

"You heard me."

Dan looked to René, who stared hungrily through a gap in the headrest. He showed no sign of interfering with his friend's abrupt decision to rob them.

Dan glanced around outside. A darkening sky full of rainclouds stretched above a view of flat fields. The middle of nowhere.

"You can't do this to us!" Cathy fumed.

"Not you," Claude corrected. "You can stay." He smiled at her. The same welcoming smile he had greeted them with when they pulled up to offer them a ride.

Dan felt helpless. His crotch had suddenly tightened and he desperately needed to relieve himself. "Okay," he croaked. "I'll go." He fumbled the door open, grabbed his backpack and scrambled out of the car.

"Close the door!" René ordered. Dan did so.

The passenger door opened on the other side. "Fuck you!" Cathy yelled into the car, bursting out. She slammed the door shut.

The car accelerated away, leaving them in a cloud of dust.

Dan was so relieved to see her that a smile spread across his face.

"What the fuck were you thinking?" Cathy said, marching towards him.

His smile vanished. "Um..."

"You're the biggest idiot I've ever met! Now what are we supposed to do?"

Dan glanced left and right. The road stretched on dead straight for miles in both directions. Endless flat fields. Not another car in sight.

Thunder rumbled in the distant sky.

"I guess you need to do your hitch-hiker trick again?"

"Fuck. You."

It was the last thing she said to him for over an hour.

***

Dan's sodden shirt clung to his outstretched arm. He squinted through the drenching rain at the approaching headlights.

"Please!" he begged, sticking his thumb in the air and forcing a smile as droplets fell from his eyebrows.

The car sped past without slowing. Fine spray covered Dan, not that it made any difference to his clothes.

"Argh! Why are you so cruel?" He shouted at the red taillights of the car as they disappeared into the distance, their crimson glow slowly fading away.

"Fuck you!" Cathy answered.

He turned to her. She sat hunched on a rock, her brown hair hanging straight around her shoulders, arms crossed.

"I wasn't talking to you!" Dan retorted. "Although..."

"Although what?"

"Well, you know!"

"No, I don't!"

"We've been standing here for an *hour*!" Dan wailed, arms in the air.

"And that's somehow *my* fault, is it?" Cathy stood, glaring. Her eyes glinted with rage in the light of the only streetlight on what must be the longest stretch of road in the whole of France. Like him, she was soaked to the bone, and equally pissed off.

"Why won't you just help me?" he cried.

"No! I'm not doing that again." She looked away, re-crossing her arms. "You got us into this. We had *so much money* Dan, we could be riding First Class on the Eurolink right now instead of freezing to death on the side of the road!"

"I know," Dan scratched the back of his head. "I'll get us some more money when we reach the next town."

"Damn right you will!" She let out a frustrated grunt, which Dan couldn't help finding endearing despite the circumstances. She went on, "But I'm not getting in another car. What if a serial killer picks us up this time? Or a *rapist*?"

"I won't let anyone hurt you."

Cathy choked on her laughter. "Now I feel so much safer!"

Dan flushed. "You'd be bleeding to death in the woods back in England if it wasn't for me!" He intended to sound angry, but his voice broke halfway through the sentence, turning him into a squeaky little boy. "Ugh!" he turned away from her, searching for another car.

The rain came down. Under the streetlight, it was hard to see much farther than a hundred feet down the dark road. Thick clouds blocked the moonlight, but Dan knew they were surrounded by flat fields stretching for miles in every direction.

She's right. I couldn't protect her if anyone tried anything... I'm just a scrawny dweeb.

He stood by the side of the road in moody silence for a while.

How did I manage to screw this up so badly? Things were going fine yesterday…

The rain came down in endless sheets.

Not a single car had stopped since they were abandoned. The closest Dan had come was a couple of honking horns. He looked back at Cathy sulking on a rock. He needed her help.

He hugged himself, shivering with cold. "I'm sorry," he said.

She looked up. "What?"

"This wasn't your fault. Like, at all. You are right, I was an idiot. I'm sorry." He looked around, unable to make eye contact. "I've just been pushed around by guys like that my whole life. I wanted to show off or something, I dunno."

"They were assholes," Cathy said.

Dan raised his eyebrows. "Really? I thought you liked them."

"No. French men are arrogant. Didn't you see the way that René creep kept looking at my breasts?"

Dan hadn't noticed that at all. "Um. No."

"You wouldn't," she stood up, wrapping her arms around her belly.

She must be cold, too. Maybe I should hug her...

"I wished they'd just shut up," Cathy continued. "So I could enjoy the scenery. It's beautiful out here." She snorted a laugh. "Well, it was when I could actually see it."

"I bought you something," Dan blurted.

"What?"

"It's in my bag. I wanted to give it to you earlier, but..."

"You bought me something?" She sounded surprised.

"Yeah." He swayed over to his bag and pulled out the box. He turned it over in his hand, hesitating. The rain pattered off the lid. "It's a bit stupid, actually." He opened it. She leaned close to take a look. "See this, it's from England." He pointed to the red bus. "Your first country as a traveller. And this is from France, obviously. You seemed to like the Tower." He shrugged. "It's that bracelet you liked. You can add more keyrings to it as you go along." He held it out to her.

Cathy took it. "Dan... That's so thoughtful."

He hoped it was dark enough that she couldn't see him blushing.

When she met his eyes again, her face was lit with a lovely smile. It made Dan feel warm and fuzzy.

She leaned in and pecked him on the cheek. His right leg almost gave way.

"Thank you," she said, admiring the bracelet.

The light of an approaching car blossomed behind her head. She turned to it, and scurried to the side of the road.

Cathy stuck her thumb into the rainy darkness. The sight of her silhouette encased in an angelic glow from the headlights etched itself into the deepest segment of Dan's memory. *My first kiss.*

18
YUMA

"Yuma."

"Yuma?"

"Yes. Yuma." Henry clasped his fingertips together, gazing at the map on the big suspended monitor. "Where better to begin the solar initiative than the sunniest place in America?"

Margery considered what she knew of the small town: sun, sand and cowboys. *They will not be missed.* "America won't be an easy fix, you know." She tried to sound casual, but doubt crept into her tone.

Across the table, Henry eyed her coolly. "I thought you relished a challenge."

Heat prickled the skin on the back of her neck. "Of course I do. But there's a challenge, dear, and then there's *America.*"

"I have every faith in your ability."

"It's not *my* abilities you have to worry about. It's whether the American media will play along with Stone's report. Even she may struggle to cover this up as an *act of terror* in the country that invented the bloody term..."

"Then we won't call it an act of terror." Henry spread his palms. "Let's call it an act of God."

"Hmm." Margery held his gaze. She leaned back in her chair, swirling her pinot noir. "Well, talk me through it. What's the plan?"

He broadened his cock-sure smile. "Why talk, when we

can watch the show?"

Oh, I like the sound of this...

He aimed the remote at the lights and turned them off. The glow from the monitor cast the room in dim light. Henry eased into the sofa beside her, *clinked* her glass with his own and turned his attention to the screen. Margery noticed the stubble around his chin for the first time. *He hasn't shaved for three days.* He obviously had been busy setting up whatever it was they were about to see. A hot tingle swept down Margery's back in anticipation. She sipped her wine and gazed at the monitor.

The Yuma map disappeared, replaced by a bobbing view of a dusty street.

"Hello?" said a voice.

"Hello, Mr. Granger," said Henry.

"Hi, Mr. Zhin," said the voice on the screen. A hand appeared, waving at the camera. Whoever this Granger was, he had the camera on his head, giving Margery and Henry a first-person perspective. "Can you see my hand?"

"Just fine," Henry replied. "The signal is clear as day. How was your journey?"

"Oh, sublime, thank you, sir. I had the entire coach to myself."

"Well, only the best for Servants of the New Dawn."

Margery smirked and let out the tiniest snicker, which she immediately tried to hide with the back of her hand.

Henry flashed her a grin and waved her silent. "Where are you now?" he asked the monitor.

"I'm, uhh, just making my way down Main Street. Only a few blocks to go now, sir."

"Good, good," Henry replied, stroking his chin. "It looks like a fine day. How are you feeling, Mr. Granger?"

"Oh, sir." Mr. Granger sounded on the brink of ecstasy. If Margery were to put a word on his tone, it would be pride. He babbled on, "There is no language fit to describe my feelings at this moment, sir."

"I understand," said Henry. "Might I take this

opportunity to thank you for your dedication and commitment?"

"It is I who am filled with gratitude to you for entrusting me with this holy task. Ever since God took my wife and daughter, I have prayed for a righteous opportunity to join them in the next life."

"If only we could all serve God so admirably." Henry wiped his mouth and shot Margery a mischievous smile.

Margery pinched her lips together, fighting the urge to burst out laughing. *Good lord, where did he find this zealot?*

"You are too modest," Mr. Granger went on, oblivious. "You are serving Him by helping to reduce the strain on the planet He gifted us. Your moment of glory is just over the horizon."

"Indeed."

Margery clucked a short laugh. Granger wouldn't have a clue of the significance of that statement.

Henry regained his composure and frowned. "So, Mr. Granger. I see you are approaching the square now."

"Yes sir."

"You have the purifier?"

The camera tilted down and Margery saw the man's stomach and arms. He cradled a metal box about the size of a small beer keg. "Of course, sir."

"Excellent. Well, there is little reason for further idle talk. You know what to do."

"Yes, sir."

"God speed, Mr. Granger. I wish you safe voyage to the other side."

"Thank you, sir." His voice cracked. "May God wat—"

Henry muted it.

Margery scoffed. "*God speed?* How do you find these lunatics?"

"It doesn't matter. All that matters is they are in plentiful supply."

"I'm not entirely comfortable putting all our eggs in the religious basket, Henry."

"The other volunteers are not all zealots," he assured her. "I have theologists, environmentalists, sociopaths and a few psychopaths – all potential candidates for the other locations. Now, pay attention." He pointed at the screen and whispered, "This will be quite the sight."

Margery watched. The tingle came again, originating at the back of her neck and shimmering down her spine. *This is it… the culmination of our research.*

Granger reached a wooden bench in the middle of a square, and put the metal box down on it. He peered around, the camera panning left and right. People roamed the streets, a few dozen or so, shoppers and tourists. A few cars lined up at a traffic junction nearby.

Granger turned back to the case and unclipped the two latches. He eased the lid open, revealing a simple interface of two buttons, one green, one red, and a digital display of red numbers. Margery recognised the device. The prototype had been installed at the Swiss facility's test chamber, and subsequently destroyed during the purge. This one was supposedly a hundred times more powerful.

His hands appeared in front of the camera, clasped together in prayer.

"Oh, for fuck's sake man, don't draw attention to yourself," Henry muttered.

The prayer went on for an uncomfortable amount of time.

"Get on with it, you fuck," Henry fumed. His clenched fist rested on the armrest, and Margery feared he may spill his whiskey. She reached for Henry's fist, covering it with her palm. He didn't seem to notice, but touching him sent another pleasurable shiver through her, and that was more important anyway.

Henry unmuted the screen so they could hear the video feed. Granger was muttering incomprehensible gibberish amid the general hustle and bustle of a workday afternoon.

"He can't hear us anymore," Henry said, pointing the remote at the screen. He brought up a menu and clicked through a few options. When he was done, the monitor was divided into several sections, five squared off images of different locations around the town, with Mr. Granger's headcam taking up the largest portion of the screen.

In the other segments, Margery spied people walking down the street. A couple with their young son in a pushchair strolled up a road towards one of the CCTV cameras. The mother wore a bright orange dress that Margery found horribly garish.

In the square, Granger finished praying. He pushed the green button on the device, and the 10-second countdown timer began to beep.

Boop. Boop. Boop. Boop.

The headcam jerked around abruptly and aimed at the floor.

"What the fuck?" Henry asked, but then Granger himself suddenly appeared on the screen. He was placing his camera down on the bench beside the bomb so they could see him, as well as the square behind him.

Henry exhaled.

Boop. Boop. Boop.

Granger took a few steps back and faced the camera. Margery had expected a robed middle-eastern man in a turban, so was surprised to see Granger sporting blue jeans and a cowboy hat instead.

Margery spied more people walking about behind him. Aside from the occasional glance, nobody took any notice of Granger.

"The new dawn rises," he announced. He wiped away a tear and sniffed.

Boop. Boop.

Granger spread his arms wide, palms raised to the sky, and closed his eyes. He smiled from ear to ear and wept.

Boop.

Margery held her breath.

Boooooooooooooooooooooooooop.

The monitor flashed white.

She squinted against the blinding brightness, gripping Henry's fist.

After a few moments, the visual feeds came back. Granger's cowboy hat fell to the ground on top of his boots. In the adjacent window, the empty pushchair wheeled to a halt. The hideous orange dress tumbled down the street, caught by the breeze. Small bundles of clothes littered the ground in the deserted square. A car mounted the curb and bounced across the sidewalk before crashing into a storefront. Another one ploughed into the back of a parked pickup.

Silence.

Margery's jaw dangled loose. Her arms trembled. She became vaguely aware of a wetness in her underwear. *Oh my god.*

Henry squeezed her hand.

"It worked." He wasn't smiling. "It worked better than I had hoped. Look at that," he pointed to the screen. "Not a single piece of structural damage. The car crashes were inevitable, I suppose. But it *worked*."

Margery's body tingled all over. "Henry..." She pulled his hand up and kissed it lightly.

He spun toward her, and she knew that he felt as hungry for her as she did for him.

He wrapped a hand around her neck and pulled her close, squashing their lips together.

Margery dropped her half-filled wine glass on the sofa. Henry's hands caressed her neck and weaved through her hair, tugging at it and kissing her with an overwhelming intensity. Margery grabbed his shirt collar and tore it downwards, popping off all the buttons. He reached under her dress and ran a hand up the inside of her thigh.

They tumbled to the floor, intertwined.

Between breathless kisses, Henry said, "My Margery. You know this was only the first phase?"

"I know." She raked her fingers across his bare back.

"There is no turning back now. We have mounted the

lowest step, and we must now climb to the top."

"I know." She rolled him onto his back, straddling his waist. "The top is where I belong." She pulled her dress over her head and tossed it aside. He grabbed her waist as she arched her back.

He means to be king of the ashes. And I will be his queen.

19
CAPTOR

Sid hunched over the desk in front of his computer in his hundredth floor office. His red raw eyes sagged above his drooping mouth, forty more stressful hours without sleep hanging off his face.

"What do you mean, you lost her!?" he wheezed down the phone. "Why didn't you stay and look for her?"

"I tried, sir," said Arnie, his voice distant and tinny, barely audible above the engines. "But Europa sent helicopters and these fucking idiots set off the EMP to get rid of them. The bloody thing disabled my legs."

Sid's mouth flapped in a wordless, seething rage. "*What?*"

"I'm sorry, sir."

"Do you know how much those prostheses will cost to repair?" Sid hissed.

"No, sir. But I am bringing back a bargaining chip, one that may help us keep Europa off our backs."

"What do you mean by that?" Sid asked.

"Shit! Europa's still on our tail. I'll call back when I can!" The line went dead.

Sid slammed the phone back onto the receiver and collapsed in his chair. *He had her. He had her in his arms and now she's gone again.* With the tracker mysteriously vanished, Sid now had no idea of Catherine's whereabouts or whether she was even alive. His entire rescue plan had failed catastrophically, *and* he'd need Gunther to repair the prototype combat legs before he could think about trying again. Things could not get any worse.

He lifted himself out of the chair, his back giving a nasty *click* as he stood up straight, and gazed out of the wall-to-wall window overlooking the twinkling Berlin skyline. He thought of Catherine, out there somewhere. *How will I ever find you now?*

His phone rang again.

Sid dived on it. "Arnie?" he croaked.

"Sorry, sir. It's only me," said Julie, his personal assistant.

"Julie, tell me you have some good news?"

"I have the Chief of Europa on the line for you."

Sid's stomach plummeted. He gulped. "Put her through." The line *clicked*.

"Am I speaking to Mr. Blunt?" said a stern, British, female voice.

"Yes, that's me. What can I do for you?"

"This is a private line, Mr. Blunt. Nobody but the two of us can hear this conversation. I want you to know that."

What game is this? "Okay," he said, trying to sound bemused. "What's this about?"

"Don't play coy, Mr. Blunt. You just attacked a government holding facility. Your man, so to speak, killed three of mine, injured a dozen others, and shot down two of my helicopters during his escape. I need this to end right now."

Sid collected his thoughts. *She knows it was me. Which means she knew about Catherine.* "So it was *you* who sent me the photographs of my daughter. You wanted me to come. Why?"

"I assumed you would have the balls to come for her yourself, but I underestimated your fatherly commitment."

"How *dare* you question my commitment to Catherine?" Sid sputtered. "I would do anything to get her back to me. You had no right holding her prisoner like that. I could report you to the police and have you arrested for misconduct and kidnapping."

"I *am* the police." The chief let that hang in Sid's mind for a while until he felt a gnawing sensation in the pit of his bowels. She went on, "If you want to play that game, how about I arrest you for fraud? You declared your daughter dead six years ago, remember?"

"What's stopping you?" Sid asked.

"It would implicate your ex-wife, which is a complication I don't need."

So Margery paid the Chief of Europa to have me taken out? This is overkill, even by her standards. "Should I expect a Europa SWAT team to crash through my window at any moment?"

"I'm hoping that won't be necessary. I'd rather come to a quiet arrangement with you."

"I see. How much? I'll double whatever she paid."

"Margery Blunt didn't *pay* me… but I'm glad you are a man that sees reason. Shall we say, thirty million Euros in an off-shore account? Get it to me by midnight. In return, I'll make the Plumpton incident disappear."

She's as corrupt as they come. No wonder Margery used her. "Call off your hunt of my aircraft immediately. When my men return safely, *then* I will make the transfer."

"Consider it done. I'm glad we could come to such a swift understanding. Goodbye, Mr. Blunt."

Sid hung up the phone and inhaled a deep breath. *Arnie's bargaining chip had better be good.*

***

The cold wind buffeted Sid in the night air, flapping his tie around his head. He stood on the roof of the skyscraper as the VTOL swooped down to land on the helipad.

The ramp opened and five men exited the cargo bay. Arnie dangled between two mercs, his big arms draped around their necks. The lead mercenary, a man called

Barnes, led the bulky fifth man by gunpoint.

"Who are you?" Sid asked, looking the stranger up and down. He stood a foot taller than Sid, sported a stubbly chin and a mean scowl. He was clutching his right arm, clearly in a lot of discomfort.

Barnes answered for him. "This is Agent Frank Hawkins, a Europa infiltrator."

So this is Arnie's chip. "Hawkins? You're the one who kidnapped my Catherine from the facility. What happened to your arm?"

"Your guard dog attacked me," Frank growled, cocking his head towards Arnie.

Barnes snorted a laugh. "Yeah, Arnie took his chance to get even."

"We're not *even* yet, bro. Not by a long shot," Arnie spat as they carried him past.

Sid swallowed back bile at the sight of Arnie, bare chested and legless. "Stop."

The mercs carrying Arnie froze and spun him around to face Sid.

"Who gave the order to trigger the EMP when Arnie was within the blast radius?"

Barnes exchanged a glance with his comrades, but then manned up. "Me, sir."

Sid clenched his fist. "What were you thinking?"

Barnes swallowed, and gave a feeble shrug. "I hoped you could just give him a new pair."

"Those legs cost six hundred *million Euros!* They're a prototype. Do you understand what that means?

"Err," Barnes mumbled.

"There isn't *another pair*! It could take *days* to repair the damage you've done."

"Shit. I'm sorry sir, I—"

"*You're fired*! Get the fuck out of here." Sid turned on Arnie. "And you. I sent you there to bring Catherine back. You *had* her. What on earth happened?"

Arnie pointed fiercely at Frank, squeezing the neck of

one of the mercs that was holding him in the process. "That Europa bastard came back for her. Him and some kid. They ran into the woods together and just disappeared!"

Sid's temples throbbed. He whirled on Frank. "Was this kid another agent of yours?"

"Something like that," Frank grunted.

"So, where will he take her?" Sid grabbed his shoulders and shook them. "*Where's my daughter?*"

"Fuck *me* that hurts," Frank shoved Sid away with his left arm. "Get the hell off me!"

Sid stumbled backwards and bumped into someone, who steadied his fall. It was Hugo, the VTOL pilot. "Easy there, sir. It's no good interrogating him up here. He needs medical attention. And you look like you haven't slept in a week."

Sid composed himself, inhaling deep gulps of frigid air. *His arm... A man with his training could be an ideal candidate.* "You're right. Take the elevator down to medical. I want Doctor Gunther to examine his arm."

Gunther strapped Agent Hawkins down into a reclining medical chair, watched closely by Sid, Arnie in a wheelchair, and Harrison, one of the mercenaries.

"All this really necessary?" Frank said.

"It is for our protection from you," explained Doctor Gunther. "And your protection from yourself."

"Why would I need to protect myself?" Frank asked.

"He's the best limb surgeon in the country," Sid assured him. "If he can't fix your arm, no-one can. But while he works, I want to ask you some questions."

"Okay," Frank said.

"Europa sent you to my ex-wife's facility, correct?"

"Yeah. I was there," Frank said. "I rescued Cathy."

"You *kidnapped* her," Arnie corrected.

"No, I didn't even know she was there until I was

escaping for my life." Frank kept eyes on Sid. "What *was* she doing there, Mr. Blunt? The world thinks she died six years ago... murdered by her best friend."

Annie. "You are in no position to ask q-questions, agent." Sid wagged a trembling finger at him.

"You might want to cooperate with me, Mr. Blunt. Europa has evidence that your daughter is alive, a secret kept from the world, but for what purpose? A scandal like that could seriously harm the public image of a company like yours, couldn't it?"

"You can't blackmail me, agent," Sid gave a nervous laugh. "I've already negotiated that issue with your boss. Now, where did your partner take Catherine? You must tell me."

"I honestly don't know. Dan's a hacker. A proper nerd. He's got no street sense, so I have no idea where he would think to take her. That's assuming they even found each other in those woods." He looked at Harrison. "Your buddy Barnes might have squashed them both by the fucking helicopters for all we know."

Sid inhaled sharply. "Is that possible?"

"Yeah," Arnie admitted. "They crash landed right on top of where I told Catherine to hide."

"Oh my god," Sid squeezed his forehead with a palm. "I have to know for sure. Harrison, find Hugo and ask him how long it would take to refuel the VTOL and get back to England."

"Will do, sir," Harrison left the room.

"You think the chief will let you fly back to their doorstep?" Frank asked.

"She will when I tell her I have you as a hostage."

Frank burst out laughing. "You don't know the chief. She'll disavow any knowledge of my existence before negotiating with you. We ain't exactly on the best of terms, she's probably *looking* for a reason to retire me."

Sid studied him. "What would you suggest, then?"

"Help me."

Sid frowned. "What?"

"What do you know about *Horizon*?"

"Never heard of it," Sid said impatiently. "What makes you think I can help you with your spy work?"

"We found numerous references to something called Horizon in your ex-wife's facility. You were married to Margery Blunt for almost twenty years. If anyone was aware of a secret project that she was invested in, I figured you might be one to know."

"We divorced after she took Catherine hostage," Sid reminded him. "I've spent the last six years developing my prostheses project. I have no time to worry about what my ex-wife is up to."

"Why did you carry on the cyborg program?" Frank eyed him. "Were you hoping to regain the Neo-Asian military contract?"

"No," Sid insisted.

"You realise how suspicious that looks, considering how your father made his fortune in the first place?"

"Yes, yes, I know."

Frank pierced him with interrogating eyes. "I saw first-hand how *Blunt* rose to prominence during the Second Cold War. Your father secured more technology patents than every other big player in the world during those years. And when I saw your cyborg lapdog running across those fields and jumping hedges like a fucking tin-man Olympian, I got the same sense of dread that I felt back then. Mr. Blunt, are you conspiring to initiate a Third Cold War?"

"No!" Sid screwed up his face, shaking his head. "I carried on the prostheses program with the goal of creating a soldier that could infiltrate that place and rescue Catherine." He furrowed his brow, and met Frank's eyes with anger. "I had the prototype legs working a week before Europa sent you in. The facility was purged before I found a suitable candidate to wear them." *He's a trained special agent. Even with a broken arm, he's showing very little sign of the pain. He's perfect for what I need.*

"Hmm," Frank nodded in thought. "So you've had no contact with Margery at all during this time?"

"Only when she needed something, would Margery call me. Whether to steal some of my employees, or to have my manufacturing plants build her a batch of new computers. How could I refuse while she held my Catherine hostage? I've no idea what she was working on in that god-forsaken facility."

"You provided them with equipment?" Frank cocked his head. "I'm sorry Mr. Blunt, but that means you are obligated to help me here. You might have unintentionally contributed to a conspiracy."

"Don't talk to me about obligations," Sid snapped. "If it weren't for you, I'd have my daughter back by now. If you want to know what Margery was doing, why don't you just ask Horatio Zhin?"

Frank raised his eyebrows. "Zhin?"

"I suppose it's not exactly public knowledge," Sid muttered. "Well, here's some juicy intel for you. Margery has been fucking that Korean diplomat ever since she left me. Well, before she left me, if you must know…"

"Really? What's a highly respected politician got to do with all this?"

"He retired from politics after the Korean unification. He and I were business partners for a while. He helped me establish a retail presence in Neo Asia." Sid clenched his teeth. "Then he and Margery betrayed me, and stole the entire market for themselves."

"Was that part of your divorce settlement?"

Sid flustered, uncomfortable talking about these personal matters. But the allure of badmouthing his ex-wife and old business partner overcame him. "Yes. She forced me to split the company in two. Any profits made in the newly established Asian market went directly to her. I was left with the single Euromerican market."

"Fuck me," Frank exclaimed. "So, they secured

themselves a huge income of financial support." Frank frowned at the floor, lost in thought. "Maybe he's the one behind Horizon…"

"I don't have the foggiest idea," Sid said. "All I care about is finding Catherine. I am sending my pilot back to England to inspect those woods."

"Take off these restraints," Frank said. "Let me speak to my boss, and I'll convince her to let you carry out a search. You've been very helpful, I'm sure she will repay you for this valuable information."

"No," Arnie said. He hadn't said anything for a while, and Sid had forgotten he was there. "Remember if it wasn't for this guy, I'd still have my real legs. I don't trust him, sir, and neither should you."

"Relax, Arnie," Sid said. "I don't trust him. Not yet." He turned back to Frank. "Thank you Mr. Hawkins, but I will speak to the chief myself. You're going to help me in another matter." Sid turned to Doctor Gunther, who had a mad grin plastered across his face, and held up a syringe full of clear liquid. "You may proceed with the operation, Doctor."

"With pleasure." Gunther walked up behind Frank.

Frank jerked his head back, gaping in fear at the doctor. "What the fuck?"

"Now you understand the reason for ze restraints, ja?" Gunther said, holding the needle up to Frank's face.

Arnie gave him a smug smile. "After the doc has dealt with that busted arm, *then* we'll be getting closer to even, bro." He wheeled about and rolled out of the room.

"No!" Frank roared at Sid. "What the fuck gives you the right?" He heaved at the strap around his good arm, but he couldn't break his way out of the chair.

Sid looked him in the eye. "You lost me my daughter. Tomorrow, you'll help get her back."

The doctor jabbed the needle into Frank's neck. Frank's eyes rolled and his head drooped to one side.

"Sleep now, agent Hawkins. I'll see you on the other

side."

20
DERUNOX

Cathy insisted they take the Eurolink train for the last leg of their journey. She'd had her fill of hitch-hiking with thieving Frenchmen and smelly truckers for the last three days.

"We can't risk you being seen, especially in Germany," Dan argued. "You grew up here!"

"Don't patronise me," she said. "If we catch the train, we can just buy a private room where nobody will bother us. That's safer and will be less exhausting than making small talk with another nosey truck driver. I'm sick of pretending to be called Zoey."

He relented at that. After hacking another ATM to replenish their cash—withdrawing only a modest 500 Euros this time—they boarded the train at Stuttgart and locked themselves away in their own cabin.

"Thanks, Dan," she said when the train was under way.

He glanced up from his phone. "For what?"

"I don't know. For this." She gestured to the window view of rural houses rolling past. "This trip is the closest I've come to a holiday in years."

He smiled sadly. "It doesn't feel like that to me. I need to know what my brother died for."

She touched his arm in sympathy. "That's why we're going to see your hacker friend. He'll be able to help us, right?"

Dan perked up. "Oh yeah, Derunox is the best. He'll go

nuts when he meets you. I still can't believe he was right this whole time. About you, I mean."

"So, was he the only person in your group who believed I was still alive?"

"Not the *only* one…" He looked at her. "You knew a guy named Ben, didn't you?"

Cathy's heart skipped a beat at the sudden reminder of Ben. "Yeah. He worked with me at the facility."

"I knew it," Dan said. "He posted about you on the Eye's forum. He claimed to be, um… dating you." Dan added softly, "What happened to him?"

"He was killed." Cathy looked down at her lap. "It was my fault. I shouldn't have gotten so close to him. My Mother had him murdered right in front of me."

"Jeez," Dan said.

She laughed sardonically. "Yeah. Add him to the list of people who I've seen die. She killed my friend Annie before that, too." She looked at Dan, who was watching her with puppyish brown eyes. She shrugged. "I guess we've both lost people in this."

"Yeah," Dan said. "But it wasn't your fault, Cathy."

"It's okay, you don't have to try and make me feel better."

"No, seriously," Dan said. "Ben leaked information about Horizon. That's where I first heard about it. I know it's still terrible what happened to him, but he was probably killed because of that, not you."

Cathy blinked. "I didn't know that. Oh god," she lifted a hand to her mouth. "So *that's* what he was doing in the cabin that night…"

"What night?" Dan asked.

"We stayed in a cabin on the mountain," Cathy said. "He was acting weird, I caught him setting up a transmitter on the roof. He said he was using it to access the Shadow Net."

"When was this?"

"About two months ago."

"Oh man, that's it then," Dan said. "You were there the very moment he leaked knowledge of Horizon."

"Yeah," Cathy said. "And my mother had him killed for it." A hollow realisation washed over her. "So, she didn't kill him because of me. It was to protect herself."

"Yup, I think so."

Cathy felt numb. "She made me think it was my fault."

Dan leaned forward. "So, um, are geeks your type?"

She snorted a laugh. "What? You're asking me that now?"

"Err, no. I mean, you know." He fidgeted, and turned away. "You liked Ben, so I just thought…."

"Are you *jealous* of Ben? He's dead, Dan."

"I know," he scratched the back of his neck.

"That's a bit fucked up."

"Yeah," he looked down at his phone, his cheeks blushing.

"Dan, how old are you?"

"I'm nineteen, why?"

"No reason."

He stood up. "I'm gonna go to the bathroom." He unlocked the door and disappeared into the carriage.

Unbelievable. A smile tugged at Cathy's lips. *He is rather cute.*

***

Cathy and Dan disembarked at *Praha hlavní nádraží,* Prague's international train station.

"We made it." Cathy gave a satisfied sigh. She hoisted her backpack over a shoulder, the buzz of excitement showing on her ear to ear grin. "So, where does Derunox live? You should call him and tell him we've arrived."

Dan chewed on a finger nail. "Not yet."

Cathy's smile waned. "Why not?"

Still biting a nail on one hand, he pointed with the other to the long queue of people at the far end of the platform. They were all waiting to be seen by a Czech immigration officer sitting in a booth.

"Oh."

There was no avoiding it. They had to get through that security checkpoint. They joined the end of the line and queued in silence. Dan exhaled a long breath, clearly agitated.

"Will you relax?" she whispered sternly. "We've got this far without Europa catching us, haven't we?"

"Yeah," he said, flexing and clenching his fingers at his side. "The fake passport should be fine. It's the cameras, though." He glanced up, raking his eyes across the ceiling like a stoner paranoid about UFOs.

"Stop fretting! You look guilty."

He's such a kid. Only four years separated their ages, but Cathy sometimes felt like Dan's mother. She decided she'd have to be the confident one here, and slipped her sunglasses onto her nose. She figured it would be harder to be recognised if they couldn't see her eyes.

Dan browsed his phone, reading some news article. "Holy shit," he mumbled.

"What?" Cathy said, stepping forward to keep up with the queue.

"There's been an incident in Yuma, Arizona."

"What happened?"

"They're calling it a *supernatural event*. Everyone in the town has mysteriously disappeared."

"Let me see," Cathy scanned the headline and saw an ominous photo of a bunch of clothes lying in a deserted sunny street. "That's pretty strange."

"Yeah, man. That picture gives me the shivers."

One by one, travellers approached the front desk until their turn arrived. Dan went first.

A strong sense of anxiety overcame her as she watched Dan hand over his legitimate passport. *Oh, God, please keep it together. Don't let them catch me now.* She looked at the fake one in her hand. *Dan got this for me. He knows about that kind of stuff. It'll work…it has to.*

She chewed her lip, and ran a hand down the length of her arm, butterflies jittering in her stomach. Her fingers brushed against the miniature Eiffel Tower dangling on her bracelet. Her "freedom" bracelet, Dan's gift to her. She smiled.

"Next!"

Cathy gave a start. Dan had disappeared through the gate and the officer was giving her an impatient wave forward. She scrambled up to the booth and handed over her forged passport.

The man grabbed it, shaking his head. "Business or pleasure?" he asked in a thick Slovak accent, studying the photograph.

"Pleasure," she replied. She twisted so he could see her bag. "Just backpacking."

"Please remove your glasses," he said. He compared her face to the photograph.

Cathy held her breath.

The guard flipped the passport open to the back page and scanned her ID. The computer *beeped* and a small green LED flicked on.

Thank God.

The officer held the passport out to her, but didn't let go when she tried to take it.

"Um," she met his eyes.

He squinted at her and cocked his head. "You look like somebody."

Oh, shit.

"Really?" She uttered a nervous laugh. She tugged at the passport, but he didn't let go.

The immigration officer lifted a thoughtful finger. Cathy could practically see the list of names flashing behind his eyes.

"Have you ever been on television?" he asked.

"No. I mean, I don't think so."

"Hmm," he pondered.

"*Oü, pospěš si!*" Someone behind her in the queue shouted.

The officer let go, and ushered Cathy through. "Go, go. Next!"

She stuffed the passport into her pocket and hurried to join Dan on the other side of the barrier.

"What happened?" he asked, falling into step.

"Oh my god, he almost recognised me." She slipped the sunglasses back on.

"No way!" he said, tensing up.

"The passport worked, though," she said.

"Does that happen a lot?" Dan asked. He quickly added, "I mean. Did it? You know, before you were a hostage?"

Cathy clenched her jaw. "Subtle. You know, you have a real way with words."

He frowned in confusion.

"Not often, no," she answered, sighing. "I stayed out of the spotlight growing up. My father didn't want me to be a public figure. I guess that officer guy recognised me as the dead girl he saw on the news or something?" She wrinkled her nose at that thought. "That's actually kinda creepy."

Outside the station, they hailed a cab. Dan showed the driver an address he had stored in his phone and the driver set off.

Cathy gazed out of the window at the surreal mix of buildings both modern and gothic. "Wow, check out this place. It's so weird!" She turned to share the moment with Dan, but his face was buried in his phone.

"Mm-hmm," he mumbled. "This Yuma thing is crazy. They think it was caused by solar flares from the sun. How is that even possible?"

Cathy rolled her eyes. *He'd rather look at his phone than admire where we are.* She planted her elbow on the window frame and rested her chin in her palm, soaking up the view. The car crossed over a wide river towards a hillside dominated by a monstrous cathedral. It looked so old and out of place, surrounded by red-roof tiled houses. She whispered, "This place is beautiful."

The cab took them up and over the cathedral hill and into the suburbs. They drove along gridded streets that reminded Cathy of tree-lined roads she had seen in American movies when she was younger. The only thing missing was the white picket fences. The cab pulled up outside a four-storey block of apartments.

Dan paid the driver and after they retrieved their backpacks from the trunk, Dan whipped out his phone again.

"I'll email him."

"Uhh, what's wrong with the doorbell?" Cathy suggested.

"This'll be quicker."

Cathy shook her head, dumbfounded. "You are such a geek."

She followed Dan, typing on his phone, down the path towards the front door. By the time they reached it, the intercom crackled to life.

"Bergazoid? Is that you?"

"Yo dude, I'm here," Dan replied.

"Heeeey," the man on the other end welcomed him warmly. "Come in, my friend. Apartment number six."

The lobby door made a buzzing sound, followed by a *click*.

Cathy frowned. "Did he call you *Bergazoid*?"

"Yeah. " Dan shot her a quick red-cheeked glance before pushing through the door with his head down. "My hacker name. He doesn't know my real name. I don't know his either, he's just Derunox."

Cathy snickered. "I'll never be able to call him that with a straight face, you know that, right?"

A chubby bald man in his early thirties popped his head out of a door as they walked down the corridor. Chillout jazz music poured out of the door with him. "Hello, my friend," he said in a softly spoken Slovakian accent. He held a thick fingered hand out to Dan and slapped him on the back. "It is good to finally meet you in person. You look even younger in real life!"

Dan laughed. "And you look older. And fatter!"

Derunox released Dan from the man-hug and feigned offence with an exaggerated gasp. He wore a black t-shirt emblazoned with a white logo—a burning wall with a bulging eye peering through the brickwork—that fitted rather tight across his round belly. He spotted Cathy over Dan's shoulder. "Bergazoid! Who is your lady friend?"

"Well," Dan scratched the back of his head. "I didn't want to tell you over the Net. Don't you recognise her?"

Derunox frowned for a moment, then studied her more closely.

Cathy tucked both thumbs under the straps of her backpack. *Well, if this isn't the most awkward greeting ever...*

"Should I?" Derunox asked, rubbing his chin.

Okay, enough. Cathy put on her most disarming smile and strolled forward to take his hand. "Hello. My name's Catherine Blunt. I used to be dead."

Derunox blinked and his mouth dangled open. He stared at her, unable to speak for some time.

"Fuck." His friendly manner turned to efficient urgency. "Quickly, come inside." He looked left and right down the corridor as Cathy followed Dan into the dimly lit apartment.

Derunox shut the door behind them and ushered them through to what Cathy assumed was the living room. It was difficult to tell because of all the computers.

Three rows of monitors stacked neatly on top of each other covered two walls of the square shaped room. There were over twenty screens, and no two were alike, each one displayed something unique – several feeds showed news reporters in a studio, others seemed to show CCTV footage, one showed animated robots locked in a space battle, and a few showed nothing but black and white text scrolling up the screen in an endless loop. Together, they cast the room in a flickering glow of soft light, but thankfully they were all muted except the one spitting out the jazz.

Derunox muted the music, and dropped into a high-backed office chair in front of the monitors. His girth filled the chair like a foot in a slipper. Cathy suspected he spent a lot of time in that chair.

"Please, sit," Derunox offered, gesturing to a beanbag on the carpeted floor and a two-seater sofa which was half occupied by a stack of hard drives.

Dan plonked himself into the sofa, leaving Cathy with the beanbag. *Such a gentleman.* She opted to remain standing.

"You have an awesome setup here, man," Dan gazed around the room. "I had two of those at my place in Korea." Dan pointed towards a stack of micro-servers under the desk. Cathy recognised them because they used the same ones in her lab – *Blunt* brand, of course.

"They are very reliable," Derunox nodded. He turned to Cathy. His voice had a warm, knowledgeable tone. "I cannot believe I'm looking at the daughter of the man who created half the equipment here in my humble control centre."

This is what he calls humble? "Don't give him all the credit," Cathy said. "It was my grandfather who started the company. Dad just took over the reins. Um, can we talk about something else?"

Derunox nodded. "You don't like your father." It wasn't a question. He eyed Cathy with a sad smile. "My father disowned me when I was eleven, and it was the best thing that ever happened to me."

"Why?" Cathy asked.

"He did not approve of my sexual preferences." His matter of fact tone caught Cathy off guard.

"Oh?" she uttered.

"I am gay."

"Really?" Dan said, sounding surprised.

"Yes, I hope that doesn't make you uncomfortable?"

"Uh, no." Dan scratched the back of his head.

Cathy recalled her mother's terrible reaction to her and Annie's 'study session.' It was the most humiliating moment of her life. *This guy went through the same experience.*

Derunox chuckled. "To cut a long story short, I left home, and found a new one online. The digital world is far more liberating than the real, and the members of *Binary Eye* are some of its defenders. I felt drawn to the world of programming, and joined their ranks as an underling."

"And now you're one of the elite," Dan gushed. He told Cathy, "Derunox can hack *anything,* any time."

"Heh. You and J-Lord are not so bad yourselves." Derunox added cautiously, "How is the padawan? Did you manage to locate Agent Hawkins?"

Dan hung his head.

He doesn't know about Jimmy...

"Uhh, that's pretty much why we're here," Dan said. His brow furrowed, his mouth opened but he couldn't seem to find the words.

Cathy lowered herself onto the sofa armrest and placed a hand on Dan's arm. She explained, "Jimmy died helping me to escape from the facility."

Derunox exhaled a sad sigh. "I'm sorry to hear this."

"It's okay," Dan gave a little shrug. He sniffed and wiped his eye. "I won't let him die in vain, man. Did you download the datapacket yet?"

"Oh yes," Derunox said with a glint in his eye. "But I was waiting to hear from you about J-Lord before I touched it. It's *heavily* encrypted."

"I know. That's because it contains information about Horizon."

Derunox grabbed the armrests of his chair. "*The Horizon Conspiracy?*" he whispered.

"Exactly," Dan said with a knowing smile. "You saw Bennit0's article, didn't you?"

"Oh, boy. It's my latest obsession." Derunox leaned forward rubbing his pudgy hands together. "He leaked it two months ago. It was around the same time he claimed—" He cut himself short and stared at Cathy.

"What?"

"He claimed that *you* were still alive. And that you two were a couple."

"Yeah," Cathy said at length. "My mother had him killed."

"That is just terrible," Derunox said. "The question is, what is she trying to keep secret? I'd very much like to know that."

"Heh. I knew you would," Dan said.

Derunox leaned back in his chair and steepled his hands in front of his nose. He peered over his fingers at Cathy and Dan. "I am glad you've come to me," he said. "Together, we will figure out this conundrum. I think to start, we must pool our knowledge. If you don't mind, Miss Blunt, I'd like to hear your story. Your involvement in these events must be troubling, I think, so you can say no if you prefer."

"No," Cathy shook her head. "It's okay. What exactly do you want to know?"

Derunox leaned forward in his chair again. "Everything." His kindly eyes gleamed with curiosity. "Start at the beginning. How did you end up working for your mother in that facility?"

Cathy inhaled a deep breath. "Well, eight years ago, when I was in college, I made a friend called Annie Earnshaw…"

She recounted the whole story, from her parents failing marriage, the horror of seeing her best friend violated by her father and her mother's resulting wrath, ending with her working underground for the past six years. It felt oddly satisfying to explain it in depth. Derunox was a stranger, but his interest in her and his friendly demeanour made him easy to open up to.

Dan listened too, which she didn't mind. He may be a socially awkward nerd, but he had gotten her across Europe and his occasional incompetence forced her to find an inner strength she didn't know she had. She felt confident around him. She couldn't remember the last time she felt confident about anything. By the time she had finished her tale, her eyes were sticky with tears and a small pile of snotty tissues rested at her feet. *Gross*, she thought.

"Anyway, we made it through security and now we're here," she finished, spreading her palms. "Dan wants to avenge his brother. I want to avenge Annie and Ben. My parents *deserve* punishment..." She met Derunox's eyes, cast in shadow by the screens behind him. "Will you help us?"

Derunox didn't hesitate. "Of course. And I know how to begin."

"Jimmy's datapacket," Dan said. His eager eyes flickered with the reflections of the monitors.

Derunox grinned. "Yes. Oh yes, this is getting exciting. I'll need your help with the decryption. Are you ready for the challenge, Bergazoid?"

Dan leapt to his feet. "Hell yeah."

Cathy felt a shiver at the raw determination in the air.

"Take a seat next to me, padawan." Derunox rolled over to his bank of monitors. "Let us see what we will see."

21
THE BRIDGE

Dan took a seat next to Derunox, thoroughly distracted by the thought of Cathy in bed with a girl called Annie. *I thought she was into guys.*

"I will use my TX7 to keep us in a walled environment, to be safe," Derunox explained. "There's no knowing what booby-traps might be contained within this data."

"Makes sense," Dan agreed. *Is she into girls as well? Like a lesbian?*

Derunox punched a few lines of code into a terminal and partitioned a safe zone for them to begin decrypting. The files appeared in a long list, thousands of randomly sized chunks of digital information.

"Try this sector," Dan pointed at one particular cluster. "That's where I first spotted the name Horizon. You see?"

"Nice," Derunox said, nodding his head. "Look at that, it's a video file."

Dan frowned. "How can you tell?" *She liked Ben, so surely I have a chance… Don't think about that! Gotta focus, man.*

"I've seen this naming structure before," Derunox tapped the screen with a finger. "It's security footage, you see this is a single part of the video. There should be dozens more like it." He extracted the file and dropped it into another window.

An animation of a key opening a padlock appeared on the screen, above a percentage counter that ticked up to 100% in the blink of an eye.

"Wow, that's fast," Dan said. "But it's only a few megs. That'll be, what, barely a second of video?"

"More like half a second. Watch." Derunox played the clip. An image of an empty observation room appeared, overlooking a white-walled chamber with a set of restraints secured to the wall.

"What is that?" Cathy blurted. Dan jumped. She was leaning over, just behind his ear.

"Seems to be some kind of test chamber," Derunox said.

"Yeah," Dan agreed. "But testing for what?"

"Those restraints," Cathy pointed. "They're for a human..."

All three of them silently digested that.

Cathy gulped. "Is there any more footage?"

"There will be," Derunox said. "I have a piece of software determining where the rest of the fragments are now. It has to sift through trillions of bytes, but it will slowly piece together the whole video."

"That's a good start," Dan said.

"How long will it take?" Cathy asked.

"Who knows?" Derunox shrugged. "I have no idea how long the video file will be. It's from a CCTV camera, so it could be hours."

Dan's stomach grumbled.

Cathy and Derunox both looked at him.

"Heh, I guess I'm hungry?" he said, abashed.

"We are in for an all-nighter I think, no?" Derunox slapped his belly. "We should fuel up."

"Good idea," Dan agreed. "What's the number for a good take-out round here?"

"Take-out?" Derunox shrilled. He broke into a fiendish grin and laughed. It was an absurdly infectious, high-pitched chuckle that made both Dan and Cathy smirk. "No, no," he went on. "I will cook us a meal." He pushed himself out of the chair and ambled into the kitchen.

"A dork who can cook?" Cathy remarked, following him out. "You're full of surprises."

"Is it safe to leave that running?" Dan called, pointing at the padlock animation as it replayed over and over with each newly decrypted segment.

"It's safe in my quarantine zone," Derunox called back. "We can leave it for now. Come."

Dan followed Cathy through to a compact kitchen with a small counter, a sink and an electric oven. Coming from the dark living room, the late afternoon sun shining in through the kitchen window dazzled Dan as it shimmered between the tops of the trees enclosing a communal lawn outside.

"Do you like *goulash*?" Derunox asked.

"I've never had it," Cathy said, propping her butt against the counter.

"Me neither," said Dan. *I don't even know what it is...*

"Ah, you are in for a treat." Derunox laid out several cartons with indecipherable labels and a bowl of brown stew from the fridge. "It is the perfect meal to fill you up after a day on the road. I made this yesterday, but we will need some fresh dumplings. It won't take long."

"I'll help!" Cathy said as she rolled up her sleeves.

Dan watched for a while as the two busied themselves with flour and eggs. *She gets on well with him. Is that because they're both gay?* He felt pretty confused after hearing Cathy's story and he couldn't see any way of being useful to the dinner preparations. "Hey," he said to Derunox. "I'm gonna keep an eye on the decryption. Mind if I surf the Net?"

"Go ahead, Bergazoid. Don't go peeking at our findings without me, though."

Dan held up his hands. "No chance, man. Your gear, your rules."

He returned to the control hub and sat down in Derunox's chair. It was soft and wide and moulded to the shape of the hacker's butt, so Dan had to squirm to find a comfy spot.

He grabbed the mouse and quickly worked out which of

the twenty-four screens responded to it. He went straight to the Eye's forums and skimmed over all of the latest underground happenings.

He found a thread about the Yuma incident and, as usual, nobody could agree on what really happened.

JonJi: it's alien abductions! the hole town is gone. 1 sec ur walkin down the street, next POOF aliens sucking you up. they took every1 for probing.

Deciple_of_the_New_Dawn: Open your hearts to the Lord and give thanks to the sun. For only the sun can bring the Dawn.

GardAX: who invited the God Bot? i saw on the news it was a chemical spill at the oil fields. they had to evacuate everyone for safety

Transient_MetaFour: Duh. What do you expect to happen to the oil plant when everyone working there dies? The oil rigs need people to maintain the coolers. The spill happened AFTER the incident, they're just using that as the excuse to cover it up. Its obviously some terrorist attack.

Frellig: Actually, a phenomenon known as *Z-class Solar Emittance* has vapourised everyone in a concentrated vicinity. Yuma is the sunniest town in America. This event was inevitable.

KRUG: Look At this!! [*Attached picture of a Yuma street littered with clothes.*] WTF how can the sun steal ur clothes? It was EXPERIMENTATION. they injekt u to find out if u hav cancer and then EVERYONE GOT SHRUNK

Herbert472: Good grief. Did none of you learn English?

Roofey: It's happened again! Dongola! LOOK UP DONGOLA.

Transient_MetaFour: Yeah, same shit happened in Dongola. Who the fuck cares about those sand monkeys? Africa is fucked up anyway, their always blowing each other up.

Dan's stomach growled as the scent of baked dough balls and beef stew wafted out of the kitchen.

Cathy and Derunox soon followed, carrying trays of steaming food.

"Look at this, guys," he said, standing to let Derunox reclaim his throne.

The big man took a seat and placed his bowl of goulash next to the keyboard.

"Here, Dan." Cathy handed him a bowl.

"Thanks," he said with a smile.

Cathy bee-lined for the sofa, so Dan dropped into the beanbag.

"This is just terrible," Derunox said, referring to an article about the Dongola incident. "Another town full of people has completely vanished."

"Yeah, just like Yuma," Dan said.

"What caused it?" Cathy asked.

"Nobody seems to know," Dan said. He ate a spoonful of the meaty stew, which warmed him to the core. "Mmm, dude, this is really good."

"Yeah," Cathy said between slurps. "It's delicious."

Derunox spread his palms and beamed. "Yes, let us forget these troubles for now. Feast, my friends!"

By the time they had finished eating, Derunox's software had decrypted a large portion of the security video footage.

He scrubbed through it until two men in lab coats zipped across the room, moving from right to left.

"Hello there, Mr. Scientists," Derunox said. He rewound the video, played it again at normal speed, and turned up the volume so they could hear what the two men were saying.

"According to our analyst, compound G was most effective when applied to the electromagnetic emitter," said one man holding a tablet computer. *"She was right about scrapping compounds K through O as well, so I'm willing to give it a try."*

"Okay then," the second man agreed. *"I'll have them prepare us a new subject."*

Both men disappeared off-screen to the left.

"Well that sure sounds ominous," Dan said.

"Compound G..." Cathy said softly. "I analysed that."

"Really?" Derunox said.

"Do you know what they were talking about?" Dan asked.

"Not really. I mean, I know what compound G was for. They were trying to determine an effective method for targeting human tissue with concentrated electrical impulses. A new form of cancer treatment."

"Did you ever get to see them test it?" Dan said.

"On mice, yeah," Cathy said. "But it didn't work, not the way they intended, anyway. The mice kept dying."

"Would they ever test something like that on people?"

"No!" Cathy said. "At least, they weren't supposed to. Oh god, do you really think...?"

"I can't say for sure until we decrypt more of this footage," Derunox said.

"Fuck," Dan said. A cold shiver rushed through him.

"I think I might take a walk," Cathy said.

Dan darted around. "Right now? Don't you want to find out more about what those people were up to?"

"Um, not especially, no. I *worked* there, Dan. If it turns

out I had something to do with human experimentation… I feel sick just thinking about it."

"We don't know anything yet," Derunox assured her. "Maybe a walk is a good idea. Prague is a beautiful city. You should see the Charles Bridge at night. This decryption will take a while, why don't you both go?"

Dan hesitated. He turned to look back at the screen. The padlock animation replayed in rhythmic repetition with every fragment of decrypted data. This was the data that Jimmy gave his life for, and Dan wanted to see as much of it as possible. "But I—"

"I need to use the bathroom," Cathy said, and walked out of the room.

Derunox slapped him on the arm. "What are you doing?"

"What?" Dan blinked.

"Go with her."

"What?" Dan's cheeks flushed. "No, I…"

"*Ha!*" Derunox squeaked. His voice had a habit of breaking when he got excited, Dan noticed.

Dan scratched the back of his neck.

"I saw her bracelet," Derunox said. "She told me you bought it for her. She wants to add a Prague souvenir to it. That's why she's going. You should go help her choose something!"

"What if someone recognises her?"

"Pah, it's getting dark, and Prague will be full of partygoers, beggars and *milovníci.*" Derunox bounced an eyebrow at that. "Nobody will recognise her tonight."

"What's miloven…mila… whatever you just said?"

Derunox jiggled his shoulders to the beat of an unheard song, and sang, "*Loverrrs,* ooh. *Sexy sexy people.* Yeah!"

Dan stared, horrified.

The toilet flushed.

"You can stay here with me, Bergazoid, or you can go with her." He continued to dance provocatively in his chair. Dan made up his mind.

"You coming or what?" Cathy said, appearing in the door with a hand on her hip.

"Message me the second you find anything, okay?" Dan jumped up from the chair.

Derunox chuckled, shooing him away. "Yes, yes!"

Dan and Cathy left the apartment and walked back through the suburbs to the cathedral hill overlooking the city. The setting sun cast the grand cathedral in sheets of orange and set the river ablaze far below as it wound through the city centre. It was a beautiful view, but Dan was drawn to Cathy's smile, radiant in the glow of the setting sun.

"Have you ever seen such a pretty view?" Cathy cooed.

"No," Dan said. She caught him staring and he averted his eye back to the city.

"Come on," she said. "I want to walk along the river."

They set off down the hill side by side.

Am I having a romantic walk right now? He couldn't think of anything to say, but Cathy didn't speak either, so Dan thought it best to try and enjoy the scenery.

They reached a cobblestoned pedestrian bridge, illuminated by streetlamps and decorated with many statues. At the far end of the bridge rose a gothic clock tower, piercing the clear navy sky, now twinkling with a few bright stars.

They strolled across the ancient cobblestones in the direction of the clock tower. They weren't alone; dozens of other people were enjoying the bridge, many of whom held hands, Dan noticed. *So this is where all the milovníci's go...*

Statues of old priests, kings, and Jesus watched them amble by.

"This is amazing, isn't it?" Cathy said. She wandered over to the edge and rested her forearms on the wall, gazing across the water.

Dan leaned next to her. Her hand rested invitingly on

the cold stone, and Dan fought the urge to touch it. Instead he casually slid his hand closer to hers, feeling the beat of his heart pounding in his chest.

"*Oh!*" Cathy exclaimed.

Dan froze mid-reach and looked up.

She was studying something on the ground to her right. Dan leaned back to peek around her.

There was a lump under a blanket near her feet. When it moved, Dan realised it was a man kneeling on the cobblestones, doubled over with his head low to the ground. He held a paper cup in both hands, outstretched in front of his head.

"Is he begging?" Cathy wondered. "Dan, give him some money."

Dan hesitated. "Okay." He pulled out the wad of notes from his pocket.

"Dan!" Cathy grabbed it. "Remember last time? Be more subtle, please." She glanced around at the couples strolling past.

"Sorry," Dan whispered, tucking most of the notes back into his pocket. Cathy took a ten and placed it into the man's cup.

His head tilted to see, then he nodded vigorously, mumbling something in Czech.

"Look," Cathy said. "There's more."

Sure enough, every twenty paces or so, another beggar knelt on the side of the walkway, hunched over with his head pressed low to the ground, holding out a cup, or a cap, or just his bare hands.

"They're *real* beggars, aren't they?" Dan said. "They look truly humbled."

"Yeah," she cocked an eyebrow at him. "Wouldn't expect that from you."

"What?"

"I dunno. You said something poignant."

Dan flushed.

"Come on, let's share that money. It's not like it's ours,

anyway."

They strolled along the bridge, and Cathy placed a note into each beggar's cup they passed.

"Dan, what's your mother like?" she asked as they walked.

"My mom? Err, she's nice. Why'd you suddenly ask me that?"

"Just curious. What did she think of you going to live in Korea?"

"She didn't know. I didn't tell her until after I got there. She was pretty upset."

"Why didn't you tell her?" Cathy asked, bending down to place another note in a cup.

"I had to keep her safe." He stuffed his hands into his pockets. "Jimmy and me were learning some heavy shit back then. This one time, I even hacked into the FBI. We were becoming real members of Binary Eye, and one of the things they mention is the safety of living alone. It made sense to me."

"Why live by yourself?" Cathy asked.

"It's just better that way. Hacking into big companies is dangerous. Sometimes, if you find out something you shouldn't, they'll send people to your home. Not always police either, but hired thugs, y'know. I'd never forgive myself if someone like that came to my mom's house because of me. So, I left."

"I think I understand."

"Yeah, I mean, look what happened to Ben..."

"Yeah," she said, turning away. "You must've been pretty lonely out there by yourself?"

"Um, yeah. I guess." *Oh boy, talk about an understatement.* "But Korea has some of the fastest Net access in the world. I didn't mind it."

"Heh," she smiled. "So, after this, are you gonna go back home? Your mom must really miss you."

"Probably," he said. "But not before I find justice for Jimmy." He looked at Cathy. "Which might involve, you know, putting *your* mom behind bars."

"She deserves worse than that," Cathy said, clenching her jaw. "I wanted to kill her, after what she did."

"Yeah," Dan said. "I guess I would too."

Her voice grew very soft. "Do you think you could... you know?"

Dan whispered, "Kill someone?"

She laughed. "Never mind, I think we already established you're not built for that line of work." Her smile wavered. "I bet Frank Hawkins has killed people..."

"Yeah, probably." He stuffed his hands back into his pockets. *She must think I'm a total dork.*

A man and a woman making out by the bridge wall caught Dan's eye.

"Dan," Cathy said, stopping in front of him. "There's something I wanted to say to you."

He shivered inside. "Oh, yeah?"

"It's been a long time since anyone treated me with such respect. I'm very grateful to your brother for getting me out of that horrible place. But it's been you who gave me this sense of freedom. I really needed this."

She reached for his arm and pulled one hand out of his pocket, squeezing it in her warm hand. "Thank you, Dan."

He felt his right leg quivering and fought to hold it still. "You were my first kiss," he blurted.

She uttered a laugh, but cut it off. "What?"

She doesn't remember? "You know, back on the roadside, after I gave you that." He glanced at her bracelet.

"Oh," Cathy said. She smiled sympathetically. "Dan, it was only a kiss on the cheek."

His eyes flicked to the couple behind them, still engaged in a passionate embrace.

Cathy turned to follow his gaze. "*That's* a kiss, Dan." She still held his hand, squeezing gently. "I don't want to give you the wrong idea... I think you're sweet, I do."

Dan's heart sank. "But you're actually a lesbian."

She scoffed. "What? No, I'm not."

"Really?"

"No. Why would you... oh, because of my friend Annie?"

"Yeah," he said, heat creeping up his neck.

"A lot of girls go through that, um... phase."

"Oh." Dan felt very out of his depth. "Man, you're right. I'm such a dork."

She cocked her head and wrinkled her brow. "No, don't say that. I'm only teasing when I say things like that."

"Listen, I don't really wanna lose my focus," Dan said. "I'm in this to get payback for my brother."

"And I want the same," Cathy said, pulling his other hand out of the pocket. Now, she clutched both of his hands between them. "We both want the same thing."

I'm not so sure. He knew what he wanted, but had a strong idea what she was thinking of. "Do you want revenge?" Dan said.

She nodded.

For a while, Dan stared into her big, pretty eyes. She chewed her lip.

"Oh, fuck it," she said. Cathy leaned in and planted her lips on his.

Dan's right leg cramped and he toppled sideways, pulling Cathy with him.

She shrieked as they hit the cobblestones.

"Uhh," Dan spluttered, "I'm sorry."

Cathy tittered. "Dan, what the hell?" She laid half on top of him with a hand on his chest.

Several passers-by laughed and commented, and the making out couple stopped to give them a quizzical stare.

"You *are* such a dork." Cathy grinned, staggering to her feet. "Yeah, hope you enjoyed the show," she remarked to the onlookers. She offered Dan a hand, and helped pull him to his feet.

He brushed himself off, his cheeks burning. "Shall we, uhh, go home?"

"No! I haven't even found a new keyring for my bracelet

yet." She held it up to remind him. "Come on, let's go that way."

She took his hand and led him under the clock tower arch, heading deeper into the city.

They discovered an old town square lined with restaurants and gothic architecture. On one side, a merchant stand was selling the usual tatty junk, and Cathy found a tiny keyring of the Charles Bridge.

"It's perfect," she exclaimed.

"Isn't that getting a bit heavy now?" Dan asked as she fitted the new ring.

"Nah, it's okay." She gave a cheeky smirk. "You should get one too." Before he could protest, she snatched up another of the tiny bridges, and bought it. She held it out to him. "This will forever remind you of your first *real* kiss."

He smiled and took the keyring. "Did that count as a real kiss?"

He meant it sincerely, but she gave him a gentle shove. "Don't push your luck, mister."

Just then, Dan's phone beeped. He had hardly given it any thought in the last hour. A message popped up on the screen, an email alert. "It's from Derunox!"

"Oh yeah? What does it say?"

"It's a video." Dan glanced around. "Maybe we shouldn't watch it here..."

"You're right." She pointed to a bench in a dark corner of the square, and they hid in the shadows to watch the video.

The screen showed the observation room with two scientists sitting in chairs overlooking the white test chamber. A man wearing a loose patient gown was escorted into the chamber. He seemed to be heavily tranquilised, or just high, because he offered no resistance when the technicians strapped him to the wall standing up.

Cathy gasped. "No…"

"*Clear the area,*" ordered one of the scientists.

272

"*Initialising.*"

The room cleared of all personnel, leaving the test subject alone on the screen.

"*5-4-3-2- and 1...*"

The chamber lit up bright white and the camera hissed static for a moment.

Dan stared at the screen holding his breath. The static cleared and the test chamber reappeared. There was no sign of the subject, but his gown dangled loose, hanging from the straps on the wall.

A scientist returned and peered in through the chamber. He must have liked what he saw, because he let out a startled cheer. "*Success!*"

The video ended.

Dan swallowed the lump in his throat and slowly turned to Cathy. "I think your mother attacked Yuma."

She covered her mouth with trembling hands and gaped. "Oh, god."

22
SPEECH

In the lounge of their secluded lodge, nestled in the Swiss mountains, Margery draped a red velvet tie around Henry's neck.

The spacious living room resembled a temporary film studio. Cables ran across the floor and reporter Louise Stone was making her final adjustments to a big green canvas against the back wall. The luxurious sofa had been pushed aside to make room for three bright LED lights and a tripod mounted camera.

Henry had donned his best suit for his speech. Now that he'd shaved, he looked elegant and handsome. But Margery couldn't bury the apprehension in her gut.

"This is a very big gamble," she muttered, threading one end of Henry's tie into the other. "I hope you realise the gravity of what you are about to do."

Henry tweaked his cufflinks and gave her a wink. "Relax, Margery. I know what I'm doing."

The wink made her gape in disbelief. She'd never seen him do that. She clamped her mouth shut, determined not to let him see how flustered he was making her. "You do understand that if this backfires, I won't be able to manipulate it for you? The public will see *exactly* what your intentions are."

"And that is why it's going to work," he insisted. "The world is ready for me."

She completed the final thread and eased the Windsor

knot up to his throat, then stepped back to admire him.

Henry put one arm behind his back and stood straight as a post. His dyed black hair reflected the studio lights with a waxy sheen, combed back and neat above his smooth forehead. Dark brown eyes studied her with a cool confidence. Rather than ask what she thought of him, he simply said, "Yes, the world is definitely ready for me."

Henry strode away. He took up his spot in front of the camera.

Louise, bending down to check the tripod, had her arse pointing right at Henry, who promptly started admiring it.

Margery cleared her throat loudly. "Shall I just leave you to it?"

"No," he waved a dismissive hand. "I want you to see this."

Louise finished whatever she was doing and stood up to address Margery. "Just please remain quiet during the recording."

Margery shot her a glare. "I know that."

The young reporter gave a curt nod, unable to maintain eye contact. She scurried around to join the cameraman behind the tripod.

"Just do your job." Margery left it at that.

Henry chuckled.

She redirected the glare his way. "Don't laugh. Nobody is going to take you seriously if you have a cock-sure grin on your face."

"Yes, dear. Now please, sit over there and watch your man address the world."

Margery clenched her teeth. She glanced at Louise, to see if the bitch dared say anything else, but the little whore was fiddling with cables and pretending not to notice. Margery stalked into the shadows behind the camera and sunk into the sofa, where she had a clear view of Henry.

"Okay, Mr. Zhin," the cameraman said. "I think we're good to go. Shall we do a trial run?"

"No need. I want this done in a single take," Henry

explained.

"Oh. Well, it's not live," said Louise. "So we can edit it if we need to."

"No. One take," Henry raised his index finger for emphasis. "Just go for one of those slow zoom-ins on my face towards the end, you know the sort?"

"Uh, yes." Louise exchanged a look with her cameraman. "Sure."

Oh, Henry, you beautiful, arrogant bastard. It wasn't a live broadcast, but Margery still felt nervous enough to want a glass of wine. But it was too late now.

"Make sure you get it right," Henry instructed the cameraman. "I mean it when I say *one take.*"

"Nothing ever goes right on the first take," the cameraman whispered to Louise, not quietly enough.

Henry clapped his hands once. "Enough." The smirk had finally gone from his face, to Margery's relief. Henry gave the pair behind the camera a stern gaze which sent a pleasant shiver down Margery's spine.

After some final adjustments to the camera and lighting, Louise put on her headphones and gave Henry the signal to begin.

A moment of silence fell upon the room. From her seat, Margery admired her man, standing against the green screen, bathed in hot light. He stood straight, rigid yet obviously comfortable, his posture radiating a fearless authority.

"Greetings, brothers and sisters of the world," Henry's clear voice pierced the air as his declaration commenced. "What I am about to say is going to change your life. So, please stop what you are doing, make yourself comfortable and listen. My name is Horatio Zhin and I want to talk to you about the Horizon Initiative."

There it goes. Horizon was the codename they had been using for this project ever since its inception. To date, there had been only one instance of the name leaking to the Net, by Catherine's young IT monkey no less, but

Margery had quelled it early. Still, you could never be too careful, and by using it in his speech, Henry's intention was to reclaim the word in a new, positive light.

Henry smiled right down the lens, oozing charm as he addressed the camera. "Some of you may well be thinking, *why should I listen to this man*? Let me show you something."

He spread his left palm and gestured at the green screen behind him. Margery imagined the Korean War images that would be displayed behind him as he talked the audience through his family history.

"These are my ancestral countrymen. For a great many years, my home country of Korea was split into two warring factions. My mother was a southern *wainbu,* a 'comfort woman,' otherwise known as a prostitute. She was assigned to my father, a northern general. Unlike the other generals, he treated her well, and rescued her from a life of torment and misery. But it would not last." Henry gave a long, mournful blink.

Margery stifled a laugh when she thought he might be about to shed a tear. She knew the story of his parents—a northern man, a southern girl, the most unlikely of love stories. He'd told it with a tone of romanticism which fell on her like a stone in wet sand. She didn't care about his past. All she wanted from him was a better future, one that she could help him build. A future free of the worries that plagued the insignificant masses. Henry's vision of a new world, with the two of them mounted upon its peak.

Henry's speech went on. "At the risk of execution, my father deserted his countrymen and took my mother away from the conflict. Two opposites, united by a powerful force, in this instance, love. And this, friends, is what I want to talk to you about today." He clasped his hands together in front of his chest and slowly interlocked his fingers to emphasise the word. "Unification."

Margery's inner thigh tingled. She crossed her legs in an attempt to subdue the untimely arousal. *I'm going to show you some unification after this, my dear.* She gently bit her lip as it curled in a smile, amused by her own wit.

"Unification is in my blood," Henry continued. "I united my countrymen. But now it is time to unite the world."

Margery leaned back in the sofa, taking it all in. Henry spoke about Yuma and Dongola, and the shitty Australian village with the forgettable name. The three targets of the Horizon Initiative's first phase. Somehow, the peons had successfully bombed all three locations without mishap, and now the global news corporations were beginning to suggest there may be something more to it than mere acts of terrorism. Henry believed the world was ready for a global catastrophe, one that would bring people together for a common cause. Terrorism was so last century...

"The New Dawn believes the sun is flaring up," Henry said. "It seems like something out of science fiction, does it not? Whether true or not, I believe it is a question for the scientists of the world to try to answer. They will be first to benefit from the plan which I have set in motion."

Now we're getting to it, Margery thought. This was it, make or break. So far, Henry had successfully spoken his entire speech without stutter. Maybe he would record it all in one take, after all.

"One thing I know for certain: the power of the sun is a power worth utilising. I believe those innocent citizens should not have died for nothing. In each of the three disaster locations, noted for their yearly abundance of uninterrupted sunlight, the Horizon Initiative is establishing a network of solar power stations. Every man, woman and child who has lost their life to these tragic events shall have a panel erected in their honour, so that even in death they can continue to contribute to the world. In harnessing the power that may have killed them, I like to think we are giving them a little piece of justice." Henry's eyes shone with sincerity as he frowned at the camera.

Margery nodded silently. *This might just work.*

"And what of the energy that we generate? Currently, the

world uses 25 terawatts of power at peak times. The three new super stations that I propose would generate 12 terawatts of power by themselves." He paused to let that sink in. "Yes. In one swoop, we will have nearly halved the demand for fossil fuels, *globally*. For decades, we have searched for a solution to the Carbon Crisis, and here in the wake of tragedy, comes progress. Before the unification of our great continents, such an endeavour would not have been possible, but it is *today*."

Henry briefly outlined his plans for distributing the power across the three continents, with a portion going directly to all the major scientific research establishments in the world, including CERN.

That should keep the boffins from looking too closely at the true cause of these "atrocities", Margery mused.

Henry's voice became soft and reassuring. "To those in mourning, I bid you not to dwell on your losses... But do not forget, either. The memory of our fallen brothers and sisters will live on, powering future generations. Let these terrible events be the spark that triggers a new age of abundance." Henry's head tilted down a fraction but his eyes pointed ever surely down the lens of the camera. Margery hoped the cameraman remembered his cue to commence the slow zoom-in, as this was Henry's big finale.

"For a century, the world has been cast in a shadow of suffering and fear." Henry spread his palms, his voice rising to a crescendo. "Let Mr. Z show you the light beyond the horizon."

Margery choked on her laughter. *Mr. Z? I gave him that!*

The silent aftermath was deafening. Margery's crotch felt tight and pulsing. She held her breath, drinking in the sight of her man bathing in the spotlight.

"Cut," Henry said.

Margery exhaled and stood up. She brushed her skirt down and wiped the corners of her mouth with two delicate fingers, then strode forward onto the makeshift set.

"Well done, Mr. Zhin," Louise was saying. "One take!"

Henry gave a satisfied smile, and met Margery's gaze as she entered the light. "What did you think, beloved?"

"You were exquisite, Mr. Z."

He gave her a sly grin. "Did you like that? My homage to you, my dear."

Margery took him by the hand and pulled him away from the green screen to the back of the room. She was about to march him into the hallway when a thought occurred to her.

She stopped, and turned back to the reporter. "Louise, get the footage into post-production immediately. I want it headlining in every country first thing in the morning."

"Yes, Margery. Of course."

Margery whisked Henry from the room, pulling him behind her. He didn't say anything; there was nothing more to say.

They reached the bedroom. Margery shut the door behind them, and grabbed Henry by the tie.

He held a palm out to her. "Wait."

She froze.

"This is a very expensive suit." He ambled to the wardrobe and slowly, agonisingly slowly, removed his jacket. He slid it onto a hanger and shut the door. "Now, wh—"

Margery shoved him hard in the chest, and he tipped backwards onto the giant bed, laughing. He pulled her down onto him, and tore open her top with a spray of buttons.

She fell upon him, and they devoured each other.

When they were finished, they lay together naked under the canopy of silken bed curtains. Margery nestled her head against his shoulder and draped an arm across his chest. The few hairs he had there were grey, betraying his true age. His Asian heritage, not to mention numerous plastic surgeries, gave him younger looks, but Henry was over sixty. Yet he demonstrated the vigour of a man in his forties when they went to bed, which pleased her enough.

It wasn't his looks that she admired in him, anyway. She admired Henry's soul. He harboured a darkness that she saw reflected in herself, and that brought them closer than she and Sidney had ever been. Sidney was chosen by her parents in an arranged marriage when she was just eighteen. She'd had no say in the matter. How could Henry even compare to that? He had been her choice. And he *was* hers, she told herself. Nothing could tear them apart.

"Phase two will be a resounding success," he said.

She lifted her head to look at him. He was gazing thoughtfully across the room.

"I think so, too," she agreed. She pinched his chin gently between thumb and forefinger, and tilted his head towards her. "Your speech was incredible." She kissed him on the lips. "The whole world will be behind you after that."

He smiled, stroking her shoulder. "Phase three will pose the real challenge," he said.

Margery stiffened ever so slightly. She didn't know anything about phase three. Henry had organised it by himself with his team. He'd kept her in the dark, which only fuelled her suspicions. That frightened her.

Foolish woman. Don't think about that, not here, not now. She hugged his chest, trying to get as close to him as possible. "It's nothing we can't handle," she said, more to convince herself than him. He didn't need convincing of anything.

"I know," he said, as if it were obvious. "You don't doubt me, do you dear?" he asked.

She nuzzled her head against his chest. "No."

He didn't speak. She thought he was waiting for her to say more, but she daren't. She'd already said too much.

"What is it?" he asked, shifting beneath her.

No, don't move, just stay here.

He lifted her chin to meet his eyes. His gaze bored into her, as if searching for something. "My Margery, I do not recognise that expression in you. What's on your mind?"

Margery swallowed. She suddenly felt rather cold, so she pulled the covers up around her chest and leaned against the headboard. "Henry, it's just… Phase three."

"Yes?"

She chose her words very carefully. She couldn't afford to show weakness to him, not now. She wouldn't lower herself to that of some petty wench worried about trivial matters. "It has to do with the population problem, doesn't it?"

"Yes."

"I am not clear on the details. You haven't explained it to me." She inhaled a short breath, and forced herself to meet his eyes. "I want to know everything."

Henry eyed her for a moment, reading her. A sly smile crept across his mouth, and his hard gaze softened. "Of course you do. Simply put, our solar plants will only sustain half the planet's energy consumption. It's an impressive figure, but there's still that other half to consider. Once governments realise how much money we are saving them, they will endeavour to build their own plants across the globe, and reclaim a large percentage of our control."

She nodded. This part she understood already. Henry didn't have the manpower to sustain control across all three continents for long. It was too much. They would be forced to construct more plants, which would be unfathomably expensive. This was the point where her calculations ceased, because she couldn't see an easy answer to that predicament.

No, *easy* wasn't the right word; she couldn't see a *moral* answer…

"Phase three is where we ensure our control," he went on. "The people must require *our* service, and not their governments. But, given the choice, they are not guaranteed to choose us. So, we must give them only one choice." He paused, giving her time to consider that. "Phase three is where we establish our empire."

She liked the sound of that. Margery wanted nothing more than to be queen of her own empire. But he was still being coy over the specifics.

She was disturbed to find a tightening in her stomach. She recognised the sensation, because she had felt it once before, back when she was very young, about to be thrown into a marriage that she didn't want.

It was anxiety. She felt anxious about the unknown. Not knowing was the worst part. Back then, she didn't know whether she could love a man she had never met, even if he was a rich businessman. And now, Henry was keeping something from her, something important, and the fact that she didn't *know* was starting to drive her mad.

I have to know.

"Henry, if phase two is successful, we will provide energy for just over four billion people."

"Four point two five billion," he corrected.

"Right. That's half the population of the planet. So... how do you plan to gain control of the other half?" She stared into his eyes, the butterflies in her stomach reaching a fluttering crescendo.

"I will remove them," he said.

He's going to murder four billion people.

The butterflies dropped dead. Margery went numb, starting in her toes and rippling up through her midriff and ending with her face. She shut her eyes. Her breath had become short, tiny bursts. A blank void had engulfed her core. *He's going to murder four billion people...* The tingling began in her pelvis. It intensified the moment she recognised it, and soon spread across her waist, down her legs, up her spine and pulsed its way through her chest. She moaned and shuddered.

When she opened her eyes, Henry was gazing at her with a boyish grin on his lips. "Did you just come?"

She flushed beetroot red and nodded, breathless. There were no words to describe how that felt. Her anxiety had vanished. She felt no fear. In that moment, she believed she would never know fear again. So long as she and Henry were together, there was nothing they couldn't accomplish.

PART FIVE

23
REARMED

Frank jolted awake as blinding light stabbed through his retinas.

He tried to shield his eyes but found his arms numb and unresponsive, strapped down against the bed. He flopped his head back into the pillow and clamped his eyelids shut again.

"Where am I?" he croaked. His throat tasted like he'd swallowed a bucket of gravel and his demand turned into a hacking cough. He tried again, "*Where am I?*"

He eased his eyes open and squinted against the row of intense spotlights embedded in the concrete ceiling. He winced and surveyed the room. Four solid grey walls surrounded him. To his right was a long mirror next to a metal door.

Then he noticed his new arm.

He stared at it, slowly looking down its length from shoulder to fingers. It was sleek, polished titanium, painted black and streaked with stainless steel. The arm connected to his shoulder via a moulded cup that had been grafted into his collarbone. It lay beside him, strapped to the bed at the wrist and elbow.

The pain behind his eyes vanished in an instant. He tried to swallow and nearly choked. All the moisture had gone from his mouth, and a spine tingling shiver crawled down the length of his back.

He tried to move his fingers, but they didn't respond.

The arm was heavy and lifeless at his side, a lump of cold, dead metal.

Fuck you, Blunt. Fuck you.

He glared at the mirror, wondering if anyone might be watching him. "Are you out there?" he yelled, his throat burning. He sputtered and coughed, spitting bile. "Who the *fuck* do you think you are? *Get in here you bastard!*"

His head started to spin, a dizziness brought on by overexertion. He lay back and forced himself to steady his breathing.

How dare he do this to me?

Ten years Frank had been a Europa infiltrator and never suffered an injury like this. A few near misses, sure. He'd been shot a couple of times, but he prided himself on his ability to deal with pain and get on with the job.

Replacing his arm was a massive insult.

It looked to be a very expensive and highly advanced prosthetic, but it didn't change the fact that Frank hadn't been given a choice. When they captured him in England, he'd assumed Blunt would offer him medical treatment so long as he cooperated. A splint and some aspirin, that's all he needed. Not this.

A bubble of rage formed in the pit of his stomach. It simmered as he lay motionless in the bed, too furious to react.

A tinny voice filled the room. "Hello, Agent." A thick German accent, it had to be the doctor. Doctor Gunther, Frank recalled.

"Fuck you!" Frank said, and broke into another fit of coughing.

The mirror shimmered and turned transparent. Gunther wagged a finger at him through the glass. "Now, now, Agent, your throat must be very sore. It's a side effect of the anesthesia. I will bring you a glass of water soon. But first, there is something I would like you to do for me."

The only thing I'm doing for you is breaking your neck the moment you walk through that door. The question was how to bring

Gunther into the room? The door looked solid, and was no doubt locked. The concrete walls lent the room a cell-like claustrophobic air. *It's a quarantine chamber*, Frank realised.

"I would like you to move your arm, Agent," the doctor continued. "The new one," he clarified, with smug authority. "I'm switching it on now."

Switching it on? What the fuck?

A hot shock zapped down the length of his metal arm. Frank's eyes bulged and he gave an involuntary grunt. In an instant, the dead arm had become part of him. He could *feel* it waking up. The nerves around his shoulder sang, tingling with energy. It didn't hurt, it felt incredible. Frank sensed the arm coming to life, merging with his organic sensory systems.

"Please try to move your fingers, Agent."

He felt an overwhelming desire to move the arm, to experience its power, to allow that pleasurable sensation that was happening at the joint of his shoulder to spread throughout his body at the mere wiggle of a finger.

No. Make him think it's broken, then he'll have to come in here.

Frank resisted, and with an almighty effort he held the arm dead still.

"It's not working," he wheezed. He focused on breathing, long and slow, steadying himself until the temptation settled. The arm felt ready, like a snake poised to strike. His left hand, meanwhile, had clenched into a fist so tight that every knuckle had gone pale.

"Hmm," the doctor mused. "One moment." The intercom *clicked* as he shut off the speaker and the window shimmered back into a mirror.

The door unbolted and swung open.

A submachine gun barrel entered first, pointed at Frank's head. Frank recognised Harrison, one of Blunt's mercenaries. "No sudden moves now, Agent."

A doctor followed him in, but it wasn't Gunther. An assistant, Frank assumed. He had receding hair and pallid skin, suggesting a man in his late fifties, but his appearance could easily be the result of too much time spent in a lab away from sunlight. The door closed with a heavy *clunk*. The assistant walked around the bed to the right hand side where Frank's arm lay.

Gunther's voice came loud and clear through the intercom again. "The doctor is going to examine your arm. Please lay very still, Agent."

The assistant didn't even look Frank in the eye, his attention went straight to the arm. He bent to study it like a man fretting over a wounded pet. He mumbled something in German, his voice sounding confused and worried. Frank felt his body tightening with anticipation as the assistant loosened the restraints to gain access to the arm's underside.

I'm gonna throw you into Harrison.

To Frank's surprise, his new arm responded to the thought. He tore free of the restraints and grabbed the assistant by the belly. He felt the pudgy fat squeezed within his fingers with remarkable clarity, as the doctor's face wrinkled in an expression of extreme pain.

Frank launched him across the room.

The assistant's body slammed Harrison against the concrete wall and they both landed in a heap on top of one another.

Frank ripped off the restraints holding his natural arm and leapt out of the bed. He marched across to Harrison and wrenched the gun from his grip. Frank pulled the assistant up by the collar, and spun him around. Aiming the gun at Harrison with one hand and squeezing titanium fingers around the pudgy assistant's throat with the other, he turned to the mirror.

"*Open the door!*" Frank bellowed.

Silence.

Frank coughed and spat on the floor. "Open the door, or I'll *break his fucking neck!*" He squeezed tighter. The doctor's eyes bulged and he made a desperate grunting sound, feebly pawing at Frank's metal arm.

The intercom crackled. "Please do." Gunther didn't sound surprised. He didn't sound upset, or concerned, or anything close. He sounded *curious*.

Frank frowned in disbelief. *Are you kidding me?* Gunther's disregard for the assistant's life only intensified Frank's fury.

He threw the assistant towards the wall, but the arm was stronger than he realised. The man's skull went *crack* and a spatter of blood sprayed onto Harrison's face.

"W-why'd you do that?" Harrison stammered.

"I didn't mean to." Frank held up his hand, in awe of its absurdity.

Frank had no time to feel remorse. This was Gunther's fault, not his. *If he won't open the door, I'll just punch through the window.*

He turned to the mirror and thrust his fist straight towards the glass.

Something alien within his nervous system switched on before the fist could make contact. Frank's arm froze in mid-punch, his clenched fist barely an inch away from the mirror.

Frank couldn't move it.

"What the shit! *How can you do that?*" he shouted. The arm was frozen solid, hanging in front of him. He bellowed at his reflection, "Let me the fuck out of here now you piece of sh—!"

The arm moved of its own accord. The fingers unclenched and flew towards his face. It grabbed around the neck and squeezed. Frank stumbled backwards, choking.

In a mad panic, he fired Harrison's submachine gun at the glass, the gun jackhammering in his feeble off-hand grip. The glass cracked but didn't break, and bullets ricocheted all over the room.

Frank fired until the clip was empty then dropped the gun. He writhed, grabbing at the arm with his natural hand

and tried to pry it away from his throat. The hand squeezed tighter, and he felt blood pulsing in his forehead.

He stumbled to his knees on the hard concrete, then slammed his metal elbow against the floor, which only resulted in jabbing the fingers deeper into his throat.

He was strangling himself to death.

Tears filled his eyes and the room went fuzzy. He rolled onto his back, the bright lights glimmering through the watery haze.

Fuck. I'm gonna die.

A dark acceptance settled over him, the fiery rage in his belly extinguished as he felt the last of his energy draining from his body. His new arm pulsed with an alien presence, nothing like the pleasurable sensation he felt when Gunther first switched it on. This was an outside force, an invader telling the arm what to do.

Frank gasped for air, fighting for a few more seconds of life. The fingers loosened a fraction, and a trickle of air found its way to Frank's lungs. He rasped on it, sucking it down as hard as he could. Then he exhaled, long and strained, like blowing through a clogged straw. In and out, he wheezed long, painful breaths, barely getting enough oxygen to stay conscious.

He could breathe. He was still alive.

Gunther's head loomed into view above him. Frank had succeeded in luring him into the room, but now he hadn't the energy to do anything about it. His hearing tuned in and out as Gunther spoke to him. "It seems to me the prosthetic is working just fine." With a satisfied smile, Gunther held up a device and pressed a button.

Frank's metal fingers unclenched themselves from his neck. He gasped, sucking in deep lungful's of air, before all his energy went into another fit of coughing. He rolled onto his front, trying to push himself off the floor, but couldn't. The arm had gone limp by his side, a dead weight hanging from his shoulder.

"You were right about installing that failsafe, doctor."

Blunt's voice. He sounded clearer, Frank's hearing seemed to be coming back, now that the blood was circulating his head again. "Although, it was too late for Harrison."

Frank turned and saw that the mercenary had caught a stray bullet in the eye.

Frank cleared his throat and spat out a thick blob of blood and phlegm. He slumped onto his butt and leaned back against the wall, dragging his arm with him. "What the fuck have you done to me?"

"Improved you!" Gunther exclaimed.

Blunt pointed to the arm. "That is my latest prototype. You won't find anything like it outside of my test lab. Even the military haven't got this technology yet." He hunkered down in front of Frank. Frank wanted to knock his head off, but he was too drained to try. "I trust you understand the situation you're in, Agent Hawkins?"

Frank scoffed. "Yeah. I get it. I'm your hostage."

"What? No." Blunt frowned. "You're my new asset."

"I don't think so."

"I have spoken with your chief," Sid explained. "You were right about her. As soon as she knew that I had you, she classified you as KIA. Officially, you're now dead."

"Oh, I'm not dead yet."

A flash of worry passed across Blunt's face. "I know. But I hope that little demonstration proved how easy you could be. If I wanted it."

Frank couldn't deny it. Strangling himself to death with his own arm had to be among the top five ways he didn't intend to die. It was up there with being eaten by a shark or drowned in a vat of molten plastic.

He nodded at Blunt.

"Good." Blunt stood up. "I'm glad we have an understanding. So, your first task will be to help me find Catherine. I hold you personally responsible for her disappearance. You will do this for me, won't you?"

Cathy...where could she be now? Frank did want to see her again. He could do this. Find Cathy, bring her home, then see what happens. Better than being dead, after all. "Okay." He coughed, and spat again, aiming for Gunther's shoes. The doctor stepped back and screwed up his face. "But like I told you before, I have no idea where she is."

"Well, fortunately, your boss has some questionable morals," Sid said. "Her help was expensive, but I suppose everyone has their price."

"You bribed her?" *What the fuck are you playing at, Chief?*

"Yes. She is making efforts to find Catherine for me. No doubt covering her own rear end, but at least you two won't be searching alone."

"Two?" Frank frowned.

"Every asset needs a partner, Mr. Hawkins," Sid said. He waved at the mirror.

Arnie Dillon rolled into the room on a wheelchair, examining Frank with all smugness and no pity.

"You gotta be kidding me," Frank muttered.

Arnie admired Frank's arm, nodding with approval. "Looks like we're even now, bro." He said to Gunther, "Come on, doc. You're finished with him, now it's my turn."

24
SUSPICIONS

"There's been a third incident," Derunox said as soon as Cathy and Dan stepped through the front door.

"A third?" Cathy gasped. "Where?"

She followed him through the apartment back to the control hub. Derunox fell into his chair and pointed at one of the monitors.

"A small village in Australia called Tarrow Creek," he said. "Several hundred people missing, presumed dead."

"That's much smaller than Yuma and Dongola," Dan pointed out.

"But why those places?" Cathy asked. "What's their connection?"

"There's not a lot to compare them," Derunox said. "They're on three different continents and as you say, their sizes don't even relate. Yuma's a city, Dongola is a small town, and Tarrow Creek is barely a village. The only link I could find is that each place rests in a geological suntrap— they all have over 90% year-round sunshine. Apart from that, there's seemingly no correlation."

"We saw the experiment video, dude," Dan said. "Tell me you've noticed the similarities? Horizon has to be some kind of weapon, right?"

"We don't know that yet," Cathy insisted. She didn't want it to be true. How could she? If they had really developed a mass-killing device, then was *she* partially responsible for all these deaths? "I think I'm gonna be sick."

"New Dawn are loudly supporting this mad theory about sun flares," Derunox went on. "A group of professors have spoken out to verify it, and it's gained a surprising amount of traction online."

"The sun doesn't vapourise people!" Dan cried. "That's just fucking insane. How can people believe that?"

"Well, New Dawn have shown an increase in supporters over the past few months," Derunox said in a worried tone. "The CERN disaster has fuelled their influence massively this week. They believe that God is punishing us for meddling with science, and people are taking them seriously."

"What has that got to do with the sun?" Cathy said.

"Nothing," Dan snorted. "It's bullshit."

"But people want answers," Derunox shrugged. "Religion always manages to explain the unexplainable."

"What are the authorities saying about it?" Cathy asked, hoping for some reassurance.

"All three locations have been quarantined," Derunox said. "Nobody's being allowed in to investigate, but take a look at this. A journalist managed to sneak into Yuma and upload a video. It's not been seen outside of the Shadow Net, which suggests the mainstream media don't want to touch it. Make of that what you will…"

Derunox pointed at another monitor and maximised the video.

It started with shaky footage of feet running along a dusty road. Distant shouting could be heard, and heavy panting. *"I just made it through the barricade,"* the reporter wheezed. *"I'm running down Main Street towards the town square. I can't believe what I'm seeing."* More huffing and puffing. He slowed, and panned the camera around.

The town square looked like a film set from a disaster movie. Black smoke billowed out of burning buildings, and abandoned cars littered the scene—some overturned, others jutting out of shattered shop windows where they had crashed.

"I only have a few seconds before they catch me. But look… where is everyone?"

There wasn't a person in sight, only clothes. Jackets, shirts, shorts, all either scattered or lying in small heaps. Cathy found the shoes really harrowing. Pairs of them lying next to the clothes, one in front of the other, as if the owners had all decided to go barefoot mid-stride and leave them in the street.

She put a hand to her mouth. The piles of clothes bore a striking resemblance to the test subject in the security footage they had seen earlier that night. She swallowed, her throat dry as sandpaper.

"That's so fucked up," Dan said. "The clothes man, it's just like—"

"Don't!" Cathy blurted. "Don't say it, Dan. How could they? *How?*" A cold flush crept up her neck so she hugged herself tight. "We still don't know anything for sure. It might be a coincidence."

Dan chewed his lip.

We both know it's not.

"You're right," he said. "We don't know anything for definite yet. I'm going to stay up and keep looking for evidence."

"I can't watch anymore," Cathy said, stepping back away from the screens. She hugged herself.

"It's okay," Dan said. "You don't have to. Just rest."

"I don't have a spare bed," Derunox said, apologetically. "But you can borrow my sleeping bag, and the couch is very comfortable."

Dan flicked his eyes to the sofa and scratched the back of his neck. "I guess I'll crash on the floor, then."

"Thank you," she said.

Derunox hauled himself out of the chair. "I'll get you that sleeping bag."

Cathy's mind whirred as soon as her head hit the sofa cushion. All night long, she shifted in the sleeping bag trying to forget the image of the man in the lab that haunted her thoughts. Her colleagues had murdered him with some kind of experimental weapon.

If only I had known...

But even if she had known, what could she have done about it? Ben suspected something, and when he tried to leak it to the Shadow Net, her mother executed him. Margery knew everything, it seemed.

No matter how much she tossed and turned, Cathy couldn't find a comfy spot, even though the couch was as soft as the big man who owned it. The overwhelming guilt made it feel like a bed of nails.

Then there were the shoes. The shoes of Yuma, accompanied by the scattered clothing, reminded her of the test subject's empty gown dangling from the restraints—the only evidence that he had been there at all. Could the same thing have happened to the people of Yuma, Dongola, and Tarrow Creek?

It's not the same. That was a small, localised experiment. It wouldn't be big enough to affect an entire town.

Two ghouls looked down at her accusingly. It was Dan and Derunox's shadows, cast against the ceiling by the computer monitors' ambient glow. The guys were whispering, reading more threads and watching video reports.

Cathy turned over, letting out a groggy moan. *Please, I just want to fall asleep.*

In a rare moment of social grace, Dan finally suggested they shut down the computers so that Cathy could get some sleep. She heard him rustling about as he made a bed out of spare cushions and a sheet, followed shortly by Derunox's heavy feet padding past. Finally, the room went dark.

But she still couldn't sleep. Images of the test subject and all those abandoned shoes crept into every thought, and she felt an ache in her chest, a soreness that intensified whenever her brain tried to link the two together.

If this is Horizon... then why?

When dawn finally came, Cathy silently cursed the morning sun that poked through the blinds, slowly filling the room with hazy light.

She lied there, exhausted and anxious, waiting for Dan or Derunox to wake up.

Dan didn't stir until 9:30. She envied him for his ability to completely switch off his brain. *Stupid boy.*

He yawned and sat up, rubbing his eyes. "Mornin'. Did you sleep okay?"

Cathy looked at him sideways, her ear against the cushion and the rest of her body snuggled up inside the sleeping bag. She nodded once. "Mm."

He gave her a sleepy simper, then shambled to the bathroom.

Cathy closed her eyes, willing herself to sleep, but her body clock refused to acknowledge the request. It was time to get up.

She pushed her zombified body out of the sofa, and stretched. Her back clicked, making her wince. After pulling on her hooded sweater, she wandered into the kitchen.

Dan walked in after and poured himself a glass of water. "Wow, you look really bad," he said.

She glared at him. "Thanks!" *What a jerk.*

"Sorry, I didn't think—"

"No, of course you didn't." She folded her arms. "You just say whatever pops into your damn head."

He looked like he was about to say something else, but then gulped his water instead.

"Good morning!" Derunox beamed as he flowed into the kitchen wearing a big white dressing gown. He moseyed over to the fridge and pulled out a bottle of banana milkshake. "Help yourself to whatever you like." He ambled back out into the living room. Cathy heard the whirr of his computers powering up.

Despite herself, she smiled. Derunox's merry demeanour had somehow brightened her mood a little. She felt bad about snapping at Dan, he hadn't really done anything wrong. She was just exhausted.

Dan helped himself to a bowl of cornflakes and sat down at the kitchen table to eat it.

Cathy stared at the contents of the fridge blankly for a while, but decided she didn't even want anything.

She closed the fridge, pulled out a chair and sat down opposite Dan. "I'm sorry," she said. "I actually didn't sleep very well... I don't feel too good."

He met her eyes and blinked, chewing on his breakfast. "It's all right."

Cathy stared at the tablecloth. "So, um. Did you find out anything?"

"About the disasters? Yeah, a bunch. They've counted over two hundred thousand people missing now. *Two hundred thousand!* It's the worst disaster, natural or otherwise, in recorded—" He stopped when he saw her horrified face. "Um, but we... there's still no solid proof... You know, there's no evidence of Horizon yet. A lot of people are buying the solar flare argument. Can you believe it?"

"I want to," Cathy said desperately. "Anything to prove I didn't help murder two hundred *thousand* people." She buried her face in her hands and pulled her cheeks downward. "Ugh."

Dan reached out and squeezed her hand. "This is not your fault at all. Don't worry. Please don't worry."

She looked at their hands, hers cupped within his. *He feels much more than I do. Maybe I shouldn't have kissed him.* She sighed, unable to look him in the eye. He squeezed a little harder and caressed the back of her hand with his thumb.

"Aren't you hungry?" he asked.

"Not really. Maybe later."

A voice drifted into the kitchen from one of Derunox's

computers. *"What I am about to say is going to change your life."*

"What's he watching?" Dan said, peering towards the door.

"My name is Horatio Zhin, and I want to tell you about The Horizon Initiative."

Cathy sat bolt upright. *Zhin? My mother's partner!*

Dan gaped. "Did he say *Horizon?*"

They scrambled out of their seats and darted from the kitchen.

"I'm speaking to you today not as a politician, or entrepreneur, or even a Neo Asian, but as a humble human."

"What the fuck is this?" Dan said, leaning over Derunox's shoulder.

"It's trending all over the Net," Derunox replied. "It was uploaded this morning and already has over fifty million views. Shh, let's listen."

Cathy gaped at the image of Horatio Zhin on the video, superimposed against a backdrop of planet Earth, drifting through space. The background zoomed all the way into Korea, replaced by snapshot images of its citizens.

"These are my fellow countrymen," Zhin said.

The scene changed to ancient black and white archive footage of the Korean War from nearly eighty years ago; soldiers fighting in forests and fields and cities, scenes of devastation and lines of marching troops.

"Oh yeah, it's him!" Dan grabbed his hair with one hand and pointed at the screen with the other. "He's the guy who orchestrated the Korean Union. He's a fucking hero over there."

Cathy hugged her stomach, a nasty knot had begun to tighten inside. "He always seemed like a bit of a creep, to me."

"Oh shit, of course," Dan said. "He worked with your father, didn't he?"

"Yeah. I never met him though." Her tone was distant and flat. "He was my dad's business partner. And then my mother's sexual partner."

Derunox turned his head to face her. His eyes were wide, but he said nothing. Slowly, he turned back to continue watching the video.

"*Unification is in my blood,*" Zhin was saying. "*I united my countrymen, but now it is time to unite the world.*" The background changed to show a series of well-known international disasters, including hurricane Katrina, the 2010 Haiti earthquake, and the Asian tsunamis of 2004 and 2022. "*Since the turn of the century, we have faced many catastrophes, and it seems Mother Nature has struck again. No doubt you will have seen the reports from Yuma, Dongola and Tarrow Creek...*"

Cathy's stomach hit the floor.

Dan folded his arms and hunched himself up, staring intently at the video.

Cathy tasted acrid bile in the back of her throat. She swallowed it back down.

"*My heart goes out to all of those affected in this most recent of global tragedies.*"

"My ass," Dan muttered. "How can anyone believe this bullshit?"

Derunox gave a casual shrug. "People haven't seen the video we have seen. If they had, well..." He made a see-saw motion with his hand.

"But *why* is he doing this?" Cathy said.

"*The three new super stations that I propose would generate 12 terawatts of power by themselves. Yes. In a single stroke, we will have nearly halved the demand for fossil fuels, globally.*"

"Woah," said Dan.

"*Of the energy generated from the stations, twenty percent will be directed to all of the major scientific research establishments around the world – ICSU, UNESCO, CERN, the L.R.A, and CSIRO – these global organisations, among others, are striving to understand the world we live in, and perhaps will one day uncover ways to prevent such disasters as these recent calamities. To those in mourning, I bid you not to dwell on your losses. But do not forget either...*"

"What a clever bastard," Dan scathed. "He just secured

himself a global energy contract and bribed all of the people capable of proving his guilt with the same dice roll."

Derunox frowned. "What do you mean?"

"Think about it!" Dan spread his hands. "This guy fucking bombed those towns. You know it, I know it. Yet half the world thinks it was the goddamn sun, and instead of being hanged for genocide, he's gonna be marked a hero... listen to this shit!"

"*For a century, the world has been cast in a shadow of suffering and fear. Let Mr. Z show you the light beyond the horizon.*"

"Oh my god, he's not even subtle!" Dan cried. "*Mr. Z?* He's acting like a fucking supervillain!"

The video came to an end with Zhin fading out to reveal a spectacular cosmic sunrise appearing behind the Earth before the whole image burned out white.

Cathy didn't know what to say. She felt numb from anger. It occurred to her that the nausea had passed, replaced by a terrible sense of hurtful rage. She wasn't to blame for those deaths. Zhin had designed it all.

"He must be Henry," Cathy said with realisation.

"Henry?" Dan said.

"Yes. Back in the facility, right before the explosion, my mother called to warn me about getting out. I overheard her talking to a man called Henry… he was the one who gave the order to destroy the facility."

"You think Henry is actually Horatio?" Derunox mused.

"His real name is Hyun-Ki," Dan pointed out. "Horatio is his adopted western name."

"I see," Derunox said.

If Zhin was the mastermind, then Cathy's mother was the accomplice. She had the contacts and the power over the media to spin this her way. It all made sense; they were perfect for each other. *No wonder she left Dad...*

Cathy clenched her jaw, trembling with anger. "We have to stop them," she said softly. "I think I know how."

Derunox and Dan turned to her. "How?" Derunox

asked.

"You said it yourself," Cathy went on, "The people need to see what we've seen. We have to release our own video, one that will draw the media's attention away from Zhin, and cast him in a darker light."

"Yes," Dan exclaimed, his face lighting up. "We expose them! We have video evidence of their weapon test."

"Not only that," Cathy said, showing off a cunning smile. "We show *me*. The world thinks I'm dead, so let's show them the truth."

"Ooh," Derunox said.

"You worked there, you can be a whistleblower!" Dan cried.

"I have a camera," Derunox said. "I sometimes make home movies, we can give it a bit of spark, just like Zhin's."

"Ahe," Cathy said, not wanting to think about the sort of home movies Derunox might enjoy making. "We'll need more than a single clip, though. Dan, do you think you can find more evidence of their experiments?"

"Sure. How much did we decrypt last night, dude?" he asked Derunox.

"All of it," Derunox grinned. "I had it running overnight in my TX70. Everything is revealed to us now."

"That's brilliant!" Cathy said. "You guys are the best. Together, we're going to reveal Horatio Zhin's true colours. He needs to pay for what he's done." She clenched her fists in giddy excitement at the best part. "And as a bonus, his downfall will destroy my mother."

25
HACKING

Dan cracked his knuckles and wriggled his fingers to loosen them up. He clicked open a window, displaying every single file from Jimmy's datapacket. With the decryption complete, everything was now there in plain readable formats – documents, emails, photos, videos, web browsing history, phone logs, address books, employee details; there must have been years' worth of archived data.

While Derunox and Cathy were outside in the communal garden recording her video, Dan had the job of finding more evidence of the vapourisation experiment. If the weapon was capable of wiping out an entire city, they had to have tested it on a larger group of people first. Cathy was relying on him to find something like that for her video.

He filtered through the files, watching snippets of the same laboratory over and over. Most of the videos showed nothing but an empty test chamber, but finally, after twenty minutes of tedious search, he struck gold.

An entire flock of scientists had gathered in the observation room, all watching as seven gowned men were secured to the wall of the test chamber.

"*Initialising in ten...nine...eight...*"

The countdown reached zero and the camera went fuzzy for a moment, blinded by a bright white light. When the image refocused, all seven men inside the chamber were gone. Their gowns lay in crumpled heaps along the floor.

Dan squeezed his cheeks with a hand, feeling a little sick. "This is so fucked up," he muttered.

He considered searching for another clip, but he didn't really want to see any more murders. *I wonder if Jimmy was caught on camera?* The chance to see his brother one last time was too tempting to resist.

He filtered the videos into reverse-timestamp order, so that the newest videos were at the top. Scrolling through, he found a video taken from a camera just outside the main server farm. *That's where Jimmy sent me the files from.*

Dan scrubbed through the video until a red pulsating light started flashing through the corridor. Dozens of technicians began filing past the camera, all heading in one singular direction. But then two figures emerged from the server room, and forced their way through the crowd.

Dan hit pause.

He leaned closer to the screen. Frank Hawkins was the man in front, and following behind was Jimmy. *There you are, little bro.*

Dan swallowed the lump in his throat and a tear welled in the corner of his eye. The thought that Jimmy died just minutes after this video was taken filled Dan with an empty sadness.

If only Jimmy could see what Dan was doing now. He was on the brink of uncovering a bona fide global conspiracy. They'd fantasised about this sort of shit so many times, back when they were learning how to hack. Binary Eye's entire philosophy was built around the concept of illuminating the evil that lurked in the world's shadows.

But Horatio Zhin was hiding in plain sight.

A crazy idea struck.

Zhin's home address might be in the employee files. What if I found out where he lives?

He glanced about the room, a bout of paranoia sweeping through his bones. He swallowed. Surely Zhin wouldn't be that stupid to record his address?

After a final look at Jimmy's face on the frozen video, he clicked it shut. *You didn't deserve to die there. I'm doing this for you, Jimmy.*

Dan brought up the records, and ran a search for 'Hyun-Ki Zhin.'

```
0 results.
```

Of course, he usually went by 'Horatio' Zhin. He tried searching that, and then 'Henry' Zhin.

```
0 results.
```

He tried just 'Henry.'

```
16'382 results.
```

The name was too common. Dan exhaled a long, frustrated grunt.

So, Zhin wasn't stupid enough to leave any trail of himself. Dan rubbed his chin. He brought up the address book files and ran a search for Zhin, boss, CEO, leader, all to no avail. He tried searching for *egotistical maniac douchebag* as well.

Nothing.

No trace of the guy. Dan blew air through his teeth, squinting with one eye. There had to be *something* here about him. He was their leader, after all.

"Think man, think." He poked his tongue into one cheek, then started making fish noises with his lips. This was seeming like a dead end, and a big waste of time.

In a flurry of blasé hope, he ran a search for *Mr. Z.*

```
1 result.
```

Dan read the line and assumed it said 0 at first. He did a double take and nearly fell out of the chair.

The file was an email. It had been sent from none other than Margery Blunt. He grabbed the mouse and pounced onto the file.

The email was dated June 6th 2027, last summer. It contained just a few sentences, which read:

```
Hello Mr. Z. ;) Guess who just got
home? That's right, our new home. I'll
be here all day, waiting for you.
```

`Enjoy this teaser.`

There was a picture attached to the email. Dan hesitated, his cursor hovering over it. He clicked it, and immediately wished he hadn't. A stark naked older, uglier version of Cathy smiled seductively back at him, on her hands and knees across a large bed. Her breasts sagged and she was slathered in makeup. Dan gagged and closed the image.

He stuck his tongue out in disgust and shut his eyes but the image of Margery had burnt into his retinas like a sun spot.

He made a whimpering sound and shook his head.

The window. You have to look again.

Despite the hideous woman taking up the vast majority of the photo, Dan had been vaguely aware of a large pane glass window behind her. He knew that in order to confirm where that building was, he'd need to check the photo again.

With an excruciating effort, he dragged his cursor back to the file and reopened it.

He held both palms out to hide the terrible witch and squinted at the window behind her. Pine trees and snow-capped mountains. It was difficult to tell for sure, but the house seemed to be secluded and nestled within a forest.

Dan smashed *Escape* to close the image, and slumped back in his chair.

"Ugggh," he said, and shook his head. "Right. Focus." He checked the sender's ISP stamp and punched it into the Net to see what organisation claimed it. SwissNet. *Okay, so Switzerland. Now, how to pinpoint the exact location?*

The email had been stamped with a local IP address, which wouldn't help, because they could be used repeatedly on multiple machines. But if he could access SwissNet's logs, he could find out where the contract was assigned. That would give him Horatio Zhin's address.

Dan shivered with excitement. He lived for this shit.

How the fuck am I gonna hack an ISP?

ISPs provided the digital infrastructure that allowed the

Net to exist. Their security was beyond military grade, it was the strongest, most secure software in the world, constantly changing and shifting to deter all but the most professional and expert hackers. Breaking into their system undetected would be like trying to pick a flea off the back of an angry gorilla on a trampoline.

Time to bring in the master, methinks. He stood and went outside to find Derunox.

***

Cathy was standing under a small tree talking to Derunox, who held a handheld camcorder up close to her face. Dan didn't want to disturb her flow, so he approached as quietly as he could.

"This footage was taken from the lab where I worked," Cathy said. "It's rather… disturbing. But please watch it. Watch it and understand how evil these people are!"

Dan smiled proudly. She was really giving it her all.

"At this point, we'll let the security video play," Cathy said.

"Yup," said Derunox, lowering the camera. "What are you going to say next?"

"I dunno," Cathy bit her lip. "Something about how they kept me hostage, and something about the avalanche. All those people who died, and for what? Just to protect their horrendous schemes. God, it makes me so *angry*. After Annie, and then Ben, I knew my mother was messed up, but this?" She trailed off, shaking her head.

"I found something," Dan said.

"Yeah?" Cathy said, looking up.

"Another video. This time, seven test subjects. They all died, just like the first one. It's pretty horrible."

"Good work." She chewed her lip. "Ugh, this is so bad, isn't it? Are we getting in over our heads?"

"Maybe." Derunox gave a nervous chuckle. "But it's exciting, isn't it?"

"Yeah, man," said Dan. "This is real shit."

Cathy eyed them both. "Will this really work? I mean, a counter video. Will it be enough to expose them?"

"It's hard to say. The Net is a fickle place," Derunox brooded. "All we can do is put this online, and hope it attracts some attention. I have friends who specialise in virals, they will help it to spread."

"I might have a backup plan," Dan said. They both raised their eyebrows at him. "It's uhh... I might need your help with it," he said to Derunox.

"Really?" Derunox lit up. "That sounds interesting. What do you have in mind?"

"I have a lead on Zhin's address. His house. Or, well, you know, one of them."

"Really?" Cathy exclaimed. "How did you find that?"

He tried to suppress his smugness. *She's impressed!* "Well, you know, I dug about in some employee emails, found an IP address." *And a photo of your naked mother...*

"Wow, Dan. That's brilliant," Cathy said. "So, what do we do next?"

"Well," he looked to Derunox. "This is the catch. We might need to hack into SwissNet."

"What?" Derunox fumbled with the camera and almost dropped it, gaping at Dan. "*Hovno*, are you serious?"

"We can match the IP to the building. I know it's in the Swiss mountains somewhere, but we need a street name at least."

"How do you know it's in the mountains?" Cathy asked.

"Oh, um." The photo. That was how. "I just, err. The email... the person said they were in the mountains. I think."

"You think?"

"No. I know."

"Can I see it?" she asked.

"No!"

She flinched.

"Maybe we can help you decipher it?" Derunox suggested, unhelpfully.

Ohh man. Dan's face started flushing. He fidgeted with his hair. "Just trust me." He avoided eye contact with Cathy. "We need to hack SwissNet and I can't do it without you, man. You wanna do the hack of your life and help me take down these bastards and go down as mother-fuckin' heroes or not?"

A silence fell. The birds tweeted under the midday sun.

"Yes." Derunox said.

"Good. Finish the video and let's go." Dan marched back into the apartment.

While Dan made preparations for the most dangerous hack of his life, Derunox and Cathy cobbled together the video footage and turned it into a three minute long damnation of Zhin, as well as Cathy's terrible parents. Derunox posted it to the Eye's forums and told his friends to start spreading it around on all the social media and news sites they could.

"Now we just have to wait." Derunox's chair creaked as he leaned back in it, cradling his head within two pudgy hands.

"I'm ready to do this," Dan said. "Are you?"

Derunox made a high-pitched whine. "Ready to risk my home and my life to expose the terrible truth to the world?" He shot Dan an evil toothy grin.

Does nothing faze him?

"Yes, young Bergazoid," he went on. "Let's fuck someone up!" He raised his hand for a high five.

Dan reached over and slapped it.

"All right then!" Derunox beamed, swivelling the chair to face the control hub. He pulled out a keyboard and planted it on his lap, then took out a strange wiry glove with buttons on the end of each fingertip.

"What the hell is that?" Dan asked.

"It's my nav-glove. I save it for special occasions," Derunox said, slipping the glove onto his right hand. He laid his elbow on the armrest and held his gloved hand in mid-air. "The speed advantage is incredible."

"Huh. I've only ever used a keyboard," Dan said. "Did that thing take long to learn?"

"*Fwooo!* About six months. I'm not like you padawans, I can't learn things so fast. But I'm glad I did... you'll see." He flicked Dan a confident smirk.

Dan couldn't have asked for a better partner. He looked over his shoulder to Cathy. She was sitting on the sofa, watching.

She raised her eyebrows and uttered a nervous laugh. "Good luck, guys. If you need anything, just ask."

"How about a coffee?" Derunox said, sticking his tongue out at her.

"Okay then." She laughed and headed for the kitchen.

Derunox opened a command console on his screen.

"Okay, Dan. How is your defence management?"

"What do you have in mind?" Dan opened his own terminal. The cursor blinked at him.

"Well," Derunox flicked his nav-glove, and a globe appeared on the screen. A red dot marked their location, on the outskirts of Prague. Dan recognised the program. It was a modified version of a robust bit of software that cloned a user's ID stamp, fooling the target into thinking the hack was coming from somewhere else. It was designed to make tracing difficult, ensuring you left no footprints that could lead back to you. Anyone could hack, but the key was staying invisible.

"I've used that before," Dan said, pointing at the globe on the screen.

"Good." Derunox's voice had subtly shifted to a serious tone. His facial features had hardened and he spoke now with his lips pressed tightly together. "Okay, you keep us hidden, and I'll break us in."

"Got it," Dan said. He punched in a few commands and set himself up a dual-window workspace. In one window, he could see their ID stamps and identifiers, with Derunox's network location and firewall. The second window was blank, but very soon would fill with details of the target. "I'm good to go."

Derunox paused to compose himself, inhaling a deep breath. Their target was SwissNet, the ISP provider of the home where Margery Blunt emailed Horatio Zhin. SwissNet's ID stamp was written inside his console, next to a blinking cursor. "Here we go." Derunox hit *enter*.

Reams of text appeared on Dan's console as the hack started. He scanned through it, checking for signs of defence. He quickly recognised the system. It was some serious shit. "It's a *heat-seeker*," he told Derunox.

It was a slang term for a dynamic firewall defence system. It had a constantly shifting algorithm that sought out intrusions by locking on to anything that shouldn't be there. As soon as it recognised a presence that wasn't on the whitelist, it honed in and severed the connection, but not before sending a detailed log all about the intruder to the firm's security team.

"Not surprising," Derunox said. "Keep it off us."

"I will." Dan's fingers blurred across the keyboard, *taptaptaptaptaptap*.

In order to break into SwissNet's system, they needed a disguise, and the ID stamp was it. The only way to avoid the heat-seeker was to continuously alter the stamp on the fly. A program could be setup to do this automatically, but eventually the system would recognise it as a virus because the stamps would change too quickly or too regularly. Within a few alterations, you'd be caught.

The best way to avoid detection was to utilise the Human Error Concession, or *Hec*. The heat-seeker's scan took a microsecond to calculate, but there was always a window of two or three seconds before the system took any evasive action. This was the *Hec*, the time given to the user, usually an engineer, to undo whatever change he's made to the code. It refers to the gargantuan difference in time it takes for a human to manually press his or her keyboard, compared to the time the computer would take to enter a potentially devastating loop. If the code caused the system to loop, it would crash, often resulting in fried hardware and loss of data. For a big company like SwissNet, this risk had to be minimised. So, the *Hec* was a unique opportunity to sneak inside a system, so long as you were capable of keeping up with it.

Dan's longest streak was fourteen minutes on a 3-second *Hec*. That was the time he broke into the FBI a couple of years ago.

SwissNet's *Hec* was just a single second.

He nearly shat himself when he saw the heat-seeker, conveniently visualised on his globe GUI as a red line shooting out from Zurich and heading straight towards Prague, flashing red almost as soon as the hack began.

Dan frantically punched in random letters, tweaking their stamp, and the red line darted to somewhere on the other side of the world. Then he had a single second to do it again. And again. And again.

He hammered the keys, altering the numbers and letters with lightning reflexes. After just twenty seconds, his fingers went into auto-pilot, but he was vaguely aware of a tightening across his forehead as he frowned in deep concentration at the screen.

"It's a one-second *Hec*," he said, matter-of-factly.

"*Fwooo!*" was all Derunox could say. Dan didn't dare take his eyes from his monitor, but in his peripheral vision, he could see Derunox's nav-glove flicking back and forth as the big guy maintained his attack.

After a few minutes, Cathy came back. "Coffee's up," she said cheerily.

Derunox made a loud hissing noise.

Cathy's arms appeared between the hackers wielding two steaming mugs, which she placed on the desk. "I'll just—"

Derunox hissed again.

She whispered, "...stay out of the way."

Dan's eyes started to water after ten minutes. He didn't dare to blink. Every second, he was punching in random combinations of characters, tricking the heat-seeker into thinking they were just harmless netbots in Detroit, then Havana, then Melbourne, then Moscow, then Birmingham, then Lyon, then Johannesburg... he had no idea where each combination would point to, but so long as he didn't let it linger on the same spot for more than a second, the heat-seeker would never figure out they were breaking in.

Twenty-two minutes, and still the hack continued. He vaguely registered that he had broken his old record, but wasn't able to acknowledge it beyond a feeble wheeze.

Finally, Derunox found something. He knew because he heard a squeal come from the big guy's throat.

"I'm into the customer accounts," he said. "Decrypting now." His nav-glove jerked and spasmed as he worked through the files.

Sweat dripped from Dan's forehead. He needed Cathy to wipe it off. But his brain couldn't connect to his mouth. It was too busy processing numbers and letters. He made a questioning grunt.

Cathy didn't respond. *Is she there?*

"Found an account tied to Zhin," Derunox said.

Dan's heart thumped against his ribs. *Holy shit, he's almost there.*

He blinked, and a sweat droplet fell into his eye, fuzzing his vision. He squinted it shut and peeled the other eye as wide as it could go, his vision now severely hindered.

"Cathy!" he blurted.

"What?" she yelped, surprised. He heard her get to her feet and come up behind him.

"Eye!"

"Yes? You what?"

Dan pounded the keys. An alteration came dangerously close to the one second mark. The red line on the heat-seeker flashed red again, and he managed to divert it just in time. The onslaught continued, relentless.

"My eye!" he wheezed. His open eye was getting fuzzy too. He couldn't hold out much longer.

Cathy leaned around him. Her hair fell across the corner of his screen, partially blocking his view.

"No!" he cried. He floundered for half a second, but that was enough.

"I've got it!" Derunox roared. "Cloud Lodge, Valais region!"

Cathy darted away. The heat-seeker flashed red. The globe spun around to Prague and a big red dot appeared over the city. They were traced.

"*Fuck!*" Dan cried, punching the keys. It no longer responded. The program had crashed and they were disconnected from the hack.

Derunox's console seized up. "What?" he looked at Dan's screen and his eyes bulged. He kicked the chair backwards and dropped to the floor like an earthquake. He rolled under the desk and Dan heard a heavy *thunk*.

Fwwummmmmm. All the screens went black. Derunox had killed the power.

A deathly quiet settled over the room as the whirring of the fans died out. Derunox scrambled back out from under the desk, his breathing rapid and raspy. "Cloud Lodge, Valais," he mumbled. "Cloud Lodge…"

"I… I'm sorry man…" Dan stuttered.

Cathy stood over Derunox. "Is that the address? You got it, right?" She hadn't quite caught up yet, it seemed.

Derunox mumbled the address again. "Write it down. My phone." He pointed to it on the desk. Cathy grabbed the phone and tapped the words onto it.

Dan felt numb, he sat in front of the dead monitors, hands trembling. "It traced us…" He gulped.

Derunox was slumped on his side half-under the desk, eyes wide as plates and his jaw dangling open like a suffocating fish.

"I'm so, so sorry man…" Dan repeated.

"Why are you sorry?" Cathy said, holding up the phone. "We got the address, look!" She handed it to Derunox, who took it in a feeble hand.

"Thank you Cathy," he said softly. "Get your things together. We have to run."

Dan closed his eyes. *I fucked up so bad.*

"What?" Worry crept into Cathy's tone. "What happened?"

"I fuc—" Dan started.

"We were caught," Derunox interrupted, graciously taking his share of responsibility, even though Dan entirely blamed himself.

"The *fedz* will know we are here now," Dan mumbled.

Derunox drummed it home. "Europa will be coming for us."

No-one moved for a few stunned moments.

It was Cathy who kicked them into gear.

"Get up then!" she cried. "Let's get out of here! What can I do to help?"

Derunox hauled himself off the floor, and Dan sprang to his feet.

"I need to wipe my drives," Derunox said, slumping into the chair again, and rolling across to a different set of monitors.

"Do we have time?" Dan asked.

"I don't know." He pried open a computer case with a screwdriver.

Dan felt a horrible wave of guilt wash over him. "Man, I can't believe it. I mean, dude, I'm so fucking sorry."

"It's fine, padawan. We got what we wanted." Derunox had his back to him, distractedly pulling out cables. He froze, and hung his head. Dan thought he was crying. But when he turned around to face him, Derunox had a huge smile across his face. "That was my best ever hack."

Dan barked a laugh. "Yeah. Me too."

They shared a proud nod.

"Now, let's make it worth it. If we get caught here, it will have been in vain," said Derunox. He frowned with a Czech curse. "I have to destroy the drives. Help me, Bergazoid!" He gestured to the rest of the control hub.

Dan set to work on the computers around him. They frantically ripped out drives and handed them to Cathy.

"Take these to the garden and make a pile," Derunox ordered, turning to the next case.

Cathy ferried handfuls of equipment to and from the garden as Dan and Derunox tore the control hub's innards apart. When the last drive was out, Derunox pulled a jerry can out from beneath his sink and carried it outside, where Cathy had made a heap of metal in the grass.

"Um, that guy is watching us," Cathy pointed to a man on a balcony overlooking the garden.

"Screw him," Derunox said, and doused the pile of hard drives with the gasoline.

The neighbour shouted something at them. He pointed and gestured wildly to the sky, yelling in Czech.

Derunox ignored him, so Dan tried to as well, which was difficult. He sounded very angry. Then he was gone, disappeared back inside.

"What did he say?" Dan asked.

"He's calling the police," Derunox answered, upturning the jerry can.

"Shit."

"Stand back." Derunox threw the empty can aside and struck a match. He crept forwards and tossed it onto the pile. *Fwump-sshhhh.*

The metal heap went up in flames, black smoke billowing into the air.

"Time to disappear."

They left the pile burning and ran back through the apartment, past the semi-dismantled control hub, now mostly blank monitors with dangling cables, and out the front door.

Each carried a backpack. Derunox had no time to pack

much, just a few essentials like his laptop and cloned passport. Dan also had his laptop, some clothes and one of Derunox's old nav-gloves, which the big guy let him keep. Cathy took the EMP gun in her bag, since she barely had any belongings as it was.

They marched into the street in bright sunlight. A few parked cars lined the roadside, neighbours and resident vehicles, but they were the only people in sight. They started to jog down the road just as a sleek black car with tinted windows pulled around the corner. They skidded to a halt.

"Shit," Dan said, lowering his head. "Slow down. That might be them." They slowed to a brisk walk. The car passed them by and pulled up behind them, outside the apartment block. Dan heard the car door open and close.

A man's voice called out. "Petrov Clitski!" Footsteps ran up behind them.

A hand grabbed Derunox on the shoulder and spun him around. Dan wheeled about and came face to face with a pistol barrel.

"You're coming with me, Petrov," the man said, pointing the gun at Derunox. "By order of Europa. Put your fucking hands up. All of you."

They obeyed.

Fuck, fucking, shit, fuck!

The agent glanced at Dan and Cathy. "These your accomplices?"

"No," Derunox said immediately. "Just friends. Let them go."

The agent took another look, this time with a squint of recognition. His eyebrows shot up. "Wait, you're Daniel Bergman. I recognise your face, you were working with Hawkins."

Ah hell, seriously?

Then, as if it couldn't get any worse, he shifted focus to Cathy. "And you're Catherine Blunt. What the fuck?" he muttered. "Don't you dare move." He waved the gun across each of them and took a step backwards, keeping it trained on them. He touched his ear and spoke. "I got a positive ID on our SwissNet suspect, but get this. He's got Blunt and Bergman with him." A pause. "Yeah, Catherine fucking Blunt."

"I'm not going back there," Cathy mumbled.

Derunox, standing between Dan and Cathy, blew air through gritted teeth. He whispered, "You two, get ready to run."

"What?" *Is he thinking about doing something crazy?*

"Get. Ready," Derunox ordered in a firm tone.

"No, man, I—"

"Affirmative," the agent said, and ended his call. "Miss Blunt, please come with me." He lowered the gun and offered his empty hand to Cathy.

"You only want her?" Dan said, dropping his arms to the side. "Does this mean we're not under arrest?"

The agent gave him a look of disgust, but otherwise ignored the comment. To Cathy, he said, "I have orders to bring you in. Your father will be informed."

"No," she murmured, retreating a step.

"You're not taking her," Dan stepped between them. His heart pounded in his chest. He was acting on impulse, a desire to protect the girl he loved. *Fuck, am I in love?*

"Step aside, Bergman," the agent demanded and aimed the gun at him. "You're lucky I don't haul your ass in with her."

"I'm not moving," Dan said, feeling his bowels tighten.

The agent shoved Dan out of the way. "Miss Blunt, I won't ask nicely again. Come with me. Now." He swung the gun towards Cathy.

Dan clenched his fist and gritted his teeth. He felt the blood rushing through his veins, his pulse pounding against his temples. "I said, you're not taking her!" He shoulder charged the agent into the road, and both of them tumbled to the tarmac.

Bang! The gunshot pierced the air.

Dan's anger drained out of him, replaced by a cold flush of terror.

A high-pitched whine overloaded his hearing, which slowly faded. The distant sound of sirens replaced it. A sharp twang of smoke stung his nostrils as it drifted from the barrel of the gun. The agent shoved him and he fell to the hard ground, staring up at the sky. Thick black smoke wafted across the blue canvas, spewing from behind the apartments.

He felt no pain. The bullet must have missed him.

"Fucking moron, you want me to shoot you?" The agent loomed above him, pointing the gun between Dan's eyes.

He feebly shook his head.

The agent glared at him, then looked up. "Miss Blunt! *Come back here!*"

Dan spun his head to see Cathy sprinting down the road.

The agent hesitated. He looked from Dan, to Cathy, back to Dan. "Argh! Where's fuckin' backup when you need it." He took one step, about to charge after her, when Derunox body-slammed him into the ground. The gun tumbled from his hand and bounced away. Derunox pinned the agent against the road. "Run!" he shrieked at Dan. "Go after her!"

Dan didn't waste any time debating it. He scrambled to his feet. The agent flailed beneath the big hacker, swinging his elbows and trying to roll him off.

Dan bolted after Cathy. She was already at the end of the road, and before he'd taken four strides, she disappeared from sight around the corner. A Czech police car with flashing red and blue lights careened into view, heading in his direction. He carried on running, hoping the car would speed past him. But it skidded to a halt in front of him, and out popped a uniformed officer, who immediately trained a pistol on Dan.

He yelled something in Czech, which Dan assumed to mean *"freeze."*

"Fuck!" he shouted, raising his hands and slowing to a

walk. He looked at the empty corner where Cathy had disappeared, and his heart sank to his knees. *She's gone!*

26
TENSIONS

Forty levels up, in the middle of Sid Blunt's skyscraper, Arnie ran laps around the cavernous sports hall on his newly repaired legs.

One end of the hall looked out onto Alexanderplatz and the Berlin skyline, while the other showcased a state-of-the-art gymnasium covering three floors, separated by sleek glass windows.

He would have liked to use the rowing machines on the second floor, but his legs would mangle them up. Gunther had ordered him to run gentle laps around the hall instead to get accustomed to the replacement sensors.

At least I'm not chewing up the floor anymore.

Back home in New Zealand, he had been raised on rugby, training every week with his hardass father, so exercise came naturally to Arnie. Not that his prosthetics needed exercise—they could probably run a hundred miles and he would barely break a sweat.

He had the hall to himself at this early hour, filling it with the *cu-thunk, cu-thunk, cu-thunk* of his feet bounding across the hard surface.

I feel good.

The nerves around his waist adapted to the sensors as if he were born into them. Arnie didn't have a clue how the system worked, only that it responded to his thoughts, and that if he wanted to run faster all he had to do was think about it.

The legs picked up speed and he grinned to himself. "Easy now," he said to them, slowing to a steady jog again.

As he passed by the outer window on his way around the hall, he glanced outside. A thick layer of grey cloud hovered above Berlin, drizzling rain over the city.

I wonder if it's raining where Catherine is.

Arnie last saw her back in England, fleeing with some scrawny kid into the woods. He didn't understand why she chose to run off with a stranger, for the second time. Arnie had broken her out of that Europa bunker to free her, but as soon as that bastard Hawkins showed up, all thoughts had turned to revenge, and she fled while he was preoccupied. By now, she could be almost anywhere in the world, if she was still alive.

I just hope you're safe…

A door opened across the hall and Frank Hawkins entered with Doctor Gunther, escorted by an armed merc. The merc stayed by the door, watching guard.

Arnie jogged across and came to a stop in front of them.

The doctor nodded enthusiastically. "Good, good, Mr. Dillon. You have made excellent progress. How do they feel?" he gestured to the legs, admiring them with keen eyes.

Arnie loomed above them, so he retracted the legs. They brought him down almost to eye level with a hydraulic *hissss*. "They feel good, doctor. I mean. Not a patch on my real legs." He flicked an accusing glance at Hawkins. His pelvic nerves fluttered in pleasant tingles; it almost felt as if the legs were eager to run again. "But they have some advantages…"

Hawkins' new arm appeared to be the same design as Arnie's legs, so far as he could tell. Black, sleek, and shiny. Streaks of stainless steel ran down the length of the forearm, just like his thighs.

"You seem a natural amputee," Hawkins said in a flat tone. His metal arm dangled at his side, giving him lopsided posture. Gunther probably didn't trust Hawkins with the arm switched on until he was safely out of reach.

Arnie ignored the comment and asked the doc, "What brings you here?"

"I thought you might help our new asset." He gestured to Hawkins, who was shaking his head in disbelief.

"You're joking," Arnie said. "Why would I help him?"

"Because Mr. Blunt requests it of you. And you are the most experienced person for the job. The perfect mentor."

"I don't need any help," Hawkins stated. "Especially not from him."

"Right," Arnie agreed.

"Why don't you play a game?" the doctor suggested, unfazed by their reservations. He went to a wall-cabinet full of sporting equipment, opened it and pulled out a rugby ball.

"Fuck's sake," Hawkins muttered, looking down at the floor.

The doctor held the ball out and wiggled it. "Mr. Dillon, please *go long*." His eyebrows bounced up and down above a childlike grin.

"You're not listening, doc." Arnie snorted. "I'm not helping *him* do a bloody thing."

The doctor's smile faded and he sighed. "Miss Blunt is out there somewhere. Do you know where?"

Arnie stiffened. "No."

"Well, it's your job to find her, need I remind you?" Gunther studied him with hard, grey eyes. "Both of you."

Neither spoke.

Gunther motioned to Frank's metal arm. "Mr. Hawkins needs to get accustomed to his new prosthetic, and this is part of the training. Surely you can empathise with him?" He cocked his head at Arnie, and lightened his tone. "You must show a little, how do you say... team spirit!"

He's the one that fucking broke me in the first place. And yet, seeing Hawkins in his current state, defeated and helpless… he did feel a bit sorry for him. A tiny bit.

"Perhaps you can become friends, yes?" Gunther went

on jovially, patting them both on the arm at the same time.

Hawkins shrugged the doctor away and pinched the bridge of his nose. "Will you just go long, mate?" He looked at Arnie with a hint of desperation in his eyes.

Arnie considered the request for a long moment. "Fine." *But he needs to know I could squash him like a bug any time I like.* Arnie extended his legs until he towered over them both again, well over eight feet tall.

"Cripes," Hawkins said, wiping his mouth and looking away. "Gimme the bloody ball." He snatched it from Gunther's hand.

"Ahh, heh heh, very good," the doctor tittered. "Mr. Dillon, I want you to kick, while Mr. Hawkins throws. Practice your accuracy." He stretched the word out in his thick German accent: *ack-u-rassy.* "You must learn to be subtle, to control your strengths. Throw and kick, simple *ja?*" He rubbed his hands together. "I will be watching!"

Gunther scurried away through the door, the merc following close behind.

Arnie stared Hawkins down for a few more seconds, enjoying the discomfort in the agent's body language.

Hawkins blinked and moved his arm all of a sudden. His posture straightened and he flexed his fingers. "Let's get this charade over with," he said, swivelling the metal arm around his shoulder joint as it came to life.

Arnie grunted and jogged away.

Hawkins made his way to the opposite end and stood with his back to the gym's windows.

Doctor Gunther appeared on the second floor and squeezed between a pair of treadmills to stand at the window overlooking the hall.

Arnie clapped and showed Hawkins his open palm. "Right here, then. If you can." His lip curled in a smirk.

Hawkins took the ball in his metal hand, leaned back and threw it.

The ball sailed high over Arnie's head and struck the outer window with a *twang.* It bounced off the glass and ricocheted away. "What was that?" Arnie scathed.

"This thing's ridiculously overpowered," Hawkins said.

Arnie collected the ball and faced Hawkins. *Okay, keep it subtle.* He'd done a thousand drop kicks in his time, an essential skill for any rugby player. He thought about letting the ball drop gently in front of his foot, connecting with it a fraction of a second after it touched the floor. If he hoofed it indoors, the ball would crash right into the ceiling, so he concentrated on keeping control.

The legs obeyed. They adjusted their strength perfectly as he kicked the ball back towards Hawkins. It arced through the air and came down right on top of him. He reached to catch it with both hands, but fumbled and it smacked him in the cheek.

"Argh," Hawkins cursed, as the ball bounced away.

Arnie chuckled. "You Brits. Never know how to handle your balls."

Hawkins muttered something incomprehensible as he picked it up. Arnie glanced at Gunther, who was taking notes on his tablet.

Arnie felt a leathery hot slap on his cheek—the ball smacking him in the face like a brick.

"Argh!" he grunted, reeling and blinking stars.

"Wakey, wakey," Hawkins mocked.

The agent was probably grinning, but Arnie couldn't see properly. Everything was blurry.

"No wonder you're such a piss-poor shooter with those blinkers," Hawkins said.

"Fuck you," Arnie retorted. He shook his head clear and picked up the ball. "Think you're the man, eh? Well, catch *this.*" He booted the ball hard and low. It shot straight down the hall like a tank shell.

Hawkins dived sideways and rolled out of its way.

The ball smashed into the sound-proof glass and popped like a balloon, leaving a thick crack in the window.

"Now, now, gentlemen," Gunther's voice crackled over a tannoy, echoing off the walls. "You must learn to work together. Fetch another ball, if you would, Mr. Hawkins."

"Roger that," Hawkins muttered and retrieved a new one from the closet. "Listen, it's Arnie, right?"

"Yeah."

"Let's get the elephant out of the room, shall we? I don't like you, and you don't like me. And the reason's pretty fucking obvious."

"Too right it is mate. If it weren't for you, I wouldn't be—"

"A cripple," Hawkins said.

"I am no fucking *cripple*," Arnie growled, deeply offended.

"Yeah, you are. That's just a fact."

"Are you *trying* to rile me up?" Arnie clenched his fists. "Because it's working."

"You got a shit deal," Hawkins went on. "I meant to kill you on that train, but somehow you survived. I'm sorry."

Arnie blinked. "You're sorry?"

"Yeah. No man deserves what happened to you."

Arnie frowned. "Are you serious? You're *apologising*?"

"Yes, for fuck's sake. If it wasn't for me, you'd still have your legs." He launched the ball in a swooping arc across the hall.

Arnie plucked it out of the air. "I don't know what to say to that."

"Whatever," Hawkins said. "You got even. We're both cripples now."

"Stop calling me that." He kicked the ball and this time Hawkins caught it. *Damn, he's a fast learner.*

"Seems like you have a problem facing reality," Hawkins said. "Just accept it."

Maybe he's right. "It takes courage to admit responsibility," Arnie said. "I appreciate your apology, but I don't accept it."

"Why not? I'm fuckin' trying here." He chucked a decent spinner straight into Arnie's midriff. "We need to try to get along. Cathy's depending on us."

"Cathy? You speak as though you know her."

"We talked a bit," Hawkins said. "I felt kinda sorry for her."

"Why?"

"Privileged kid, brought up in a house like that. Worst parents I could imagine. It's a wonder she isn't a complete whack job."

"Mr. Blunt is a good father," Arnie insisted. He squeezed the ball between broad, solid fingers. "It's Margery that was the problem."

"Don't I know it? I lost a good kid because of her."

"She's psychotic."

Hawkins put one hand on his hip and pointed at Arnie with the other. "Huh. Now there's something we agree on. You gonna kick that, or what?"

Arnie studied the ball in his hand. "Catherine means a lot to me. I've known her since she was young." *My Ruapehu...* "I could work with you, if it means finding her quicker." He clenched his teeth and forced his head up to meet Hawkins in the eye. "Will you work with me, bro?"

Hawkins scoffed. "Yeah. Why not? Maybe you can teach me that crazy battle chant. You gave me the willies, mate. I ain't above admitting that, either."

"Heh," Arnie chuckled. "Some tough guy, you are."

"Hey, I'm just a bloke. Now that Europa thinks I'm dead, I've not even got their resources at my disposal to help us track down Cathy. All I got is a skysuit, a zip-winch, and this fucking arm."

"Mr. Blunt has resources of his own."

"True," Hawkins said. "That stealth VTOL is something else."

The side door burst open. Four mercenaries marched into the sports hall. They wore pistols in their belts, but the leader of the group pulled his out and aimed it at Hawkins.

"You killed Harrison, you son of a bitch!" he shouted.

"No," Arnie roared. "Stop!" He bounded across the hall

in three steps and blocked their path. They all stopped dead in their tracks.

The leader glared up at him. "Move it, Dillon. This guy murdered our buddy and one of the doctors."

"Harrison deserves payback," a second glaring merc added.

Arnie empathised, but he couldn't let them hurt Hawkins. "No. We need him. Listen, I get that you're angry."

"Like fuck you do. Move aside." The leader sidestepped to get past, but Arnie stamped his foot down an inch away from the merc's boot. The floor cracked outwards like a spider web beneath his metal foot.

"No." Arnie crossed his arms. "Did you see the doctor's assistant?"

"What?" The merc squinted. "Yeah, his head was caved in."

Arnie nodded. "He did that with his arm. What do you think I could do with these?" He extended the legs a few inches, towering over the men, who seemed to shrink, both physically and mentally. "You wanna touch him? You go through me."

The leader watched the legs warily. "Ugh," he grunted, holstering his pistol. "Let's go, boys."

The other three shot mousey glances between Arnie and Hawkins before trudging off behind the leader. The last one out of the hall slammed the door shut.

"Does this mean we're friends?" Hawkins said from behind Arnie. He was staring at his metal palm, slowly flexing the fingers. "I didn't mean to kill either of them."

"You just gotta get used to it," Arnie said. "It gets easier."

"Oh yeah?"

Arnie knew how he felt; he'd been there. His own bitterness faded more and more each day as he adapted to his new legs. They were strong, fast, not to mention virtually indestructible.

"You look like you admire them already," Hawkins said.

"I wouldn't go that far," Arnie said. "But I can't keep denying the advantages. It's like you said, I gotta accept reality…"

"Ugh, *fuck!*" Hawkins outburst came out of nowhere.

"What?"

"My arm's dead again. That *bastard.*"

His arm flopped by his side, putting his posture off balance again. A moment later, the doctor strolled in with Julie, Sid's personal assistant.

"I'm glad my legs don't have that feature," Arnie said.

"They told you that, did they?" Hawkins muttered.

"Huh?" Arnie hadn't even considered that before. He looked up at Gunther. *Can he control my legs, too?*

"Hello Arnie," Julie said, stopping just in front of them. "Mr. Blunt would like to see you both in his office."

"What for?" Arnie asked.

"We've had contact from…" She glanced at Hawkins. "Europa."

"Oh, have they changed their mind about letting you keep me as a hostage?" Hawkins quipped.

"No," Julie said, straight-faced. "They've sighted Miss Blunt."

"*What?*" Arnie said. "Where is she?"

"Prague, I believe," Julie said. "Mr. Blunt has the details. Please follow me."

Arnie's spirit soared at the news. But Hawkins' comment had cast a shadow dark enough to give him doubts. *Am I really just a puppet?*

27
REUNION

Frank seethed all the way up the elevator to the hundredth floor. His heavy, lifeless arm hung off his shoulder, pulling him sideways. He leaned against the elevator's shiny wall in an attempt to relieve the pressure, but what he really wanted was for that bastard Gunther to switch it back on.

"I won't hurt you," he muttered through gritted teeth.

"Hmm?" Gunther turned to him with that permanent slimy smirk plastered across his face.

"Turn my arm back on, this is really uncomfortable."

"Ha," he scoffed. "In this enclosed space? I don't *zink* so Mr. Hawkins."

Arnie offered Frank a sympathetic shrug. He didn't exactly look comfortable himself, with his neck crammed up against the ceiling. Even with the legs retracted, he still had to hunch down, looming over the four of them.

The mercenary next to Gunther didn't take his eye off Frank once for the duration of the ride.

"We're here," Julie said, as the elevator went *ding*.

The doors opened and they filed out into a plush, carpeted corridor leading straight to Sid Blunt's private office.

Julie led them inside, a sprawling space decorated with high tech gadgetry and a few exotic pot plants. A single piece of glass covered one entire wall, overlooking Berlin. Sid sat at a grand mahogany desk with his back to the breath-taking view.

"Gentlemen," he said, rising to greet them.

Gunther approached first and handed Sid a small device that looked like a smartphone. "Here's Mr. Hawkins' controller. I shall return to the lab now."

"Thank you, Doctor," said Sid. "Kevin, would you mind waiting outside, please?" he said to the mercenary.

"Are you sure that's a good idea, sir?" Kevin asked, eyeballing Frank.

"Yes, I think we'll be just fine. I'll call if you're needed."

Kevin leered at Frank one last time before he stalked out, following Gunther.

"I have a lead on Catherine's whereabouts," Sid announced.

"Wait just a bloody minute," Frank said. "You seriously gonna treat me like some tool you can just disable when it's convenient? Turn my fucking arm on right now."

Sid stiffened. He looked at the device in his hand as if it might grow teeth and bite him.

"Sir," Arnie said. "I'm here if he tries anything."

Sid hesitated. His glance flittered between Frank and the device. Julie took a step backwards away from Frank.

What cowards.

Sid jabbed the screen with his index finger, and Frank's arm woke up. His shoulder sang at the connectivity, a thousand nerve endings sparking to life. The arm became weightless, and the AI inside fused with his synapses, ready and waiting to receive instructions.

Frank flexed his fingers, standing upright again and heaved a sigh of relief. "Thank you."

Sid watched Frank with a wary eye, but seemed to relax after a few moments had passed and Frank hadn't snapped his neck.

"Where is Catherine?" Arnie asked, breaking the silence.

"Yes," Sid jerked a finger up. "I had a call from a Europa agent in Prague. He told me he had sighted Catherine when he was called to arrest a hacker."

"That must have been Dan," Frank said. *Shit, the little*

twerp got caught.

"What about Catherine?" Arnie said.

"She got away, somehow," Sid explained. "But they wouldn't tell me anything more."

"Give me a phone and I'll call the chief," Frank said.

"I tried that," Sid went on. "It seems the Chief of Europa has mysteriously vanished. I had a direct line to contact her with, but now that number has been disconnected and I can't get hold of her."

"I have my own access code," Frank said. "Just give me a phone, I'll find out."

Sid sidestepped away from his desk and gestured to the phone. Frank picked up the handset and dialled in the number.

An automated voice on the other end said, "*Input now.*"

Frank punched in his access code. Usually, he'd be required to enter a second code after that, but this time, the phone went dead. He frowned at the handset. "I was cut off. Let me try a different one."

He did the same thing, using his backup access code, but the same thing happened. The phone line *clicked* and died.

"Shit," Frank muttered. "I've been disavowed." *What the fuck's going on, Chief?*

"I thought you already knew that," Sid said. "I told you when I last spoke to her, the chief said you'd be classified as killed-in-action."

"There's a big difference between KIA and disavowed," Frank said irritably. "Even KIA, my access code should work in an emergency. It's an agent's lifeline in the field, a direct line to the chief. But I've been cut off completely… It's like I no longer exist."

"Um, sir?" Julie said.

They all looked around to her. She was holding her tablet computer, her brow furrowed. "I think you should see this," she said, and held the tablet out to Sid.

He gasped when he saw the screen. "Catherine! Put it on the wall."

Julie swiped a finger on the screen and an image of Cathy projected itself onto the wall where they could all see.

What is she doing?

She was standing in a garden, underneath a tree, framed in a close up of her head and shoulders. Wide, fearful green eyes gazed out at Frank, and her dirty brown hair hung in a loose ponytail. Her face looked darker than when Frank had last seen her, grubby but also lightly tanned.

"It was uploaded an hour ago," Julie explained. "One of the techs downstairs just sent it to me."

Julie pressed play and Catherine started to speak, addressing the camera.

"Hello there. My name is Catherine Blunt, the daughter of Sidney Blunt, CEO of Blunt Electronics Incorporated. Six years ago, you were told that I had died, but it was a lie. I'm alive, and on the run. There's something very important that I need to tell you. So please listen."

"Good grief," Sid exclaimed. "How many people have seen this?" Julie brought up the view counter which displayed over seven million and was ticking upwards at a steady rate.

Cathy went on, *"Horatio Zhin is not who he says he is. Don't believe his promises of a better world. I know, because he is partners with my mother, who murdered my best friend, Annie, and framed her for my fake death."* Cathy's voice was cracking up.

"Oh my sweet girl, what are you *doing?*" Sid cradled his head in both hands, transfixed on the video.

Frank took no small satisfaction in watching the man squirm. *She's exposing his little lie.*

"Annie, I'm sorry for what happened to you. I wish I could have saved you..." She was on the brink of tears, but a flash of anger washed it away. *"It was my father's fault. He slept with Annie, and as punishment, my mother divorced him and had her killed. He did nothing to stop it."*

"No," Blunt wheezed, his voice pained and high.

"And then he let Mother take me away, to an underground facility, where I was forced to work on Zhin's secret project. I was stuck there for six years. Years I will never get back."

The camera cut to a wider shot of her whole body. Frank thought the maroon hoody and khaki shorts suited her; the ragged look of a modern traveller. Her slender legs still bore a few scratches from when he'd base jumped off the cliff and landed in a tree with her.

"At least I'm alive." She spat the word *alive* like an accusation. *"Unlike everyone else who worked there, and the poor souls who were being experimented on. This footage was taken from the lab where I worked. It's rather... disturbing. But please watch it. Watch it and understand how evil these people are!"*

The video cut to footage of a laboratory where a hospital-gowned man was tied up against a wall. A blinding flash of light disrupted the feed for a few seconds. Afterwards, nothing remained of the man but his gown, dangling from the restraints that had secured him.

Fuck me.

"This was not just a one-off," Cathy continued. More footage, another experiment, this time with seven sedated men, all subjected to the deadly light.

Frank considered where Cathy might have gotten the footage. *Could only be Dan.* Jimmy had transferred the data to his brother, and the kid must have been able to dig this out. Jimmy hadn't died in vain, after all. Frank's guilt about his involvement in the facility's destruction waned. If *this* was the shit they'd been doing down there, then destroying the place was a blessing and Frank felt a lot better about the entire clusterfuck of a situation.

"My god," Sid muttered, staring in horror at the disturbing images.

"My friend Ben worked there with me, and he knew they were up to something. He tried to leak information about it on the ShadowNet, but my mother killed him too. Why? Because she couldn't allow Horatio Zhin's secret plan to be revealed. The secret of Horizon!"

Frank cupped his chin in concentration. *Did she and Dan figure all of this out by themselves?*

Cathy continued, "*I believe he's responsible for murdering hundreds of thousands of people in Yuma, Dongola, and Tarrow Creek... it's not the sun. It's Margery Blunt and Horatio Zhin! It's Horizon and this terrible weapon. Don't listen to them, and don't support them. They have to be stopped. Please send this video to everyone you care about.*"

The video faded to black.

Sid dropped Frank's arm controller on the desk as he staggered to his chair. He collapsed into it with his back to them all. He ran his fingers through his thin, dishevelled hair, seeming to forget that Frank and the others were still in the room.

Has he snapped?

"Uh, sir?" Julie prompted.

"Julie," he spun around, jerking back to the situation.

"What should we do?" she asked.

"We have to get to Prague!" Arnie said as if it were obvious. He said to Frank, "You know where they might be holding your hacker buddy?"

"Yeah, I think so," Frank nodded, glancing at the little gadget on Sid's desk. "I knew a guy stationed there, once."

"Well, then, what are we waiting for?" Arnie said.

"Julie," Sid said. "Please ready the VTOL, I want them taking off as soon as possible."

"I'll go find Hugo and let him know." She strode out the door, tapping away on her tablet.

"Arnie, get to the lab and put on your combat armour. Please," he pleaded. "Bring her home."

"What happens if we do?" Frank demanded, stepping closer to the desk. "Say I help bring her back, what happens then?"

"I'll let you go?" Blunt tried weakly.

"Damn-fucking-right you will," Frank agreed. "But that's so easy for you to say. It's just that I don't trust you."

Blunt went to speak, but Frank silenced him with a

wave. He snatched the controller off the desk and held it up. "Listen, pal. You want me to help you out, then no more of this bullshit." Frank crushed it like a coke can within his titanium fingers.

Sid jumped out of his chair and stepped backwards.

"Yeah," Frank said, planting both hands on the desk and leaning towards him. "Not so tough now. You gave me this arm against my will, the least you can do is let me use the thing without turning me into a bloody marionette."

Arnie grabbed Frank by the shoulder and pulled him away from Sid's desk. "Easy, bro. We ain't friends yet."

"Oh relax you twat," Frank shrugged him off. "I'm not gonna hurt him. No matter how much I *want* to. I just won't be anyone's puppet. And neither should you." Frank glared at Sid. "Where do you keep *his* controller?"

Sid gulped. "Arnie doesn't have a control chip…"

"Lying comes easy to you, doesn't it, Mr. Blunt?" Frank said. "You're just shit at it."

"Is it true?" Arnie said. "Can you control my legs?"

"Arnie, please," Sid said, rubbing his forehead. "Look, it was Gunther's idea! He insisted on installing a control chip as a safety precaution, because he didn't know how the AI would react to the human interface."

"So I'm just a guinea pig, sir?" Arnie sounded dejected.

"No," Sid whined, wiping his mouth. "You're my most trusted friend. And I'm sorry but we just don't have time for this right now. Catherine is out there, and I need you both to help me bring her back."

Arnie was silent, his brow creased. He turned away, his legs making a hydraulic *hiss-click, hiss-click,* as he walked across the office, heading for the elevator.

"Where are you going?" Sid asked.

"To the lab, to gear up. See you on the roof, Hawkins." He ducked under the door frame and disappeared, leaving Frank alone with Sid.

Frank stood between Sid and the door, the only entrance or exit in the room. He had a strong urge to pick Sid up by the throat and throw him through the window. His metal fingers twitched in anticipation, so he forced the thought out of his head.

I may be disavowed, but I'm still a professional. And I'm in too deep to throw this mission away now…

Sid was watching him like a rabbit caught in headlights.

"So where's Arnie's controller?" Frank demanded.

"I-I don't have—"

"Bollocks."

Sid flinched.

"You may have convinced that loyal chump, but I'm not blind. This is the same model. If you expect me to go into the field with a partner whose ten-tonne legs might turn to stone in the middle of a firefight, or crush me into jelly the second we've got Cathy back... you can fuck right off."

"All right! G-Gunther has it. I'll have him d-destroy it."

"Not good enough. I want to see it happen. Send him up here."

"Okay!" Sid fumbled with the phone, spoke briefly to Gunther and hung up.

"Happy now? He's on his way, then we can get this over with and send you both to Prague to look for Catherine…"

"Have you even considered that Cathy may not *want* to come back?" Frank asked.

"What?" he said. "She's my daughter."

"So? You consider yourself a loving father. You've convinced yourself of it. Yet you're only willing to send us out there to find her."

He stared back at Frank, his eyes giving a nervous twitch. "What else can I do?"

"I don't know, when was the last time you even left that desk? I ain't got any kids. But I sure as hell wouldn't have let this happen to them if I did. I'd be out there, doing whatever I could to protect them."

The office door opened and Gunther strolled in with that knowing smirk on his face. "Hello again, Agent. Here is the controller, as requested." He offered it to Frank, who snatched it out of his hand.

He was about to crush it, but something about Gunther's eager smile made him hesitate. "What are you grinning at, you mad old cretin?"

"*Ziz* is my universal controller," he said. "It can control any limb in the CBP208 range—that's your arm and Mr. Dillon's legs. I built two of these, and gave the other one to Mr. Dillon just now."

Frank stared at him in disbelief. "You're fucking kidding me. Is *this* your idea of trust?" he demanded of Blunt.

Blunt was frowning, deep in thought.

"Exactly, Mr. Hawkins. It is all about trust," explained Gunther. "Now you'll have no choice but to trust one another. It should help you to focus on the task at hand, and bring Miss Blunt back safely."

He looked so smug. Frank wanted to punch him square in the – *No. Bloody control yourself, man.*

Twang!

They both jerked their heads at Blunt.

The snivelling wreck had risen to his feet so fast that his chair wheeled back and struck the glass window. "I'm coming with you," Sid declared. "I want to see her. If anything happens, you can kill me. Will that satisfy your trust, Mr. Hawkins?"

Frank didn't know what to say. He searched Blunt, looking for a lie, a hidden meaning. But for once, the jabbering mess of a man seemed to have full composure. Frank believed he had finally found some bollocks.

"Huh," he snorted. "I guess so."

"Right, then." Blunt straightened his tie, his eyes wide as plates. "Let's get to Prague."

***

Blunt's VTOL cruised across the border and into the Czech Republic within the hour. Frank, Arnie, Sid and three mercenaries disembarked on the outskirts of the city, where Europa had a modest three-storey holding facility. The low sun poked through gaps in the clouds casting godrays across the square concrete building, reflecting off the windows in hues of yellow and orange.

"You all wait here," Frank said. "Let me speak to them."

"I'm coming too," Arnie said. "Not letting you out of my sight with that controller."

"It was your idea to keep them," Frank said. "I still say we should destroy the bloody things."

"Nah," Arnie shook his head. "You're growing on me, Hawkins, but we aren't buddies yet. Until we've found Catherine, we come as a package."

"Team spirit, eh?" Frank quipped, parroting Doctor Gunther.

"Exactly, bro."

Frank sighed and led the way towards the Europa building. They approached the lobby door where an armed guard stood watch.

"That's far enough," the guard said, un-holstering his pistol. He pointed it at Arnie's chest. "What the fuck is that?"

Arnie was doing his Terminator thing again. A combat exoskeleton covered his upper torso, made of black titanium to match his legs. The pistol in the guard's hand would be like a flea bite to the big Maori.

"Relax, he's not here to attack us," Frank assured him. "And if he was, you think you could stop him with that?"

"We heard about you," the guard said to Dillon. "You killed five agents in England breaking the girl out. I should take you in right now."

Arnie's legs went *hsssrkkk* as they extended. He towered over the guard, blanketing him in shadow. "I'd like to see you try."

Frank stepped between them. "Easy. We're not here to

cause trouble. I spoke to your officer on the way here. Lukas should be expecting me."

The guard held his aim steady, but glanced at Frank. His gaze fixed on Frank's arm for a while. "You must be Agent Hawkins."

"Yeah."

"Wait here." He ducked inside and a moment later, emerged again with the grizzly moustachioed officer.

Frank smiled at the familiar face. "Good to see ya, Luke."

"Likewise, Frank," Lukas said, taking a long look at the Maori Terminator beside him.

Frank offered his hand to shake, but Lukas balked. "It's all right," Frank said. "I won't crush it."

Lukas shook it and said, "You two make an imposing pair. What's the story behind that arm?"

"A long one. No time for it now," Frank said. "I need to see Daniel Bergman."

Lukas grunted. "You can enter, but he stays outside. I'm not having a repeat of Plumpton here."

Arnie growled like a bear.

"He's a bit on edge," Frank explained. "No chance of a favour for an old comrade?"

"Listen Frank, I don't know what you've got mixed up in, but you're disavowed. There's no record of you ever being a Europa agent. I'm letting you in to speak to this kid because I *do* remember. That's all the favour I can risk. Either you come in alone, or you both get the hell out of here."

Arnie crossed his arms and muttered something in Maori that sounded very much like a threat.

"Just relax, man," Frank said to him. "We ain't leaving here with nothing, so just stay out here while I go talk to Dan. We're doing this for Catherine, remember?"

"Yeah," Arnie rumbled. "Just be as quick as you can."

Lukas led Frank into the building, and escorted him to the holding cells. "You want to speak to the fat one as well?"

"Fat one?" Frank asked.

"Petrov Clitski. He's the one we arrested. Bergman just happened to be with him at the time."

"Let me see Dan first."

"Right in here," Lukas opened a cell door and Frank ducked inside.

"Frank!" Dan cried as he saw him. Handcuffs clinked at his wrist as he tried to stand up, but they were chained to the desk.

Frank said to Lukas, "Give us a minute?"

Lukas nodded and walked out, closing the door behind him.

Dan wore his usual attire of baggy jeans and a grey hoody. His greasy bird's nest of black hair looked like it hadn't seen a comb for a week, and he also sported a mild tan that suggested he'd been on the road for a while.

"You gotta get me out of here!" Dan said. "I know where Horatio Zhin lives, but we have to get there before Cathy does!"

"All right, slow the fuck down," Frank raised his hands. "What are you talking about?"

"I found out what Horizon is, Frank. Aren't you listening? It's all a plot by Horatio Zhin to take control of the world's energy supply. He's the one responsible for Yuma and those other towns!"

"What happened in Yuma?"

"You haven't *heard*?" Dan gaped.

"I've been a bit preoccupied being held captive the last few days." He held up his metal arm for Dan to see.

"Woah," he muttered. "Did Sid Blunt do that?"

"Yeah," Frank said, flexing the fingers. "Still getting used to it."

Dan gawked at Frank's arm, leaning closer, but his restraints didn't allow much movement. "Can I see it?"

Frank circled the desk and held the arm out for Dan to inspect.

He marvelled at it, reading the tiny text embossed in the metal at the shoulder. "An R52 chip? Holy shit. Dude, you have a supercomputer in your arm."

"Really?" Frank asked nonchalantly.

"Does it feel like your real arm?"

"No. But I *can* feel. Sensory receptors, or something."

"That's awesome. Is it easy to use?"

"There's some AI inside that reacts to my thoughts." He remembered the sound of the assistant's head cracking against the wall. "It's pretty responsive..."

"It looks the same as that big metal guy's legs."

"Yeah. It's the same prototype. He and Sid are waiting outside with the VTOL."

"Oh my god that's perfect," Dan cried. "He can fly us to Zhin's house!"

"You sure that's where Cathy has gone?"

"Yes!"

Frank rubbed his stubbly chin. "All right, catch me up with what you've been doing since Plumpton." He took a seat opposite Dan. "Tell me everything you know. The quick version."

Dan recounted his adventure across Europe with Cathy and explained the events in Yuma, Dongola and Tarrow Creek, which Frank found pretty goddamn disturbing.

"We hacked into SwissNet dude," Dan boasted. "We found Zhin's secret home address in the Swiss Alps. Frank, we have to get there before Cathy. Who knows what kind of protection that psychopath has?"

"Why would she go to his house?"

"Where else is she gonna go? She wants to murder her mother! There's a good chance that's where Margery retreated to, after the incident at the facility. Cathy talked to me about wanting revenge..." Dan spread his hands as wide as the handcuffs would allow in an attempted shrug.

Horatio Zhin, Frank thought. The Korean unifier, Sid Blunt's ex-business partner, Margery's fuck buddy, and possibly the mastermind behind Horizon.

Frank's mission had started six months ago when one of Dan's peers had leaked information to the ShadowNet about a super weapon being developed in the alpine facility. Now, the bodies had piled up, spreading to all three continents, and once again, thanks to the skill of a kid in Binary Eye, Frank had a major clue as to what the fuck was really going on.

If Horatio Zhin was the man pulling the strings, then he'd been ahead of them the entire time. This was Frank's chance to catch up.

"What's the address?" he asked.

"Cloud Lodge, Valais region. Up in the Swiss mountains. Ask Derunox, man. He's the one who found it."

"Deru – what?"

"Derunox! My buddy, he's stuck here too."

"Is he as good with computers as you?"

"Dude, he's a Jedi."

Frank leered.

"He's better than me," Dan elaborated.

So, he'd be useful to have around. "I have to get you both out of here." Frank stood and left the cell. Lukas was waiting outside, leaning against the wall.

"How did your talk go?" he asked.

"Good, thanks. Listen, Lukas, I'm gonna need to ask another favour…"

Lukas cocked an eyebrow. "What?"

"I have to take these boys with me."

"You know I can't do that, Frank."

"It's important," Frank said. "I've been investigating a conspiracy these past few weeks, and thanks to those two, I finally have a lead on the people behind it. You gotta let me take them."

"There's nothing I can do, Frank," Lukas said, stepping away from the wall. "You're disavowed. That makes you a civilian. What do you think would happen to me if I let a civilian walk away with Europa prisoners?"

For fuck's sake. "Have you *seen* what's happening in the

world right now?" Frank seethed. "People are dying in the thousands because of Horatio Zhin. I might actually be able to stop it."

Lukas held up his hands. "I'm sorry, Frank. I let you in here, I could already lose my job for that alone. This is a difficult position you put me in, comrade."

Gah. "I know. All right."

Frank glanced up and down the corridor. At the far end was a concrete wall, which by his judgement, had to be an outer wall of the building.

He turned back to Lukas. "Just gimme a moment to tell Dan."

"Make it quick," Lukas urged. "That metal guy outside is making my men twitchy."

There's a good reason for that.

Frank ducked back inside the cell and eased the door shut. He looked at Dan, chained to the desk, and shook his head dejectedly.

"Not letting us leave, huh?" Dan said. "Figures."

Frank believed his arm could rip the chain off the desk with ease. But not yet…

"Dan, take a look at this." He pulled out the universal controller Gunther had given him. "Do you think you can operate it?"

Dan held it in his handcuffed hands and his eyes lit up. "Holy crap, this can control you?"

"Not just me. See if you can access our Terminator friend outside."

Dan flicked through the touch screen interface and an image of the Europa building's front door appeared on the screen. "No way," Dan said in awe. "Dude, this is metal-man crotch-view. He has a camera in his dick!"

"Can you control him?"

"I think so."

"Okay, bring him around the side of the building."

Dan fiddled with the control interface and the camera moved.

'What the fuck?' Arnie said, his voice sounding tinny through the controller.

Dan spun him left and marched Arnie across the grass around the building's left side, which was where Frank believed that outer wall was.

"Frank, you bastard. If this is you, I'm gonna rip your fucking balls off."

Dan gave Frank a worried look.

"Ignore him. Bring him up to that wall, just *there.*" Frank pointed at the screen, as the camera bobbed right up to the brickwork. "Kick that wall."

"Seriously?" Dan gaped.

"You want to get out of here or not?"

"Yeah, but—"

"Kick it."

Dan pushed a button on the screen.

A tremor shook the cell.

Outside the door, Lukas shouted.

"Kick it again," Frank said.

He saw Arnie's leg thrust forward on the screen and knock a hole in the wall.

"Keep going, we're gonna be escaping through there in thirty seconds."

He left the cell again and saw Lukas calling for backup. "Sorry comrade," Frank chopped him on the neck, and Lukas went limp. Frank caught him and eased him down onto the floor.

He peered through the adjacent cell door and saw a fat man sitting at the desk, also handcuffed. Frank punched the door's lock and it flew open on its hinges.

"Agh!" the fat man yelped.

"Derunox, I assume?" Frank said.

"I, yes."

"I'm getting you out of here." Frank grabbed the chains and tore them out of the desk. "Move it!"

Derunox followed him out of the cell and into the corridor.

CRASH!

A metal foot exploded through the wall at the end of the corridor and Arnie roared through the gap. "*Frank, you bastard!*"

Frank ducked into Dan's cell and ripped his chains from the desk. "Go!"

They piled out of the cell and sprinted for the broken wall. Frank shoved Derunox through the rubble, followed by Dan. A man behind them yelled "*Freeze!*"

Frank dived through the gap into sunlight.

"Run!" he shouted, pulling the fat man to his feet.

Arnie clomped ahead of them acting as a shield, as Europa guards opened fire from the lobby entrance.

"Keep your heads down!" Frank barked as they ran towards the gaping maw of Sid's VTOL. Sid's mercs started returning fire from the aircraft, providing cover.

Derunox stumbled and fell on his face in the grass.

Dan slowed.

"Keep going!" Frank ordered, shoving Dan forwards, his legs burning from the low-crouched sprint.

They reached the VTOL and scrambled up the ramp.

"Get us in the air!" Frank bellowed at Sid, who was cowering at the front of the hold.

Sid nodded and disappeared through the cockpit door.

The VTOL's engines screamed to life. Gunfire peppered the craft's hull. The mercs retreated inside, popping off shots.

"What about Derunox?" Dan cried.

"I'll get him," Arnie said, and ran back down the ramp. "Hold the doors open!"

He clomped across the grass towards the fat man, drawing fire from the guards. Bullets clanged off his armour like a hail of deadly stones.

Arnie and Derunox disappeared from sight as the VTOL lifted into the air.

"Petrov!" Dan cried.

Frank stopped him with a hand and pushed him down

into a side bench. "It's too late."

Shit. Frank collapsed into the bench and clung to the cargo netting.

A moment later, Arnie leapt into view again and landed on the edge of the open ramp, holding Derunox over a shoulder. The aircraft rocked at the force of his weight. He stepped forward and dropped the big man on the floor.

Dan stumbled to his feet, grinning like an idiot. "*Holy shit!*"

The ramp closed and the cabin quietened.

Arnie cast a dark glare at Frank from across the hold.

"Derunox!" Dan cried, dropping to his knees beside the big lad.

Frank spotted blood seeping out from under his stomach, and spilling across the floor. He jumped down next to Dan and lifted up Derunox's shirt. Three seeping bullet holes dotted his stomach, oozing bile and blood. *Fuck. Three gutshots.* Nobody could survive that.

"Dan," Derunox croaked, spitting up blood that ran down his double chin. "I am glad... we met, padawan." He wheezed a few ragged breaths, staring up at Dan. Then his eyes rolled back and he stopped moving.

Dan clutched his friend's shoulder, and shook it lightly. "Derunox? Petrov? No. No..."

Dan fell back onto his arse and buried his face in his hands.

PART SIX

28
ON THE RUN

She ran all the way back to the city centre, until her lungs felt ready to burst. Wheezing and panting, she reached the bridge where she and Dan had kissed the previous night, and slowed to catch her breath. She inhaled slowly, trying to relieve the stitch in her side.

She listened for sirens. Checked over her shoulder for people following her.

Nothing.

I'm alone…

She hastily crossed the cobblestoned Charles Bridge, ignoring the beggars, and entered the old town. She passed through the gothic square and weaved through alleys until she came to the modern part of the city. On the high street, a protest march was taking place. Several dozen people wielding banners and pickets were walking down the middle of the road, blocking traffic and causing a scene.

Cathy didn't understand what they were chanting, because it was in Czech, but she recognised the emblem on the banners – a yellow sun rising over a red field. The symbol of the New Dawn religious organisation.

I have to get out of Prague.

But how? Hitchhiking seemed dangerous. She couldn't trust anyone now. She had to find her own way out of the city. Maybe she could acquire a car. But where to go?

She gulped, squeezing between the crowds of onlookers,

making her way down the road. Her freedom bracelet *clinked*, Dan's gift to her. A hollow sadness wafted through her at the sight of it, which she forcefully buried, trying to focus on the terrifying, but exciting reality: she could go anywhere she liked.

Right now, I'm actually free.

A smile played on her lips, then she wondered about Dan and Derunox. They'd been captured, after risking their own safety to give her the chance of escaping. There was nothing she could do for them without getting caught herself.

She couldn't let their capture be for nothing. *I have to finish what we started. I know where I need to go...*

She spotted a bank nearby and weaved her way through the onlookers to get to the wall-ATM. Peeking left and right, she made sure nobody was watching her, and pulled out Dan's EMP gun from her backpack.

"How does this thing work?" she muttered, aiming the device at the card reader slot. She squeezed the trigger and nothing happened. "Shit, shit, *shit.*" She turned it over in her hand, and found a little button on its side. *A safety switch?* She flicked it on and tried again.

Zrrrrap!

A spark shot out of the nozzle and arced into the slot. The money hatch opened and notes spewed out. She grabbed a handful and stuffed them into the bag, but the money kept coming.

A deafening alarm blared out of the building. She panicked and stepped backwards, tripping on a paving slab and landed on her butt. People in the crowd turned around to see what the commotion was, eyes drawn to the bank.

A man offered her a hand. "Are you all right?" He spoke with a deep, British accent. He glanced at her open bag, with the gun and a splay of notes spilling out of it. He frowned, then recognition flashed across his grey eyes. "Holy moly, Catherine Blunt?"

Shit! He recognises me!

Another man shouted something in Czech, and ran towards the ATM. It was spitting out notes like an electronic poker card dealer. They sprayed out in the air and fluttered to the ground. As more people noticed, they swarmed around the machine, plucking money off the pavement and cheering.

The British man was bumped aside, and Cathy took her chance to escape.

She scrambled to her feet, zipped up the bag and bolted into the road. She plunged into the New Dawn march, barging past the protestors as she crossed the road and fled into an alleyway on the other side. At the far end of the alley, she emerged on a narrow side street lined with shop fronts.

Cathy's heart pounded against her ribs, so she slowed to a brisk walk, wary of causing another scene by sprinting. Mingling with the tourists, she strolled down the street, clutching one strap of the bag over her shoulder.

Ahead of her, she spied a shop selling cheap sunglasses and baseball caps on a rotating stand. *I could use that as a disguise.* The busy side street bustled with activity, tourists shopping and sitting in café verandas. As she passed by a café, she noticed a small group of people huddled round a cell phone, watching a video.

Cathy caught a soundbite as she walked by, and heard her own voice talking through the tinny little speakers.

Oh my god, they're watching my video.

She risked a glance at their faces, and saw a mixture of confusion, horror and bewilderment on their expressions. It was impossible to tell if they believed what they were seeing. One of them, a young girl looked up and made eye contact with Cathy. Her heart jumped and she quickly turned away, bee-lining for the sunglasses stand outside the store now only a few more paces away.

She made it another three steps before a heavy hand fell upon her shoulder.

"Oi!"

She spun around, a jolt of ice shivering through her.

"It *is* her!" said the British guy from before. He was in his early twenties, and turned to a young black haired girl about the same age. "Look, Laura. It's really Catherine Blunt."

"No way!" said Laura, clutching her hands to her mouth.

Cathy stepped back away from them. "Are you *following* me?" She looked past them, checking for bank security, or police, but it was just tourists and shoppers milling around. The group at the café had finished watching their video, and now the girl at the table was saying something, and pointing right at Cathy. Her companions all turned at once and looked at her. "Leave me alone!"

She turned and started walking away.

"We saw your video," the British guy said, his deep voice rolling through her. "Is it true about Horatio Zhin? Did he murder all those people?"

She froze. They had seen her online as well. Was that good or bad?

"Yes." She spoke softly, talking over a shoulder. "I'm trying to stop him."

"That's amazing," Laura said. "And were you really held hostage underground? That sounds just awful..."

What would Frank, or even Dan do in this situation? They're sympathetic. Maybe I can use that.

Cathy turned to them. "Who are you and what do you want from me?"

"Nothing," the guy said, raising his hands in defence. "My name's James. This is my girlfriend, Laura. We're on a road trip together." He squeezed Laura round the shoulder and smiled.

Behind them, Cathy spied movement, as the girl had left her friends at the café table and was weaving through the crowd towards them.

"That's nice," Cathy said. "But I don't have time for this. I need to g—" She paused. "Wait, do you have a car?"

"Yeah, of course," Laura said. "Can't exactly do a road

trip without a car, can you?"

Cathy thought about the stack of money she had stored in her bag. "How much do you want for it?"

"Huh?" James said, frowning.

"Your car. I want to buy it from you. I'll give you cash right now."

"Excuse me?" The café girl stepped up beside James, speaking in a heavy Eastern European accent. "I just saw you go by, and had to ask... are you Catherine Blunt?"

Cathy gulped, the hairs on the back of her neck standing rigid.

"Yes, she is!" said Laura.

"I, uhh," Cathy stammered.

"I thought so!" the café girl's face lit up. She turned and waved to her friends at the café and two more of them stood up to approach.

This is getting weird.

"Look, I just need to get out of here," Cathy said apologetically. "You all should too."

"Why?" asked James.

"Wow!" said one of the men from the café as he joined them. "Je to naozaj ona!"

"Yes," said a third. "Sorry. His English not good. We see you on line! You amazing!"

"Thanks," Cathy said, chewing her lip.

"Why should we get out of the city?" James asked.

"Look," Cathy said. "I'm trying to *stop* Horatio Zhin from killing more people. I think those New Dawn people may even have something to do with it..."

"Really?" Laura said, glancing at James with worry.

"You think Prague is next?" the café girl said. "Oh god!"

"I don't know," Cathy admitted, raising her hands.

Passers-by were eyeing the gathering quizzically. Now the other three people from the café were coming over, and Cathy felt eyes on her from all angles.

I haven't got time for this! She turned to walk away, the New Dawn march nagging on her mind. If Zhin was using them to spread the vapourisation bomb, she had to get out of the city as fast as she could.

"Where you going?" cried the café girl.

Cathy looked at all of the people around her. She watched their shoes, and their clothes, imagining them strewn across the streets, their bodies turned to dust. She ran both hands through her scalp, a gnawing sense of fear burrowing into her gut. *How can I just leave without warning them?*

She turned back to the group. "You need to run. Get away from the city or you might all die!"

They just gawked at her.

"You're crazy," said one of the men from the café. "Horatio Zhin is helping people by making those solar plants. Soon, everyone will have power, even poor countries."

"Did you *watch* her video?" James interjected. "He's built a weapon that vapourises people!"

"That's bullshit. Have you ever heard of Photoshop? That video was fake as hell."

"It's not!" Cathy cried, clenching her fist. "You must believe me, Zhin is a dangerous man. I have to stop him and my mother no matter what."

"What are you going to do?" asked Laura.

"I know where he lives. I'm going to go there and…and k—" *Kill them?* It sounded ridiculous. How was she going to murder her own mother, let alone a world famous politician turned businessman. The place will be crawling with security.

I'll never be free unless she is gone! She owed it to Dan and Derunox, Annie and Ben, as well as all the people in the facility who died. She had to *try*.

"Look," she said to the gaggle of strangers in front of her. "I have to go. Just get away from the city, for your own sake."

Cathy turned and strode away, clinging tightly to the shoulder strap of her backpack. *Should I try and buy someone else's car?* There had to be a used car shop somewhere. But that would take too long, and she didn't have a license. She weaved through the bustle and came to a wide main road. Cars cruised by, heading out of the city.

Here we go again.

She took up a position on the sidewalk, let down her hair and stuck out her thumb.

A few cars went by, then one pulled over. A black saloon with rusty wheel arches parked up beside her and the window rolled down. The driver, a thirty-something man with sunglasses and rolled-up sleeves leaned out to analyse her. "Where to?" he spoke accented English, toking on a cigarette. A pungent aroma of smoke poured out of the car.

"West?" Cathy replied vaguely. There was no way she'd tell this guy exactly where she wanted to go. Thinking quickly, she added, "A friend is meeting me in… Munich."

"Germany, ja?" The man smiled, rubbing his chin as he gazed forwards at the road ahead, taking another deep drag of his cigarette, before tossing it on the ground at Cathy's feet. "Get in."

"Thanks," Cathy said, gulping.

Don't do it. Don't get in that car. Remember what happened last time? The two French boys had robbed her and Dan blind, and left them for dead on the side of the road. But that was Dan's fault. She was smarter than him when it came to social behaviour.

She hesitated. Other cars were passing by. It would be easy to wait for another one. A woman driver might be safer, surely?

"Catherine!" a deep voice boomed behind her. "Wait!"

She turned around and saw James and Laura running towards her.

"What are you doing?" James said as they reached her.

"Hitchhiking," Cathy said. "I told you, I have to get out of here."

"Come with us," Laura said. "We'll take you wherever

you need to go."

Cathy's heart skipped a beat. "Really? You'd do that? You don't even know me."

"Well, we kinda do," James smiled. "That video you posted was pretty shocking."

"I can't believe they were experimenting on people," Laura said with an airy tone of worry.

"Listen, I'd totally regret it if I let you get in that car and drive away," James said. "I know we can help you. Right Laura?"

"Yeah, it's not like we have a set plan or anything." Laura shrugged. "We've been winging it this whole trip. Taking us where the wind goes."

"She's right," James grinned. "Nothing quite like being on the open road. You never know where you'll end up or who you'll meet. Case in point!" He gestured to Cathy.

Cathy sucked in a breath, hardly believing her luck. She never thought her video would prove to be so helpful. She expected it to go mostly unnoticed, but she'd bumped into these two, plus the others at the café who had all seen it. How many others had it reached?

The greasy saloon driver made a remark in Czech. It sounded rude. He was eyeing James up and down. Then he turned to Cathy. "Well?"

"Uh, sorry," Cathy said. "I guess I have a ride."

He frowned at James, closed his window up, and drove off.

"I think you made the right decision," Laura whispered conspiratorially, and wound an arm between Cathy's elbow.

Cathy couldn't help but smile. There was something curious about these two that put her mind at ease.

"Our car's this way," James said, cocking a thumb over his shoulder.

"Lead the way," Cathy said.

Their car was a pristine, white Landrover Discovery 4x4. It had one of those GB stickers on the rear bumper and an English style license plate.

"Woah, this is not what I expected from a couple of backpackers," Cathy said.

"It's my dad's car," James explained, as he clicked a key fob to unlock the car.

Laura unwound herself from Cathy's arm and opened the back door. Cathy said thanks, threw her pack into the middle and climbed in after it. Laura went around to the other side and joined Cathy in the back.

James got into the right-hand driver's seat. "Oh, abandoning me for our famous guest, is it?"

Laura grinned, "Of course! You can be our chauffeur."

"Righty ho," James said, straightening his shoulders and lifting his chin. He mimicked a butler's voice, "Where to, m'ladies?"

Cathy had the absurd thought that he'd make an excellent blues singer with those gravelly tones. It somehow didn't match his clean-shaven, boyish face. He and Laura had the air of a privileged upbringing, not too dissimilar to Cathy's own.

"I, uhh…" Cathy started. "I have to get to Switzerland."

"*Switzerland?*" he gaped at her in the rear-view mirror.

Laura giggled and reached forward to type it into the GPS. "I always wanted to go there!"

James' mouth flapped like a fish. "Uh, so which part?"

"The Valais region, a place called Cloud Lodge." Cathy felt a pang of guilt. "Is it too far for you?"

James read the GPS. "Does that say *nine hundred kilometres?*"

Cathy's heart sank. It was too far. She should never have come with them. How could she expect two strangers to just drop their plans and take her on a cross-continent road trip on a whim? "Are you guys sure about this?" she asked. "That's a really long way."

"Looks like we can finally see the Alps, sweetie," Laura

said, kissing James on the cheek, before gliding back into the rear seat next to Cathy.

"Seems so," James smiled, shaking his head. "We got a 9 hour drive ahead of us. Better get comfy."

"Onward!" Laura pointed both hands towards the windscreen.

Cathy laughed. "You two are something."

"Oh, I know," Laura grinned.

They joined the nearest highway and set off west out of Prague.

They made polite small talk for a while as they cruised smoothly down the highway. The leather seats were spacious and comfortable, and Cathy had plenty of leg room behind the driver.

Despite this, Laura sat with both feet hunched beneath her butt, her entire body facing Cathy. Her long black hair flowed like a frizzy waterfall down past her shoulders. "We're from England, in case you didn't guess already."

Cathy chuckled. "The accent was a bit of a giveaway."

"Ooh you're half German, right? You must like beer!" She reached over the back seat and rummaged in a cooler box. She came back with two beer bottles. "Want one?"

It seemed rude not to say yes. "Sure, thanks."

Laura twisted the cap off and handed it to her. "None for Mr. Chauffeur, I'm afraid," she pouted at James.

"Gee, thanks, hope you girls are enjoying yourselves back there," he griped teasingly.

"Don't mind him. I'll make it up to him later." Laura winked, and held her bottle out to clink it with Cathy. "Cheers!"

"Cheers," she said, taking a swig. It tasted a bit like fizzy metal. "So, are you guys on holiday or something?"

"We're post-grad students, celebrating our successful graduation," Laura explained. "We met at Oxford University."

Cathy took another swig and forced it down. "What did you study?" she croaked.

Laura laughed. "Not a beer drinker? Sorry, it's all we've got."

"It's fine," she said, taking another swig. That one went down easier.

"We're Bachelor of Arts graduates in Modern Media." James bounced his eyebrows at her in the rear-view.

"What does that mean?" she asked.

He scoffed in disappointment.

Laura waved a hand lazily through the air. "It means we're film buffs."

"Oh," she said. "That's interesting." The truth was, Cathy hadn't seen many movies in her time at the facility. She hoped they wouldn't ask her about anything recent.

She took another sip and stared out of the window at the scenery. They were alongside an industrial train line, and pylons kept whizzing past.

"Are you scared?" Laura asked.

Cathy turned sharply towards her. "Um. Yeah, a little, actually."

"I thought you might be." She had a chilled out, almost lethargic way of speaking. She rested her head sideways against the headrest, looking at Cathy with sincerity. "I can't believe they locked you up in a facility all these years…"

"That must have been horrendous," James agreed.

"Yeah." Cathy felt hot blood rushing to her cheeks. "It was awful."

"What are you going to do if your mum is at this Cloud Lodge place?" Laura asked.

"I…" Cathy started. *I want to kill her.* She took a long swig of beer, and wiped her mouth. "I'm not sure yet."

"It's okay," Laura said, touching Cathy's arm. "Let's talk about something else." She glanced down at Cathy's wrist. "Oh my god, where did you get that bracelet?"

"It was a gift. To celebrate my freedom, Dan said. Each

little piece represents a country we visited together."

"Aww, that's so cute!" Laura clutched one hand to her chest. "Who is Dan?"

"A guy I met after escaping from the facility."

"Oooh," Laura grinned, propping her head up with her hand against the seat. "Do tell."

Cathy smiled. "He's the biggest geek I've ever met."

"He sounds like my kinda person. Where is he now?"

Cathy's face dropped. "He got captured by Europa, along with one of his friends."

"Oh no…"

"He's a hacker, you see. He's the one who helped me get that information about Horatio Zhin. If it wasn't for him, I wouldn't be here now. I had to leave him behind, otherwise they would have caught me, too… he must have been so upset with me."

"I think he'll understand," Laura said. "He obviously thinks highly of you."

"I have to do this for him. I can't let his capture be for nothing."

Laura was smiling. "This is so sweet. It's just like a romantic spy story."

Cathy blushed. "It's not like that."

"Like what?"

"Me and Dan," Cathy stammered.

"What, you don't like him?"

"I do. He's so caring, and sweet. I'm just…" Her mind flicked to memories of Annie and Ben, the only meaningful relationships she'd ever had. "I've not had much luck with love in the past. It never seems to end well."

"Well, it won't if you're always worrying about the ending!" Laura said. "You have to enjoy the moment. Just go with it. Things either work out or they don't."

"Yeah. I agree with that. That's why I kissed him yesterday…"

"Oooh, look at you."

James shook his head at them both in the rear-view. "Like a couple of gossiping school girls."

"Ignore him!" Laura shrilled, leaning closer. "So, how was it? Spill the beans!"

Cathy chuckled. "We were on that old bridge last night, this one." Cathy held up her bracelet, pointing to the miniature Charles Bridge.

"So romantic!"

"He was looking at me like this lost little puppy," Cathy explained. "Sometimes I find it cute and sometimes it pisses me off. But last night, I just felt like I needed to try it, y'know?"

"Of course."

"So, I kissed him. And you know what he did?"

"No, what?"

"He fell over."

"Ha!"

"Yeah. We just fell right onto the ground in front of all these other people. It was so embarrassing."

"But you enjoyed it. I can tell."

Cathy pushed her hair behind an ear. "Yeah. I'd try it again."

It dawned on her that the past few days spent with Dan had created some of her most exhilarating and happy memories. She'd evaded her father's capture and travelled across Europe, sharing some memorable sights with the geeky but caring guy. He was similar to Ben in some regards, but she'd never felt as confident around Ben as she did with Dan. He had this way of bringing out the best in her, somehow. It saddened her deeply to think of him stuck in some cell.

Laura sighed dreamily. "I hope you two reunite after all of this."

"Me too…"

Laura reached over and hugged Cathy. It was awkward with the seatbelts, but Laura seemed to be the sort of girl that relished awkwardness. Cathy liked her.

"Thank you for doing this." She leaned forward. "And you, James. Seriously, just, thank you."

"It's nothing," he said. "When we started this little adventure we agreed on one solitary rule, didn't we, hun?"

"Yeah we did!"

"What rule?" Cathy asked, intrigued.

"Do whatever will make the best story," James said.

"The best story?" Cathy asked, snorting a laugh.

"Yeah!" Laura said. "What's so funny?"

"It just seems like a...well, an odd way to make important decisions."

"It's exciting!" Laura said. "And it's made this trip way more memorable than it could have been."

"Back there in the street," James said. "I saw two options: let you go alone, or offer to help you. It was an easy choice."

Laura was nodding in agreement.

"Heh," Cathy said. "I like that a lot. It sounds like real freedom."

The scenery gradually grew more rural as the hours ticked by. The sun was setting behind the hills, as they cruised along a German autobahn under a deep orange sky dotted with fiery clouds.

"So you haven't seen *Star Wars Episode Twelve: The Black Star?*" Laura asked, slumped back in her seat.

"Nope," Cathy shrugged. Three bottles of beer in, and her head was swimming pleasantly. She didn't even mind all the movie conversation, even though it seemed she had missed an entire generation's worth of entertainment.

"Shocking," Laura said, shaking her head. She closed her eyes and fell quiet.

After a while, Cathy heard gentle snores to her left.

"Has she passed out?" James asked from the front.

Cathy chuckled at the sight of Laura, wedged in her seat with her head dropping forwards. "Yup, just you and me now."

"Wanna ride up front? Keep me company."

"Sure," Cathy said. She downed the last sip of her beer and left the bottle in the cup holder. Unclipping her seatbelt, she wriggled between the seats and sat next to James in the front.

As soon as she was seated, she let loose a ferocious yawn.

"Oh, you too? Gonna just leave me to drive alone?" James quipped.

"Sorry," Cathy said. "I didn't get much sleep these past few days." She wriggled in the seat, trying to find a comfy spot, but got stuck sideways, pinned by the seatbelt. She slouched, resting her head against the headrest, watching James drive. He had a square chin and a button nose, with a crop of short, tidy black hair close-shaven around his ears and neckline.

"That doesn't look very comfortable," he remarked, without looking at her. His deep voice was more penetrating now that she was next to him. It rumbled through her core.

"It's okay." She fought the urge to fall asleep, and figured his voice might keep her conscious, so she forced some more conversation on him. "Did you say this was your dad's car?"

"Yup. Do you like it?"

"It's fancy. What does your dad do?"

"He owns some golf courses."

"Wow." Cathy didn't know anything about golf. Nor any other sport, for that matter. "Your dad must have very nice golf courses..." She felt her eyes trying to close. "Because this is a very, very fancy car."

"He's done alright for himself," James nodded. "Not a patch on your father, though."

Cathy jerked awake. "My father is a prick."

James opened his mouth, then closed it again. He gulped. "Sorry. We don't have to talk about him."

Cathy frowned. All of a sudden, her happy, tipsy state of mind had soured. She loosened the seat belt, and readjusted herself to sit properly in the seat, facing the front. Up ahead, she could see the dark outlines of small mountains looming in the distance.

"Wanna see something cool?" James said.

"Sure."

"Open the glove box."

She did, pleased with the distraction. The lid tipped forward, illuminated by a small light, revealing a pistol strapped to its underside. "Um. Why do you have a gun?"

"It's my father's. Don't worry, it's licensed. We have to show it at every border crossing. It never leaves the car."

"Are golf courses really that dangerous?" she asked.

He laughed. "No, it's mostly to scare the deer. Dad sometimes drives around shooting it to scare them off. They eat the long grass around the edges and their hooves chew up the fairways." He eased into the chair, clutching the wheel with one hand and rubbing his chin with the other. "Wanna hold it?"

She gave the gun another brief once over. "Is it loaded?"

"Yeah."

"Then no." She closed the box.

"Fair enough," he said coolly.

"What was university like?" she asked, trying to keep the conversation going. Anything to push the niggling thought of her father away a bit more.

"Fun. Really fun." He thumbed towards the back. "Met her there. We just clicked. Had the best time of our lives."

"Really?" Cathy breathed, feeling a little jealous. She and Annie had hoped to one day go to university together. That entire part of her life had been stripped away by her mother.

Fuck! First father, and now *her*. She wriggled her butt, somehow the seat had gotten much less comfortable.

"Why don't you get some sleep?" James suggested.

"I can't."

"Try."

She found her eyelids sagging again, giving in to his suggestion. She tilted her head back against the soft headrest. "Won't you get lonely?"

He chuckled. "I'll be fine."

"No," she insisted. "I'll stay awake…" But the last twenty four hours were catching up with her, and as the sun dipped beneath the hills, casting the car into a dim shadow, she lost the battle with exhaustion.

***

When warm sunlight caressed her cheek, gently easing her into consciousness, she felt refreshed and at peace. The car was parked up next to a lake. Outside, pine trees surrounded them on both sides, growing up the slopes of the looming mountains all around.

Laura and James were in front of the car, sitting on a rock beside the lake, watching the sunrise.

"Oh my god," Cathy said, rubbing sleep from her eyes. *Are we there?*

She opened the car and stepped outside.

James turned around at the sound of the door closing.

"Good morning!" They both beckoned her over.

Cathy wrapped her arms around herself, the chill dawn air giving her the shivers.

"How long was I asleep?" she asked.

"All night," James said. "I parked up here just after midnight and snoozed. Didn't wanna wake you both."

"Check it out," Laura said, pointing across the lake.

Cathy followed her finger and spied a grand wooden building nestled in the forest on the opposite side of the lake.

"That's your Cloud Lodge."

Butterflies fluttered in Cathy's stomach, churning her

insides to butter. "Oh, god." *Mother's over there.*

A hundred thoughts flashed through Cathy's mind. Now that she was almost here, it occurred to her that she had no idea what to expect. Would they have guard dogs? Armed mercenaries? Would the house be a fortress, impossible to even approach? Supposing she did manage to get to the front door, what the hell was she going to say to her mother, or Horatio? What would she do? Or most importantly, what would they do to *her?*

Maybe it was a mistake coming here.

No. I need to do this. I need to confront her.

"You okay?" Laura asked.

"Having doubts?" James said.

"We're here to help, remember. We'll take you all the way to the front door if you like."

"Thank you guys," Cathy said. "But I need to do this alone." She gazed across the water and the lodge, thinking about what she might do if her mother was there. "I have one more thing to ask of you, though."

"What is it?" James said.

"I want to buy your gun."

29
CLOUD LODGE (I)

Derunox's body lay atop the side bench in the cargo hold, covered by a sheet of tarp. Dan sat in the row opposite, next to Frank, staring at the lump that used to be his friend.

Sid Blunt, Arnie and Frank were engaged in a heated debate with the three mercs, but Dan was barely paying any attention to the conversation.

A numbness had settled over him. His eyes stung from crying, and his clogged nose made it difficult to breathe, but he didn't care. He sat on the bench leaning forward on his knees, just staring, and waiting.

They had landed in Switzerland around midnight, and Blunt's VTOL sat cloaked, halfway up a lakeside mountain. Cloud Lodge was far below them, a secluded oaken manse, hidden within the trees.

Frank and Arnie had disagreed about the best way to approach the house. Arnie wanted to bust right in and secure Cathy as soon as possible.

"She might be dead already!" he argued.

"We don't know if she's even there," replied Frank. "And we have no idea what kind of defences they have."

Blunt fidgeted. "He's right, Arnie. We should listen to him. He's the expert in this sort of thing..."

"Europa didn't recruit me as an infiltrator for nothing," Frank agreed. "If we're doing this, we do it *my* way."

"So, what do you suggest?" brooded Arnie.

"A Keno jump at dawn."

"Dawn?" cried Arnie. "That's over six hours away!"

"Let's assume they have guards. Dawn is the end of a night shift. It's the time when they are at their most vulnerable, and least alert. We have five trained men here, and two civvies." He gestured to Blunt and Dan. "Not exactly an army, is it? We need every advantage we can get."

"I'm not listening to this bullshit," Arnie jerked a dismissive hand. "We go in hard, and we go in *now*."

"Arnie," Blunt pleaded. "No-one wants to get Catherine back more than me. But if we go in gun's blazing, and she gets hurt, or worse... I'll never forgive myself."

Arnie submitted, resentfully.

They agreed to get some rest before assaulting the lodge at sunrise and putting a bullet between Horatio Zhin's eyes. At least, that's what Dan hoped. The man was responsible for so many deaths, how could he possibly be allowed to get away with it? Derunox would still be alive too if they hadn't been dragged into this, and he could put that responsibility at Zhin's feet too.

Not to mention Jimmy. *Things are coming to a climax, little bro...*

Frank nudged his shoulder. "You alright with heights?"

Dan pinched his lips together and shook his head.

"Well, I'll be with ya the whole time. You're gonna tandem with me."

Dan didn't know what that meant, but he grunted an agreement and went back to staring into space.

Frank leaned closer and spoke more gently. "Sorry about your hacker pal." Frank clasped a heavy hand around his shoulder. "Try to let it go, for now. I need you out there. Chances are they have some heavy security. Might need your computer skills."

Dan licked his lips and took a deep breath. He felt a small pulse of energy, the tiniest glimmer of excitement. "Sure," he said, turning to Frank.

Frank patted him on the back. "Good lad."

The VTOL took off in the dim light of dawn, rising high into the sky. A bulb filled the hold with a red glow, illuminating the line of men as they waited for the ramp door to open. Arnie was at the front, fully armoured and wearing double parachute packs. Behind him were two of the mercs, then Dan, strapped at the waist to Frank behind him. Blunt took up the rear with the last merc, and his nervous mumbling drifted down the line.

"For Catherine... I'm coming Catherine... Just stay safe... I'm on my way... I can do this...I can do this..."

That's when it occurred to Dan what he was about to do, and his bowels loosened. "Um, Frank?"

"Get ready," he replied. "Any second now."

"You mentioned heights?" Dan gulped. "Yeah, I'm actually, you know... I don't really, like—"

The red glow turned green and the ramp opened.

Dan's feeble voice was drowned out by a storm of wind that ripped through the hold, tugging at the black jumpsuit around his body. Frank flicked a button on the side of Dan's face and a visor flipped around, casting everything in a tinted shade of dark orange.

Arnie leapt out of the back and disappeared. The two mercs jumped out after him.

And then Frank was bundling him towards the hole. Dan gaped at the sky beyond, and as he came close to the edge, he saw the mountains and trees far below.

"Come on, Dan!" Frank nudged him again, but Dan's feet had decided to stay on the aircraft.

He tried to shout *I'm terrified of heights!* But nothing came out. Frank shoved him and they lurched forwards, somersaulting into oblivion.

Dan's senses overloaded.

The world became a hurricane of gushing wind and screaming as he fell through the sky, slowly settling on a face and belly-first plummet towards the ground. He choked on freezing air that tried to cram its way down his throat and clung to the shoulder straps for dear life. All around, the vast mountain ranges stretched to infinity. Directly below, growing steadily larger, a tree-lined glassy lake reflected the dim grey sky.

Frank stretched his arms out in front of them both, guiding their flight towards the lodge. From so high, it seemed little more than a wooden matchbox, nestled within the forest. A patch of lighter green stretched away from it towards the lake. Dan had just enough control of his mind to work out that it was a lawn, their landing site.

The lawn approached at a sickeningly rapid rate. *Why isn't the chute opening?* Dan dry-retched as a pair of giant's hands squeezed his shoulders. The pressure was the Keno-chute deploying, slowing them to almost a standstill in a matter of seconds. His feet dangled below him and they landed in the wide sloped garden of Cloud Lodge. Frank released the straps connecting them and Dan tipped forwards, falling onto his hands and knees. He squeezed the grass between his fingers, relief and adrenaline gushing through every vein in his trembling body.

Gunfire rattled through the frigid air.

He searched for it and saw two of the mercs bracing against the wall on either side of a door to the house, shooting into it. Shouts could be heard from indoors, then the mercs darted inside and out of sight.

Arnie stomped past, chewing up the pristine lawn, bellowing "*Ka mate!*" as he went.

Dan struggled to take it all in, frozen in terror. *I'm gonna die here!*

"Get up!" Frank ordered, hauling Dan to his feet. Their noses almost touched as Frank pulled him close. "I'll keep you safe, but for fuck's sake, stay on me." He drew a pistol from his belt.

A trail of bullets spattered the grass at Dan's feet, spraying dirt into his face.

"*Move!*" Frank yelled, tugging his arm and firing wildly up at a second storey window. Glass shattered and rained down onto the patio like deadly hailstones.

Dan ran behind Frank to the door and took cover on one side. Frank leaned around the door frame, glanced left and right. "Clear." He slipped inside and Dan stuck to his back like glue.

They stalked through a spacious living room furnished with lavish sofas and a grand fireplace. More gunshots *popped* from somewhere deeper inside the house. They passed a corpse, a suited man with three seeping bullet holes in his chest and neck. Dan went weak at the knees and looked away.

He followed Frank through a door and into a hallway. Movement at the top of a staircase to his right caught Dan's eye. He thought he saw a woman disappearing around a corner. But it was dim, and his pupils hadn't adjusted to the light yet. He remembered the visor, and flicked it open. The house lit up, his sight no longer hindered by the tinted lens, but when he searched for the woman, she was gone.

"Frank," he jabbed the agent's arm, and pointed up the stairs.

Frank aimed the gun up and started ascending the staircase, hugging the wall. Dan followed.

An armed man came around the corner at the top of the stairs and almost ran into Frank on the way down. Frank swiped his metal hand. He snatched the gun out of the henchman's grip in one direction, before backhanding him across the head on the return blow. The man's limp body slammed into the bannister and flipped over it, plummeting to the floor below with a disgusting *crunch*.

At the top of the stairs, Frank paused to peer around the corner. "Fuck!" he dropped to one knee as the wall opposite them exploded in a hail of plaster and wood chippings, accompanied by the *rat-tat-tat* of a sub machine gun. Frank lowered his arm to ankle level, aimed around the corner and fired a burst.

Someone grunted in pain and Dan heard the dull thud of their body collapsing to the floor. Frank darted to his feet and stormed around the corner, firing twice more as he went.

When Dan came through, he saw the dead man sprawled out on the landing, still holding his gun, a thick pool of blood seeping into the carpet.

They passed by several doors, bathrooms and storage cupboards, before entering a small but luxurious bedroom at the end of the corridor. "Empty," Frank muttered.

"*You fucking bitch!*" Arnie's shout came cascading down the corridor at them, followed by his stampeding footsteps.

Frank and Dan hurried back the way they had come just in time to see Arnie bounding up the second flight of stairs.

They raced after him. At the top, a short, narrow corridor led to the master bedroom. Dan recognised it from the photo he had seen of Margery. Arnie was there, looming over the emperor-sized bed. He bent down, gripped the bed and tipped it over like it was made of cardboard.

Nobody there.

"Arghh!" He kicked a bedpost, snapping it in two.

A cry came from the landing. They ran out again, chasing two of Blunt's mercenaries into a study.

"She went through here! She's trapped," one of them said. They were both standing beside a closet door, guns aimed at it. "This is the only way out."

Arnie crashed through the door behind them. "Well, what are you waiting for?" he thundered.

The mercs pulled the closet door open. A secret room lay beyond, a short innocuous-looking corridor. The mercs stormed in.

A blinding light flashed through the room.

Dan's ears popped and he lost sight of everything. His

heart leapt into his throat. *The weapon!* He blinked again and again, until the study came back into focus.

He shook his head, gasping for breath.

Arnie stomped back a step and nearly crushed Dan's foot. "Stay away!" he cried, panic in his tone.

Dan skipped out of the way of his crunching metal feet, and looked into the closet. A pair of machine guns and mercenary gear lay sprawled on the floor. At the other end, he could see a second door, this one solid grey and metal. A small, round security camera watched over the tiny room from a corner just above the door.

"Fuck!" Arnie shouted. "You cowardly bitch, get out here!"

"It's a panic room," Frank said.

"No shit," Arnie retorted. "She's probably calling for backup as we speak. We need to get her out."

"Why don't you kick the door in?" Frank suggested.

Arnie glared at him. "How stupid do you think I am, bro? This closet's a death trap."

Blunt and Kevin came up behind them into the room. "It's all clear, nobody left alive," said the merc.

"What is it?" Blunt asked, looking across their faces.

Dan pointed at the tiny secret corridor that led to the panic room. "I think Margery's in there."

Blunt's eyes went wide and he gulped. He strode forward, but stopped when Frank planted a hand against his chest. "Not so fast, it's rigged." He cocked his head at the clothes on the floor. There weren't any other remains of the two mercenaries.

Kevin groaned in despair. "Is that John and Carl? Shit!" He gritted his teeth in a snarl of anger and grief.

"Margery!" Blunt shouted. "It's over! Come out." He was clearly trying to sound authoritative, but Dan had heard more guts from his old pet hamster.

No reply came from within.

Dan leaned closer, and thought he could hear the faint muffled sound of a voice. "She's on the phone." He looked to Frank. "She's on the damn phone!"

Frank slammed the pistol into his holster and rubbed his chin. "Gah. We need to get through there, and fast. We need..." He snapped his fingers and pointed at Arnie. "We need a puppet."

"Oh not again! Don't you even *think* about it!"

"Get out of the legs," Frank said. He pulled out the controller and handed it to Dan. "We can use the legs as a battering ram."

"What?" Arnie sounded shocked. But realisation slowly dawned on his face, and he frowned. "Ohh man, you're loving this, ain't you?"

"No," Frank assured him. "Hurry up."

Arnie avoided eye contact with everyone as he unclipped the combat suit that connected his torso to the legs. He reached down to his crotch and unfastened a series of cables that disappeared into the pelvic bucket.

Dan gave a nervous glance at the security camera in the death room. *You see us, don't you Margery?*

Frank noticed the camera and aimed his zip-winch at it. "Let's take out her eyes." He fired the grappling hook at the camera and yanked it off the wall. The movement triggered the weapon to flash again, forcing Dan to shield his eyes.

"Someone give me a fucking hand," Arnie demanded, holding his arms out.

Frank and Kevin grabbed the big Maori under each armpit and hoisted him out of the legs.

Dan studied the screen. It had a simple interface with a round *On/Off* button, which was currently green. Another icon said *Advanced Actions*. He pressed it and an array of icons spread out across the screen. Directional arrows, speed indictors with sliding bars and all manner of other options.

Arnie perched awkwardly on the study desk, one arm draped around Kevin's neck for support. "Do it," he said. "Smash the fucking door in."

Dan tapped an arrow and the legs stomped towards Frank.

"Other way!" he cried.

"All right, all right, gimme a second." Dan fidgeted with the controls, clomping the legs around until they faced the closet.

"Woulda been easier if you'd got into position first," Frank pointed out to the angry Maori.

"Fuck you."

Dan pushed forward and guided the legs into the closet. They squeezed through, tearing a panel of wood frame off the wall as they entered. Immediately, the room flashed white again as the weapon triggered.

"Argh!" Dan stumbled, shielding his eyes with his hands. No sooner had they readjusted, the weapon triggered again. And again.

"Fuck!" Frank cried through the blinding light. "Do it already!"

Dan staggered backwards out of the room and planted his shoulders against a wall. He rubbed at his eyes until they focused again and he could see the controller, and the crotch-camera view of the metal door on the screen. He cranked the power slider to full and pressed forward. The legs stomped across the floorboards and–

CLANG!

Margery shrieked.

The blinding light ceased. Dan re-entered the study and peered into the closet. The metal door to the panic room was half on its hinges, the titanium legs wedged between it and the floor at an angle. Inside, Dan spied a metal desk, chair and computer screen, blank but for a progress bar creeping from left to right. Whatever it was doing, it was already 43% completed.

Her hard drives! She was wiping evidence, destroying her files. The others were still recovering from the flashes, but Dan felt a surge of bravery and urgency.

He had to stop that computer. He ran into the death

closet.

"Dan!" Frank cried.

He made it to the mangled metal door and squeezed between the legs into the panic room.

POP!

Margery shot him with a pistol.

Dan's vision went white.

The room disappeared.

Dan felt blood pour down his face. He tumbled to the floor.

He sensed Frank bursting into the room.

BANG!

A second gunshot.

"*Ohhh!*" wailed Margery.

Dan's vision faded back into focus. He was shaking violently, filled with panic. He lifted a trembling hand to his face and pulled away blood on his fingertips.

He searched for Frank. He had a pistol trained at Margery, who was unarmed, leaning to one side. A red rose blossomed on the sleeve of her silver night gown, which she clutched with the other hand, a look of extreme shock bursting from her gaping eyes.

She shot me. The panic dissolved to rage. Nobody had ever meant him such irreversible harm.

Dan clenched his teeth. Pain flared through his scalp. He hauled himself up, clutching his head wound, leaning against the table for support. *She shot me in the fucking head.*

"Dan!" said Frank. "Are you all right?"

"I think so," he managed. *I'm alive.* He turned to the screen, blinking blood out of his left eye. *56%.* He lurched sideways and reached for the chair to steady himself, flopping into it.

He grabbed the keyboard and punched Escape. The progress bar disappeared, and the view returned to the computer's desktop.

"Up," Frank said behind him.

"Get your *fucking hands off me,*" Margery shrieked.

"Yeah, yeah."

Dan swivelled around in the chair and staggered to his feet.

He glared at Margery point-blank. This hateful woman was the cause of so much pain. He wanted to say something, make her realise how bad she was. *Jimmy might be alive if it wasn't for you.* He couldn't find the words.

She gave him a withering look of disgust.

"Out," Frank barked, forcing her head down and shoving her past the mechanical legs and under the buckled doorway.

She cursed and stumbled out, barely concealed rage spread across her Botox-ridden features.

Frank inspected Dan's head. "Just a nasty graze, you lucky bastard. You okay?"

Dan grimaced. "It feels like my hair is on fire."

"Wait there, I'll get you a medkit." He turned to go.

"Frank," Dan blurted. "Thank you. You... just saved my life."

A smile played on the agent's lips. "Not losing another one."

A commotion started out in the study. Frank grimaced and said, "Stay still, okay?" He ducked under the mangled door and walked out.

Dan turned to the computer. *Who was she talking to?*

Wincing against the pain in his bleeding head, he sat back down and his fingers went to work on the keyboard. He brought up log files for outgoing connections, and found a solitary record.

Mr. Z.

She had been talking to Zhin moments before Dan broke through the door. He found the communication software and opened it up.

"Thank fuck," he muttered. The data wipe Margery had instigated hadn't reached this sector. He quickly found an IP of the incoming connection. He wrote down the IP address and ID stamp onto a scrap of paper on the desk.

With that, they could trace the call and find out Zhin's current location. He stuffed the scrap into his pocket, gritting his teeth in satisfaction.

But it wasn't enough. He felt compelled to savour the moment even more.

He opened the communication console, and hit *redial.*

He recognised Horatio Zhin's voice immediately. "Margery. Are you all right? What happened?"

Dan said nothing. A grim sneer spread across his lips.

"Margery, say someth—" Zhin cut himself off. "Who is this?" He made the question sound like a threat.

Dan let it linger for a moment, hoping to inspire a little fear in the hubric asshole. "She's ours now. What are you gonna do about it?" He cut off the call.

He slumped back in the seat, the pain in his bleeding head forgotten. *I just threatened the mastermind himself, little bro. How badass am I?*

The computer beeped again, signalling an incoming call. Zhin was calling him back. A cold flush seeped through Dan's body.

After a big gulp, he answered the call.

"You little shit," Zhin spat down the line. "You think Margery means anything to me? Whoever you are, you can wipe the smug look off your face. The world *needs* the Horizon epoch. Nothing can stop it now. I suggest you relish these final moments of your pathetic life."

The call went dead.

Dan's pride washed away like water down a drain at his parting words. *Final moments?* What did he mean? Did Zhin have the whole place rigged or something? Dan flinched, half expecting to be blown up in a storm of fire, or vapourised by another hidden weapon. But nothing happened. *Not yet, anyway.*

"We have to get away from this place..."

He jerked upright, wincing as a gush of blood dribbled down his face. As he made for the door, his eye snagged on the pistol Margery had shot him with.

Could you really shoot someone? Cathy echoed in his mind.

Dan gulped.

He bent to pick it up, stuffed it into his belt and staggered under the door.

30
CLOUD LODGE (II)

In the study, Sid's hands trembled with hysterical anticipation as Margery cursed and swore her way towards him out of the panic room closet.

"Who the fuck are you people, anyway?" she shrilled.

She strolled out with her head high, wearing a blood-stained, flowing night dress which hugged her hips and revealed more than a little cleavage.

Sid lost his breath at the sight of her. The taut skin around her face suggested surgery, and her hair was dyed black instead of her natural brown. It gave her a plastic doll look which aged her more than the six years it had been since he last saw her in the flesh.

This was definitely not the woman he had once loved.

"You?" She halted and stared at him agape. "*You?*"

Sid lifted his chin, but couldn't control his quivering lip. All the pain this woman had caused him, it boiled up inside threatening to burst out of his chest. There was so much he wanted to say to her, many years' worth of stored up anguish. But in seeing her, all he could manage was a feeble, "Hello Margery."

Her face contorted in a savage snarl and she whirled on him, screaming. Sid yelped as she raked a clawed hand across his cheek and slapped him, kicked him, scratched him.

"Grab her!" Arnie barked.

Kevin, Sid's last surviving mercenary, came to aid him

with a sharp pistol-whip across the back of Margery's head. She grunted and fell to her knees, giving Sid a brief respite.

"That's for John and Carl you psychotic bitch." Kevin spat on her.

Margery's glare could have shattered glass. She wiped the spittle off her cheek and flicked it onto the carpet. Her night gown had come undone, spilling a breast.

"What the fuck's going on?" Frank came out of the panic room with a look of confusion.

Sid slowly uncoiled, his cheek and head throbbing from Margery's onslaught. Specks of Margery's blood dotted his arms.

"Get up," Frank hauled his ex-wife to her feet and ruggedly closed her gown. "Move it, downstairs." He shoved her towards the study door. As she passed by Sid, he met her cold, hateful gaze and shivered.

"Call your pilot, Sid," Frank said. "I need supplies for Dan; she bloody shot him."

"What about me?" Arnie said, perched on the desk.

"Kevin, help him back into the legs," Sid said. He turned and followed Frank out of the door.

They went downstairs and into the living room. Frank led Margery towards the sofa and pushed her into it. She landed at an awkward angle, clutching her bullet-wounded shoulder. She brushed herself down and straightened, restoring as much dignity as she could. She glowered from Frank to Sid. If she was scared, it didn't show. She betrayed no emotion other than raw loathing.

"Margery..." Sid started.

"Oh, fuck off, Sidney." She crossed her legs and leaned back in the chair, eyeing him as she might a cockroach.

"Please, Margery. It's been six years."

"How the *fuck* did you find this place?"

"Does it matter? I'm here now. And Catherine is probably on her way, too."

"Really," she snorted. "Well, won't this be a jolly family

reunion?" She turned to Frank. "So, who are you, the Tin Man's cousin?"

Frank clenched his metal fist. "I'm from Europa. We came here for Zhin, but I suppose you'll have to do." He said to Sid, "Call your bloody pilot. I need that medkit, and then we're out of here. No reason to hang about."

"What about Catherine?"

"She ain't here, Sid. We don't know where she is. Best if we're in the air before any more goons show up."

Margery showed the hint of a smirk, but she hid it as soon as she noticed Sid studying her.

"Are there more men coming?" he asked. He remembered the original mercenaries that she hired and brought back to the house on the day she took Catherine away. The same day she committed her first murder... "More of your kill squad?"

She eyeballed him, shaking her head in disbelief. "What do you think, Sidney?"

"We were married for sixteen years, Margery... doesn't that mean anything to you?"

"I did not choose you," came her quiet reply.

He winced.

"Sid," Frank gestured towards the back door. "Call the fucking pilot."

"Okay." He dragged himself away and walked outside to make the call. High above, he made out the black silhouette of the VTOL, hovering far above the lodge.

His pilot, Hugo, answered, "*Yes sir?*"

Sid opened his mouth to speak, when movement caught his eye. Someone was walking down the driveway towards him. A young woman.

Sid forgot about the phone call and gaped at his daughter. He thought he was seeing a mirage.

Catherine spotted him and stopped dead. She turned around and started to run, but froze again, her head lowered.

"Catherine?" Sid whispered.

"*Sir, is everything okay?*" Hugo asked in his ear.

Sid flustered. "Yes. Get down here Hugo. Quickly." He ended the call and approached his daughter, standing with her back to him. As he approached, she turned to look at him and his heart melted.

She was so beautiful. Her long brown hair hung in a ponytail past her shoulders. He'd never seen her in such scruffy clothes before, but her green eyes were the same as he remembered. Had it really been six years? He reached out to her, a dazed smile spreading across his face.

She recoiled violently away. "Don't *touch me*!"

He retracted the hand to his chest. "I... It's me, Dad. It's so good to see you."

She didn't respond. Her eyes searched the lodge, instead.

Sid swallowed. "Catherine, my sweet girl. Won't you talk to me?"

Her lips squeezed tightly together, forming a thin line as she squinted at the house in an obvious effort to not acknowledge him.

"I knew I would see you again."

"I didn't come here for you," Catherine snapped, finally looking at him. "I was looking for Mother."

Sid's heart sank. "She's inside. We have her captive."

Catherine was moving before he'd finished speaking. She stormed across the lawn, making for the back door. He caught her scent as she flowed past and he inhaled a sharp, nostalgic breath. She left him standing there alone, and entered the house.

Sid gathered himself and followed her inside.

"So, you're still scurrying around," Margery scoffed, speaking to Catherine.

Frank jerked around. "Cathy?"

"Yes, Mother. I'm still alive."

"Don't look so smug, my dear," Margery said. "None of you will be for much longer. That little stunt you pulled, broadcasting yourself to the Net." She was shaking her head in bitter disappointment. "I'm afraid you've forced our hands."

"What are you talking about?" Sid said.

"No-one forced you to murder thousands of people in those cities," Frank growled, clenching his fist. "You're going to spend the rest of your days locked in a cell."

Margery cocked an eyebrow at him. "I doubt that."

Catherine had her back to Sid, watching Margery across the room. She marched forward, reaching behind to lift up her shirt and pulled out... *A gun!*

"A cell is too good for what she deserves!" Catherine stalked right up to Margery, aiming the gun at her.

"Cathy!" cried Frank. He took a step to intervene, but thought better of it and froze.

"You miserable, horrible woman," Cathy pressed the barrel into Margery's forehead. Margery didn't even flinch. "What kind of mother are you, you fucking bitch? This is for all those people you murdered. Like Annie, and *Ben!*" She jammed the gun with such force that Margery's head craned back.

Sid rushed up behind her, his heart thumping like a drum. "Catherine! No!"

The hacker kid bolted into the room, panting and bleeding from a head wound. "Guys, we have to get out of here! I think she called Zhin and he's gonna... Cathy!?"

Margery and Catherine stared each other down.

"Well?" Margery prompted. "It's no good threatening someone with a gun if you aren't willing to pull the trigger. What are you waiting for?"

Catherine pressed harder, the gun shaking in her trembling hand.

The room held its breath and everything went deathly still.

Catherine's face twisted into a grimace. "Mnnnnnn-*uugh!*" She clutched her forehead with one hand, wheeled about and stormed away.

Catherine's blood curdling shriek lingered in the air.

Dan ran towards her, and she fell into his arms. "I can't

do it, Dan!"

"You don't have to," he said, squeezing her in a tight embrace. Catherine wrapped her arms around his back, still clutching the pistol, and buried her face into the crook of his shoulder. Muffled sobs escaped.

Margery snorted into the quiet aftermath. "Gutless. Like father, like daughter."

Sid gave a long blink, ignoring the hateful remark. He wondered what circumstance had brought the hacker kid and his daughter into contact. They were apparently close. Why couldn't he be the one to comfort Catherine? He would do anything to hug her like that. And where on earth did she get a gun from? *I'm so completely detached from her life and I have no idea how to fix it…*

The room seemed to settle, the tension easing over everyone but Sid.

"Dan," Cathy said, pulling away to look at his face. "You're hurt."

"Yeah, she shot me…"

Sid found his voice. "Hugo is landing now. We can tend to it on board."

The steady throb of rotor blades pounded the air outside as the VTOL descended onto the lawn.

"Time to go," Frank said, moving towards Margery.

Frank grabbed her arm but she slapped his hand away. "I can walk myself." She stood, clutching her wounded shoulder, and brushing her front down. She gestured to her bloodied night gown. "Might I get changed first?"

"Umm, seriously," Dan said. "We should go, Frank. Zhin told me—" Margery spoke over the top of him, loudly and angrily, glaring at Sid.

"You're going to let them drag me to the dungeons in my fucking nightie? I suppose you're so proud of yourself, Sidney."

He prickled. "Don't call me that."

"It's your name, you silly man," she retorted.

"You lost the right to call me that the day you filed the

divorce papers and abandoned your family!"

"And you lost the right to call yourself a husband the day you *fucked* a high school slut."

"Her name was *Annie!*" Catherine hurled back.

Margery ignored her completely, her icy glare fixed on Sid. "You have no idea what I went through, do you? I had my entire life ahead of me when Mother arranged our farce of a marriage. *'He's a good match, Margery, you'll do well by him.'* Mother didn't care about what *I* wanted, she only knew what was best for her."

"And you think you're any *better?*" Catherine said.

"I *never* wanted to be a parent. Who would?" She sneered. "But your grandfather insisted on an heir by his son. Someone worthy of the precious Blunt name." Her lip curled in disgust. "He died while I was pregnant, the decrepit fool. Third trimester, too late to have you aborted."

Catherine let out a pained, shuddering gasp.

"What have you become, Margery?" Sid's voice cracked. "We were a family. I loved you..."

"Well, it just wasn't enough, dear," she scathed. "Your worth ended with your father's empire." She shrugged a single shoulder. "I wanted my own."

"Is that what this is about?" Sid said, astonished.

"Henry and I were to rule the world. If we can't have that, then nobody will."

"All right, enough, for fuck's sake." Frank grabbed her arm again. She thrashed in vain, unable to break out of his titanium grip.

"What do you think you'll achieve here?" she shrilled, eyes wild with fury. "You want to take me away and lock me up? Under what charges? What exactly do you think I've done wrong, other than marry the most pathetic man in the world, and give birth to that useless *cunt?*"

Catherine screamed and stepped forwards.

BANG!

Margery's head jerked back. Blood spattered the

window. She slumped over and her body went limp in Frank's grip. A thin trickle of blood oozed out of a small, round hole beneath her left eye.

Sid gaped at Catherine. She hadn't aimed the gun yet.

Dan whimpered next to her. He held Margery's pistol in two outstretched arms. A tendril of smoke drifted from the barrel. "You're the cunt," he said.

31
AFTERMATH

The gun wobbled in his trembling hands as he stared at the dead woman dangling in Frank's metal grip.

"Fuck me, Dan!" Frank let go and Margery's corpse slumped to the floor like a sack of meat. Frank reached him in two quick strides and wrenched the guns from both he and Cathy's hands. "What the hell did you do that for?"

For Cathy. And for Jimmy.

"I... I..." Dan blinked, struggling to find his voice. His bullet graze throbbed across his head in flashing bursts of pain. "She deserved it," he murmured at last.

And for me...

Frank pulled out the guns' magazines and popped the last bullets out of each chamber.

"She was a murderer," Dan said, his voice barely above a whisper. He looked Frank right in the eye. "She deserved to die, right?"

Frank tossed the guns on the sofa and looked away, rubbing his chin.

Cathy had her back to him, staring at the corpse of her mother. He gulped and stepped forwards, into her view.

She was looking at Margery with wide, shocked eyes and her lips quivered as if she was about to speak. But she said nothing. He half expected thanks, or something akin to gratitude. Margery was the root of so much of Cathy's pain.

I took the pain away for you.

Her silence instilled a sense of empty numbness in him.

"I killed her for y..." He choked.

The abrupt whine of the VTOL's whirring engines drowned out his tiny voice.

Frank brushed past him, heading for the door. "Where the fuck is he going?"

Cathy took a microscopic glance at Dan, just long enough to see the fear in her eyes. She covered her mouth with a hand, turned and fled out of the back door.

Dan's scalp gave a sharp singe of agony. The bullet graze throbbed its most violent pulse yet, and he nearly keeled over from the intense flood of pain. He slumped to the ground on his hands and knees.

Arnie came stomping down the stairs with Kevin the mercenary. "What happened? I heard a gunshot!"

Dan looked up at him from the floor. "I… It was me…"

Arnie loomed over him. "You been shot?"

Dan clenched his teeth and gave a feeble nod.

Frank yelled into the room from the doorway. "Dillon, get him up. We have to move, *now!*"

Arnie called to Sid, "Sir! Leave her. Kev, get the boss on his feet!" He cocked his head at the merc, who promptly obeyed. Arnie's legs hissed as he retracted them and hunched over Dan. He scooped Dan up, triggering a yelp and a fresh jolt of pain, before clomping out through the back door.

Cathy was bent over, clutching her knees. The grass at her feet was wet with puke. She wiped her mouth and looked at Dan and Arnie.

"Catherine!" the big guy exclaimed.

"Hello, Arnie," Cathy had to shout to be heard over the noise of the aircraft's engines.

The *wub-wub-wub-wub-wub* of the VTOL's propellers throbbed down from overhead. Dan, cradled in Arnie's arms, watched the lumbering plane flicker and fade as its hull blended with the sky. It turned completely transparent, and became a glassy, clear shape rising high above them.

"Where's he going?" Arnie cursed.

Frank craned his neck, scanning the sky. "He knows something we don't." He pointed upwards. "Shit. There."

Dan followed his arm and spied three distant black shapes soaring into view over the peak of a mountain. Each shape left a short tail of white vapour behind them.

"What is it?" Arnie said, squinting into the sky.

Dan gulped. "Fighter jets," he said. "I think Zhin sent them."

"Blunt!" Frank barked. "Get your arse out of there!" He gestured to a gap in the trees at the lower end of the sloped lawn. "That way, head towards the lake."

Fwush! Fwu-whoosh!

The sounds came from the sky. Three bursts of air in quick succession. Arnie mumbled, "Oh, shit."

Vapour trails broke away from the jets, accelerating ahead of them.

"*Incoming!*" Arnie roared.

A car horn honked.

Everyone turned to see a white 4x4 pulling into the driveway.

Who the fuck's that?

"Oh no!" Cathy cried, running towards the car.

Frank, Sid and Kevin ran the opposite direction, into the trees.

"Cathy!" Arnie called. "Where are you going?"

"I have to warn them!" she replied.

She knows them? The vapour trails in the sky were rapidly careening towards them.

"Go with her!" Dan croaked, squirming in Arnie's grip.

Arnie's legs pounded the grass and Dan bounced in his arms as they fled across the lawn after Cathy.

She waved her arms frantically, screaming at the car, "Get away from here! Go! *Go!*"

Arnie plunged under the trees, running up the dirt driveway towards the car.

The missiles struck Cloud Lodge behind them.
HhssSSH-BU-BOOOM!

A fiery explosion lit the forest, shaking the trees and showering them in splintered chunks of oak and glass. Arnie stumbled against the shockwave and Dan slipped from his grasp. He fell to the ground and rolled in the dirt.

Searing pain ripped through Dan's head from the bullet wound, enveloping him in fiery agony. It hurt so badly that it sucked all the air from his lungs and he had nothing left to scream. He came to a thumping halt in the bottom of a ditch. Dan's face hit the dirt as burning splinters rained down through the canopy, thudding into the ground all around him.

Thunderous gun fire echoed across the sky.

"Holy shit," Dan slurred. Above him, tracers streaked through the air, bullets ploughing into the woods behind the burning lodge.

Dan caught a glimpse of one of the jets through the tree canopy – a sleek, black machine with two rotating thrusters on the wings that allowed it to hover and pull off manoeuvres similar to a helicopter. Its engines roared like a never-ending thunderclap as it drifted just above the tree canopy.

Dan crawled to the lip of the ditch. Cathy was lying on the track, slowly pulling herself to her feet.

Two people emerged from the car, now dented and scratched from the explosion's debris, and ran towards them both.

"Oh my god!" a young woman said, reaching Cathy. "Are you all right?"

The man ran towards Dan and hunkered in front of him. "Shit, you're bleeding," he said. "Quick, get up." He held out a hand and hoisted Dan out of the ditch.

They fled towards the car, Dan's mind churning like scrambled eggs from the shockwave. The pungent smell of burning wood invaded his nose as they ran.

Dan and Cathy bundled into the back seats, as the two

strangers piled in the front. The car reversed rapidly up the driveway away from the lodge.

Tracer fire rained through the canopy and thudded into the dirt in front of the car. Dan's stomach turned over as the deadly hail veered towards the car's hood and pounded straight into the chassis.

They all screamed.

Multiple heavy calibre bullets tore holes as big as tennis balls through the windshield, the roof, and the driver…

The car lost control. It veered sideways, reversed off the track and crashed into the ditch.

Dan smashed his head on the window and blacked out.

"*Cathy!*" Arnie roared.

The metal Maori faded into Dan's view, tearing off the rear door on Cathy's side.

Cathy's head lolled to the side, and her limp body tumbled out into Arnie's arms.

Dan struggled desperately to regain control of his mind, all thoughts bent on her. "Is she okay?" he mumbled, slurring every word.

Arnie dragged her out of the car and laid her on the ground.

Dan crawled uphill across the back seat, the car seemed to be lying half on its side in the ditch. He caught a glimpse of the driver, whose face had been reduced to a mushy pulp of red meat. Dan gagged, and hauled himself out of the door. He fell in a heap on the ground.

"Arnie!" Frank shouted from somewhere down the track. "Heads up!"

A deafening roar filled the air above Dan's head, as the low-hovering jet came back for another pass.

The jet opened fire again, its guns sounding like a furious beehive. Bullets smashed into the ground, tracing up the track towards them.

Arnie hunkered and pounced. He leapt high over the jet

and landed on one of the wings, his legs punching straight through the flimsy metal. The plane veered sideways, tugging its aim into the forest. Arnie was wedged into the wing as the craft banked sharply to the left and tumbled out of Dan's sight.

Frank ran out of cover and reached the car crash. He stared in horror at the mangled wreck, then hunkered beside Cathy and pressed his ear to her mouth.

"Cathy…" Dan mumbled, crawling closer.

"She's breathing," Frank said.

Dan groaned with immense relief.

"Come on, Cathy." Frank gently eased her up into a sitting position.

She was stirring, and issued a soft moan.

Something heavy shook the ground somewhere in the forest behind them. An almighty explosion ripped the sky.

"We can't stay here." Frank said. "Both of you, on your feet!"

Dan pushed himself up, and using the car for support, managed to stand up.

Frank helped lift Cathy up. "Oh no," she said, seeing the driver through the window. "James… Laura!" She felt her way around the hood of the car to the passenger door, and opened it.

Inside, the young girl was lying motionless with her head buried in the airbag.

"There's nothing you can do for them!" Frank's voice cracked.

Cathy leaned in and pulled the girl away from the bag, and she slumped back in the seat. "She's alive!" Cathy cried.

Frank hauled the girl out of the seat. She was bleeding from her nose, but otherwise seemed unhurt. He lugged her over his shoulder in a fireman's carry and set off down the track.

Holding each other for support, Dan and Cathy followed him down the hill towards the lake front, away from the carnage of the burning lodge and exploding fighter jets.

"Cathy…" Dan croaked, as they stumbled along. "Your mom…"

"Shh," she said, her voice strained. "Not now."

He held her tightly around her slim waist, not wanting to lose her again.

"Who were they?" he said.

"Just strangers," she replied, watching the unconscious girl on Frank's shoulder ahead of them. "They just wanted to help…"

They reached the edge of the forest and stopped where the dirt turned into a pebbly beach beside the lake.

Sid and Kevin were hunkered behind a fallen tree.

Frank gently eased the girl onto the ground next to a different tree. He scanned the sky, peering out from the edge of the tree line. "Where's our fucking pilot gone?"

Cathy and Dan lowered themselves next to Laura, who was finally stirring.

"Wh… what happened?" Her eyes flicked about. "Where's James?"

"Sit still," Frank said. "Cathy, how's he doing?"

She looked at Dan, studying his head. "He's bleeding."

Dan saw Sid staring across at them, his eyes fixated on Cathy. She seemed to be avoiding looking in that direction, even had her back facing them so that she didn't have to acknowledge him. Tears were forming in the corners of her eyes.

"Swap with me," Frank said. Cathy got up, tears forming in her eyes and went over to the girl.

Frank came over and blocked Dan's view. "Easy, Dan." He rolled down his skysuit and tore a piece of his undershirt. He wrapped it around Dan's head like a kamikaze headband. The pressure hurt like hell at first, but then it seemed to calm and Dan could see a bit more clearly. "That'll keep the blood where it's supposed to be for now." Frank turned away and shouted at Sid. "Blunt!

Call your bloody pilot right now!"

Sid could barely speak. His eyes flicked restlessly and he kept wiping his mouth as he scanned the forest around him, seemingly too shaken up to comprehend what was happening.

A jet roared overhead, spinning on its axis to aim at some unseen target. Dan spied a glimpse of Arnie leaping over the trees, away from the gunfire.

"Blunt!" Frank got to his feet and stormed over, grabbing him by the shoulders. "Wake the fuck up. Those planes are trying to *kill us*. Your pilot has a fucking EMP on board. *Call him!*"

Sid blinked a few times and finally uttered a response. "Yes." He bounced a raised finger in the air in agreement with Frank's suggestion, before his eyes fell upon Frank's prosthetic. "Um. Your arm…"

Dan vaguely understood. If the VTOL came back and triggered its EMP, Frank's arm and Arnie's legs would be taken out along with the jets.

Fwoooooooosh. The engines roared above them again, and another burst of gunfire rattled out. The planes fired away from the lodge down towards the lake. Dan followed the tracers and spotted Arnie sprinting faster than a train along the shoreline. Sand and pebbles sprayed up behind him as the jets attempted to gun him down.

"He's leading them away," Dan pointed. "Look!"

"Nice one," said Frank. "Crazy bastard's actually doing something smart."

Blunt's communicator rang, making him jump. He quickly tapped the screen on his wrist to answer the call. "Hugo! Where are you?" he said, looking up.

Dan hauled himself upright, swaying on his feet. Now that the jets had moved away, a steady *wub-wub-wub* became audible once more. *The VTOL!*

He searched the sky until he spotted a fuzzy shape shimmering through the air.

It accelerated towards the semi-hovering jets, which

were focused on Arnie, now just a tiny speck sprinting around the bank on the far side of the lake.

"Yes, get as close as you can," Sid ordered into his wrist. "Use the EMP, shortest-range frequency. I don't want to lose my assets!" He waved frantically at Frank in a gesture of *get away from here!*

"Oh, fuck." Frank turned and fled, cutting a path through the trees.

The jets were at least a kilometre away. Dan wondered whether Frank would manage to get out of range in time, but his eyes were fixed on the blurry patch of sky that marked the VTOL's location. It shifted out of stealth, the rotor blades spinning above each wing, and dived into the airspace between the two jets.

A deep hum cascaded down from the sky and Dan's ears popped.

The thrusters of the jets cut out one after the other. One plane nose-dived and crashed into the lake with a mighty splash. The second jet had been skirting the edge of the forest, and it plummeted into a tree. It toppled sideways, stripped the branches as it scraped down the trunk and careened into the ground. A huge fireball engulfed it, the boom splitting the air and the shockwave trembling the pebbles at Dan's feet.

"*All clear*," hissed Sid's communicator. "*Gonna find a new LZ.*"

The throbbing propellers of the VTOL rumbled across the lake, the sound mingling with the crackle and hiss of the burning lodge.

Sid staggered to his feet, haggard and drained.

The sight of him formed a lump in the back of Dan's throat. The way Sid had longingly looked at Margery, and the way he kept looking at Cathy now... Dan recognised the sense of loss that he was going through. *I think he still loved her. And I killed her. And now...* He felt physically sick, and had to look away from the man, wiping the crusting blood from his eye.

397

"Where's James?" the girl said again.

Cathy was hunkered beside her. They looked at each other, and Cathy simply shook her head slowly. "I'm so sorry, Laura."

***

Within the hour, they were back in the air, all piled into the cargo hold of the stealth VTOL.

Dan sat along one side with Cathy and Laura. Cathy had her arm draped around her, who was staring into space, clearly in a state of shock. Dan watched from the corner of his eye, itching to swap places.

Don't be so petty, man. The poor girl just lost her boyfriend... But he couldn't help it. Cathy might have been holding him now, instead. He wanted desperately to talk to her, but had no idea how to start the conversation.

Sitting opposite was Blunt, Arnie and Frank, just along from Derunox's tarp, now joined by the dead British guy, James.

How had things gone to shit so quickly? How many more people had to die?

Cathy caught him looking and said, "Are you okay, Dan?"

"Uh, yeah," he lied.

She gave a slow nod.

She's asking me if I'm all right? I just shot her mom. "Are you?"

"No," she whispered. Their eyes locked, and he lost himself in the sadness that he saw there. The usual sparkle in her pretty green eyes had dulled.

She shifted in the seat and spoke to Laura. "I need to talk to Dan now."

Laura gave a feeble nod.

Cathy shuffled along until she was sitting directly next to

Dan. She reached up to his head and touched his headband gently. "This needs changing." She stood, took hold of his hand and said, "Come on."

She led him towards the front of the VTOL's hold, to a corner where there was a bathroom, not much bigger than an airliner's restroom. She sat him down on the toilet seat, so she could inspect his head.

Dan swallowed. *I have to talk to her.*

She unwound the makeshift bandage and dropped the bloodied rag into the sink. "I'm so sorry about Derunox," she said, her tone soft.

"Me too."

She found a real bandage inside a first aid box and wrapped it with great care around his head. Dan looked out into the cargo hold through the open door as she tended his wound.

"Ow," he winced.

"Sorry."

She tied the bandage in a knot at the back. "That's better. Dan, are you sure you're okay?"

"Yeah. Shouldn't I be asking you that?"

She gave a weak smile. "I guess so."

Dan's head was level with her stomach. He reached around her back and pressed his forehead against her belly. "I…" he started, but choked on the words.

She cradled his head, squeezing softly. He felt like he could stay there forever, breathing in her scent.

But he wanted more.

"Cathy, I…" Choked again. His heart jackhammered wildly against his rib cage.

"Dan, I need you to know something."

He pulled back, tilting his head to look up into her face. "What is it?"

She stared down at him. "What you did… I need you to know that I don't… blame you."

Don't blame me? He frowned.

"And," she went on. "I don't hate you for it."

Is this her way of saying thanks? "That's a relief," he said, still frowning.

She sighed. "What do you expect me to say, Dan? 'Thanks for murdering my mother'?"

"I, uhh... I'm not sure."

"You killed her, Dan. Are you sure you're okay with that?"

He started to feel agitated. Why did she keep asking him that? "I told you, I'm okay. I had to do it... She had no respect for you! She plotted and schemed, she killed Jimmy, she—" A guttural sob escaped his throat. *Of course I'm not okay.* His vision went blurry as tears finally came, streaming down his face. "I killed her. I did it for you, Cathy. I fucking killed her for you because I thought it was what you wanted."

She covered her mouth with a hand and closed her eyes. "I know. I know."

He reached around her and buried his face in her belly again, squeezing her tight.

I killed her. I have to live with that. Please don't tell me it was for nothing...

He remembered what she said to him, moments before kissing him on the bridge. The words echoed in his head.

Fuck it.

He staggered to his feet and planted his lips on hers.

She recoiled. "Dan!"

He held her tight, her face right next to his, blurry through the tears in his eyes.

"I love you," he sobbed.

"I know you do," she sobbed back.

"I'd do anything for you, can't you see?"

She pressed her hands against his chest, not quite pushing him away, but not allowing the gap to close either. "Dan…"

What does she want?

He leaned forward and kissed her again, tasting salty tears, unsure if they were hers or his.

"I *killed* for you."

"Oh, Dan..."

Something changed. Cathy's resistance floundered. She blinked, and all at once, the spark there returned. It was like she'd been woken from a daze, and where a moment ago was sadness, now Dan saw hunger.

She reached back and pulled the bathroom door closed.

Cathy's hand moved to his crotch, and immediately he reacted, a bulge forming in his pants.

His tears ceased as she pressed her tongue against his. The VTOL disappeared, there was only Cathy.

She pushed him backwards and he sat down on the toilet seat again. Cathy leaned down, unzipping his flies. He fumbled with her shorts, tugging at the zipper, but it wouldn't budge until she swiped his hand away and did it for him. She pulled her shorts and panties down, then sat down in his lap. With surprisingly dexterous fingers, she slipped him inside her, pressing her breasts down against his chest.

She was wet, and warm, and tight, and that was enough to finish Dan. He let out a shuddering, wheezing groan. Cathy shuddered with him. She panted into his ear, her hair draped across his eyes. He hugged her tight, never wanting to let her go.

32
FLIGHT

Sitting on top of the pastey dork with him still inside her, Cathy's heart slowly calmed. What just happened, exactly?

Dan breathed in her ear. "That was amazing."

Was it? One thrust hardly seemed *amazing*, but the intensity of the moment had swept her up.

Dan was devoted to her. He'd sacrificed an irreplaceable part of himself and he'd never be the same. *He'd killed for me.* That was fucked up, but she found it so alluring. Cathy wasn't sure that she loved him, but she knew that she needed the boy close to her.

Huh. I guess he's a man, now.

The freedom bracelet clinked softly as she cupped his face in her hands and kissed him on the forehead. His flushed face beamed in a blissful smile.

A knock sounded at the door.

Cathy went rigid, gaping at Dan. He peered around her to look at the door. "Who is it?"

"It's me," said Frank.

Cathy stood up, and Dan winced as his penis sprang out and flopped onto his pant leg. "Put it away," she snapped in a hushed whisper. He fumbled it back inside and zipped it up as she redressed herself. Checking herself in the mirror, she brushed her hair behind an ear and turned to open the door.

Frank stood, leaning against the wall with his metal arm pressed against his hip. He gestured vaguely behind him.

"We were just, you know, discussing our next move." He cleared his throat. "Seems like you two already decided yours."

Cathy fought and failed to hide a smirk. "Maybe."

Dan chose that moment to stand up, and bumbled into Cathy's back in the process. She shuffled forwards and moved aside to let Dan out.

He gave a sheepish grin to Frank, who cocked an eyebrow.

"Um," Cathy said. "I'll be right there. I need to use the bathroom first." She slipped back inside and closed the door.

She found all of the men in the comms station between the cargo hold and the cockpit.

Dan was sitting in front of a computer screen, while Frank peered over his shoulder. "Zhin is in Georgia," Dan declared, fist pumping the air.

"Georgia?" Frank repeated. "Are you sure?"

"That's where the ID stamp corresponds to," Dan leaned back in the chair, clutching a scrap of paper with some numbers written on it.

"Can you get a more precise location?" Arnie asked.

"Already on it." Dan's fingers danced across the keyboard. He radiated confidence and smugness, ruling the chair and the attention of the rest of the group.

Cathy hugged herself as she watched from the back, listening. The small room was lined with flashing lights and buttons, screens displaying maps and coordinates. Her father's VTOL was state of the art, and connected to a high-speed GPS network.

She felt Sid glancing at her from the corner of her eye, and Cathy made a point to avoid eye contact.

Uncomfortable didn't even come close to describing how she felt around him. Yet, for his part, he seemed to have taken her hints, and he hadn't tried speaking to her since Cloud Lodge. Which was good, because she had nothing to say to him.

"There," Dan said, crossing both hands behind his head.

Frank leaned closer, peering at the satellite image. "It's Inguri Dam..."

"You know it?" Arnie asked.

"Yeah. Biggest power station in the region." He squinted at Arnie. "What's Zhin doing there?"

Sid was chewing on a finger nail. He gave a nervous chuckle. "The man wants to control all the power in the world." He shrugged as he added, "Must be something to do with that?"

"Probably." Frank didn't sound pleased. "How long will it take to fly us there?"

Her father made a dry choking sound. "Into Asia? I don't have the authority."

Frank spread his palms. "We're in a stealth craft, aren't we? Who the fuck needs authorisation?" He turned back to Dan and pointed at the screen. "Go in closer, I wanna see what our assault options are."

They started studying the area around the dam, searching for roads and potential entrances.

Cathy felt significantly useless, so she wandered back out to the hold, where Laura was sitting on the side bench, hugging both of her knees. She looked up when Cathy entered. "Are they going to take me home?"

"I don't know." She perched next to her. "I think we're going to Georgia."

Her eyes flapped wide. "Oh."

She patted her arm.

To her surprise, she pulled away.

"What's wrong?" she said.

Laura cast a wary glance over her. "You're not who I thought you were."

"Oh." She wasn't sure what else to say, but she clearly didn't want her sitting there, so she stood back up to go.

"Wait," Laura said. "I'm sorry. That was rude of me."

"It's okay, you're grieving."

"Yeah, and you're not."

Cathy half-scoffed. "No."

Laura watched her with a searching gaze. "She was still your mother."

That hit Cathy like a punch to the stomach. She clutched her belly. "Don't you think I know that?" Her tear ducts threatened to open up, which served only to anger her. *I'm not mourning* her. "You have no idea what I've been through."

"No," she agreed. "But if I'd just lost my mother, I wouldn't mark the occasion by getting laid."

Cathy flushed red with deep embarrassment. *She figured that out?* But why did that bother her? Laura was the one living in the moment, making decisions based on creating a good *story*.

"I think I get it, though," Laura said. "Heat of the moment, and all that. I'm glad you found each other again…"

Cathy's heart melted at that. "I'm so sorry about James, Laura. Please forgive me for dragging you into all of this."

"There's nothing to forgive," Laura said. "We made our choice."

Cathy leaned in and they hugged each other very tight. They stayed like that for some time, Cathy feeling Laura sobbing gently into her neck.

Laura said softly, "I need to go home."

"I know."

"Can you ask your father if he can drop me and James somewhere?"

Cathy tensed up. She gulped. "Yes. I will speak to him."

"Thank you."

They unwound. Cathy inhaled a deep breath, before standing up. She went back to the comms room and stood in the door frame. Sid immediately looked up at her when she entered.

"Dad."

The room fell silent. Everyone turned to look at her.

"I guess we should talk."

Sid nodded and smiled. They left the comms room and walked back across the cargo hold.

"Laura needs to go home. I want to land somewhere so she can leave."

Sid glanced at Laura, sitting by herself. "Of course. Catherine… it's so wonderful to see you."

Oh, god.

Cathy stopped and hugged her midriff. "Really."

"I haven't seen you since... since the day that, you know... Annie."

"I haven't forgiven you for that. She was my best friend, Dad!"

"I know," his tone was pained and taut. "I am so, so sorry for what happened... It was all my fault. I want to make amends, Catherine."

"Make amends," Cathy repeated flatly. "Annie's dead. How can you possibly make amends for something like that?"

"Please Catherine, let me try. Ever since that day, all I ever wanted was to have you back."

Her eyes narrowed in disbelief. "You left me to rot for six years."

He looked at the floor, nodding.

"You don't even deny it. In six years, you didn't even *try* to get me out. Why didn't you send Arnie sooner? Why didn't you do something, *anything*? You just let me with *her!* I can't even look at you, Dad!"

She stormed away towards the back of the hold, and leaned on a support beam, out of sight. She clenched her fists and thrust them down at her sides, desperately fending off the urge to cry. *She deserved to die. Dan did the right thing. Why should I mourn the woman who didn't even want me?*

The tears came then. Uncontrollable, like a flood, they poured down her cheeks in wretched droplets. She slumped on the floor and buried her face in her hands.

And laughed.

She's dead. She's dead!

A hysterical grin broke through the distressed, painful convulsions. She held it for a few moments before the anguish tore it down and the sobbing continued. "Uuugh!"

Sid came and plonked himself down in front of her, barely two feet away. "Catherine, please…"

"Dad," she spat, palming the tears away. She didn't want him seeing her like this. He opened his mouth to answer, but Cathy's floodgates had been flung wide open. "When I first arrived, I thought you might come for me. A week went by, then a month, then six more. I even remember one specific day, a year later, I still had a hope that you might be out there, negotiating for my release, working to free me. But I heard *nothing* from you. I *remember* the day I gave up, Dad. I gave myself up to being a hostage, resigned to work for Mother without any hope of getting out. " She wiped her nose, sniffing up snot.

"I was waiting for an opportunity."

"*Waiting?* How long were you going to wait, Dad? Another six years? The *only* reason I escaped was because of Frank and Dan's brother!"

"I was preparing. I was!" Sid insisted. "I developed technology, the legs that Arnie now has, and Frank's arm. I hired a bigger team, scraping all the funds I could manage to aid Doctor Gunther. He said he could make me a weapon that could give me an edge against them. I spent billions trying to get you back. Please, try to understand –"

"I understand perfectly well. You could have offered a trade. Mom wanted your business, that's the only reason she took me. You could have given her *all of it,* in exchange for me. But you gave her half, instead. The other half you kept, because it was worth more than your daughter."

Sid's jaw dangled in horror. He looked like a scared rabbit caught in the headlights of a speeding car.

His silence tore Cathy's heart out. For six years, she'd suspected it, and now his lack of denial proved it. She was an orphan, in all but name.

Her upper lip curled in a sad, depressed sneer, and she turned away from him.

He slipped closer and wrapped an arm around her shoulders. "Catherine..."

She barely heard or felt his attempt at comfort. She was beyond comfort, now. His touch only instilled a deep repulsion, which she absorbed like a sponge until it soaked into her every thought.

Darkness churned within her mind.

Her bitch of a mother's death had awoken something sinister. It felt similar to the day she jumped on the back of Frank's snowspeeder and escaped from the facility. The sense of freedom, but magnified to a dangerous level. She recognised the depravity of it, and willfully allowed it to run wild in her head.

"Now that Mother is gone, who gets her half of your business?"

He frowned. "Well, I haven't even thought about it yet. But Horatio never married her, so I suppose it would be you."

"And would I get full control, if anything were to happen to you?"

"Yes," he smiled. "But don't worry about me, darling. I'm not ever going to lose you again."

"You still love me. Don't you, Dad?"

His face went as soft as a pillow. "Of course I do, my sweet Catherine. I never stopped loving you." He caressed her hand, his voice cracking.

"Prove it," she said.

"Of course." He squeezed her hand and propped himself up on his knees, adopting a beggar's position. "How shall I prove it to you?"

She stared into his eyes and whispered, "Die."

He blinked. "What?"

She simply nodded, her eyes like stones.

Sid's jowls slowly sagged, and his lower lip trembled.

Cathy held his gaze until he released her hand and recoiled away, falling back, cushioning his fall with one hand on the floor.

Yes. Just like that. Rejection is painful, isn't it Dad?

"Cathy?" Frank called out from the front of the hold.

"I'm here." She got up and stepped around the beam, leaving her father propped against the floor. "What's happening?"

"Just making sure you're all right."

She smiled. "I'm fine. Have you guys come up with a plan?"

"Well, Dan's located Zhin," Frank said, putting both hands on his hips. He glanced past her at Sid on the floor.

"Show me." Cathy walked past him and entered the comms room. Frank followed her in.

"Zhin is somewhere in there," Dan said, pointing at a satellite image.

She leaned against the back of Dan's chair, peering at his screen. The image showed the top-down view of a grand, curving concrete dam, surrounded by a canvas of green forest. A crystal blue lake spread out behind the dam, splitting the forest into two. It looked a paradise of bright colour.

"What are you going to do?" she asked.

"We have no idea what Zhin's using that place for," Frank said. "There could be anti-air defences, so we can't risk flying directly to it. Instead, we'll air-drop a few clicks out, and make our way on the ground."

"I can approach the base, through this section of the woods," Arnie suggested, pointing to the trees.

"Right," Frank agreed. He ran his finger up the screen, gesturing to the opposite side of the river. "I'll follow this dirt track and move in here. We'll pincer Zhin in. Can't be many ways in or out of a place like that. Dan reckons he can hack the CCTV cameras, which will give us a dozen more eyes once we're inside."

Cathy shook her head in disbelief. "You're going to just walk right up to the front door?"

"What other choice is there?" Frank shrugged. "We don't know what Zhin's doing, or how long he intends to stay there. So we have to move fast if we want to catch him. Hugo says we can be there in two hours." He checked his wrist watch. "Let's hope the bastard's still there."

Just then, a red light engulfed the little room and an alarm went off.

"What the fuck?" Arnie said.

"Warning. Pressure dropping. Cargo ramp open." A computer voice spoke through unseen speakers.

Frank pushed open the door to the hold and a torrent of wind whipped through Cathy's hair, tearing her hairband out. The tarpaulin around the bodies flapped violently and came loose, revealing the bloody ruin of James's face, lying next to Derunox.

The hydraulic ramp was lowering. Wind buffeted the inside of the hold, forcing its way around the comms room.

"What the fuck's going on out there?" cried Hugo from the cockpit. Cathy braced herself against the doorframe as the craft rocked forwards, braking in midair. The VTOL eased to a gentle hover and the air pressure calmed.

She stepped into the hold and made eye contact with her father. He was standing at the far end, one hand on the ramp controls.

Sid said something, but the wind swallowed his words.

"What's he doing?" Frank said from behind her.

"Sir?" said Arnie, ducking under the door and stepping beside Cathy. "What's going on?"

"I'm done!" Sid cried. His eyes were on Cathy. "I'll do it. I'll do it for you."

Clouds drifted by outside. Cathy could see the land stretched out thousands of feet down.

Frank brushed past her and gestured for her to stay back, as he approached her father. "What the fuck are you talking about?" Frank barked. "Close the bloody ramp and get back in here. This isn't over yet, we're going after Horatio Zhin."

"Yes." Sid nodded enthusiastically. "Get him, take the VTOL, take whatever you need, and stop the bastard. You're free, now, Mr. Hawkins." He looked back at Cathy, with trembling lips and tearful eyes. "I failed you, my sweet Catherine. I leave everything to you. I only hope you will forgive me now." Sid sidestepped towards the edge of the ramp. He turned his back to her and took another step forward.

She stared at him in a daze. Is this what she wanted? Doubt crept in. Could she really be so cruel as to watch her father take his own life for her? What sort of a daughter could do such a thing? "Wait!" she screamed.

Too late.

Sid's panicked eyes turned to meet hers as he slipped over the edge and disappeared from sight.

"*Dad!*"

PART SEVEN

33
ONWARD

Frank reacted too slow to do anything. He ran and dived at the ramp, landing on his belly, reaching out his metal hand, but Sid was long gone.

"Sir!" Arnie cried, clomping to the edge and gaping into the void.

Frank peered over the precipice and barely made out the tiny shape of Blunt's body tumbling through the sky. "Fucking hell." He pounded his fist against the ramp, stood back up, and went to the controls to seal the door.

Cathy ran at the closing gap, but Frank held her back. "Don't. He's gone, Cathy."

"He jumped! Because of... I didn't—" She clapped a hand over her mouth, staring at the closing door with wide eyed horror.

Frank held her face in his palms and said, "Hold it together. This isn't your fault, you understand?"

She trembled, wriggling free of him. "Yes it is." She covered her mouth again as her tear-stained cheeks puffed out. The cargo ramp sealed shut with a *tssst*, just as Cathy bent over and vomited.

"What happened?" Arnie blinked, looking left and right. "Why did he do that?"

Frank had no idea. They both looked at Cathy, kneeling on the floor.

Arnie dropped to one titanium knee beside her. "My Ruapehu..." He laid a gentle hand beneath her chin and tilted her head to look at him. "Why would he do that, after finally getting you back?"

She wiped her nose. "I…I told him…"

Frank squinted. "What did you tell him?"

She broke down into wracking convulsions. Arnie wrapped his bear arms around her and hugged her tight. He looked past her shoulder at Frank. "Do you know anything about this?"

"No," Frank said, annoyed by the accusation in Arnie's tone. "He's barely spoken since we took off from Cloud Lodge." He turned to Laura, who witnessed the whole thing from her seat. "You were here when he opened the ramp. Did he say anything?"

"N-no," Laura said. "I just asked her to talk to him, so I can leave. She pointed a trembling finger at Cathy. "Th-they were talking for a bit. Then he was just sitting there a while. He made a call on his phone, and all of a sudden, he opened the ramp."

"And you just *sat there?*" Frank hissed.

"I didn't know he was going to *jump!*" She hugged her knees up to her chin.

Frank gritted his teeth. "Fuck me, I knew the guy was broken, but this…" He shook his head, frowning.

Cathy let out a choking cry of anguish.

Dan came out of the comms room, followed closely by Hugo the pilot, and Kev, the last mercenary.

"What's going on?" Dan ran to Cathy.

Hugo crossed his arms and said, "Would someone mind telling me why the cargo door was open just now?"

"Where's Mr. Blunt?" asked Kev.

"Your boss just killed himself. Threw himself out the fucking hold," Frank said. He took an uncomfortable glance at Cathy. "We don't know why."

"Wha-?" Hugo said, dumbfounded.

"We need to keep moving," Frank brushed past, heading for the cockpit.

Hugo followed him. "Are you serious? After what just

happened?"

"It changes nothing," Frank said, glancing around the cockpit. A curving array of buttons and consoles lined the dashboard below a wide windscreen looking out onto clouds and sky. "We still on course for Georgia?"

"Yeah. But I don't have authorisation to cross the border. It's technically Asia."

"You as well? Why not just turn invisible and we can fly wherever we want?"

"The stealth system can't run forever, it needs time to recharge," Hugo explained, taking a seat in the pilot's chair. He pointed to a gauge with a fancy battery symbol on it, which read 27%. "Sooner or later, we'll have to un-cloak, and if we're seen over Neo-Asian airspace, Russia won't hesitate to shoot us down."

Frank scanned the dashboard. He pointed to a cabled handset hanging on a hook. "That a phone? Pass it 'ere."

Hugo handed it to him.

Frank might be disavowed, but he still knew Jones' cell phone number. He punched it in and after a few rings, the Europa comms technician answered. "Who is this?"

"It's Hawkins."

"Frank?" Jones sounded startled. "I thought you were dead!"

"Not yet."

Jones switched to a hushed whisper. "I can't be seen talking to you, Frank."

"Why the fuck not? I need your help."

"Well, where are you?"

"I'm on board Sid Blunt's VTOL. I need you to get us authorisation to enter Neo Asian airspace. Can you do that?"

"Are you kidding me? Do you have any idea what's going on down here?"

"No, what?"

"The chief went AWOL, Frank. She literally disappeared overnight, and Europa is falling apart. There's rumours of a deal with Horatio Zhin. Have you heard what he's done?"

"Yes, what the fuck do you think I've been doing the last few days? I'm going after him, Jones. He's hiding out in Georgia, and you need to get me that authorisation."

"I can't!" Jones said. "Zhin is off-limits. Europa can't touch him."

"What the hell are you talking about?"

"Why do you think you've been disavowed, Frank? Everyone associated with the Horizon mission has been either declassified or forced to resign."

"What about you?"

"I disassociated myself with the mission after you went rogue."

Frank couldn't believe what he was hearing. Hugo offered him a quizzical look. Frank turned his back on him and gave a savage whisper into the receiver. "What was the price, Jones? How much did Zhin offer to buy Europa out?"

"The order didn't come from Europa. The Euromerican government has accepted a proposal from Zhin, and we have to comply. The Horizon Initiative is set to generate so much electrical power, that he's undercut all of the remaining oil firms. They've all joined with him now, under a global conglomerate. Anyone who doesn't sign on to the scheme will be cut off within the year."

Politics. It always came down to fucking politics. Frank snorted. "There's the issue right there. How can we allow one man to have so much control? What was Europa founded for if not to stop men like that?"

"What the hell can anyone do, Frank? Zhin's not even denying the possession of some superweapon. Half the world thinks he might kill us all if we don't side with him. We have no choice!"

"There's *always* a choice!"

"Frank, let this one go. He's holding the entire world hostage. It's over."

"I'm going after him, Jones. It's not over until Zhin's in the fuckin' ground."

He jammed the off button and slammed the receiver back onto its hook. He told Hugo, "We have authorisation." Frank gestured vaguely out of the cockpit window. "Get us to Georgia."

Hugo shook his head. "I took my orders from Mr. Blunt, not you. If he's dead, then I'll answer to his daughter." He turned back to the control panel, pressed a series of buttons, and the cockpit went into some kind of lockdown mode. Hugo stood up, eyeing Frank. "We're not going anywhere without Catherine's authorisation. Let's go see what *she* wants to do."

Gathered in the cargo hold, all eyes were on Cathy. Frank leaned against the wall pinching his chin between thumb and forefinger. The others sat along the side benches, except for Arnie, who towered beside Cathy standing in front of everyone.

"What about his body?" she asked softly. "My father should be buried…"

"There's no time for that," Frank said.

She looked at him with sad, wide eyes.

"Besides," he added with an outstretched hand. "We're fifteen thousand feet up, there won't be a…" Frank cut off when he saw Dan vigorously shaking his head, but he'd already said enough.

Cathy's face dropped. "Oh."

"Catherine," Arnie said. "We all worked for your father. That means, we work for you now. If you want us to land and look for him, that's what we'll do."

The big gruff Maori tended to scowl, but his face was soft and concerned as he spoke to Cathy.

"There's no time," Frank repeated. "If we're going to catch Zhin, we have to get to Inguri Dam as fast as possible."

Kev the merc spoke up. "He's probably long gone by now. When those dead fighter pilots don't report in, he'll know we escaped."

"Right," agreed Dan. "He's probably halfway to Mexico by now, or the damn moon." He shrugged. "But man… I hate the thought of getting this far and not catching the bastard."

"I'm really sorry about your dad, Cathy," said Laura, the grieving English girl. "But I can't go with you this time. Whatever you decide to do, can you let me go?" She sounded tired and miserable.

"Of course," she assured her. "Hugo, where's the nearest suitable place to land?"

"I know a spot," Hugo said. "We can recharge the cloaking generators too."

"Good," Cathy nodded. She offered Laura a sympathetic look. "I'm so sorry I got you into this."

Laura shook her head vigourously. "Don't be. I told you, this was our choice. Not every story has a happy ending… James would understand." She cast a sad glance at the lumps under the tarpaulin.

Shame they got caught in the crossfire… This had nothing to do with them, but Frank believed that if Zhin was allowed to control the world's power, their deaths would be a drop in the ocean. Zhin had something up his sleeve, Frank just didn't know what it was yet. They *had* to stop him, nothing else mattered at this point.

"Just so we're clear," Kev raised a hand. "About this plan of yours, you'll be bringing along some backup, right? A small army of your Europa buddies should suffice to take on a maniac's stronghold."

Frank inhaled a deep breath. "They won't help us. Europa have struck a deal with Zhin and discharged anyone investigating Horizon."

"Seriously?" said Arnie. "Zhin bought them out?"

"Afraid so," Frank said with an air of frustration. "If we go in, we go alone."

"Right," said Kev at length. "Well, I'll get out when she does." He gestured to Laura.

"You what?" Arnie scowled at him. "Mr. Blunt hired you. Your contract isn't over yet."

"Yeah, well, Mr. Blunt is dead. No offence, and all that," he said to Cathy, in a tone thoroughly lacking empathy. "I lost my buddies too, one to this guy's own hand," he accused Frank. "No pun intended."

Frank crossed his arms. *What a prick.*

"So, without Mr. Blunt, I won't even be paid, and if you think I'm feeling any obligation to join your fight without backup?" Kev blew air through his teeth. "Fuck that."

"You shitbag," Arnie expanded his legs and started to march towards the mercenary, but Cathy's voice broke through the air freezing him in his tracks.

"Stop it!" she demanded. The hold fell silent. "We've lost friends, too," she said, pointing to the tarpaulin. "And family," she added, exchanging a solemn glance with Dan. "You'll get your money, Kevin. But if you don't want a part of this, I won't force you. I will only ask you one small favour. Go with Laura."

At the mention of her name, Laura looked up from the floor and met Cathy's eyes.

She continued, "Escort her home to England safely, and find James' parents. Bring them his body. After that, return to Blunt HQ in Berlin and ask to speak to me directly. I will ensure you are compensated."

Kev seemed satisfied with that. "All right."

Frank was impressed by how well she was taking all of this. He'd never imagined her capable of commanding such authority. *When this is done, I'll need a new job... Might give her my CV.*

She gazed across each of them in turn, settling her eyes on Frank. "This all began when you rescued me from my imprisonment. You have no idea how grateful I am for that, Frank."

A warm sensation coursed through him. "I was just

following orders, you know."

"You could have left me, but you didn't," she said. "I owe you my life." She straightened, clasping both hands in front of her. "Will the plan still work without Kevin?"

"Better, I reckon," Arnie muttered.

Cathy's tone was wary. "What do you think, Frank?"

"I think we can do it," Frank nodded. "Either way, not much choice now."

"You can still go home," Cathy reminded him. "We could all go home…"

Frank thought about his "home". The soulless London apartment issued to him by Europa. He wouldn't be allowed back there now. And even if he did, what was there for him, anyway?

Maybe working for Catherine would plug the void that Europa had left behind. There was just something about her that he hadn't put his finger on until this very moment.

He respected her.

As the unlikely result of a terrible upbringing coupled with bad circumstances, she'd still managed to come out on top. She was a survivor. He could stand by a person like that, and feel proud about it.

She read his mind. "You're in this to the end, aren't you, Frank?"

"Bloody right I am."

She nodded thoughtfully. "If there's anything I can do to help, I will do it." She turned to Hugo. "Set a course for that landing spot. We will drop Laura off, and recharge the cloaking generators. After that, we are flying to Georgia."

"Roger that," said Hugo. He left the group and returned to the cockpit.

"Thank you," Laura's voice was warm and soft.

Frank exhaled a breath.

She looked at him and nodded. "There's a chance to end this today, and we're going to take it."

***

Laura and Kev departed in a private airfield outside Venice in northern Italy. They took James and Derunox's bodies with them. What remained of their dysfunctional team continued on towards Georgia on the easternmost edge of the Euromerican continent. Georgia bridged the gap between old Asia and Europe. Frank had been there once before on an assignment, but never to the Inguri Dam.

There was little to do but go over the plan with Arnie and Dan several more times as they flew. Arnie retired to the cargo hold to psyche himself up for the fight ahead, so Frank sat with Dan and Cathy in the communication room.

Dan had managed to download blueprints of the dam's structure, which was hardwired with redundant tech. He claimed he'd be able to hack the security cameras and open locked doors remotely from the VTOL.

Why did Zhin choose this place, if it's so easy to hack into?

Frank didn't like going into a mission without decent intel. But he had no choice this time. Whatever Zhin threw at him, Frank would have to improvise.

"New Dawn are in Berlin," Dan said. He was reading news articles on the computer.

"New Dawn?" Frank sat down next to him and looked at the screen. The screen showed pictures of demonstrations across various cities around the globe. "What are they doing?"

"Marching, protesting," Cathy chewed her lip. "Zhin is an open supporter of them…"

Frank raked his fingers across his stubble. "I don't like it." He scanned the news website. New Dawn were in London, Paris, New York, even Bangkok and Tokyo, where it was the middle of the night… some of the most densely populated cities in the world. *Did Zhin organise this?*

"Oh my fucking god," Dan said.

"What?" Frank turned to him.

"That's how he'll do it… that's how he'll take full control. Do you remember the photos, Cathy? Of Yuma and Dongola?"

"I won't soon forget that," she said morosely.

"Remember that one picture we found, of Dongola, I think. There was a New Dawn flag in it. Zhin's using *them* to deliver that vapourisation weapon!" Dan grabbed his hair with both hands. "How many people live in all of those cities, Frank?"

Frank swallowed, his throat had gone very dry. "Billions," he muttered. *He's been building up to this. Yuma, Dongola, Tarrow Creek… they were his testing grounds.* "You got family in any of these places?"

Dan leant in close and read the names. "My mom lives in Boston. There's no mention of New Dawn being there." He breathed a sigh of relief.

"Call her anyway," Frank said. "Tell her to get out of there."

"Why?" he frowned.

"You might not get another chance. I have a bad fucking feeling about today."

Cathy and Dan exchanged a worried look. Dan turned to the computer and put on his headset.

Hugo popped his head through the cockpit door. "We're thirty minutes out."

"Roger that," Frank stood and opened the door to the cargo hold.

Dan said into his headset, "Hi, mom. Heh, yeah, it's me…"

Frank eased the door shut. He joined Arnie near the back of the cargo hold, and they both suited up. Frank donned his black skysuit, attached his zip-winch and shrugged on the Keno chute pack.

"You ready, bro?" Arnie said. He was doing his Terminator thing again, wearing his combat exoskeleton.

"Yeah," Frank said. "Just hope we haven't overlooked

something obvious."

Arnie slapped his elbow with an open palm. "*Ka mate!*"

Frank snorted a laugh. "That again? You're pumped for this, ain't you?"

"Say it with me, bro. *Ka mate!*" He slapped his elbow again.

Frank gave it a try. "Ka matey."

"*Ka ora!*" Arnie chanted, and stamped a foot.

Frank repeated it. He stamped and laughed, appreciating the energy of the big Maori.

"*Ka mate, ka mate! Ka ora! Ka ora!*" They bellowed together, stamping their feet and clenching their fists.

"Good work, bro. Now you look ready."

"So, what's it mean?" Frank asked.

Arnie grinned. "I may die. I may live."

Frank gaped, then snorted laughter. "Brilliant."

"Okay, we're here," Hugo announced over the intercom. "Inguri Dam awaits below."

"Testing comms, you hear me okay?" Dan's voice came loud and clear through Frank's earpiece.

"Affirmative, I hear you Dan."

"Me too," Arnie said, flicking his helmet visor down over his face.

The red light in the hold turned green and Frank opened the cargo ramp. Wind and rain howled into the hold, as thunder rumbled in the distance.

"Bad bloody day for jumping," Frank muttered.

Arnie made a circle with his thumb and forefinger in a gesture of *okay*. His voice buzzed in Frank's earpiece, "See you inside, bro." Then he turned and clomped to the edge of the ramp, and jumped.

The light turned red again. Hugo said, "Moving to next LZ. Stand by, Frank."

Cathy's voice filled his ear. "Good luck Frank!" He turned and saw her standing by the door to the comms room wearing a headset. She shot him a nervous smile, and waved.

Cathy had transformed from the jabbering damsel that he'd pulled out of the shaft atop the alpine facility into something resembling a leader worthy of following.

The jump-light turned green again.

He gave Cathy a casual salute, before jumping into the stormy sky.

The rough weather made it the most dangerous Keno jump he had ever done. Lightning flickered around him as he plummeted between menacing electrified clouds. A forest stretched for miles below, impossible to see properly under the dark sky, but illuminated by distant lightning flashes. *The bulk of the storm hasn't arrived yet.*

The chute deployed at the last moment, rapidly slowing his descent and he dropped onto a grassy bank next to the reservoir.

The chute folded into itself and retracted inside the thin compartment lining of his skysuit. Frank made his way into the forest and followed a dirt track towards the southern end of the dam. A raised bank followed the curve of the track's left side, and he crept along the ditch for cover.

"Frank," Dan crackled in his ear. "You got company heading your way. Looks like a truck."

He crouched down. "What kind of truck?"

"Dunno, man. Delivery maybe? Gimme a sec, I've almost hacked their comms… got it!"

Frank peered back the way he had come. Approaching headlight beams refracted through bulbous raindrops and illuminated the shrubbery in a harsh white glow. "Might be a way in."

He scrambled up to the top of the bank and pressed his body against the ground, just before the truck rumbled into sight. From there, he had a good vantage point to jump onto the truck.

"Uhh, maybe…" Dan sounded apprehensive. "I'm listening to their chatter. From what I can tell, this truck should have arrived two hours ago. No word on what they're carrying though, dude. Do you see it yet? It's almost on top of you."

"Affirmative. Stand by."

Dan made a high pitched, excited noise. "Roger, roger, sir! Dude, this is so awesome—"

"*Quiet!*" Frank hissed. He'd only get one shot at this. He glanced at a tree branch overhanging the track, hoping it would take his weight.

The truck bounced along the track, a medium sized cargo transport, like the sort FedEx used to deliver parcels. Its tyres pushed muddy water into the ditch in a lazy spray; he guessed its speed at fifteen miles per hour.

Lightning lit the world.

The truck's cabin passed him by and Frank fired his zip-winch at the overhanging branch. He swung out over the top of the truck and released the cables, dropping a few feet onto the slippery roof just as a clack of thunder shook the sky.

Lucky, he thought.

He reset the winch and the cables almost whipped him in the face as they sucked back into the cylinder on his wrist. The truck's speed remained constant, so the driver must not have heard his clumsy landing. Frank crouched low, shielding his face against the onslaught of rainy wind.

He crawled towards the back of the truck, lying flat on his belly and peered over the edge. The rear loading door was padlocked at the bottom.

"Any idea what Zhin's delivery is?" Frank asked Dan.

"Not yet, man."

Frank grimaced. "I'll try to find out."

The truck lurched over a bump and Frank was flung sideways. He slipped and fell over the side of the truck. His metal hand squeezed the corner of the truck's roof so hard that it indented a hand print. His feet scrabbled for grip against the slick surface and he swung his leg up, hauling himself back onto the roof.

One of the men must've opened his window because

music poured out of the cabin. Frank heard a voice say, "I thought I saw something."

Frank pressed down as flat as he could on the roof. *Please…*

"Must've hit a branch," said the truck's passenger. "There's nothing there." The music dulled and muffled as he closed the window.

Fuck me. He exhaled a sharp breath.

"Frank?" Dan said warily in his ear. "You okay?"

"I'm all right. Thank fuck for this hand." The relief of the situation made the words tumble out before he had a chance to consider them, and they filled him with a sense of self-betrayal. His prosthetic arm was turning out to be more useful than his natural arm ever was. "Ugh. Dan, you still got a visual?"

"Right above you, dude. Arnie's made it to the dam." He added, "Hugo says we gotta get out of this storm, it's getting really choppy up here." His voice fluctuated, as if he were speaking on a rollercoaster.

Frank glanced up at the darkening thunderclouds. The hammering rain didn't look like it was letting up anytime soon. "What kind of range do these earpieces have?" Frank asked.

"Dunno man, but you're gonna be at the dam in like, sixty seconds. The road goes right under it. Not sure if they'll work anyway through all that concrete. Oh *shit!* There's a security checkpoint up ahead. The guards will see you!"

"Fuck." Frank considered climbing down and smashing open the padlock to hide inside the truck. It would easily break between his metal fingers, but if the guards saw the truck tampered with, they'd suspect something and probably find him. He opted to stay on the roof.

He caught sight of a tunnel ahead leading into the side of the dam, overlooked by a guard box and barricade.

The truck slowed and Frank pressed his belly against the roof to stay out of sight. As the truck pulled up, he cocked his head to listen.

"Finally, welcome to Inguri, boys," said a gruff American voice.

"Fuckin' storm cost us two hours," the driver griped. "The pilot refused to fly in this weather. He stayed behind."

"Reckon he'll regret that decision, come tomorrow, eh?" The truck driver and guard shared a brief, knowing laugh.

"Get your asses into the tunnel and—" The guard was cut off by a burst of activity on his radio.

"Intruder spotted on the north side. He's wearing some kind of body armour, requesting assistance!"

Good work Arnie, Frank thought.

"Shit, what's going on?" grunted the American guard. Frank saw the barricade lifting in front of the truck. "Get going. Unload as quickly as you can." He started speaking louder to some other unseen men. "Pack it up here, boys. Let's kill the intruder and get ourselves to the bunker, pronto. Move it!" The truck started moving again and rolled out of the rain into the sheltered tunnel lit by rows of orange electric bulbs.

The tunnel gently curved, following the shape of the dam itself, and descended underground. Frank stayed low with his arms and legs spread-eagled on the slippery roof of the truck.

"Frank?" Dan asked.

"What?" he whispered.

"You're inside the dam. Signal's getting weaker, I'm getting a lot of interference." Dan's voice was becoming faint and tinny. "Uhh, the goons in there are really eager to get whatever's in that truck…"

"Any word on Zhin?"

"Not directly, but they keep mentioning a Mr. Z. He's still here, Frank."

"Good."

"Arnie's engaged…" The earpiece hissed over the top of Dan's words. "…giving them hell! Good…" Dan's voice

was swallowed by incomprehensible static.
  On my own now, then.

34
INGURI ASSAULT

CWUMP-sshhhh.

Arnie's hydraulics contracted as they soaked up the impact of his landing in the slick mud. The rain pattered against his titanium legs, *clinking* as he unclipped his chute-pack and abandoned it on the ground. He had a lightweight sniper rifle strapped to his back and a pistol in his belt.

"Touchdown," he said.

"I got you on the tracker," replied Dan. "This tech's amazing."

Arnie didn't have much to say about that. "Yup. Mr. Blunt builds the best." He frowned. "Or, he did…" He could've done without the reminder of Sid. He took a deep breath. *No time to mourn you now. I'll pay my respects after I kill Zhin, sir.*

"Moving up," he relayed to Dan, as he clomped into the dark woodland.

Arnie approached from the east, following the river outlet at the bottom of the dam. As he emerged from the shelter of the trees, a silent flash of lightning greeted his arrival. Looming before him, the grand concrete structure lit up bright as day for a split second. The dam was a solid wall of curved concrete rising several hundred feet into the air, reaching for the thunderclouds. The lightning lasted barely a second, before turning the dam back into a shadowy behemoth.

A couple of seconds later, thunder ripped across the surrounding hills.

Nobody was in sight. A couple of watchtowers overlooked the forest atop the dam, but he fancied his chances of not being seen. Arnie charged at the base of the dam. He made for a maintenance door in the side of the structure. Another flash of lightning blinded him but it lingered unnaturally long. He slammed into the wall beside the door and realised he was still bathed in light.

Oh shit, a spotlight!

Gunfire rattled above him and bullets ricocheted off the ground and clanged against his helmet. Arnie had been seen by one of the watchtower guards, who trained the powerful searchlight right down on top of him.

Arnie kicked the maintenance door off its hinges and darted through into cover. Inside, a short corridor led to a metal stairway which took him to an underground chamber full of noisy industrial machinery.

His ear piece crackled. *"You're insi... pumping station... break... distraction?"* Some of the words were cut off, but Arnie got the gist of Dan's suggestion.

"On it now," he replied, not knowing if Dan could still hear him.

He eyed the machinery. Bulbous cylindrical pipes fed water through a series of generators and pumps. Some had pressure gauges connected to valves that looked like 18-wheeler steering wheels. A deep mechanical *humm* emanated through the air which rumbled Arnie's bones.

He studied one of the huge round valves, and considered turning it. Maybe he could increase the pressure or something. That would bring the guards down here and keep the attention away from Frank.

"Oi! Vin khar?"

Arnie turned towards the startled voice. An engineer was pointing down at him from a gangway.

"Uh oh," he muttered, and abandoned all subtlety. Arnie kicked the pipe below the valve causing a deep indentation. Despite the gargantuan strength of his mechanical legs, the pipe was made of some thick, strong metal, not to mention full of pressurised water, and he recoiled away in surprise.

"*Ara! Ras aket'eh?*" The engineer gaped in alarm and ran along the walkway heading for a staircase that would bring him to ground level with Arnie.

The valve hissed and the gauge needle shifted a little to indicate a rise in pressure. Arnie leaned back and kicked the valve so hard it snapped off and flew into the air. The engineer was coming down the stairs on the far end of the room, heading for Arnie, so he legged it back the way he had come.

As he retreated, he booted every pipe he could see and snapped the valves off. The plant's deep steady *hum* turned into a higher-pitched whine. Arnie glanced back over his shoulder to see the engineer flapping his hands in the air and talking into a walky-talky. He stared at Arnie in bewildered confusion, but didn't come after him.

Arnie kicked another pipe, and booted a nearby rotary generator for good measure. The spinning engine within ground to a screeching halt as its blades snagged on the protruding metal.

The high-pitched whine escalated to a deafening whistle, and a nearby gauge indicated the pressure had reached the 'danger' level. An alarm blared out from the ceiling high above, and intermittent pulses of red light flashed across the pumping station. "*Warning. Warning. Evacuate,*" boomed a loud mechanical voice in accented English. Arnie figured his work here was done.

Engineers emerged from side doors and bolted for the exits. Arnie watched them scurrying across the gangways like ants fleeing a nest, faintly amused. Water splashed onto his ankles, and the sensors in his legs told his brain that his feet were getting wet. "Oh, shit." He ran for the stairwell that led back out onto the jetty in front of the dam, and re-entered the storm.

More alarms sounded from above. The guard tower's spotlight engulfed him again, and bullets mingled with the rain. A second searchlight beam swung through the rain-streaked sky to train on him from the other end of the dam.

Snapp!

A bullet struck him square in the chest, winding him, but not penetrating the armour. *A sniper.* Arnie glanced at the river below – it flowed away to the east, fed by a torrent that spilled from the base of the dam in a violent waterfall, the outlet for the dam's massive reservoir.

Arnie leapt across the outlet and landed on the other side of the river beneath the second watchtower. The spotlights swung to follow his trajectory. He had a brief moment of respite in the dark before the light fell upon him again. He had undergone sniper training, and he knew how difficult it was to shoot straight down from such an angle.

Crack!

Arnie's head jerked backwards and his vision blurred. The bullet glanced off his helmet and buried itself in the ground at his feet. He blinked away the minor concussion. "He's good," Arnie mumbled.

He darted to the side to avoid the third shot and speckles of concrete flicked up around his feet. *I have to take out those bloody lamps.*

The rain intensified for a moment, pattering against his helmet. Combined with the blinding spotlights it made it difficult to see any footholds on the face of the vertical wall. He reckoned the legs could get him up there, but it'd take at least two jumps, like the time he escaped through the elevator shaft at the Europa base with Catherine.

Crack! Arnie leapt again, soaring over the river back to the maintenance door side. He swung the sniper rifle off his back and quickly took aim at the second spotlight. It caught up with him just as he lined up the shot, filling his visor with intense bright light.

He pulled the trigger and the spotlight exploded. A sprinkling of glass reflected the lightning as it dusted the floor. In the darkness, Arnie pounced again. He landed on the jetty and turned around to face the first guard tower, aimed and fired. The second spotlight went dark, leaving Arnie in the murk out of sight.

Crack! Snapp! Crack!

The ground spat up chunks as wild bullets struck the concrete all around his feet.

Now, he thought, holstering the sniper rifle on his back.

He expected to jump, but the legs had calculated another way to the top. They sprinted straight for the curving, vertical wall. "Whaaa—?" Arnie choked as his legs leapt onto the wall and ran along it sideways. He rose higher and higher as he sprinted around the curve of the concrete dam, all the way from the lower left corner aiming for the upper right. *This is amazing!*

The feet chewed into the wall like claws, keeping him glued to the slick surface, and carried him all the way to the top.

As he reached the summit, the legs leapt and he sailed over the ridge and landed on the lip of the vertical drop, just past the watchtower. He teetered there for a moment, staring straight down the monstrous drop, before the legs took a casual step further and he dropped onto the safety of the flat road that ran across the dam.

The guard in the tower was leaning over the edge, searching for him, unaware of his climb. Arnie's blood was high on adrenaline and he wanted more. The legs sensed his intention and retracted, poised to spring.

"*Ka mate!*" Arnie pounced.

The watch tower's legs rushed by and then disappeared as he soared over the top of it and landed on the corrugated iron roof, crumpling it like paper with his weight. He smashed down on top of the sniper and crushed him beneath his titanium feet.

The noise must have caught the attention of the guard in

the other tower. A sniper shot cracked the air and Arnie took another bullet in the chest. This time, the armour dented so badly that it protruded hard, fracturing one of his ribs. "Argh!" he gritted his teeth and jumped off the ruined tower. He landed on the road and darted along it.

The sniper kept firing, but Arnie zigzagged along the tarmac, making big leaps from one side to the other as lightning split the air overhead and bullets and raindrops zipped past his face.

As he approached, he spied two support struts bolted into the rear of the tower at a forty-five degree angle. He suspected that these towers had been hastily constructed, not designed to be permanent. He charged at one of the struts securing the tower to the ground and booted it. It snapped like a matchstick. Without breaking stride, he continued on to the second strut and kicked it away. The tower gave a violent jerk as the sudden extra weight on one side caused it to lean out over the drop. The guard within screamed, but was drowned out by the screech of rending metal as the whole thing tumbled over the side. It crashed into the ground hundreds of feet below, a clattering bombardment of broken steel.

Lighting split the air, followed by a *BOOM* of thunder that rumbled through Arnie's core. He stood alone now on the top of the dam, overlooking the dark vista of trees beneath a sea of black thunderclouds. The wail of the warning siren echoed faintly below.

His earpiece crackled. He faintly heard Frank's voice, but couldn't make out the words.

"What's your status, Hawkins?" he asked.

"He's underground, Arnie," came Dan's reply. "Lost contact with him a few minutes ago. The dam's solid concrete, these transmitters aren't getting through."

"I can hear him, but it's crackly."

"Really?" Dan said. "We must be out of range then. We're above the clouds, Hugo said the storm could fry the instruments."

434

"Good thinking," Arnie said. He looked about the deserted dam, clutching his rifle as raindrops pattered against his helmet. The dent in his armour pressed against his chest, making it difficult to breathe. "Uh," he wheezed. "What should I do now?" Arnie felt a moment of disbelief that he was requesting orders from a nineteen year old kid. *Fuck's my life become?*

"Umm," said Dan.

Arnie heard scrabbling coming from the other end, as if someone was pulling the mic away from Dan's head.

"Arnie? Can you hear me?" Catherine's voice now.

"Yes, my *Ruapehu.* I hear you."

A hesitation. "A delivery truck arrived. Frank used it to get past the checkpoint. We think we know what was inside that truck."

Arnie idly scanned the base of the dam for signs of movement as he waited for her to elaborate. *She's so grown up now.* He never imagined himself working alongside her like this. *Wow, now I feel old.*

"Arnie?" she said.

"I'm here. Why's the truck important?"

"We don't know for sure," Dan said from the background, his voice small and barely audible over the pouring rain.

"It makes sense, though, right?" Cathy said to him, loud in Arnie's ear. "What will Zhin need with a hydroelectric dam once his solar plants are fully operational?"

"Yeah, but…"

"Dan, I'm sure about this, okay? It explains why Zhin hasn't fled yet, even though he must know we're coming. He was waiting for the bomb to be delivered."

"*What?*" Arnie lowered the rifle and put a hand to his ear. "What *kind* of bomb?" Arnie had seen the mercenaries vapourised at Cloud Lodge. He didn't much fancy going out like that.

"A concussive explosive. Like the one they used to destroy the alpine facility," Cathy confirmed.

"Oh," Arnie said, relieved. Then he decided he didn't much fancy dying that way either. He gulped. "Okay, well, what should I do?"

"Frank's inside already. If the bomb goes off while he's in there… I can't ask you to do this, Arnie," her voice was breaking. "If you die too—"

"Don't you worry about me or Frank. I'll find him." He slung the rifle over his shoulder. "Listen to me, Catherine. In case I don't make it out of here, I want you to know that I'm very proud of you."

A pause. "Thank you, Arnie," she said softly. "But, don't say things like that. Just be careful and you'll be okay."

Careful isn't me anymore. "I'll try," he said. "I'm going inside to help Frank. Tell me how to find that tunnel."

"Contact!" a voice barked through the rain.

Arnie turned to a hail of machine-gun fire coming from a squad of men taking cover behind the crumpled ruins of the first watchtower. Bullets clanged off his armour.

Flinching and roaring, he clomped into the fray.

35
CONTACT

Frank rode the truck into a wide open parking lot at the end of the tunnel, supported by rows of pillars. He was now deep below the dam, countless tonnes of thick concrete above his head.

The truck pulled into a parking space, and the driver and passenger got out. They wore black clothes with combat boots and pistols strapped to their belts. Not delivery men, definitely mercenaries. They approached a nondescript grey door and pressed an intercom button.

Frank slithered off the side of the roof and dropped silently down in cover behind the truck. He duck-ran into a shadowy corner of the parking lot and crouched behind a pillar, where he could watch them.

Three more mercs appeared at the door and the group of men walked back to the truck, unlocked it and started unloading heavy-looking wooden crates.

"Be glad when this is all over," one muttered, lugging a crate over a shoulder.

"It will be, come morning," another replied, with considerably more cheer.

One by one, they carried crates through the door and into the dam's structure.

The last box was different because it was made of stainless steel. The truck driver said, "Careful with that one. We don't wanna start the fireworks early."

One merc hunkered to pick it up and Frank noticed that

he had a prosthetic arm, not dissimilar to his own. The driver locked the truck and followed the last mercenary through the door and closed it behind him.

Frank was alone in the parking lot.

He waited a few moments to ensure they weren't coming back, then crept along the wall towards the door. He spotted a circle of clear glass embedded in the ceiling just above the entrance.

"Dan, got a security camera I need disabled. Do you read me?" No answer on his earpiece. "Arnie, what's your status?" The earpiece hissed useless static, so he switched it off.

Shit.

Frank dashed across the lot and punched his titanium fist in an uppercut through the ceiling glass and smashed the camera within, raining glass around him. He shrugged off the fragments and raised his left wrist to the keypad beside the door. His skysuit's wrist scanner took a few seconds to break the door's lock code, and Frank half expected the mercs to come crashing through the door and catch him. *Someone will come to inspect their broken camera.*

The keypad beeped and the door clicked. He darted inside and shut the door behind him.

Voices echoed to him, the mercs chatting somewhere ahead.

"Hear what happened at Cloud Lodge? Whole place was blown to bits."

"Wasn't Margery there?"

"Yeah. Looks like you got out just in time."

"You're telling me. Won't miss the bitch. At least Zhin doesn't ask me to murder kids."

"If she's dead, who'll get the second pod now?"

"Beats me. Fat chance it'll be any of us, though."

Frank followed the voices down a damp, musty concrete corridor. A thick black pipe ran along the ceiling, and he passed several closed doors, but the men carried on, heading deeper into the structure.

Someone shouted up ahead. Frank only heard two words, but they were enough: "...*following you!*"

He froze. Standing in the corridor with no cover, he quickly scanned for a place to hide and spotted an alcove in the ceiling where a second pipe jutted out from the wall. He jumped and pulled himself up, wedging his body into the tight space between the pipes.

Two men ran past, clutching sub-machine guns. They headed for the parking lot. Frank held his breath, listening for anyone else.

"Find the intruder!" someone growled, closer.

Frank squirmed to draw his pistol, clutching it in his natural hand.

A merc slowly crept into view. He was looking warily about, scanning the ceiling... their eyes met.

Frank was already aiming at his head. He pulled the trigger and brain spattered the floor. Frank spun his leg around the pipe and dropped down into the corridor.

"*He's here!*"

Frank pressed his back against a door, the frame of which provided almost zero cover. Bullets sprayed up the corridor, whizzing right past Frank's nose. One bullet tore a chunk out of his left arm, instantly trickling with blood.

"Agh!" he grunted. He swung his metal fist into the door as hard as he could. It crashed open and he tumbled backwards into a dark office. He tripped and landed on his back, his wounded arm spurting blood across the carpet.

Frank scrambled to his feet and took cover behind the broken door, hanging off its hinges.

"He's in there!" someone shouted from the corridor.

He heard sets of feet pattering up the corridor from both directions. Frank took aim at the doorway.

As soon as one fool leaned in, Frank shot him in the face. He slumped to the ground with a *thud*.

"Shit!" someone else said.

The office erupted with gunfire as the mercs peppered the doorway with machine gun fire. Frank dove behind a desk and took cover, shielding his head with his metal arm. Bullets tore chunks out of the wall, spitting plaster dust into the air.

The gunfire ceased.

"Did we get him?"

"I dunno."

"If you can hear us, give up!"

"We have the door covered, there's no way out."

Only two different voices. *So, where's the fifth guy?* Frank scanned the room for an alternative exit. There was a ceiling vent, but Frank would be exposed for too long if he pried it open.

"Come out!" a voice barked.

They're standing to the right of the door.

"All right, I'm coming out," Frank called.

He clambered over the desk, keeping his pistol trained on the doorway.

"Throw your weapon out here," a merc ordered.

Judging the sound of the merc's voice, Frank shimmied along the office wall, and stopped in line with where he thought the man was waiting on the other side.

"Okay," Frank said. "Here comes my weapon."

Frank leaned back and punched straight through the wall.

The merc yelped as Frank's metal arm wrapped around his face and yanked him backwards against the wall, cracking his skull.

Bullets pelted against Frank's arm, the sensors simulating the intense pain of being shot multiple times and Frank's synapses overloaded. Something in the arm's AI switched off, and the pain vanished in an instant. He let go of the merc, whose body slumped lifelessly to the ground.

Frank peeked through the hole in the wall and saw the truck driver gaping through, the sub-machine gun rapidly going *clik-clik-clik-clik-clik-clik*. Frank pointed his pistol through the hole and shot him in the forehead.

He reloaded his pistol before exiting the office. He tore a

strip of shirt off one of the dead mercenaries and used his teeth to tie it around his wounded arm, before continuing down the corridor at a jog. His left arm burned from the bullet graze. Blood oozed through the fabric, down the length of his forearm to drip from his fingertips.

When he came to a metal door with a round glass window, he peered through, spying a red carpeted corridor. The fifth merc, the one with the metal prosthetic arm was standing next to the stack of unloaded wooden boxes, holding the stainless steel crate over a shoulder. He was speaking animatedly into an intercom next to a set of elevator doors.

Frank kicked open the door. He marched towards the merc aiming the gun at his head.

The merc darted around to face him, fumbling the metal box and almost dropping it. "Woah!" he cried, holding the box out in front of him. "You don't wanna shoot the package."

Frank eased his finger off the trigger and halted a few feet away.

"What's going on?" buzzed the intercom. "The intruder's there, isn't he…? You useless fuckwits are on your own now." The intercom made a ruffled *click* noise and went silent.

The prosthetic merc gave a long blink.

"Was that Zhin?" Frank demanded.

"Yeah."

"Where is he?"

"He's down there. The elevator leads to the bunker. But he's disabled it, so nobody can get down there now."

Frank snorted. "I'll find a way. Move aside."

"No." The merc wiggled the metal crate. "You know what this is?"

"I have my suspicions, yeah."

"It's very sensitive. All I need to do is drop it and it'll go off."

Frank narrowed his eyes. "You won't do that." He still

had the gun aimed at his head, and his finger tightened on the trigger again.

"How can you be so sure?"

He's bluffing. That crate took a beating in the back of the delivery truck. If it is a bomb, it's a stable one. Time to put this bastard down.

Frank fired.

The merc lifted the crate to shield his face and the bullet ripped a hole in its side.

Frank hesitated for a beat, just long enough for the merc to launch the crate towards him.

Shit!

Frank caught it full in the chest, knocking the wind out of him. He fumbled the gun and dropped it and the heavy crate on the ground.

The prosthetic merc pounced on him. He swung low, glancing a blow to Frank's gut. Frank staggered backwards off balance and tripped onto his arse. The merc loomed over him and tried to stamp on Frank's face.

He blocked it with his metal hand, grabbed the guy's boot and twisted it.

"Agh!" the merc yelped and fell sideways, crashing head first into the corridor wall.

Frank rolled onto his belly and pushed himself up. The dazed merc swung a wild right hook towards him but Frank jerked his neck to dodge it and the fist struck the wall instead. Chunks of concrete and dust exploded into the air.

Frank tackled the merc in the abdomen and charged forwards. He pushed until the merc's legs collided with a wooden crate and he tripped over it, laying sprawled out on top. Frank grabbed the guy's throat with his metal fist and popped the guy's nose with his left.

The merc's eyes bulged in their sockets as blood streamed down his face and into his gaping mouth.

Frank's left arm throbbed with intense pain as his bullet wound tore open further. He winced and his vision flared for a moment.

The merc's metal arm came out of nowhere and slammed Frank's forearm away, freeing him from the throat-hold.

Frank stumbled to the side, thinking *I have to end this right now before we kill each other.*

He lifted his fists in a guard, turning to face the blurry merc again. He had his back to Frank, scrambling towards the elevator doors. Frank saw him through a shimmering haze of pain, jamming his arm between the doors and prying them open.

Frank blinked.

The merc opened the doors. A dark shaft lay beyond.

Push him.

Frank stepped forwards and shoved the merc in the back.

The merc half turned as he did so, reaching out desperately with his metal arm. He fell over the precipice and grabbed Frank's arm, both their hands locking around each other's forearm.

Frank fell to one knee and braced himself against the elevator doorframe with his bleeding natural arm, and took the weight of the merc, who slammed into the shaft wall.

"Ack!" he grunted, as the merc dangled over the maw of the cool, dim plummet. It stretched straight down, the bottom far beyond sight.

"You're coming with me!" the merc growled.

The merc squeezed Frank's arm, causing the metal to bend under the pressure.

Frank glared at him and squeezed back. Frank's fingers crushed the merc's forearm like a soda can.

"No!" the merc wailed, eyes bulging in terror.

"You need an upgrade," Frank quipped. He clenched his teeth and twisted the guy's arm away from the elbow. The metal buckled beneath his titanium grip, splaying open in a jagged rip of wires.

He tore the arm off and the mercenary plunged

screaming into the darkness.

Frank stood, allowing the doors to slide shut, and tossed the ruined prosthetic on the floor. He winced as more blood seeped through the fabric on his wounded arm.

He flipped open one of the wooden crates to examine its contents. Inside were canned foodstuffs and vacuum sealed packets. He opened another and found it full of bottled water.

Planning to hide underground, are we, Zhin?

He hunkered down beside the metal box, and considered opening it. It was locked with two clips and padlocks. His metal hand would make short work of both locks, but what if it was booby trapped?

Find Zhin first, then come back for this.

Frank pressed the elevator's call button, but was not surprised when nothing happened. *He probably cut the power.*

Frank wedged his hand in between the doors and forced them open again. Cool, dry air seeped out of the shaft. It went deep underground, illuminated by a few intermittent dim bulbs, and taut elevator cables dangled down the centre.

Frank grabbed the thickest cable with his titanium hand and stepped over the edge. He slid down the dark shaft all the way to the bottom. His eardrums contracted uncomfortably at the extra pressure.

He landed on the roof of the elevator next to the splattered corpse of the dead mercenary. He crouched down and listened. Silence. Frank punched through the locked hatch in one blow. It swung inward, and the bolt clattered to the floor making a metallic ringing sound. A trickle of blood dripped down into the elevator below, spattering the floor.

"What was that?"

Frank recognised Zhin's voice coming from the room beyond the elevator. He peered through the hatch and saw that the doors were wedged open with an ornate leather sofa. *That's one way to stop a lift from working.* Frank paused at the odd sight, before a man appeared in the elevator door, his eyes sweeping from the bloodstains up at him.

"Shit! It's the intruder!" The merc fired a wild burst up at the hatch and quickly retreated out of sight again.

Frank leapt back but a bullet buried itself deep in the side of his abdomen. "Agh!" he grimaced.

"What?" Zhin's voice was shrill and panicked. "How the hell did he get down here?"

Frank drew his pistol again and yelled through the gap. "Hyun-Ki Zhin! Call off your guard and surrender. No-one else has to die here today."

There was a pause, when nobody spoke. Then Zhin said, "*Kill him!*"

Frank aimed his pistol at the elevator doors and when the merc popped his head around, Frank shot his face off.

"*Agh, fucking fuck!*" Zhin shrieked.

"Well, I tried," Frank yelled. He dropped into the elevator and took cover behind the sofa. "You got any more goons for me to kill in there?"

No answer.

Something *hissed* shut.

Frank carefully leaned over, training his pistol ahead. A tiny corridor led to a heavy-looking bathysphere-style door. Frank hopped over the sofa and shimmied along the corridor wall. He peered through the tiny round window and spied a man scurrying across a lavishly decorated living room. Clutching the central wheel, he unlocked and heaved the bathysphere door open.

The space felt more like a grand study of a mansion than an underground bomb shelter. There were bookcases and leather chairs and an antique globe mounted on a wooden base. The only giveaway that they were underground was the concrete support pillars dotted around the room.

Somewhere out of sight, a door slammed shut. Frank darted from the bathysphere door and limped after the sound, clutching the bullet wound at his side. He scrambled across the living room and caught sight of Zhin disappearing into another room in the corridor beyond.

Frank shuffled after him, kicked in the next door and came face to face with a wall full of mounted computer monitors. Standing with his palms planted on the table, leaning over the desk in front of a microphone was the man himself: Horatio Zhin.

"Initiate, Stone."

"Yes, sir."

Zhin spun towards Frank, his face shadowed by the glow of screens behind him.

The man was taller than Frank expected, easily six foot, with slicked black hair that revealed an immaculately smooth face. His tailored suit was undone at the top button and his white sleeves were rolled back from the wrists, but the man still possessed a looming sense of authority. Frank quickly scanned the room, realised they were alone, and shut the door behind him.

Zhin glared at him. "I suppose you've come to—"

"Shut the fuck up." Frank shoved him sideways into the wall, spun him around and kicked his legs apart. He frisked the man. Frank found a small, ancient-looking pistol in Zhin's belt, which he stuffed into his back pocket, and checked his legs and arms for hidden blades. Satisfied that Zhin was unarmed, he stepped back and ordered, "Sit."

Zhin turned around instead, facing the bank of monitors, ignoring Frank's command. His head jerked from one screen to the next.

Frank stepped up behind him and pressed the gun to the back of Zhin's neck. "Did you hear me? I said sit the fuck…" He trailed off as one of the images caught his eye.

Each monitor displayed journalists reporting across the world. Many were amongst New Dawn marches, but this one showed a scene of Times Square in New York. It should have been packed with people, tourists and residents shopping and bustling. Instead, it was deserted and the floor was littered with clothes.

"I suppose you came to try to stop this?" Zhin spoke

calmly.

"What have you done?" Frank said.

Zhin turned on him. Despite being unarmed and backed into a corner, he still somehow looked down his nose at Frank. "Like *you* could ever comprehend my epoch, Mister... what is your name?"

"Your epoch?" Frank's natural fist clenched, squeezing blood through the shirt tied around his forearm.

A monitor flashed white, drawing Frank's eye. When the image returned, he recognised one of the feet of the Eiffel Tower in Paris. The camera was aimed at the plaza beneath it, now strewn with empty clothes. "You have to stop it," Frank said through gritted teeth.

Zhin turned towards the monitors again but Frank grabbed him by the back of the collar and yanked him away. He grabbed the microphone off the desk and jabbed the gun into Zhin's throat, holding the microphone in front of his mouth. "Call it off now you twisted piece of shit!"

Zhin scoffed. "Call it off? It's clearly too late for that."

"Call it off right now or I swear to fuck—"

"You'll blow my brains out? You'll tear off my fingers, you'll break my legs? You think that will stop *this?*" Zhin spread his hands wide, gesturing to the bank of monitors. One after the other, flashes of white blinked at Frank, indicating another city gone. Millions of people vapourised in an instant.

The picture on the New York monitor changed. The image of Times Square retreated to a square in the corner, and two anxious-looking reporters in a studio somewhere spoke silently to the camera. A headline appeared at the bottom of the screen, *'Euromerica Under Attack?'*

Frank's stomach roiled. Bile rose in the back of his dry throat. He dropped the mic, and the pressure on the gun under Zhin's throat loosened.

"I should just kill you right here and now," he mumbled.

"Actually, you shouldn't," Zhin retorted. "The world will

need me once the… dust has settled. It is not my time to die."

"I don't think that decision is up to you any more, Horatio." Frank jabbed the gun for emphasis.

Zhin stared past the barrel, unfazed. "Of course you know who I am. But since you will not do me the courtesy of giving me your name, I will make an educated guess. Are you from Europa?" Frank didn't reply. "Thought so. But since Europa and I had come to a mutual agreement, I will assume that you have gone rogue. Yes, a rogue agent with a conscience who believes he is doing the right thing for his fellow humans." He gestured to the bank of monitors once more. "The irony being that in the long run, humanity needs this cull if we are to survive."

"Cull," Frank spat. "I think the word you're looking for is *genocide*."

"Where one sees genocide, I see ecocide. Do you know what that is, Mr. Europa?"

"No, and I don't give a—"

"It is the destruction of the world's natural habitat. A crime that *these* people commit every day. Don't you see that by removing them, I was giving future generations a chance?"

Frank shook his head, lost for words.

A grim smile crept over Zhin's face. "There are *too many people living on this planet*, Mr. Europa. You know I'm right. Somebody had to do something about it. Somebody with the power, and the *balls*. I found myself in such a position, and to not act would have been to see the downfall of my species."

"You're fucking deranged. The governments you bribed will go after you. You can't get away with murdering millions of people."

"Millions?" Zhin gave him a quizzical cock of the head. "That's a little off the mark. You truly are failing to see the bigger picture here."

Frank's mind swirled with rage at the man's unbearable

self-righteous attitude. He lost control. "Fuck you!" he slammed Zhin against the wall, squeezing his neck with a titanium grip.

"*Agh!*" Zhin squealed, scrabbling at the arm, his face contorted in pain.

"You can't justify this to me," Frank went on. "I came here to capture you. To put you on trial."

"There won't be anyone left to carry it out!" Zhin shrilled. "Circumstances changed the minute that little bitch decided to make a home movie and reveal my research. Now, the world suspects *me* as a villain. I was to be remembered as its saviour!"

"You're nothing but a murderous fucking psychopath." Frank lifted Zhin off the ground, and the man's eyes bulged with panic.

"Wait!" Zhin pleaded. He waved a trembling finger at the monitors. "Just watch. You *need* me alive. Look!"

Frank scanned the screens again impatiently. *Why the fuck are you humouring him? Just kill him and be done with it!* But something on one of the screens caught his eye.

"There!" Zhin wheezed. "You see!"

The BBC reporter, Louise Stone was speaking directly to the camera. Frank read the caption on the footage that was showing. "*America declares war on China.*"

He dropped Zhin back on the floor.

"It's started…" Zhin coughed. "I knew it would. Humans were always so predictable."

"Fuck me," Frank muttered. "You started World War Three."

36
STORMY SKIES

The VTOL hovered in a vast expanse of calm blue sky. The storm raged on below, bulbous grey thunderheads flashing with lightning, but Hugo had brought them far out of the storm's reach. Warm evening sunlight poured through the open cockpit door to the comms room and across Dan's panic-stricken face. He was hammering a message into Binary Eye's forum, a warning to his online friends.

Cathy leaned over his shoulder and read the message aloud to herself. "*If you live in a major population centre, like New York, or Boston, or Chicago…fucking anywhere! Get the hell out and take everyone you love to the countryside. NOW.*" She laid a hand on his shoulder. "I hope your friends see it before… you know."

"I know," he grimaced. He doubted many would be able to get away in time, but he had to try at least. Thirteen cities across the world had been attacked so far, and God knew how many of Zhin's vapourisation bombs were still out there. He marked the post as urgent before hitting *Submit*.

The forums were quieter than usual. They were *never* quiet. Dan tried not to think about why that was. Many of his peers lived within the cities that were being attacked. Many of them might never post online again…

"Listen, turn it up," Cathy interrupted his dark thoughts.

Dan had a livestream playing quietly in the background,

and increased the volume so they could hear it better. Most of the major global news networks had gone offline and this Turkish or Greek news station was the only one Dan could find still broadcasting in English. "...*confirmation of an attack in Shanghai. I repeat, all communications with Shanghai have ceased. It is the fourteenth major city in the world, and the sixth in Neo-Asia to go dark. Information is limited, we are struggling to communicate with any of the affected cities...*"

"My god," Cathy mumbled behind him. "He even attacked China? Is he *trying* to start a war? All those poor people..."

He spun the chair around to face her. She was chewing on a fingernail, her green eyes alert and fearful. Dan said, "What would he gain from that? I thought he was trying to unite the world, not segregate it."

She shook her head. "I don't know. Have you heard from Frank or Arnie yet?"

Her brow creased in cute little wrinkles, and Dan lost his train of thought.

"Dan?" she snapped.

"Uh, no." He straightened and turned back to the screen. With a hand on his headphones, he tried both channels, but only static hissed back down the line. "It's no good. They are both underground, and we're too high up."

Cathy gave a disgruntled sigh and went through the cockpit door. "Can we go back yet?" she demanded to Hugo. "We can't just leave them down there alone!"

Hugo replied apologetically. "It's the storm, Miss. Look out there, nothing but thunderheads for miles. We could descend, but only at risk to ourselves."

"Frank should be able to get in contact with us once he brings Zhin up to the surface," Dan said. "Even at this altitude, the comms will work so long as he's outside. I just have to listen out for him."

Cathy was silent for a while, staring out at the setting sun. She slowly nodded her head. "Okay. We'll give them both a little more time." To Dan, she said, "Tell me the second you hear from either of them."

"Of course," he said.

"God, I can't stand all this tension." She folded her arms across her chest and went into the cargo hold. Dan heard the bathroom door lock shut with a *click*.

He put his headphones on and went back to scanning the news feeds. *Quieter and quieter.* Whenever a city got wiped out, the activity online noticeably dwindled. The European reporter had nothing new to say, she was just repeating the report of the most recent attack in Shanghai. Dan scrolled through his *Chatter* feed for anything else, but that was full of questions, not answers. Everyone across the Net asking the same thing over and over: *What the fuck is happening!?*

A message popped up from the BBC. Dan frowned, and paused his scrolling. The British media had been silent for twenty minutes, ever since London was attacked. All of their reports filtered through their London HQ, so how were they managing to broadcast anything now if everyone there was dead?

Dan clicked it and a live feed of a reporter appeared on his screen. The caption said her name was Louise Stone, and she was reporting from an "unknown location."

He watched her curiously.

"*I am speaking to you live from a shelter near the Chinese border. We've just been escorted down here with several high ranking government officials under the Chinese equivalent of the Post-Defcon Protocol.*"

Dan leaned forward in the chair.

"*I can confirm that the capital city of Shanghai was attacked just minutes ago, with a catastrophic number of casualties. In response, the Chinese president authorised the launch of a Lóng-fēngbào-64 targeting an undisclosed American city.*"

Dan gaped at the screen, his mouth dangling wide open. "Holy shit! Cathy, the Chinese just launched a fucking *nuke*!"

Cathy bundled back in and grabbed the back of Dan's chair. "What! How? They shouldn't even *have* any nuclear weapons any more. Not since the treaty…" She trailed off and jabbed a finger at the screen. "*It's her!*"

Dan frowned. "What? The reporter?"

"I *know* her. She was there when…" Cathy swallowed. Her voice softened to a whisper. "She was there when Mother killed Annie."

Dan's eyes narrowed in thought. "She's the first, no, the *only* reporter saying this. None of the other networks have mentioned this yet. Could she still be working for Margery?" *No, I killed Margery.* "…or Zhin?"

"Maybe? I don't know!" Cathy spluttered. She raked her fingers across the top of her head and paced up and down the comms room. "She definitely worked for my mother in the past. Did she and Zhin use her to somehow play China against America?"

The pilot interrupted. "Miss Blunt? Could you come up here a sec?"

Cathy walked into the cockpit out of sight.

Dan wracked his brain, trying to figure out what Zhin hoped to achieve with all of this death. And why the fuck was he hiding in Georgia? *There's nothing here!* And yet he couldn't have chosen it at random; he seemed too smart for that.

"Dan!" Cathy cried, startling him.

He jerked around in the chair and entered the cockpit.

Hugo pointed out the window. High above them, skirting the edge of the atmosphere in the deepest reaches of the sky was a bright spot. It moved surprisingly quick, leaving a vapour trail in its wake. Travelling away from them, it was heading west towards the setting sun.

"Euromerica just entered Defcon One," Hugo said. "That's the Chinese ICBM."

"Fuck me," Dan uttered. "I can't believe this is happening."

"Just watch, counter measures will take it out any

453

second," Hugo assured them.

They watched and waited. The missile was now a tiny twinkling spot, clearly visible against the backdrop of the darkening sky.

Suddenly, it flared bright and disappeared.

Cathy gasped.

Dan stared at the spot. "Did it detonate?"

"No, it's been disarmed," Hugo explained. "The dead missile will drop into the Atlantic."

"What if they launch another one?" Cathy asked.

"Then we'll shoot that one down too. Our military's well prepared for this scenario, Miss Blunt. I wouldn't worry."

Dan scratched his cheek. "Yeah, but even during both Cold Wars, no country actually launched anything. How the fuck will our governments react to that? Wait, do we even *have* a government anymore?" Dan said. "There's been nothing from the US President or the EU. If they're all dead, who's in charge now?"

Cathy sucked in air through her teeth. "Don't ask me. Politics was never my subject."

"It's a good question," Hugo said. "Because someone has a mother of a decision to make now. How to react to an attempted nuclear strike…"

They were all silent for a while.

The horizon slowly swallowed the bright red orb of the setting sun. Dan looked at it and couldn't help wondering whether he'd ever see it rise again.

He went back to the safety of the computer screen.

"God, what's *taking* them so long?" Cathy said, following him out.

He tried the comms line again. Still no word from Frank or Arnie. He shook his head at Cathy.

"Ugggh!" she groaned. "We came here to stop him, Dan! Were we too late?" She gave him a desperate, pleading look that made Dan's heart flutter. He searched for the right words of comfort but nothing came. He was too cynical by nature to believe that the Chinese launch would be the only attempt. Cathy looked at the ground in defeat.

She left him alone and wandered aimlessly back into the cockpit.

He turned to the Net. *Chatter* was going wild. The hashtag *nuke* was trending.

He checked on the Eye's forums again. One of his friends in Ohio had posted a photo. Dan was glad at first to see that the thumbnail showed a serene landscape of sunny American countryside. It seemed that his earlier message may have saved at least one of his friends. But as he read the caption, his heart skipped a beat.

'Game Over. It was nice knowing ya, Earth :('

Dan clicked the thumbnail and the photo filled his screen. The bright spot in the sky was not the sun. It was the thruster glow of a missile launching into the air.

"Oh god. No, no, *no!*" Dan cried.

"What?" Cathy darted through the door.

"We got our answer! Somebody on our side just authorised a launch! What the fuck is wrong with these people? *Nobody benefits from nuclear war!*"

Not even Zhin... Dan recalled Horatio Zhin's viral video, where he claimed to be building a solar power plant, one in each of the three cities that he originally attacked with the vapourisation bomb. He was capitalising on the deaths of hundreds of thousands of people. *Could this be the same thing, on a global scale? Is this what he meant by his Horizon epoch?*

"Oh my fucking god," he said, clutching his head in his hands. "Zhin's plan has gone wrong."

"What do you mean?" Cathy asked.

"Zhin's scheme to control the world's power was only possible if he severely reduced the world's population. *That* is what he was trying to do. The vapourisation bomb...it's an alternative to nuclear weapons. He developed a *clean* nuke. There's no fallout, no destruction, only loss of life."

"Right," Cathy said at length, frowning.

"Think about it," Dan said. "His entire philosophy was to unite the world. But he only had enough resources to provide power to *half* the population. He tried to make his solar plants the *only* provider of global energy by wiping out carefully selected cities, and forcing the governments to adopt his power."

"So, he was completely full of shit," Cathy said. "His intention was *never* to unite the world, he simply wanted to control it by killing enough people, until anyone left was forced to rely on him for their power."

"Exactly!" Dan agreed.

Cathy grabbed the back of her head with both hands. "He came so close. But he'd rather trigger a nuclear war than accept defeat…"

"That's an awful big assumption to make," Hugo said. "Sounds like some nutjob conspiracy theory if you ask me."

Dan glared at him. "*Conspiracy theory?* Dude, two fucking nukes have just been launched. That hasn't happened in human motherfucking history! How much do you wanna bet that Zhin is down there hiding in a cosy little bunker beneath the dam, with a pantry full of tinned spaghetti?"

"A bunker?" Cathy said, raising an eyebrow.

"Yeah. All these old dams have them."

"Show me a map," Cathy said.

Dan clicked open a map of Georgia.

"Zoom out," she said. "Look, we're right on the border of Europe and Neo-Asia."

"Yeah," Dan said. "There's literally *nothing* here. No major cities, no military targets."

"Well, then, that's why he's here!" Cathy said.

Dan blinked. "Oh man, of course… This area will be the least affected by fallout, because we're furthest away from any of the key detonation zones."

"It makes perfect sense to hide here, especially if he has a bunker," Cathy said. "But why blow up the dam? That doesn't sound safe, if you're hiding under it."

"Maybe the bomb isn't to destroy the dam, but just to, I dunno, make a hole in it?"

"Why?" Cathy frowned.

"If he diverts the lake water over the bunker, it'll act as a seal. Protection from the fallout." Dan rubbed his cheeks. "Whatever the reason, Zhin intends to just sit down there while the world destroys itself."

Hugo interjected. "How do you know so much about nuclear bunkers and *detonation zones*, anyway, kid?"

Dan bristled. "I'm with Binary Eye. We know everything."

"He spends a lot of time on the internet," Cathy said.

More harrowing footage began to appear on *Chatter*. Cell phone videos of great rockets launching out of the ground in Pakistan, mountain silos opening up in the French Alps, British subs unleashing their payloads into the sky.

Dan leaned back in his chair, a heavy sense of defeated helplessness settling on his bones.

Cathy let out an anguished shriek from the cockpit.

Dan hauled himself out of the chair with great effort and propped himself against the cockpit doorframe. In all directions, the glow of missiles raced across a sea of navy sky. It wouldn't matter how many counter measures were deployed now.

"Sweet mother of God," Hugo muttered.

"Who's a conspiracy nut now?" Dan said, gaping out of the window.

Cathy reached back to clutch Dan's hand and squeezed hard. He squeezed back. Even in view of the horror outside, her touch sent a warm pulse through him.

"What do we do now?" Dan asked.

Hugo slowly turned his head to look at them both. "What can we do?"

Dan swallowed. He took in the scene before him. Dozens of glowing orbs drifted across the sky. There must have been thirty missiles in view. Soon, they would begin to land… There were no major towns close to the Inguri Dam, but that wouldn't make the sky any safer. The shockwaves would pluck them right out of the air.

Dan looked at Cathy. She turned to him, chewing a fingernail. There were worse people to die with, he supposed.

But I don't want to die. Not yet.

Cathy spun towards Hugo. "Take us down!" she blurted. "If we stay up here, we're dead."

"Are you *seeing* this?" Hugo replied. "This is the day the world ends." He added, sadly, "Couldn't ask for a better view."

"Are you serious?" Dan gaped. "Listen, dude. We're hovering above a structure made of fifty gazillion tonnes of reinforced concrete. That shelter will have been designed specifically to survive nuclear attacks!"

The pilot stared back at him. "You don't *know* for sure."

"I trust him!" Cathy answered, ignited with fiery energy. "Take us down. Now!"

"Okay," the pilot said. "But we'll have to be quick. There's still a deadly storm beneath us, if you remember."

Dan had forgotten. It was so calm and serene above the clouds, that it was impossible to imagine the thundering nightmare raging below.

"Take a seat and buckle up," Hugo ordered.

Cathy strapped herself into the navigator's chair leaving Dan with the co-pilots seat in the front. The seat provided him with the jaw-dropping view of Armageddon. Open sky stretched for miles ahead, lined with vapour trails and glowing missile thrusters. Swirling beneath them was a sea of brooding thunderclouds.

The view tipped forwards as Hugo tilted the flight stick. "Hold on tight!"

The VTOL plunged into the thick layer of cloud.

Immediately, turbulence rocked the aircraft, shaking Dan in his seat. He instinctively grabbed the straps at his shoulders, trying to hold himself steady. The urge to close his eyes nearly overpowered everything else.

The cabin darkened as they descended. Thickening mist whipped past the cockpit. Rain pattered against the window, droplets streaking across the glass.

They broke through the clouds and lightning flashed. The dam lit up below them, a great concrete horseshoe holding back an expanse of water that rippled and frothed in the storm.

Frank's voice crackled over the loudspeaker system. *"…in. Dan, you little shit, do you read me?"*

"It's Frank!" Cathy shouted.

"If you can hear me, get your arse back down here and pick me up. I've been shot, I have Zhin in custody, and we're on the fucking dam waiting for you."

"He's got him!" Cathy sounded surprised.

Dan's teeth chattered as his jaw bounced against the onslaught of turbulence and his stomach attempted to force its way out of his throat.

"We're coming in fast!" Hugo warned. He wrestled with the flight stick, then started pressing buttons and flicking switches around the dashboard. A warning siren wailed, accompanied by a flashing red light somewhere on the dash, but Dan saw only a purple lightning fork burnt onto his retinas.

Hugo heaved the flight stick backwards. Dan felt all his weight pull forwards against the seatbelts as the craft air-braked. His stomach heaved against the pressure. Finally, his vision cleared enough to see they were just a few hundred feet above the dam. The pilot levelled the VTOL out and the cockpit swung to look up at the sky.

The *wub-wub-wub* of the propellers throbbed through the craft and Dan's bones.

Rain hammered against the glass as Dan's stomach roiled. He suddenly tasted prawn, the aftertaste of a sandwich the Europa guards had given him in his cell the day before.

"There you are! Thank fuck—" Frank's radio cut off.

It seemed like the descent would never cease, but at last the pressure eased and they drifted down towards the dam. Screens across the dashboard showed feeds from cameras lined along the aircraft's hull, allowing the pilot to line up his landing. Dan spied Frank dragging Horatio Zhin behind him in the rain. A number of corpses lay sprawled out on the road. *Dead mercs,* Dan thought.

The world froze for a heartbeat. Dan's vision went black. His ears went *POP*. It felt like someone had switched off his brain for a fraction of a second, before everything turned back on again.

The VTOL gave a violent jolt as it struck the ground below. The whole craft started to tilt, pulling Dan to one side like an invisible hand. *Oh my god, we're gonna fall over the side of the dam.* Cathy shrieked.

Hugo wrestled with the controls and the engines throbbed harder, lifting them upwards.

"Shit!" Hugo cursed.

"What happened?" Cathy asked, her voice strained and confused.

"Lightning hit us," Hugo grunted through gritted teeth. When the craft was level again he took it down and landed on the dam. "You two, get to the cargo hold. I'm not staying here any longer than I have to!"

Dan hesitated. "What about you? You've seen what's happening out there. Our only chance of surviving is the bunker."

"Come with us!" Cathy said.

Hugo screwed up his face. "Listen kiddo, this is the end. We got about five minutes before those bombs start hitting and when they do, who's to say you won't get buried alive under a collapsing dam?" He gave Cathy an apologetic look. "Please, do whatever you think's best. I'd just sooner die above the clouds, if it's all the same to you, Miss."

Cathy and Dan exchanged a helpless look. Dan shrugged.

"Thank you," she said to Hugo.

Hugo gave her a parting nod. "I'll open the cargo ramp. You'll have thirty seconds. *Go.*"

"Come on, Dan," Cathy tugged his arm.

They left the cockpit and ran for the hold. Dan grabbed the medkit from the bathroom as the ramp lowered. Pouring rain blustered in and wind howled around the opening.

Cathy led him to the maw, and Dan spotted Frank shielding his face against the rain, peering inside. The VTOL's propellers churned the air, resonating in Dan's belly. He scrambled down the ramp with Cathy.

Dan waved his arms at Frank and shouted, "Get back! He's taking off! Stay back!" His voice was lost to the churning throb of the VTOL's engines.

"What? Where the fuck is he going?" Frank yelled, illuminated by the craft's underbelly lights.

They were plunged into darkness as the VTOL heaved itself into the storm.

"Frank, we have to get underground!" Dan shouted. "Where's Arnie?"

"I haven't seen him, only the bodies he left behind," Frank said. "My comms stopped working."

Horatio Zhin was staring at Cathy. "You're Catherine," he said. Rain droplets streaked down his unnaturally smooth cheekbones, dripping from his chin.

"You shut the fuck up," Frank yanked Zhin's collar.

But Zhin continued staring at Cathy, unfazed. "You have her eyes. Those beautiful eyes... I loved your mother, Catherine. Let's be reasonab—"

Cathy slapped him across the face.

Frank and Dan raised their eyebrows at each other.

"You *loved* her?" She curled her lip in disbelief. "I guess that's why you sent fighter jets to blow up the house she was hiding in. Is that how much you loved her?" She stuck out a hand before he could answer. "Shut up, and tell us if there's a bunker here."

"Oh, I like you," Zhin said through a slimy smile, his cheek already reddening. "Margery had a devil's temper, as well."

Cathy slapped him again. A spray of rain followed the arc of her hand after it followed through from his face. Dan couldn't help but feel impressed.

Frank interjected. "Cathy, there is a bunker. It's where I found him. I assume our new plan is to take shelter there, since our ride has left us here?"

"Yes! We should go back!" Zhin said. "It's the only way we'll be safe."

"There's no 'we' in this," Cathy said.

"You need me," Zhin said. "Only I know the way to protect us."

"We already know about the bomb," Dan said with as much condescension as he could muster. "You're going to flood the dam to seal the bunker, right?"

Zhin blinked at him. "Smart boy." He licked his lips and swallowed. He turned to Cathy. "I have something to show you, Catherine. It was meant for your mother, but I think you would be a much bett—"

Cathy interrupted, "Frank, break this man's legs."

Frank hesitated. "Um, what?"

"We don't have time! Break his *fucking legs.*"

"Roger that," said Frank, throwing Zhin to the wet concrete.

"What?" Zhin was no longer smiling. "No, please!"

"Shut up," Frank said, kicking him onto his back. He put his boot on Zhin's knee, and clutched his ankle with his metal hand.

"*No!*" Zhin wailed.

Frank yanked the foot upwards, shattering Zhin's leg at the tender joint of the kneecap.

Crack.

"*AAAAGH!*"

Dan grimaced but couldn't look away.

Frank grabbed Zhin's other foot, pinning his knee against the ground with his boot. *Crrk!*

Zhin flopped over, both legs horribly askew and protruding unnaturally in opposite directions as he lay on the ground, mouth agape and sputtering like a fish.

"We gonna just leave him there?" Frank asked.

Cathy turned to Dan. "It's up to you. What would Jimmy want?"

I promised you vengeance, little bro. Dan glanced towards the edge of the dam.

Cathy read his mind. "Frank, help us carry him."

"With pleasure," grinned Frank.

They plucked Zhin off the ground together, and lugged him to the precipice, dropping him on the concrete lip.

"I killed Margery," Dan said to Cathy. "He's yours, if you want it..."

She took him by the hand. "We'll do this together."

She and Dan placed a foot against Zhin's side.

"N-no!" Zhin wheezed, glaring at them without guilt or sorrow. Even at death's door, Zhin expressed only hatred. "It wasn't supposed to end here."

"Fuck you," Dan said, and they kicked him over the edge.

Zhin's limp body bounced off the curved dam wall multiple times before splattering on the rain soaked concrete far below.

Cathy pulled Dan into her and kissed him deeply.

He was intoxicated by her raw passion, the heat of the moment feeling both exhilarating and terrifying all at once.

She pulled away, her breathing rapid. Raindrops fell from her soaking hair, and she gazed at Dan with restrained lust. "Lead us to the bunker, Frank," Cathy ordered.

"This way," he said, marching away.

Hand in hand, Cathy and Dan followed Frank through the downpour.

37
SHELTER

Cathy took the steps two at a time as Frank led the way down a zig-zagging staircase into the heart of the dam.

Blood seeped through the cloth around Frank's forearm and dripped from a wound in the side of his belly.

"Are you all right, Frank?" Cathy asked.

"Not really," he grunted. "Sooner we get underground, the better, eh?"

"Yeah…" she said, hopping down onto another half-landing, swinging around and bolting down the next.

A deep vibration rumbled through the staircase, and Cathy lost her footing. She tripped onto her hands and knees at the next landing. Ahead of her, Frank grabbed the railing and managed to stay upright, but Dan came tumbling down and landed hard on his back.

"Argh!" he groaned, staggering to his feet.

They all exchanged a nervous glance. "What was that?" Cathy said.

"I think we're running out of time," Frank said.

"We have to get to the bunker!" Dan cried.

"What about Arnie?" Cathy despaired. When the two men had no reply, she said, "Oh god, I hope he's okay."

"Come on." Frank pulled Cathy to her feet, grimacing as a spurt of blood dripped onto the concrete floor.

"Frank, you're bleeding everywhere!" She reached for his wound.

He held her away, shaking his head. "There's no *time*!

Come on, for fuck's sake." He lumbered on.

At the foot of the stairs, they followed a concrete corridor and after piling through a metal door found themselves in a soggy carpeted area strewn with wooden crates.

"The floors wet," Dan pointed out. "Did he already use the bomb to make the leak?"

"No." Frank grimaced, pointing to a metal crate nearby. "The bomb's in there. This flooding must be Arnie's handiwork." Frank pushed the call button on an elevator and the doors slid open. "Help me with these." He began sliding the wooden crates into the elevator.

Cathy noticed blood on the floor, dripping down from the open hatch in the ceiling. She exchanged a nervous look with Dan, but neither of them dared to ask.

With the elevator full of crates, Frank ushered them inside.

Cathy stepped in, careful to avoid the dripping blood. "I can't believe this is happening again," she said miserably. "I must be cursed to live underground my entire life."

Frank paused with one foot inside and touched his earpiece. "Arnie?" He frowned.

Cathy gasped. "Where is he?"

Frank held a finger up. He stepped out of the elevator and peered down the corridor in both directions. "I don't know where that is, mate. We have to get underground right now. Can you come to us?" With each word, Frank's energy seemed to drain. He clutched his abdomen and staggered another step back towards the elevator, then his leg gave way and he fell to the ground.

"Frank!" Cathy dropped down beside him.

"I think we're both fucked, mate," Frank said. He was talking to Arnie, but looked at Cathy with pained, defeated eyes.

She paused a moment, gathering her thoughts. Like hell she was going to let them both die on her behalf when they were so close to safety. All they had to do was get

Arnie to the elevator. "Give me that," she said, holding out a hand.

Frank's eyebrows rose a fraction. He plucked the earpiece out and handed it to her.

"Dan," she said. "See what you can do with the medkit. I'm going to find Arnie."

"No, it's too dang—" he started.

"If we're not back in five minutes, get into the elevator. Don't argue with me, just go!" She darted down a random corridor and took off along it, splashing through inch-high water. "Arnie?"

A pause. Then, soft and faint, "*Catherine?*"

"Yes, it's me, Arnie. Tell me where you are."

His voice was croaky and weak; he sounded like he was dying. "*Too late. Managed to kill 'em all. Not completely bulletproof, though.*" He coughed.

She slowed to a walk, butterflies in her gut. "No, I can find you... Are you still downstairs somewhere?"

"*It doesn't matter,*" he croaked. "*I'd rather you didn't see me die. Did Frank find Zhin?*"

Tears stabbed at the back of her eyes. She stopped and slumped against a wall and slid down it onto her butt. "Yeah. Horatio Zhin is dead... Arnie, he started a nuclear war."

A long pause. "*Are you safe?*"

"Yeah," she said. "There's a shelter."

"*Underground? Ahh...*" Arnie clearly understood her anxiety.

She grabbed her hair, resisting the urge to scream.

"*You always were a survivor.*" Arnie hacked out another throaty cough. "*I'll see you on the other side, one day.*"

"No," she whined. "I have to find you... you can't die."

She heard him rasp a chuckle. "*I can for you, my Rua...*" He gargled the last word, and didn't speak again.

She covered her mouth and sobbed.

The corridor vibrated and dust sprinkled down from the ceiling.

She allowed herself a moment of devastated grief. Her eyes stung with salty tears. The water in the flooded corridor soaked through her shorts, slowly rising higher.

Enough. Get up.

She snorted a hopeless cry that echoed down the corridor, and climbed to her feet. After wiping her eyes on her t-shirt, she inhaled a few shuddering deep breaths and went back to the elevator.

Dan was hunkered beside Frank, spraying his wound with anti-septic. They looked up as she approached.

Dan said, "Is Arnie…?"

She nodded. "We have to go." She tucked an arm under Frank, and she and Dan hauled him into the elevator.

"What about the bomb?" Dan asked. "Is it safe to leave it there?"

"You wanna bring it down with us?" Frank cocked an eyebrow.

"Uhh, I guess not."

Cathy stepped into the elevator with them, and pushed the ceiling hatch closed.

The doors slid shut just as another tremor, the most violent yet, shook the dam.

The elevator descended quickly. At any moment, she expected the cables to snap, or the dam to collapse, burying them in a metal tomb. Outside, she heard the trickle of water falling down the shaft and tinkling on the elevator's roof.

Dan said, "I'm sorry about Arnie…"

She just stared ahead at the door.

They made it to the bottom. With the last of Frank's energy, he helped them drag the crates down a short corridor, through a weird submarine-type door, into the surreal living quarters beyond.

Frank collapsed into an old leather sofa.

"Seal the door," he said, coughing.

Cathy and Dan pulled the heavy door shut, and turned the big wheel in its centre until it *hissed.*

"Okay. Good." Frank spoke in one word sentences. "Alright. Safe."

And here I am… underground again. She tried to distract herself. "You need help, Frank," she said. She scanned the room, bewildered by the sight of bookcases and ornate chairs. Two doors led off in different directions, deeper into the bunker. "Dan, help me find some proper medical supplies."

They split up, each taking a door. Cathy found several bedrooms, a large bathroom with shower cubicles, and eventually discovered a kitchen. It was as big as her old lab, with half a dozen stove tops and surfaces. She estimated that the pantry at one end held enough canned food to feed a dozen people for several months. With the extra crates they had brought down, it could last even longer.

And Zhin was planning to keep this all to himself… She curled her lip in disgust. Now it was all theirs.

Cathy touched her bracelet. *So much for my freedom. It was amazing while it lasted.* She walked back to Frank.

"I think there's an infirmary back there," Dan said when he returned.

They hefted Frank up and assisted him in walking to it. An imposing set of air-lock doors separated the infirmary from the rest of the bunker. Dan and Cathy had to put Frank down on the ground to open the first door by cranking a huge wheel lock. Once inside the airlock, they had to seal the first door shut, trapping themselves in the claustrophobic seal before opening the second door.

As the infirmary door opened, a *hiss* of conditioned air enveloped Cathy, the scent of which took her back to the underground facility where she had worked for six years.

"Oh, god," she groaned, overwhelmed with the opposite of nostalgia. "Sit here," she said to Frank, easing him into a perched position on the edge of a bed.

The room was long and narrow, adorned with many glass-doored cabinets full of labelled bottles and boxes of medical supplies. Hanging on the wall were several full-body biohazard suits, complete with gas mask helmets. At the far end of the room sat two rectangular freezer chests.

"Talk about well-stocked, eh?" Dan mused. "There's enough drugs here to feed a junkie for a year."

Frank grunted in pain, clutching his side. "Morphine." He pointed to one of the glass doors.

Using some of the infirmary's equipment, Frank pointed Cathy through cleaning his wounds as best he could. But the bullet in his belly was too deep to reach. She bandaged it to stem the bleeding, but it didn't look good.

"Is that gonna be all right?" Dan asked, eyeing the already reddening fabric.

"I don't know," Cathy said distractedly.

"It'll do," Frank grunted. He sat up on the bed, inhaling deep, ragged breaths. At least he was speaking again.

The walls rumbled, fractionally, but enough to notice.

"It's really happening out there..." Cathy said, eyeing the ceiling. "How long does it take for fallout to become harmless again?" Meaning, *how long do we have to live down here?*

"Decades, man," Dan said, scratching his neck. "There's still mutant shit growing in Chernobyl, and that was like, forty years ago."

"Chernobyl was just a reactor," Frank grunted. "That," he pointed at the ceiling, "is catastrophic. Even with all these supplies, there's no way the three of us can survive long enough for the world to be habitable again..."

"Seriously?" Dan said dejectedly.

Frank was looking past them. She followed his gaze, but there was just the two freezers at the back of the room.

Frank wheezed, clutching his side. "Christ. Anyone else hungry?"

An hour later, they were sitting in the kitchen eating a cooked meal of tinned vegetables and preserved meat.

"This isn't bad," Dan mumbled, filling the morose silence.

"There's not enough," Frank replied, chewing on a chunk of something. "We'll run out within the year."

"Zhin must have known that… he planned for all of this," Dan insisted. "He was a fucking psycho, but he was smart enough to have some kind of backup plan. He's not the sort to just hide in a bunker and wait to die."

Cathy watched Frank. He was shaking his head and kept avoiding eye contact with them.

He has the look of a man who knows he's going to die.

The cutlery in the drawers rattled. A deep and far away rumbling resonated through the walls, and the light's flickered.

Everything settled again.

"That was a close one," Dan muttered. "The earth's taking a beating tonight." He gulped and rubbed one eye. "I hope my mom got out of Boston…"

"All those poor people," Cathy said. "We failed… so many people are going to die, and eventually so will us."

"You two don't have to die," said Frank. "Not yet, anyway."

"What do you mean?"

Frank swallowed a mouthful. "Did you see those freezers in the infirmary?"

"Freezers?" Dan said.

"Yeah, I saw you looking at them," Cathy said.

Frank propped his metal arm on the table. "I think they're cryopods. Hibernation chambers."

"No fucking way," Dan breathed. "I can't believe I didn't realise that. So *that* was Zhin's backup plan for him and Margery. Talk about an immortality complex. That must be what he wanted to show you, Cathy."

"Yeah, but Frank," she said, realising their predicament. "There's only two…"

"Yup," Frank said, scooping another forkful of food.

Cathy put down her fork and stared sympathetically at

Frank, trying to find something meaningful to say.

"Then how do we...?" Dan gulped.

"Listen," Frank said. "I'm done for. And this arm of mine, it won't stay active forever. Without Blunt's support, it'll cease up and die on me eventually. You two are young." He forced a grin. "Someone's gonna have to repopulate the earth."

Cathy snorted a laugh, despite herself.

"Re...populate?" Dan reddened, casting a glance at Cathy. He scratched the back of his head.

"Are you sure about this, Frank?" she asked.

He shrugged. "Not much bloody choice. At least I'll have food. There's those fancy suits in the infirmary, too. Maybe I can take a look up top in a few years if I'm still alive."

"Holy shit, just like a VaultTech dweller..." Dan said.

She frowned at him.

"It's from an old videogame." He scratched his elbow. "Never mind."

Frank ate the last bite of his meal and leaned back in his chair. "This must be how Jesus felt after the last supper." He burped, followed by a grimace. "Although he didn't have a gutshot."

"Oh, Frank," Cathy sobbed. She got up, made her way around the table and hugged him.

"I know," he said, voice cracking. He rubbed her back as he squeezed.

She glanced over Frank's shoulder, tears filling her eyes and gestured to Dan. He got up and joined them, wrapping his arms around them both.

They all hugged one another tightly, as the lights flickered and the walls rumbled.

Eventually, Frank stirred. "All right, enough of this morose bollocks. If things are to end tonight, there's something we have to listen to, first."

Frank unwound himself from the hug and staggered through to the living quarters. Next to the ornate globe was a record player, and a shelf stacked with a collection of vinyl's.

Frank sifted through them and found one that he approved of. "Set this up, Dan."

Cathy wandered over to the bathysphere door and glanced through the window. Water was seeping out through the elevator doors and was filling up the corridor. Already, it was almost two feet deep. *Thank you, Arnie. You might have saved us.*

The record-player made a *scrrp* noise, then crackled to life. Cathy broke into a grin as Monty Python's "Always look on the bright side of life" played out through the speaker.

"This is more like it," Frank said, a hazy smile spreading across his pale face.

Cathy chuckled. The song was old, but well-meaning, and she was infected by its quirk. "Dance with me, Dan."

She joined hands with him and they clumsily skipped around, hand in hand. He was crying, but trying not to show it, and had a sad smile on his face, which made her cry again.

"Always look on the bright side of life!"

Cathy laughed between sobs, and hugged Dan close as they danced up to the bathysphere door and away again, up and down between the support pillars.

"Forget about your sin, give the audience a grin!"

Cathy inhaled a sharp breath, thinking about her father.

"So, always look on the bright side of death!"

"I'll try," she said.

Dan looked into her eyes and sighed. He cradled her head in his hands and spun her gently to the rhythm of the music.

Cathy caught a glimpse of the water rising above the level of the door's window, sealing them inside for good, just as the final chorus kicked in.

"Always look on the bright side of life!"

Dan squeezed her tight, and met her eyes again with a

deep and undeniable longing.

Nobody had ever looked at her that way. Nobody had done the things he had done for her. She would never find a more devoted and caring person. She kissed him long and passionately.

I do love him.

They were still kissing when the song came to an end.

She reluctantly pulled away, hugging him tight, pressing her forehead against his. "It's time, Dan."

"I know…"

She turned to Frank. He was leaning against the wall, smiling at them both. He was deathly pale and wobbly on his feet. "Better get this over with," he said sadly.

Together, they helped him walk to the infirmary. They cranked the airlock wheels and slipped inside, sealing the door shut behind them.

Frank wandered over to the cryopods. He leaned over, studying the controls. "Looks simple enough."

Cathy and Dan looked at each other. She saw fear in his red raw eyes. Reaching down, she took hold of his hand and led him over to the pods.

"Frank…" Cathy said, a lump forming in her throat.

"No backing out now," Frank said. "There's no reason all three of us have to die down here. At least this way, you two stand a chance."

She looked at the controls. The interface was surprisingly straightforward, and even listed a set of instructions. You simply set the amount of time you wished to be asleep, pushed a button, and got inside.

"Oh, man…" Dan said, putting both hands on his hips and hanging his head. "Frank, dude…" He held out his hand. Frank shook it. "Thanks for everything."

"Nah, thank you, kid." Frank pulled him in for a man hug. "At least we fucking tried."

"Yeah," Dan wiped his eye as he stepped back. "How long should we set the timer for?" Dan said. Then added quickly, "Actually, you know what? I don't think I wanna know."

"I'll keep an eye on you both as long as I can," said Frank.

Dan and Cathy opened the lids, which popped up with a little *hiss*. Inside was a soft layer of padding with lots of little tubes running around the edge of the pod.

Cathy gave Frank a tight hug, tears leaking out again. "Thank you, Frank. You have no idea how grateful I am to have met you." She tiptoed to kiss his cheek, then hugged him around the neck.

"You too," he said, resting his chin on top of her head.

When she pulled away, he wiped a tear from her face with a delicate, titanium finger. For a while they looked at each other. She squeezed his hands, feeling skin in one and cool metal in the other. *He'll never see another woman.* Leaning up, she kissed him on the lips.

Frank gave a wistful sigh.

"Take care of yourself, Frank."

"I will," he smiled.

She turned to Dan. "Are you ready?"

"No," he said, his voice cracking. She embraced him in a hug, and he squeezed her back. She felt his heartbeat hammering in his chest and his body trembling. They pulled apart, and he reached up, cradled her face in his palms for one last kiss.

It was deep and delicate, and made her tingle all over.

Oh, Dan... I do hope we wake up from this...

They separated and with one final scared look into each other's eyes, they turned and climbed into the pods. She lied down on her back, looking up at the white ceiling.

Frank held up his hand in a wave, and hit a button. The lid slowly closed and she lost sight of him.

It was claustrophobic, but she didn't care. This was her best hope of staying alive. She knew that in her heart, and so when the cryofluid filled up around her, it brought Cathy a sense of hope.

I'm a survivor.

As the water covered her face, she held her breath and closed her eyes. A flash of light and a jolt of ice, and she slept.

EPILOGUE

She awoke violently, gasping for air.

The open lid of her pod swam into focus, illuminated in a soft blue light. The rest of the infirmary was pitch black. Air burned her lungs with every intake of breath. The cryofluid drained away leaving her soaking wet and shivering. Cathy's heart pounded erratically, beating again after… *how long has it been?*

She reached up, her arm muscles screaming as the blood recirculated. She grabbed at the sides with feeble hands, and heaved herself into an upright position.

The infirmary's lights came on, reacting to her movement. Immediately a string of bulbs *popped* off and the room went half as dark.

She brushed her wet hair back away from her face.

An infirmary bed had been wedged between the two cryopods. A pile of rotten rags was strewn across the empty mattress. On the other side of that, Dan's pod was open and he lay still as a stone.

She clambered out of her pod and collapsed in a heap on the hard floor. Goosebumps prickled her arms and legs as the stuffy, humid air caressed her frigid skin.

"Dan," she croaked and coughed. "Wake up."

No response.

She tried to stand but her legs were numb. She crawled along the floor, dragging her dead weight feet.

Cathy lifted herself onto the foot of Dan's pod and peered in at his motionless body. His eyes were closed and he wasn't breathing.

"No," she choked. "Don't you leave me here alone." She squeezed between the bed and the pod, crawling nearer to his head. "Wake up, Dan!" She thumped him weakly on the chest.

Still nothing.

She shook him feebly by the shoulder. "Dan!"

Cathy's heart accelerated.

She turned away from the lifeless boy and crawled to the end of the pod, slumping down onto her butt.

The infirmary was ghostly quiet. The glass refrigerators were completely opaque, covered in a layer of dark grime. A stack of rusty metal boxes lay piled in one corner, a wide brown stain spreading across the floor from its base.

The airlock door was still sealed, but it looked as though the door was twisted on its hinges, very slightly.

How many years have I been asleep? Is Frank still here?

Dan inhaled a wild rasping breath.

"Wah!" Cathy jumped, fell forwards and slipped onto the floor.

Dan lurched upright, wheezing and coughing, clutching the side of his pod with white knuckles.

"Dan!" she spluttered, and coughed up a thick globule of blue tinted phlegm.

He rasped, "Cathy." They both caught a fit of coughing, and it took sometime before either of them could talk again.

Dan clambered out and joined Cathy on the floor. They both leaned back against the wall to catch their breath.

"I thought you were dead," she said.

"I feel dead." He clutched his chest. "My lungs are on fire, but I feel freezing."

"Your skin is blue," she said.

He gave her a sideways glance. "You're not looking too good yourself."

They sat like that for a while, bathing in the clammy air.

Cathy's bladder clenched like a fist. "Ohh…" She

crawled on her hands and knees across the floor, behind her pod and fumbled to pull down her damp shorts and panties. Crouched in the corner, out of Dan's sight, she peed.

"Are you…?" Dan said.

"Yes," she sighed. "Oh my god, that feels good."

"Owww," he groaned. "Holy crap I'm gonna piss my pants." She heard him unzipping and then the tinkle of him reliving himself on the floor. "*Uuugh*," he sighed.

She tested her legs, and found enough strength to stand. She wobbled around to the front of her pod and checked the input screen, hoping for a clue as to how much time had passed. Its display was on, but the screen was completely filled up with black dots. She tapped it with a finger, but it didn't respond.

Dan swayed to his feet. He wandered over to the bed next to her. "Looks like Frank made himself a nest down here with us." He idly probed the flaky rags, which ripped at his touch. "We've been asleep for a long time…" His belly made a long, gurgling growl. "Ooh," he grimaced. "I think my stomach's woken up, though."

"Let's get out of here," she said.

Holding each other for support, they stumbled across the infirmary to the airlock door.

"Are we sure we want to open that?" Dan asked warily. "What if the air outside is dangerous?"

Cathy inhaled a lungful of stuffy, humid air and said, "The air in here won't be much safer if we keep breathing it." She pointed at the biohazard suits hanging on the wall.

After clambering into the plastic suits and donning the gas masks, they turned their attention to the airlock door. It took both of them hanging on the wheel lock to force it open.

The angle of the door proved to be askew, and the door snagged on the floor, making it impossible to open more than a foot. They squeezed through the gap one at a time and sealed themselves in the airlock beyond.

"On three," Dan wheezed, taking a hold of the second wheel lock with Cathy. "One, two…"

They heaved the wheel around. It screeched, before snapping like a twig and shattered on the ground in a spray of rusty flakes.

Cathy shivered, a wave of fear washing over her.

The door had parted barely the width of a finger. Through the tiny gap, a dim light seeped into the airlock.

"The power's still on," Dan said, his voice muffled by the gas mask.

With what little strength they had, Cathy and Dan struggled for forty minutes to push the door open enough for them to escape. They tumbled through the door and landed on the corridor floor.

Sticking to each other like glue, they wandered into the murky shelter. Movement sensors triggered lights to flicker on as they shuffled through the corridor, but more often than not, the bulbs popped and they found themselves stumbling in the shadows.

The walls were scarred with thick cracks. The ceilings, too. As Cathy staggered along the corridor, she sensed the floor was sloping very subtly to the right, as if the entire bunker had shifted with the earth's tectonics.

When they came to the living room, it was unrecognisable. All of the antique furniture and decorations had long disintegrated, or broken down into husks. A fine layer of dust covered the surface of everything. Looking back, she saw that they'd left a trail of dusty footprints all the way back towards the infirmary.

A pile of rotten planks lay strewn in one corner, which may have once been the grand bookshelf. Next to that, she just about recognised the skeletal frame of the ornate sofa.

And Frank's titanium arm.

She gasped.

Cathy scurried over to the sofa and hunkered down. Sure enough, Frank's arm, rusted and ancient-looking, was lying between the metal framework of the sofa. There was no other sign of his body.

Clutched in the hand was a sealed zip-lock plastic bag containing the zip-winch and a small book.

"Look, Dan."

He bent beside her to inspect it. "Oh man…"

Cathy carefully plucked the bag out from Frank's grip and lifted it up. She carried the bag over to a corner and sat down on the floor to open it. She eased the book out of the bag and examined it. It felt delicate and withered, but it was difficult to tell through the gloves of the biohazard suit.

She eased it open to the first page. Frank had written something by hand inside it. She felt a lump in her throat when she realised it was a diary of some kind.

"*Decided to make some notes for you guys. Gonna keep this in a bag to preserve it or whatever. First off, that bullet didn't kill me yet. Lucky me, eh? Must've missed my vitals when it sunk in. I can't get it out, but at least the wound healed around it. Hurts to do pretty much anything, but I don't think I'll be dying any time soon.*"

She felt a wave of emotions at this; relief mingled with sadness. Frank survived! At least for a while. But he must have been so lonely. She turned the page.

"*Had a good wander around the entire bunker today. The power's still working, somehow. I figured there must be a reactor or some kind of generator somewhere in here, but there's nothing. No idea how the place is still running, but Zhin obviously prepared for this scenario. I'm eating the stuff in the crates first, I think this was intended for Zhin's goons,*"

while all the preserved food in the
kitchen was for him and Margery when
they woke up. Evil bastards. Still, it
won't last forever, so I gotta be
sparing..."

"Jeez," Dan said, reading it next to her. "How long did he last, I wonder?"

They skimmed through the delicate pages. Many were stained and unreadable, but there were plenty more that had instructions for things like filtering water, cooking meat and preserving it.

In one entry, he said the water in the corridor mysteriously disappeared over night. That was terrifying, since he assumed it was the only thing keeping him safe from the toxins outside. But three months later, he was still struggling on. He had lived for over four years in the bunker before running out of food. But he wasn't done after that...

"What d'ya know, this arms still
bloody working. Took one of the hazard
suits, and made it to the surface
today. Elevator's stopped working, so
I had to climb the maintenance ladder
all the way to the top. Not gonna lie,
its awful out there. Sky's all sickly,
and its fucking freezing. Seems Zhin
knew what he was doing when he chose
this place, though. Whole bunch of
animals are living in the dried up
lake and the surrounding forest. I've
seen monkeys, deer, wild boars, and
loads of birds. Weird, colourful
things. Also saw a rabbit with four
ears, yesterday... not sure what that
means. But he tasted good."

It went on like this for several more pages. Cathy came to a page dated almost five years after they had gotten inside the cryopods.

"*Not feelin too good any more. Just got back from the surface again. Think I made a mistake takin my mask off out there. But I just had to try. Inhaled a good wiff and instantly knew the air wasn't ready yet. I can feel my lungs givin up now. Feels like they're fillin up with sand. I added a couple hundred extra years on your pods, just to be safe. Think that should be long enough. If it aint, well…maybe you'll never even wake up to read this. And if you do, well, you'll know I did my best. Gonna lie down for a bit now.*"

That was the last page.

"Oh, Frank…" Cathy's tear ducts were dry and they stung. She was too dehydrated to cry.

Dan laid a comforting hand around her shoulders. He helped her to stand up, and they looked around the desolated bunker. "Well, what now?"

Cathy picked up the plastic bag and swapped the book for the zip-winch. She stuffed the book into a pocket, and examined the device. It was in excellent condition, and she hoped it still worked.

"We have to get out of here."

Cathy wandered over to the bathysphere door, which led to the elevator shaft. The corridor beyond was covered in moss, but there was no water. Together, they spun the wheel and tugged open the door. They wandered down the mossy corridor and peered up the elevator shaft.

"Oh my god!" she gasped.

The dark shaft stretched up at a subtle angle, not quite vertical, pinheaded with a patch of stark blue sky.

"Dan, look!"

He joined her and craned his neck. "Woah."

Outside. I have to see it.

Cathy held the zip winch out into the shaft and pressed the button. Three cables sprang out and attached themselves to the shaft walls. She turned to Dan, apprehensive. "I'm getting déjà vu."

"Really?" he said.

"This… is exactly how Jimmy died."

She saw his face drop, even through the gas mask. "Oh."

"It's not designed for two people, Dan."

"Well, maybe you should just go?"

"Not a chance," she said. "I'm not leaving you behind."

"Look at this place…" He cast a wandering glance back down the corridor to the shelter and shrugged. "I'm not letting you die down here with me. Just go."

She shook her head. "No. I have an idea. Hold this." She threaded his hand through the strap and forced him to hold the zip winch handle. She wedged her own hand through it as well and clutched the handle beneath his hand. "If we're gonna die, we'll die together."

"Mmm," he said. "Okay then."

She looked back one last time, thinking of Frank. "Thank you," she said. Turning back to Dan, she interlocked her spare hand with his fingers. "Okay, ready? On three," Cathy said. "One…"

"Two…"

"Three!" They leapt into the shaft and Cathy hit the button.

The zip winch's cables tautened and shot up the shaft, pulling them upwards.

They flew up like a rocket, dangling beneath the cables, as the square of sky expanded above them. The blue square got bigger, and bigger, and bigger…

They reached the top and Cathy didn't let go of the button.

She shot out into the air, somersaulted forwards and landed on top of Dan in a thick patch of dense grass.

"Owww," he wheezed, as she sprawled across his belly. She unclipped herself from the zip-winch and rolled onto her back staring up at the brilliant blue sky. She'd never seen a sky so blue.

A vibrantly coloured humming bird hovered right in front of her nose. She laughed, and scrambled to her feet. The bird floated inches from her face, following her as she stood up, and stared at her with three curious, beady eyes.

Each eye blinked in unison and then the creature flew away over the flora.

Cathy lost her breath.

They were in the crater of a vast valley, rising all around them amid a sea of lush green ferns. One end of the valley was open, and the view stretched for miles ahead of them—an ocean of greenery as far as the eye could see.

This is the way the earth's supposed to be. She recalled Arnie's words, when he described his home, New Zealand. *The bluest sky you could imagine, and trees greener than emeralds.*

She'd been transported there through time.

Cathy couldn't resist it. She had to breathe the air properly.

"Cathy, wait!" Dan said, as she unclipped her gas mask.

She tore it off and threw it to the ground, inhaling deeply.

The oxygen rich air invigorated her, seeping into her deprived lungs and making them sing. She grinned from ear to ear, smelling the life all around her. Tears came now, streaming down her cheeks and she burst into gleeful laughter.

Dan took off his mask and inhaled, giving a long sigh.

"Oh, man," he said, wistfully.

She threw her arms around him and they cried in each other's embrace.

Standing side by side in the lush valley, the grief of being the only people left alive was too much to consider. Cathy simply didn't care. She was happy to have Dan, and she was happy to be alive.

THE END.

A NOTE FROM THE AUTHOR

Cripes! It. Is. DONE.

And so ends my second foray into trying to be a novelist. I sincerely hope you enjoyed my story. Unless you just turned to this back page to see the ending, in which case…shame on you.

There is no doubt that without my online writing critique group on Scribophile, this book will never have gotten finished. So, I want to thank every member of 'The New Apocalypse Now' - Devin, Henry, Bryan, Joshua, Thalia, Amailia, Shona, Jeanne, Andrew, as well as regular returners Alex, Rubin, Cormac, Pauline and Gwynn – you all provided invaluable feedback throughout, and without a doubt helped me to make sense of it all.

Special thanks goes to Jerry for running the Ubergroup within Scribophile – you do an amazing job, and I feel lucky to have been a part of it!

Finally, I have to thank my good friend Paul for enthusiastically shirking work with me as we discussed ideas and characters that ultimately ended up inspiring me to write about Cathy, Frank, Dan and co… If it weren't for those nerdy conversations way back in 2012, this story simply would not exist.

I won't lie. This one was tough. Trying to write a multiple point-of-view story with over 5 main characters, and interweaving storylines is a recipe for trauma and stress. I don't know how George RR Martin does it…

Thank you for reading, and I hope you'll join me on the next one.

M A Clarke
– November 2016

ABOUT THE AUTHOR

M A Clarke is an English bloke who quit his full-time career job in an attempt to become an author. In reality, that means he does whatever work he can find, whether its washing up dishes in a pub, milking cows on a dairy farm, or feeding sugary lumps into a conveyor belt at a chocolate factory to make ends meet. Then he stays awake late making up stories.

He's living the poor suffering artists dream, one day at a time. It's mostly awesome, he insists.

He's also an avid traveller who loves mountains, dogs, space, time travel and eats a lot of chocolate.

You might like his website:
www.mattclarke.co.uk

Other work by the author:

Lunaria

36753087R00277

Made in the USA
San Bernardino, CA
27 May 2019